THE ABOMINATION

THE ABOMINATION

JONATHAN HOLT

HarperCollins*PublishersLtd*

Published HarperCollins Publishers Ltd, by arrangement with Head of Zeus Limited.

First published in the United Kingdom in 2013 by Head of Zeus Ltd

First Canadian edition

HarperCollins Publishers Ltd
2 Bloor Street East, 20th Floor
Toronto, Ontario, Canada
M4W 1A8

www.harpercollins.ca

Library and Archives Canada Cataloguing in Publication
information is available upon request

ISBN 978-1-44342-074-7

Map on pages vi–vii © Jeff Edwards

Printed and bound in the United States
RRD 9 8 7 6 5 4 3 2 1

There is within every man and woman a core of evil only lightly held in check. Whether we call it savagery, brutality or barbarism; whether we give it some scientific-sounding label such as sadism or psychosis; whether we ascribe it to amorality or the Devil himself, it is, nevertheless, mankind's constant companion. Most of the time it sleeps, invisible and unheeded, within our breasts, and we call ourselves civilised and pretend it is not there. But only give us cause to wake the beast – give us unlimited power, for example, over our fellow man, and tell us there will be no repercussions from exercising it – and we will every one of us prove capable of acts more terrible than the imagination can conceive.

And each time we will wake, as if from a dream, saying "Never again", and each time we will lie.

Dr Paul Doherty MRCPsych

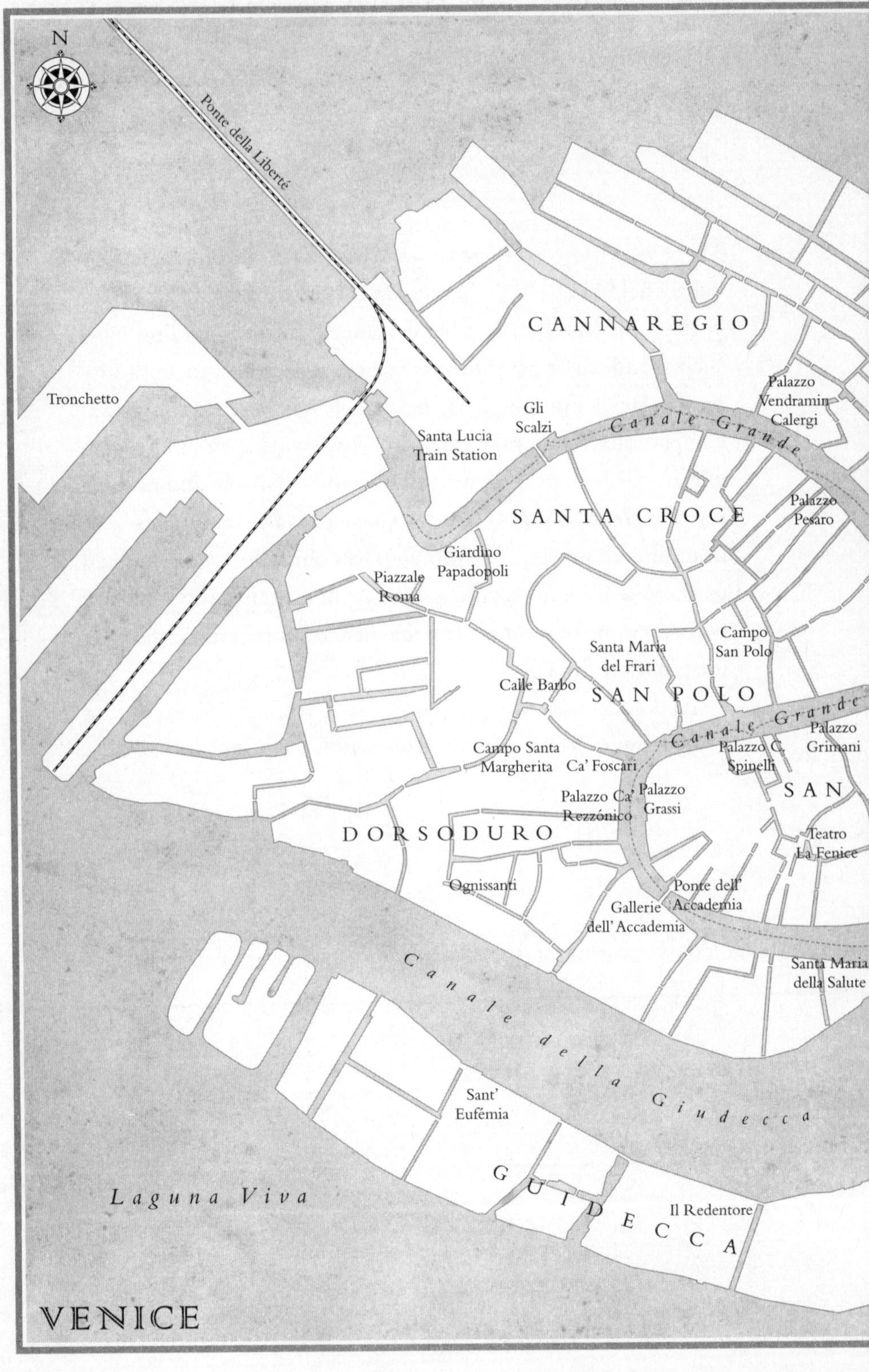
N
Ponte della Liberté
CANNAREGIO
Tronchetto
Gli Scalzi
Santa Lucia Train Station
Palazzo Vendramin Calergi
Canale Grande
SANTA CROCE
Palazzo Pesaro
Giardino Papadopoli
Piazzale Roma
Campo San Polo
Santa Maria del Frari
Calle Barbo
SAN POLO
Canale Grande
Palazzo Grimani
Campo Santa Margherita
Ca' Foscari
Palazzo C. Spinelli
SAN
Palazzo Ca' Rezzónico
Palazzo Grassi
DORSODURO
Teatro La Fenice
Ognissanti
Ponte dell' Accademia
Gallerie dell' Accademia
Santa Maria della Salute
Canale della Giudecca
Sant' Eufémia
Laguna Viva
GUIDECCA
Il Redentore
VENICE

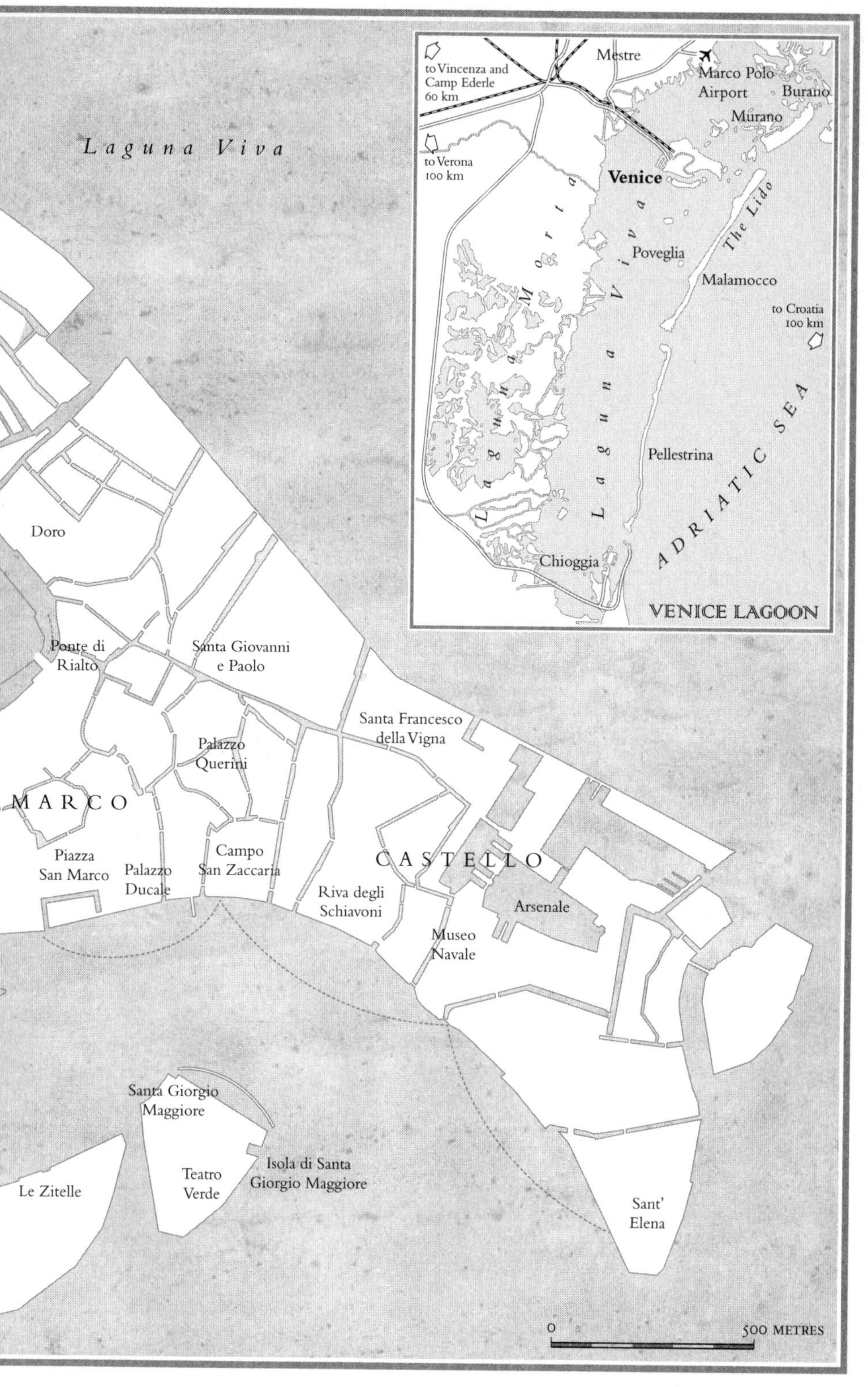

Laguna Viva
Doro
Ponte di Rialto
Santa Giovanni e Paolo
Santa Francesco della Vigna
Palazzo Querini
MARCO
Piazza San Marco
Palazzo Ducale
Campo San Zaccaria
CASTELLO
Riva degli Schiavoni
Museo Navale
Arsenale
Santa Giorgio Maggiore
Teatro Verde
Isola di Santa Giorgio Maggiore
Le Zitelle
Sant' Elena
0
500 METRES
to Vincenza and Camp Ederle 60 km
Mestre
Marco Polo Airport
Burano
Murano
to Verona 100 km
Venice
The Lido
Laguna Morta
Laguna Viva
Poveglia
Malamocco
to Croatia 100 km
Pellestrina
ADRIATIC SEA
Chioggia
VENICE LAGOON

Prologue

Venice, January 5

THE LITTLE BOAT slipped away from the quayside, its two-stroke outboard no more than a quiet splutter at the stern. Ricci, tending the throttle, steered carefully around the fishing boats and out-of-season gondolas that cluttered the tiny boatyard. He made this trip out to the lagoon every evening, ostensibly to check his crab pots. Few people knew that his excursions sometimes netted a more lucrative catch as well: packages tightly wrapped in blue plastic, attached by persons and vessels unseen to the buoys that marked each pot's location.

As the boat left the island of Giudecca behind he stooped to light a cigarette. "*È sicuro*," he said quietly into the flame. It's safe.

His passenger came up from the cramped cabin without replying. He was dressed for the weather – dark waterproofs, gloves, a woollen hat pulled low over his eyes. In his left hand he still held the metal case with which he'd boarded. A little larger than a briefcase, and oblong, it reminded Ricci of the cases musicians kept their instruments in. Except he was fairly sure his passenger tonight was no musician.

An hour earlier Ricci had taken a call on his *cellulare*. The same voice that usually told him how many packages to look out for informed him that tonight he'd be carrying a passenger. It had been on Ricci's lips to retort that there were plenty of water taxis in Venice, and that his fishing boat wasn't one of them, but something made the comment die in his throat. In all the time he'd been getting orders from the voice, he'd never heard it sound frightened before. Not even when the instructions had been to take a weighted body-shaped package out to the furthest regions of the lagoon and heave it over the side, for the crabs to feast on.

From their left came the sound of splashing, shouts. Several wooden craft, powered by oars, were racing through the water towards them. Ricci reduced the engine, idling.

"What is it?" The first words his passenger had spoken. His Italian, Ricci noted, was heavily accented. An American.

"Don't worry. It's not for us. It's for La Befana. They're practising their racing." As the boats neared, one could see they were filled with what appeared to be women, in huge frocks and bonnets; only as they passed did it become apparent that these were teams of rowers, dressed incongruously in female costumes. "They'll be gone in a minute," he added. Sure enough, the boats rounded a buoy and headed back for Venice, one narrowly ahead.

The passenger grunted. He'd ducked down as the rowers approached, clearly intent on not being seen. Now he stood at the prow with one hand on the rail, scanning the horizon as Ricci opened up the throttle.

It took an hour to reach the crab pots. There was nothing attached to any of the lines, nor had any boats come to meet them from the other side. It was dark now, but Ricci kept his lights turned off. In the distance, the humps of a few small islands broke the horizon line.

His companion spoke. "Which one's Poveglia?"

Ricci pointed. "That one."

"Take me."

Without another word Ricci set a course. There were some, he knew, who'd have refused, or asked for more money. Most of the fishermen gave the little island of Poveglia a very wide berth. But for exactly that reason it was a useful place for a small-time smuggler to be familiar with, and he sometimes landed there at night to pick up cargoes too large to be tied to a buoy – crates of cigarettes or whisky, the occasional shivering Eastern European girl and her pimp. Even so, he rarely lingered longer than he had to.

Unconsciously Ricci crossed himself, no more aware of the gesture than he was of the tiny adjustments he was making to the outboard as he steered a complex course through the sandbanks and shallows that littered this part of the lagoon. Then came a stretch of open water, and the boat jumped forward. Freezing spray lashed their faces as they crashed from wave to wave, but the man in the prow seemed hardly to notice.

Eventually Ricci slowed. The island was just ahead of them now, silhouetted against the purple-black sky, the clock tower of the abandoned hospital piercing the trees. A few faint dots of light flickered amongst the ruins – candles, perhaps, in one of the rooms. So it was a rendezvous, after all. No one lived on Poveglia, not any more.

Kneeling, Ricci's passenger unlatched the metal case. Ricci caught a glimpse of a barrel, a black rifle stock, a line of bullets, all packed neatly into their allotted spaces. But it was a night-sight, fat as a camera lens, that the man pulled out first. He raised it to his eye as he stood, steadying himself against the boat's movement.

For a moment he remained looking in the direction of the

lights. Then he gestured to Ricci to head towards the jetty, leaping impatiently but noiselessly onto the shore even before the boat touched land, the metal case still in his hand.

Later, Ricci would wonder if he'd heard any shots. But then he recalled the other tube he'd glimpsed in the case – a silencer, even longer and fatter than the night-sight. So it must have been his imagination.

His passenger was gone just fifteen minutes, and they rode back to Giudecca in silence.

One

THE PARTY IN the dimly lit Venetian *bacaro* had been going on for almost five hours, and the volume level was still rising. The good-looking young man who was trying to get off with Katerina Tapo wasn't so much chatting her up as shouting her up: the two of them had to stand very close and bellow alternately into each other's ears just to be heard, which, while it certainly robbed their flirting of any subtlety, also meant she was left in little doubt of his intentions. That was no bad thing, Kat decided. Only those who really fancied each other would persevere with small talk in such difficult conditions. For her part, she'd already made the decision that Eduardo – or was it Gesualdo? – would be coming back later to her tiny two-room apartment in Mestre.

Eduardo, or possibly Gesualdo, wanted to know what she did for a living. "I'm a travel agent," she yelled back.

He nodded. "Cool. Get to travel much yourself?"

"A bit," she shouted.

She felt her phone buzz against her thigh. It was set to ring, but such was the noise around them she hadn't heard it. Pulling it out, she saw she'd missed three calls already. "*Un momento*," she shouted into it. Indicating to her companion she'd be back in a minute, she struggled down the crowded steps of the bar into the open air.

Mother of Christ, it was cold. Around her a few hardy smokers were braving the chill: her own mouth barked steam almost as thick as their smoke as she turned back to the phone. "*Sì? Pronto?*"

"There's a body," Francesco's voice said. "You're on it. I just spoke to Allocation."

"Homicide?" She struggled to keep the excitement out of her voice.

"Could be. Whatever it is, it's going to be a big one."

"Why's that?"

Francesco didn't answer her directly. "I'm texting the address. Near the Salute. You'll meet Colonnello Piola at the scene. Good luck. And remember, you owe me for this." He rang off.

She glanced at the screen. No address yet, but if it was near the church of Santa Maria della Salute she'd need to catch the *vaporetto*. Even so, she was probably twenty minutes away, and that was assuming she didn't go home to change first, which she definitely ought to, given what she was wearing. Damn, she decided, there was no time for that. She'd do her coat up tight and hope Piola didn't wonder too much at her bare legs or her party make-up. It was La Befana, after all – January 6th, the Feast of the Epiphany, but also a celebration in honour of the old witch who brings children sweets or lumps of coal depending on how naughty they've been – and the whole city was out having a good time.

At least she'd brought rubber boots as well as her heels. Everyone had: the combination of winter tides, snow and a full moon had brought *acqua alta* to Venice, the intermittent floods that plagued them almost every year now. Twice a day the city was submerged by a tidal surge several feet higher than Venice had been built to accommodate. Canals expanded over their pavements; St Mark's Square – the lowest point of the city – became a salt-water lake, soupy with cigarette ends and pigeon droppings, and even those who tried to stick to the raised wooden walkways put out by the authorities sometimes found themselves having to splash.

She felt adrenalin sluice her stomach. Ever since she'd been promoted to the detective division she'd been pressing to work on a murder case. And now, with any luck, she had one. Colonel Piola wouldn't have been assigned to this if it was just another drunken tourist drowning in a canal. So that meant a double stroke of luck: her first big investigation would be under the supervision of the senior detective she most admired.

She briefly considered going back into the bar to tell Eduardo/Gesualdo she had to go to work, and maybe get his phone number before she left. Then she decided against it. Travel agents, even busy ones, were rarely called to their offices at ten to midnight, especially on La Befana. It would mean explaining why she didn't tell casual pickups like him she was actually an officer of the Carabinieri, and generally soothing his wounded pride, and she really didn't have time for that.

Besides, if this *was* a murder investigation, she was unlikely to have any time over the next couple of weeks to return his phone calls, let alone see him for sex. Eduardo was just going to have to get lucky with someone else.

Her phone pulsed again as Francesco texted her the address, and she felt her heart beat a little faster in response.

Detective-Colonel Aldo Piola stared down at the body. He badly wanted to break his six-day-old New Year's resolution and light a cigarette. Not that he could have smoked here in any case. Preservation of evidence came first.

"A *piovan*?" he said wonderingly, using the Venetian slang for "priest".

Dr Hapadi, the forensic examiner, shrugged. "That's what was called in. But there's a bit more to this one. Want to take a closer look?"

Somewhat reluctantly, Piola stepped off the raised walkway into the foot-deep murk, splashing gingerly towards the circle of light emanating from Hapadi's portable generator. The blue plastic wraparounds the doctor had offered him when he arrived at the scene were immediately flooded with icy seawater, despite being tied around his calves with elastic bands. Another pair of shoes ruined, he thought with an inward sigh. He wouldn't have minded, but he and his wife had been celebrating La Befana with friends at Bistrot de Venise, one of Venice's best restaurants, and as a consequence he was wearing his best new Bruno Maglis. As soon as he could, he jumped up onto the marble steps of the church, one level above the body, pausing to shake each foot dry as if he were stepping out of a bath. You never knew: perhaps they could be salvaged.

The body lay slumped across the steps, half in and half out of the water, almost as though the victim had been trying to crawl up out of the sea into the sanctuary of the church. That would be the effect of the tide, which was already receding a little, back towards the pavement that usually separated the church from the Canale di San Marco. There was no mistaking the black and gold vestments of a Catholic priest dressed for Mass, nor the two bullet holes in the back of the matted head that left purple-brown stains dripping onto the marble.

"Could this have happened here?" Piola asked.

Hapadi shook his head. "I doubt it. At a guess, the high water washed the body in from the lagoon. If it weren't for the *acqua alta*, it'd be halfway to Croatia by now."

If so, Piola reflected, the corpse was little different from the rest of the rubbish that got washed into the city. The seawater around him had a faint aroma of sewage: not all Venetian cesspits were watertight, and some residents notoriously saw high water as a chance to save themselves the usual emptying fee. "What height was it tonight?"

"One forty, according to the pipes." The electronic sirens that informed Venetians of impending *acqua alta* also warned them of its extent – ten centimetres above a metre for every note the sirens sounded.

Piola bent down to take a closer look. The priest, whoever he was, had been of slight build. It was tempting to turn him over, but Piola knew that to do so before the forensic team had finished photographing would be to incur their wrath.

"So," he said thoughtfully. "He was shot somewhere to the east or south."

"Possibly. But you're wrong about one thing, at least."

"What?"

"Take a look at the shoes."

Gingerly, Piola hooked a finger under the sodden cassock and lifted it away from the priest's leg. The foot was small, almost dainty, and it was shod in what was unmistakeably a woman's leather shoe.

"He's a tranny?" he said, amazed.

"Not exactly." Hapadi almost looked as if he were enjoying this. "OK, now the head."

Piola had to crouch right down, his buttocks almost touching the eddying water, to do as Hapadi asked. The corpse's eyes were open, the forehead resting against the step as if the priest had died in the very act of drinking from the sea. As Piola looked, a small wave washed over the chin into the open mouth before sucking away again, leaving it drooling.

Then Piola saw. The chin was without stubble, the lips too pink. "Mother of God," he said, surprised. "It's a woman." Automatically, he crossed himself.

There could be no doubt – the shaped eyebrow and trace of eyeliner around the lifeless eye, the feminine lashes; even, he now saw, the discreet earring half-hidden by a strand of matted hair. She was about forty, with a little middle-aged thickening of the shoulders, which was why he hadn't realised immediately. Recovering himself, he touched the sodden alb. "Pretty realistic, for fancy dress."

"If it *is* fancy dress."

Piola looked at the other man curiously. "Why do you say that?"

"What woman would dare to go out dressed as a priest in Italy?" Hapadi said rhetorically. "She wouldn't get ten yards." He shrugged. "Then again, maybe she didn't. Get ten yards, I mean."

Piola frowned. "Two in the back of the head? Seems a bit extreme."

"Colonnello?"

Piola turned. An attractive young woman, her face heavily made up, wearing a short black coat, galoshes, and apparently very little else, was hailing him from the wooden walkway.

"You can't come through here," he said automatically. "This is a crime scene."

She dug an ID card out of her pocket and held it up. "Capitano Tapo, sir. I've been assigned to the case."

"You'd better come across, then."

She hesitated for only a moment, he noticed, before pulling off her boots and wading barefoot towards him. He caught a flash of red paint on her toenails as she put her foot into the murk.

"Last time I saw someone try that in Venice," Hapadi said cheerfully, "they cut their feet to ribbons. Broken glass under the water."

The *capitano* ignored him. "Any identification on him, sir?" she asked Piola.

"Not yet. And we were just remarking on the fact that our victim is not in fact a him."

Tapo's eyes darted warily to the body, but Piola noticed that she didn't cross herself as he had. These youngsters didn't always have the ingrained Catholicism he'd struggled so hard to shake off. "Could it be some stupid joke?" she said hesitantly. "It's La Befana, after all."

"Perhaps. But it should be the other way round really, shouldn't it?" In Venice, where any excuse for dressing up was always seized on, La Befana was celebrated with fancy dress; not least by the boatmen and manual workers, who put on women's clothing for the day.

Squatting down beside the body much as Piola had done a few minutes earlier, Kat scrutinised it carefully. "This looks real, though." Gently, she tugged a chain out from under the robes. A silver cross dangled from the end of it.

"Perhaps it's not hers," Piola said. "Anyway, first things first, Captain. Establish a perimeter, start a visitor log, and when the *dottore* here is finished with his photographs, make arrangements for the corpse to be removed to the mortuary. In the meantime I want screens and an evidence shelter – we don't want the good citizens of Venice any more alarmed than absolutely necessary." It went without saying that it would be the fact that the dead woman was defiling a priest's robes that would cause the alarm, not just the fact that she'd been murdered.

"Of course, sir. Shall I call you when the body's at the mortuary?"

"Call me?" Piola seemed surprised. "I'll be going with it. Chain of evidence, Capitano. I was the first officer at the scene, so I stay with the corpse."

If that was impressive – Kat's last supervising officer had usually knocked off for the day not long after the end of his extended lunch break, telling her to "call with any developments" while switching his phone off even before he'd reached the door – it was nothing compared to what happened when the State Police turned up, their launch idling over to where Hapadi was packing up his kit. Kat was blue with cold now, the freezing water eating into her very bones; when she saw the words "Polizia di Stato" her first reaction was one of relief.

An officer stepped out of the boat, immaculately dressed for the occasion in police-blue fishing waders. "Sovrintendente Otalo," he said, introducing himself. "Many thanks, Colonel, we'll take it from here."

Piola barely glanced at him. "Actually, this one's ours."

Otalo shook his head. "It's been decided at a higher level. We've got some spare capacity at the moment."

I bet you have, Kat thought. She stayed quiet, waiting to see how Piola would handle this.

Visitors to Italy are often surprised to discover that there are a number of separate police forces, of which the largest are the Polizia di Stato, answering to the Interior Ministry, and the Carabinieri, answering to the Ministry of Defence.

Effectively they operate in competition, right down to having two different emergency numbers, a system which the Italian government claims keeps both organisations on their toes, and which Italian citizens are aware is actually a recipe for muddle, corruption and bureaucratic incompetence. Even so, it was a source of pride to Kat and her colleagues that most people preferred to dial 112 for the Carabinieri, rather than 113 for their civilian counterparts.

Piola did look at Otalo now, his glance one of barely concealed contempt. "Until my *generale di divisione* says I'm off this case, I'm on it," he said. "Anyone who tries to tell me otherwise is obstructing an investigation, and may well get themselves arrested."

The other man looked equally disdainful. "All right, all right. Keep your precious body, if it's so important to you." He shrugged. "I'll get back to my nice warm station house."

"If you wanted to be helpful, you could lend us your boat," Piola suggested.

"Exactly," the man agreed. "If I wanted to be helpful. *Ciao*, then." He stepped back into the launch, saluting ironically as the boat reversed into the canal.

At about three in the morning it started to snow; fat, wet flakes as big as butterflies that melted as soon as they settled on the salty water. The snow turned to slush in Kat's hair, chilling her still further. Glancing at Piola, she saw that his entire head glittered, from his scalp down to his stubble, as if decked in a carnival mask. Only on the corpse did the snow not melt, gradually covering the dead woman's open eyes and forehead with a white, blank gesso.

Kat shivered yet again. Her first murder, and it was going to be a strange one, she could tell that already. A woman in a priest's robes. A desecration, right here on the steps of Santa Maria of Health. You didn't have to be standing in freezing salt water for that to send a chill right into your soul.

Two

THE YOUNG WOMAN coming out of the baggage hall at Venice's Marco Polo Airport shortly before 7 a.m. looked very different from the other passengers who had arrived on Delta flight 102 that morning. Where they were dressed for vacations or business trips, she was wearing the combat fatigues that, since the declaration of the war on terror, all American military personnel were encouraged to wear on commercial flights as a gesture of reassurance to other travellers. Where their hair was tousled from catching some sleep on the red-eye from JFK, she had already ensured that her blonde locks conformed to US Army regulation AR670 ("Females will ensure their hair is neatly groomed, and does not present a ragged, unkempt, or extreme appearance... Long hair that falls naturally below the bottom edge of the collar will be neatly and inconspicuously fastened or pinned"). Where they wheeled suitcases with extending handles, or piled their luggage onto airport trolleys, she carried hers on her back, a bulging Molle field-pack so large it seemed remarkable she didn't overbalance with its weight. And while they clustered around the waiting travel reps, or scanned the milling crowd for drivers holding up name cards, she turned right, walking confidently – with a parade-ground gait she was by now entirely unconscious of – past the coffee shop and the Hertz rental office to where a booth tucked down an inconspicuous side corridor bore the acronym "LNO–SETAF".

Behind the counter was a man her own age, also wearing grey US fatigues. He returned her salute with a friendly "Welcome, Second Lieutenant", turning an electronic card-reader towards her so she could swipe her CAC card. "You've timed it well. The shuttle bus leaves at 0800, and it looks like you'll have it to yourself. Once you get to Ederle, report to Inprocessing. I'll notify your sponsor you're en route."

Nodding her thanks, she made her way to the car park, which to her delight was lightly dusted with snow. A white minibus was parked to one side, engine running. It too was marked only by the acronym "SETAF" in small letters on the front doors. The US Military tried to keep its presence here relatively low key: even unscrambled from its acronym, "Southern European Task Force" sounded suitably generic.

The driver, a private, jumped out to help with her bags. Taking in his passenger's face – which was kind of geeky for a blonde, but not without charm – as well as the newness of her second lieutenant's tabs, he decided to chance a conversation.

"Welcome to Venice, ma'am. TDY or PCS?" Meaning: Temporary Deployment or a Permanent Change of Station?

"PCS," she said with an eager smile. "The whole four years."

"Awesome. Must be your first foreign posting, right? Ever visited OCONUS before?"

OCONUS – that was military-speak for Outside the Contiguous United States. To many soldiers, she knew, OCONUS was just as much of a place as Utah or Texas. Perhaps that wasn't surprising, given that their experiences of all three ended up being remarkably similar.

"First foreign posting," she agreed. "But actually I was raised here."

He raised an eyebrow. "Army brat?"

"Affirmative. My dad was in the 173rd. Camp Darby, down at Pisa."

"Speak any Italian?"

She nodded. "*In realtà, lo parlo piuttosto bene.*"

"Neat," he said, clearly not understanding a word. "Listen, I'm not meant to do this, but since you're the only passenger, want to take off now and get a tour en route? There's a great view of Venice if we go by the coast road, and we'll still arrive on schedule. Ederle's only about fifty minutes away."

She knew he simply wanted an opportunity to flirt with her, and a part of her recognised that as an officer, even one with the greenest and most lowly of rankings, she should probably say no. But another part of her was euphoric at finally getting back to the country where she'd done her growing up. She'd found it hard even to walk past the airport coffee shop without pausing to go inside – a proper coffee shop! At last! With a real zinc counter to lean against while you threw your espresso down your throat, rather than the faux-college-library atmosphere and gigantic cappuccinos of Starbucks or Tully's! Even before that, on the plane, she'd pressed her forehead to the window when the seatbelt sign came on, eager after so long for a glimpse of Italy. It hadn't been a particularly auspicious one – from the glorious dawn sunshine of altitude they'd struggled shakily down through cloud, the window becoming flecked with ice, before emerging above a grey, cold-looking lagoon dotted with islands. For a moment she'd had the strange sensation that she was actually in a submarine, dropping towards a dark seabed, rather than flying. But the plane was still turning, and just for a moment Venice – that magical, extraordinary island – had been tantalisingly visible beneath her, buildings and canals crowded into its ridiculously small area, as intricate as a piece of coral or the inner workings of a watch.

"OK," she said suddenly. "Why not?"

The private grinned, certain it was him, not the promised view of Venice, which had swung the decision. "Outstanding. What's your name, ma'am?"

"Boland. Second Lieutenant Holly Boland." And then, because the place and the soil seemed to demand it, she added, "*Mi chiamo Holly Boland.*"

Despite taking her along the coast road, where the views of Venice across the water – "Regularly voted world's most romantic," he assured her – were just as remarkable as he had promised, Private Billy Lewtas's talk was all of their destination. Caserma Ederle, or Camp Ederle as he called it, had everything a soldier might need, right there on post. The PX was no ordinary store but a whole shopping mall, with a 24-hour supermarket, various clothing concessions including American Apparel and Gap, and a flower shop for those – like him – who liked to give a girl a nice gift after a date. There was a twelve-bay auto repair centre specialising in Chryslers, Fords and other vehicles unfamiliar to Italian mechanics. There was an 800-bed hospital; four bars – including the Crazy Bull, the Lion's Den, and the "outstanding" Joe Dugan's; a bowling alley, movie theatre, sports arena, high school, three American banks, five restaurants serving everything from French fries to pulled pork, a Burger King... even an Italian gift shop, so that you could buy mementoes of your deployment abroad without actually leaving the post. Best of all, he enthused, was the proximity of the Alps – look, they were visible right now, if you looked high enough, with that great coating of snow – where the military maintained its own cadre of skiing instructors for their exclusive use.

Holly had an idea that it was actually the Dolomites, not the Alps, that rose in the distance, but chose not to correct him. She was obliged to live on-post for six weeks – had in fact already been assigned a room in the rather unmilitary-sounding Ederle Inn Hotel – but after that she'd be free to move off-base, into private housing around Vicenza. Six weeks wasn't so long to wait. Until then she would drink Miller and Budweiser in Joe Dugan's, and probably even go on dates with, and accept flowers from, men like him, although not – if she could help it – after a visit to Burger King.

She turned her head to the window, drinking in every Italian street sign and licence plate, every expressive gesture of the drivers and passers-by. A teenager on his way to school, steering his moped with ridiculously exaggerated panache through the crawling morning traffic, carried a raven-haired girl on his pillion. Neither was wearing a helmet: the girl was facing backwards, the better to eat the hot slice of pizza that was folded *a fazzoletto*, like a handkerchief, in her right hand. The boy shouted something back to her; she looked up, her brown eyes alive and dancing. With a pang of mingled yearning and exultation, Second Lieutenant Holly Boland recognised herself, a decade younger, speeding through Pisa on the back of her first boyfriend's Vespa.

"This is it," Private Lewtas said.

She became aware that they were driving alongside a long, unmarked wall of bomb-resistant concrete. It was, however, hardly anonymous, being covered in long, looping scrawls of graffiti. "NO DAL MOLIN" she read, and "US ARMY GO HOME". There were people milling by the roadside – civilians, some dressed in outlandish clown-like costumes, while others were holding placards with more slogans. When they saw the minibus they shook them fiercely.

"What's going on?" she asked.

"Oh, this is nothing. Weekends we get hundreds, sometimes thousands of these guys. Camp Ederle's scheduled to double in size over the next few years, and some of the locals ain't too happy."

"What's Dal Molin?"

"The airfield we're expanding onto."

The bus slowed briefly at the gate, Lewtas exchanging swift salutes with the guards as the barrier was raised. Most of the guards were *carabinieri*, she noticed, Italian military police, working alongside an American MP.

"You'd think the ginzos would be more grateful we're here, protecting them," he said as they pulled over inside the gate to have their IDs checked. "Welcome to Camp Ederle, ma'am."

In front of her was a town – or rather, a fortified town-within-a-town, its boundaries marked by that bomb-resistant wall that ran in either direction as far as the eye could see. Italian street signs were replaced by American ones; right now they were on the junction of Main Street and Eighth. Crosswalk poles in English instructed pedestrians to "Walk" or "Don't Walk". Most people wore army fatigues, and military vehicles alternated with Buicks and Fords.

"Hey, Inprocessing's just about a hundred yards down. I can drop you right outside. They'll give you a map, by the way – everyone gets lost to begin with. This place is huge." He turned round a traffic circle where the Stars and Stripes fluttered on a pole. "Do you want to give me your number? Oh, I forgot, you won't have a European phone yet." Pulling up, he scribbled something on a piece of card and handed it to her. "I believe I'm free on Saturday night."

As she stepped off the shuttle bus, still a little amused by Private Lewtas's self-confidence, Holly Boland still saw only a vast military encampment of anonymous buildings, similar to every other US army post she'd ever been on. There was nothing to make her suspect that what happened in this place would soon test, and stretch, loyalties she didn't even know she had.

Three

THE BODY WAS in the mortuary at last, where Kat was barely any warmer, the morgue being kept at a constant nine degrees in order to prevent its occupants' flesh from corrupting during the long Italian summers. Piola still hadn't relinquished custody, and Kat, determined not to be outdone in stamina, intended to stay with him until he did, even though the colonel had suggested several times that she go home and get some sleep, not to mention some proper clothes.

The mortuary technician, a man called Spatz, was explaining why identification was going to be difficult.

"See here," he said, lifting the dead woman's left wrist in his own blue-gloved hands. "Salt water does terrible things. Fingerprints will be almost impossible."

"Is there anything you can do to enhance them?"

"We can glove her."

"Better do it then." Piola glanced at Kat. "Know what gloving is, Capitano?"

"No, sir," she confessed.

"Spatz will peel the skin from the victim's fingers and stretch it onto a hand cast." He nodded to where four or five wooden hands of different sizes, like glove-makers' mannequins, stood on a shelf. "Standard practice where a corpse has been in seawater, and something we have to do quite often in this waterlogged city of ours. In future, if you hear something you don't understand, ask, OK? This is your first homicide, but I expect you to be able to run the next one on your own."

"Yes, sir," she said awkwardly.

"Now go home and get a couple of hours' rest. This time I mean it. And next time we meet, I don't want to see quite so much of your legs." His smile – the lines beside his eyes falling into a well-worn pattern, like a fan – robbed the words of any offence, even before he added, "They're a distraction, quite frankly, and I'm a happily married man."

"Colonel?" Spatz said softly behind them. Piola turned. The technician was still holding the corpse's arm. The sleeve of the robe had fallen back, revealing something on the woman's right forearm, just above the wrist. Both officers went to examine it, Kat holding back a little since she was technically disobeying an order not to be there.

It was some kind of tattoo. Dark blue and barely more sophisticated than a child's drawing, it resembled a circle with lines coming out of it to represent the sun – except that in this case there was something inside the sun as well, a motif like a kind of extended asterisk.

Pushing the sleeve further up, Spatz revealed a second tattoo, similar but subtly different in design.

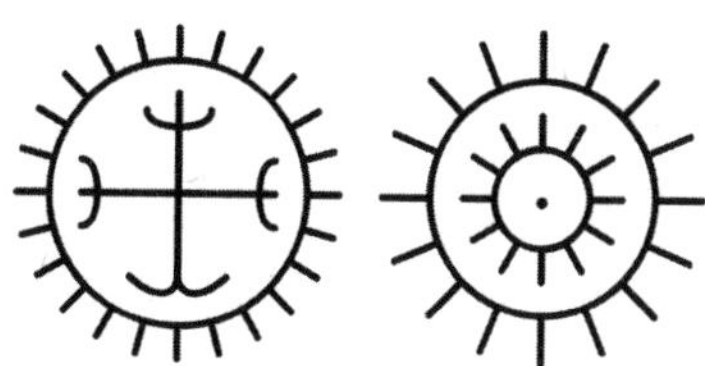

"Curious," Piola said after a moment.

"And here..." Spatz indicated the fingernails. None were

painted, the cuticles short and unpolished, but three of them, Kat now saw, were missing completely, the skin beneath lumpen and scarred. "Same on the other hand too."

"Torture?" Piola ventured.

Spatz's shrug said that interpretation of evidence wasn't his concern. "The scars look pretty old."

"How quickly can you do the autopsy?"

Spatz's eyes went to the hand. "Next week, according to the schedule. But I'll make sure it's today."

"Good." Piola's gaze turned back to Kat. "Now off you go."

As she walked to the door she thought she was conscious of his eyes watching her, following those inappropriate bare legs of hers. But when she reached the doorway, and, without quite meaning to, glanced back to check, she saw he had returned to the corpse. He was leaning over the dead woman, her hand laid in his, examining it minutely. Like a manicurist, she thought; or someone extending an old-fashioned invitation to a lover at a dance.

Four

DANIELE BARBO SAT in a cell below the Verona courtroom, reading a book on mathematics while he waited for the jury to reach their verdict. A few feet away, his lawyer went through her notes, anxiously rehearsing the different arguments that might be required, depending on what combination of charges he was convicted of. She knew better than to involve her client in these deliberations. The same book that held his attention now had rarely left his hand during the trial, the proceedings of which he had deigned to notice only with the occasional disinterested glance, and she had learnt to her cost that any attempts at conversation would be rebuffed.

Eventually her client closed the book and stared into the corner of the room.

"It won't be long now," she ventured hesitantly.

He looked at her, as if a little surprised to find her there, but said nothing. He already knew what the judge would decide. He knew it because, for the last five weeks, someone had been altering his Wikipedia profile, adding a new final section:

Conviction and subsequent life

In 2013 Daniele Barbo was found guilty of seven charges of computer hacking; failing to curtail trafficking of pornography, including underage pornography and sexual violence;

facilitating criminal enterprise including identity theft and money laundering; and refusing to allow the authorities access to requested information. He was found “Not Guilty” on an eighth charge: living off immoral earnings. He was sentenced to nine months in prison, despite his lawyer’s pleas that her client was psychologically unfit for custody – a tactic that had worked at his previous trial.

Barbo committed suicide within a year of his release, drowning himself in the canal outside the Venetian palazzo his family had occupied since 1898. His family name died with him. The future of Carnivia, the website he created, remains uncertain.

The first time he was alerted – by an anonymous email – to the addition, Daniele simply erased it. Within seconds it was back. The same thing happened the next three times he wiped it. Someone had created a bot, a simple piece of software programmed to carry out this one task repetitively, rewriting Wikipedia’s page every time he corrected it. It was, on one level, a tiny, malicious little torture, of no real consequence, but it showed the lengths that those who wanted to attack him were prepared to go to.

Or, he reflected, it showed how much they wanted him to think that: to believe there was nothing they wouldn’t do to destroy him.

He could easily have written a more powerful program of his own, to erase the final paragraphs forever and lock the page, but he had no pressing reason for doing so. There were only three or four people in the world whose opinion mattered to him, and he had little interest in what the other 6.9 billion might think. His entire Wikipedia entry, which he had never troubled to read before, was in any case littered with half-truths and distortions.

Daniele Marcantonio Barbo, b 1971, is an Italian mathematician and computer hacker. He is best known for founding Carnivia, a gossip- and information-sharing social network based in Venice, Italy, with over two million regular users.[1]

1 Early life and kidnap
2 Conviction for computer fraud
3 Creation of Carnivia
4 Growth of Carnivia

Early life and kidnap

Daniele Barbo was born into the aristocratic Barbo dynasty of Venice, whose business interests at the time included Alfa-Romeo cars. His father Matteo was a noted playboy before taking over the family investment trust. In later years Matteo devoted himself to establishing the art foundation which bears the family name.

Daniele Barbo's childhood coincided with the period of socio-political turmoil in Italy known as the *anni di piombo* or "Years of Lead". Although his father reportedly favoured progressive industrial relations, the family's profile and wealth made them a target for far-left organisations such as the *Brigate Rosse*, or Red Brigade.

Daniele Barbo was kidnapped on June 27 1977, aged seven. It was widely reported at the time that his father was under pressure from the Italian government not to negotiate with the kidnappers,[2] although it was later claimed that this was a smokescreen erected by the security forces to buy time while they located him.[Citation needed] On August 4 1977 Matteo and his American wife Lucy received Daniele's ears and nose through the post.

In a subsequent operation led by Italian Special Forces, the boy was freed and all seven kidnappers killed or captured. The three surviving kidnappers refused to cooperate with the court on the grounds that it was part of the para-capitalist hegemony.[3] They were sentenced to jail terms of between twenty and forty years each.[4]

Conviction for computer fraud

Little was heard of Barbo between the end of the trial and the early 1990s, although it is understood that he attended an institute for deaf children before going to Harvard to study mathematics. Whilst at Harvard he had the unusual distinction of having a term paper on cybernetics (specifically, on the application of Kullback-Leibler divergence to complex dynamical systems) published in a peer-reviewed academic journal. [5]

In 1994 he was one of those arrested for the Comcast Hack, in which a loose-knit group of computer activists took control of the cable giant's website, reportedly in revenge for poor customer service. The method they employed was both simple and effective, accessing the database of the company from whom Comcast had purchased the domain name Comcast.com and re-registering it as theirs. This enabled them to redirect Comcast's web traffic to a page containing an abusive message.[6]

Barbo's lawyer later confirmed that he was the hacker known as Defi@nt.[7] At his trial it was claimed that he suffered from a number of medical conditions as a result of his childhood kidnap, including partial deafness, Social Avoidance Disorder and Autistic Spectrum Disorder, making a prison term unfeasible. The judge evidently agreed: Barbo was given a suspended sentence, although this may have been because the Italian government had no wish to see the murky circumstances of his kidnap and botched rescue rehashed in court.[citation needed]

Barbo/Defi@nt was rarely seen, either in public or online, in the years after his trial, although he may have used a number of other aliases including Syfer, 10THDAN and Joyride.[8] In 1996, following the death of his father, he moved back to the family residence, Ca' Barbo in Venice, and took a non-executive seat on the board of the Barbo Foundation.[9] A 2004 newspaper report described him as "an almost total recluse", stating that he rarely leaves his home except during the Venetian Carnevale, when he wears a costume mask to disguise his facial disfigurements.[7]

Creation of Carnivia

In 2005 Barbo emerged as the programmer behind Carnivia, a 3D mirror world of his home city, Venice, notable for its obsessive attention to detail. It has been claimed, for example, that the real St Mark's Square and the version in Carnivia contain exactly the same number of paving stones. The Doge's Palace alone is reputed to have taken Barbo four years to programme.[9]

Carnivia is unusual in that users encounter almost no instructions telling them what it is for or how it should be used. It was initially assumed that it was intended as a social network for Venetians. It soon became apparent, however, that the site granted its users an unusually high degree of anonymity, and it quickly gained a reputation amongst those who preferred to conceal their real identities. It has been described as "a Facebook for hackers… an unregulated, unlicensed marketplace, not unlike its real-life counterpart once was, where anything from wild rumours to stolen financial details can be bought or sold for a price." [7]

Barbo himself claimed in a rare Usenet post that the creation of Carnivia was not driven by any particular purpose. "Galileo said, 'Mathematics is the language in which God wrote the universe.' I thought it would be interesting to program a virtual world from pure mathematical principles. What people do with that world is really up to them." [8]

Growth of Carnivia

In a move considered ground-breaking at the time, Carnivia incorporated full cross-functionality with other technologies including Facebook, Google Mail, Twitter and Google Earth. This allows the user to leave anonymous messages on other sites, a process implicated in internet stalking.[10] Users can also "tag" social networks with untraceable information, such as rumours, or send encrypted messages.

Anti-pornography campaigners have highlighted the sexual nature of much Carnivia traffic.[13] In 2011 Barbo refused to allow the Italian authorities access to Carnivia's servers to check for illegal material, in breach of national and international laws.

It was subtly done. Almost every individual fact or reference was genuine, but the whole was cleverly constructed to suggest more than was actually stated. The juxtaposition of the pornography accusation, for example – failing to mention that it came in an article that also named MySpace, YouTube and a multitude of other websites – and the judicial application by the authorities to open up his servers for scrutiny – again, an application that had been made to many internet businesses – gave the impression that it was specifically pornography they were looking for, when the real issue was whether a government had the right to pry into what its citizens were doing online. The suggestion of psychological flaws, too, was mostly between the lines. It was true that he rarely went out, but when you loathed crowds, living in the most-visited city on earth made doing so an unrewarding, even distasteful experience. As for the implication that he had created Carnivia as a kind of refuge from the real world – well, that had more merit, though probably not in the way the writer had intended.

His reverie was interrupted by the lawyer, gesturing to get his attention.

"The judge is back."

He nodded, stepping back from the door as the guards came towards him with the handcuffs. The prosecution had requested that, like some captured beast, Daniele Barbo must be chained in court, and the judge had agreed. It was yet more confirmation that the sentence would be "Guilty". That Italy's justice system was infinitely corruptible didn't surprise him; that someone was bothering to spend so much time and money using it to destroy him did.

They must be desperate, he found himself thinking. *Why?*

The courtroom would be full of people, and even when he left it there would be journalists, cameras… For a moment he found himself wishing he could stay down there, in the relative calm of the cell. But even as he was being led up the stairs his mind was already planning ahead, analysing and probing, rewriting the future as if it were a piece of software that had to be debugged and re-engineered before it would function as he wished.

Five

AS INSTRUCTED, KAT went back to her tiny apartment near the seafront in Mestre, fell into bed, and caught a couple of hours' sleep. A shot of espresso from her beaten-up stovetop Bialetti got her going again, followed by a quick shower that was even hotter than the coffee.

Her uniform was still hanging on the front of her wardrobe where she'd left it the previous evening. The Valentino-designed skirt and jacket, with its elaborately silvered collar and red-piped epaulettes, had been her second skin since she'd left the Carabinieri training academy three years earlier. Now, for the first time, she wouldn't need it: homicide investigators wore plain clothes. She reached inside the wardrobe to where a navy blue pleated skirt and a crisp tailored jacket from Fabio Gatto in Calle della Mandorla had been hanging for months, waiting for just such an occasion. Though unshowy, the fabric was impeccably tailored and had cost almost a month's wages. She wondered, briefly, if Piola might consider her a little overdressed for a captain, then dismissed the thought. Even a captain needed to make a good impression.

Hurrying from her apartment, she took a train across the Ponte della Libertà, followed by a *vaporetto* to Campo San Zaccaria, the ancient square near Piazza San Marco where the

Carabinieri's headquarters were housed in a former nunnery. Francesco Lotti, the friend who'd swung her assignment onto the case, had already established an operations room on the second floor. It was buzzing with activity.

Colonel Piola was standing in a small glassed-off office, deep in conversation with another man. Despite having told her to go home and rest, he looked as if he hadn't yet done the same. As the man with him turned, Kat saw a grey clerical shirt and white *collarino* under his dark suit. A priest.

Seeing her, Piola gestured for her to join them.

"This is Father Cilosi, from the bishop's office," he said by way of introduction. "He's kindly offered to tell us all about priests' garments."

Father Cilosi nodded. "Not that I can be of much help, I'm afraid. The robes seem authentic, from the photographs." He pointed to the pictures from the mortuary that were scattered across the desk. "This outer garment is a chasuble. All priests are required to wear one when they take Mass. And underneath that, the usual tunic and alb."

"When you say 'take Mass', Father, I assume you mean as a celebrant?" Piola asked.

"Correct. A priest attending Mass as a visitor would wear a surplice – a plain white robe."

"And the fact that the chasuble is black – could you remind us what that means?"

"The colour of the chasuble reflects the nature of the Mass. During this season, for example, we usually wear a white chasuble, to commemorate Christ's birth. Black is only ever worn for the most sombre rites, such as an exorcism or a Mass for the dead."

"So there's no possibility," Piola asked thoughtfully, "that this could be some other kind of robe, worn legitimately by a woman in a non-ordained role? An altar girl, say, or some kind of lay reader?"

Father Cilosi shook his head. "Every vestment a priest wears has a very precise symbolism. These red ribbons, for example, symbolise Christ's wounds. This long strip of silk is the stole, worn in remembrance of His bonds. Even the fringes on the ends of the stole are based in scripture. Numbers 15:38, if I recall correctly: "Speak unto the children of Israel, and bid them that they make them fringes in the borders of their garments.... that ye may look upon it, and remember all the commandments of the Lord."

Kat pulled a pad towards her and jotted down notes as Father Cilosi continued. "Each garment is accompanied during robing by a specific prayer. When the priest puts on the tunic, for example, he recites the words 'My soul shall rejoice in the Lord, for He hath clothed me in the garment of salvation, and with the vesture of gladness hath He covered me.' As he puts on the cuffs, first the right and then the left, he says, 'Thy right hand, O Lord, is glorified in strength; Thy right hand, O Lord, hath vanquished the enemy.' The rituals, and the garments, are of deep significance to us. Whoever this woman is, she has absolutely no right to be defiling them like this." He spoke calmly enough, but Kat thought she noticed a tremor of genuine revulsion in his voice.

"And can you summarise why that is, Father?" Piola asked. "The situation as regards women and the priesthood, I mean?"

"In a nutshell, the teaching of the Catholic Church, as set out by His Holiness, is that the Church simply has no authority to confer priestly ordination on women. It goes back to the original curse levied against Eve – in other words, it's a matter of divine law rather than Papal judgement. Hence any woman attempting to receive ordination, or to pass herself off as having been ordained, would be guilty of what His Holiness calls a 'grave delict'. That is, she would be a kind of heretic."

The word, vaguely medieval in its connotations, hung in the air. "And what would the penalty for that be?" Piola asked.

"Excommunication," Father Cilosi said. "His Holiness is quite clear about that."

"Meaning that to kill such a woman wouldn't be a mortal sin?" Kat said quietly. Piola glanced at her questioningly, then nodded for her to continue.

Father Cilosi had the grace to look a little discomfited. "In a purely theological sense, perhaps. But the Church teaches that murder is always against God's purpose, as well as man's laws."

"But just so I'm clear, Father," she pressed. "A woman who dresses up as a priest, even for fancy dress – she's the one who's committing the sin?"

"How would you feel if someone turned up to a party dressed in a stolen uniform of the Carabinieri?" he countered.

"Man or woman, the penalty would be a small fine. And it would be unlikely to lead to that person being murdered."

He raised his hands. "If that is indeed what happened here."

"Could she have been a genuine priest, but of another faith?" Piola suggested.

The priest considered. "If so, it isn't one that I know of. Some of the Protestant churches permit women clerics, of course, but their robes are slightly different. A Catholic cassock has thirty-three buttons, for example, to symbolise the thirty-three years of Christ's life. An Anglican cassock has thirty-nine, to symbolise the thirty-nine articles of their faith." He caught Piola's expression. "These may seem small details, even petty ones perhaps. But they evolved over many centuries of custom and debate, and serve to remind every priest of the ancient, sacred traditions of our calling."

"Capitano, check the number of buttons with the morgue. And get someone to check with the Protestant churches in the city, just in case," Piola said to Kat. He slid another photograph towards the priest. "One final question, Father. Do you happen to know what these tattoos might represent?"

Father Cilosi took the picture Piola gave him, then busied himself finding a pair of glasses from his jacket pocket. "I've no idea," he said eventually. "They seem vaguely reminiscent of occult symbols – but I should stress that's not my area of expertise. I could get you the name of someone who would know more, if you wish."

"Thank you, Father," Piola said. "That would be very helpful."

"Not at all. And please call me if I can be of any further assistance." Father Cilosi hesitated. "The bishop has asked me to convey that he regards this incident as deeply distressing for the faithful, and he hopes it can be brought to a speedy conclusion. As I'm sure you recall, a few years ago the issue of women's ordination threatened to become a divisive one for us. There are enough problems engulfing the Church at the moment without reawakening that particular controversy."

"Indeed," Piola said blandly. "Rest assured, Father, we'll do everything we can to get to the bottom of this poor woman's death." He laid a faint emphasis on the last three words.

Father Cilosi was struck by a thought. "If you would like me to say a prayer for her? Or indeed for your investigation..."

"I'm sure she would be most grateful for any prayers you

see fit to offer," Piola said, moving him towards the door. "And in the meantime, the Carabinieri will continue to pursue a more secular approach."

Kat spent an hour with tide tables, weather charts and maps of the lagoon, trying to understand where the body might have entered the water. As a Venetian, she'd grown up with the sea. But the *acqua alta* had complicated everything.

"There are just too many variables," she told Piola. "We can assume our victim came from the lagoon, but it's the currents, not just the tides, that determine the flow of the water. Some of these sandbanks change their position every month."

"So what's the answer?"

"I think we should talk to some fishermen. They'll be able to pinpoint the most likely place, and also tell us if they saw anything suspicious that night."

"Good idea. I'll come with you."

The Venetian lagoon is divided into the *laguna viva*, the part washed by the Adriatic tides, and the *laguna morta*, the more northerly inner or "dead" lagoon, a place of still, salty marshes where hunters catch wild ducks and eels. Reasoning that the body had almost certainly been washed in from the former, they caught the ferry to the fishing port of Chioggia, fifteen miles south of Venice, and went from boat to boat asking questions.

All the fishermen agreed that the body must have originated from somewhere within the long, thin sandbank of the Lido. Beyond that, it would have been washed further out to sea. It also became clear that anyone with local knowledge would have been perfectly well aware of that.

"When the *criminali* dump bodies, they take them five miles out," a gnarled old fisherman called Giuseppe told Kat with a shrug. "That way they're never seen again. It's well known."

"And who do they use to take them there? Is that well known too?"

Another shrug, even more eloquent, told her that, well known or not, there was no way he was going to share that information with her.

From then on she and Piola concentrated on asking about the area within the Lido. Did you see anything unusual around the fourth or fifth of January? Hear anything? Were there any unfamiliar boats around? They found that the fishermen – many of whom were deeply superstitious – were far more shocked by what their victim was wearing than the fact that she was dead, so they prefaced their questions by showing two pictures: the first a close-up of the corpse's face, taken by Hapadi in the morgue, and a second that showed her full-length in her priest's robes. Without exception the second picture prompted a double response – the right hand reaching for the forehead to make the sign of the cross, the left reaching for the testicles to make the *malocchio*, a gesture of protection from the evil eye.

Finally a young fisherman called Lucio gave them a breakthrough.

"The weather was bad that night," he told them. "There was the high water coming, and snow... I decided to cut my losses and get back to my girl. She's in Venice, see, in Dorsoduro? So I took a short cut."

"Show me," Piola suggested, and the young man traced a finger across the chart.

"Here. Past the Isola di Poveglia."

Piola nodded. "Go on."

"No one fishes round Poveglia. People won't buy the fish – they say they've fed on human bones. And it's forbidden to land. The authorities claim it's because the building is unsafe, but everyone knows the real reason is that it's haunted." He paused and lit a cigarette. "Anyway, as I passed, I saw lights. You know, moving, like torches. I think they were in the old tower."

"Did you take a closer look?"

"What, on the eve of La Befana? No way." Lucio shuddered. "I got the hell out of there."

Piola patted him on the shoulder. "OK, that's useful. Thanks."

"You're welcome." The young man hesitated. "Look, I got a ticket from you lot last month for not displaying my boat licence. I *had* the licence, but it had fallen off the holder. Any chance you can make the fine go away?"

"'Fraid not," Piola said. "It doesn't work like that with me. Sorry. Mind if I take a cigarette?"

The other man shrugged dourly. "Be my guest."

"It's your last one."

"It's fine, I've got more."

Piola smiled his thanks and took the packet.

"So," he said when the two of them had climbed back onto dry land. "Poveglia. I suppose you know the stories about that place?"

"Some of them. Wasn't there a mental hospital there before it was abandoned?"

"For a while. But the fishermen believed it was cursed long before that. It was a *lazzaretto* originally – a plague island. To begin with, the city authorities buried the dead there:

later, when the plague kept spreading, they tried to contain it by transporting anyone who showed symptoms out to Poveglia and dumping them in the plague pits before they were even dead. One doesn't suppose they had a very pleasant end. Not surprisingly, it gained a reputation for being haunted." He sighed. "Why they eventually decided to build a lunatic asylum there, God only knows. It's abandoned now, of course – has been since the eighties."

"Think we should take a look?"

"I certainly do." Piola looked at the cigarette packet in his hand.

"I didn't know you smoked, sir."

"I don't – not since New Year's, anyway. I've been promising my wife for years I'd give up. I was just curious about the make." He held it out to her. What she'd taken for a packet of Camel was actually something called Jing Lin, its logo a horned goat on a yellow background but otherwise almost identical to the American brand. "Counterfeit. I doubt it's connected to our murder, but you never know."

They debated how best to get out to Poveglia. Given the superstitiousness of the fishermen, it seemed unlikely any of them would be keen to offer a lift.

"Unless we agree to make Lucio's ticket go away," Kat suggested.

Piola looked at her. For a moment he said nothing, and she found herself flushing. "I only meant…"

"I know what you meant," he said, not unkindly. "You just wanted to get the job done. And I don't blame you for that. But that's how it starts – corners cut, deals done, favours offered or accepted." He sounded sad rather than angry. "And before you know it, you've been done a favour that needs to be repaid, and then they control you. It happens to nine out of ten officers. And you know what? Most of them don't even care. To most, it's just – normal. The way we do things here. *Italy*. End of story."

"Sorry, sir."

"Forget it. We'll call up a Carabinieri launch, and while we're waiting we can have some lunch. The fish restaurants round here are excellent, and after being on those boats I've got a hankering for some sea urchin pasta."

Six

"LET ME REMIND you why you're here, Second Lieutenant," Major Forster said briskly, fixing Holly with a level stare. "As you will know, this is the largest and most important US Army post south of the Alps. Through our power projection capability we provide stability, security and peace to an area of the world stretching from Africa to Iran. However, we have not always succeeded in being appreciated by the host community in which we serve."

Translation, Holly thought: *the locals hate our guts.*

"As a result, an extra Liaison Team was added late last year to further engage and integrate with the Italian population." He pronounced it *Eye-talian*, to match *Eye-ran.* "This is a hearts and minds initiative which will be on-going until the new capability at Dal Molin base is complete."

Translation: until the protestors go away.

"As a native speaker attached to Liaison Officer Team Three, you are tasked with being the civilian-facing component of our military capability. As such you will embody at all times the integrity and professionalism of the US Military."

Translation: personally I think your presence here a waste of my time and American taxpayers' money. But I've been told we need to cosy up to the natives, so get on with it and keep out of my way.

"Yes, sir," Holly said, saluting.

"Do not presume to think that because this mission is easy and safe it is unimportant or without valour," Major Forster said, in a tone of voice which suggested that he thought exactly that. He returned her salute. "Carry on, Second Lieutenant."

"Place is pretty quiet right now," First Lieutenant Mike Breedon said apologetically as he walked her from Major Forster's office to the block in which their team was housed. "The troops are still rotating in and out of Afghanistan, of course, as we transition towards an advisory role. Plus there are still peace-keeping missions in Kosovo and Iraq. But like the major said, LNO-3 doesn't have a whole lot to do with that side – mostly we're dealing with community initiatives, the Italian media, even the protestors themselves. It's not the most exciting, but it is useful."

An affable Virginian three years her senior, Mike was her team leader. She could tell immediately they were going to get along fine.

"This is where you'll work," he said, gesturing to a desk and a computer. "I'm over there. Want to get set up? I have to prepare for a briefing, but I'll come back after and show you around properly."

"Thanks."

She logged on to the computer, a process which involved swiping her CAC card through a reader next to the keyboard. The chip in the smartcard negotiated with the military-specific ActivClient software, checking her authorisation, security clearance and location before giving her access to a screen that was in every other respect identical to that of a normal PC. Unusually for a military computer, this one had been personalised: a photo of a smiling young woman in military-issue skiing gear and sunglasses adorned the background. Presumably this was her predecessor, whose name – she gathered from the numerous postcards still stuck to the wall – was Second Lieutenant Carol Nathans. It seemed Nathans had shipped out in too much of a hurry to tidy up after herself. Holly moved the photo to the trash. Personally, she felt computer screens looked more orderly when they were blank, or bore a simple military insignia.

She'd already checked in at her temporary quarters at the Ederle Inn Hotel, laying out her possessions neatly in the approved army manner, and dealt with the new-arrival paperwork at Inprocessing. Next week she'd join a mandatory Newcomers Orientation Programme covering everything from European driving lessons to basic Italian vocabulary. No parts were optional, even if you already spoke the language and knew the country well. In the meantime, Mike had said, she was to pick up Nathans' schedule and make herself useful.

Scanning the printout her predecessor had left her, it seemed Mike hadn't been exaggerating when he described what they did as unexciting. The army's idea of a "hearts and minds" offensive included interviewing a colonel's wife for the base newsletter about a reading programme she'd set up in a local primary school; inviting a local charity for disabled children to the Bombing Run, the Camp Ederle bowling alley; and organising a regular Pasta Lover's Luncheon at the dining facility. But that was OK. She'd come here in the full knowledge that this kind of thing, not the adrenalin of combat, would be her lot for now. Just being back in Italy was enough.

She'd grown up around bases like this one, eating nachos from the commissary and attending hot dog barbecues where only the children and wives weren't in uniform. While her father was moving from posting to posting she'd attended a new school every eighteen months; like all army brats, she became expert at making friends quickly, or seeming to, and even better at sniffing out the subtle gradations of rank that meant an officer's children didn't accidentally invite a private's to their home.

Then, when she was nine, her father got the PCS to Camp Darby, south of Pisa, and her parents had taken the unusual decision to live off-base, in an ordinary Italian apartment block. Holly had been put into a local school; when the Italian kids had their English classes, she was pulled out for coaching in Italian. Within a term she was fluent, although her brothers always struggled. But even more than school, it was their new neighbours who helped her assimilate, immediately welcoming the Bolands into their homes – occasions at which she often acted as translator for the rest of the family. She found herself acquiring two names: to her Italian friends, who struggled with the H, she was now "Ollie".

Grandparents, cousins and best friends were people an army brat saw once a year if she was lucky. Even fathers came and went according to the unpredictable rhythms of war. Her new Italian friends, by contrast, lived not only with their parents but often their grandparents too. Their fathers came home for lunch every day; their cousins and in-laws lived just around the corner, and everyone hung out together on the street between the hours of five and seven o'clock, chatting, flirting or playing football. Boys called their fathers *papà* rather than "sir"; fathers called their sons by diminutives and nicknames. Before she knew it, a part of her had become indelibly Italian, and as she grew older her first boyfriends had names like Luca and Giancarlo rather than the Dwights and Lewises she mixed with at military socials.

Her parents worried, briefly – the behaviour of an adolescent was held to reflect absolutely on a father's ability to command: any trouble she got into would be reported first to the base commanding officer and only then to her father, whilst if she were to have gotten pregnant, or been caught with drugs, the entire family would have been sent back home in disgrace – but they trusted her enough to let her make her own mistakes. And, Holly realised many years later, it hadn't just been her they trusted, but their Italian neighbours too. Not that she had ever really been the getting-in-trouble type. Too much of the military had soaked into her psyche for her to ever truly kick over the traces.

She'd never imagined she'd follow her father into the army, particularly after the difficult, bitter years of his illness. But when she went back stateside to attend college, she found herself in a world she didn't recognise. People her own age dressed differently from her – the gang-influenced fashions of American college kids left her Italian friends nonplussed – thought differently from her, and, for all their apparently laid-back mannerisms, their "dudes" and "mans" and "bros", were more cynical and materialistic than her. Her roommates could never understand why she tidied her room before breakfast each morning, why ten o'clock in the evening was always, indelibly, 2200 hours, or why she sometimes said "roger that" for "yes" or called the bathroom "the latrine". Just as the Jesuits were supposed to have claimed that if they were given a child until seven, they would give you the man, so Holly discovered that she was now an outsider in the civilian world as well.

As the time for choosing a career neared, she realised that if she was a mongrel, belonging fully to neither the military nor Italy, she might as well be true to one of those bloodlines. She switched to government and military science, but also pursued her talent for languages. At Officer Training College, a mentor with an eye on the long game persuaded her to take Mandarin rather than the more usual Arabic or Farsi. No warrior, she was always better in the classroom than the field: intercept, analysis and intelligence were her skills. But as a newly qualified second lieutenant, the very lowest rung on the officer's ladder, you didn't expect much from your first posting. She'd only applied for Italy on the off-chance. Later, her mentor told her that someone at the Pentagon's Personnel and Postings division had spotted her name on the list and called him up to ask if she was really Ted Boland's daughter.

Unexpectedly her computer chirruped, disturbing her reverie. Looking for the source of the sound, she saw it was signalling an appointment.

REMINDER: 12.00–12.30 Barbara Holton. WHERE: LNO-3.

There was nothing corresponding in the schedule Mike Breedon had given her. Evidently she was looking at Nathans' own electronic calendar, still active on the computer.

"Mike, who's Barbara Holton?" she called across to where her boss sat preparing a PowerPoint.

"NFI."

"Whoever she is, Nathans had a 1200 with her."

Breedon swore under his breath. "She must have forgotten to tell me. I can't do it, I have to be at this briefing."

"Want me to take care of it?"

"Would you? It's probably just a protestor with another petition. If we cancel now they'll say we messed them around."

"Roger that."

"Grab one of the rooms across the way. I'll join later if I can."

The meeting room, a small anonymous box as bland as any in the world, smelt of old air-con and stale biscuits. Holly hurriedly organised some bottles of water and a notepad, then arranged two chairs around the table. While she was doing that the guardhouse called to say Barbara Holton was being escorted over.

The woman they showed in a few minutes later was about fifty, with short greying hair. She was dressed smartly but conservatively, her only adornment a large plastic necklace. She looked more like a successful businesswoman or a college professor, Holly thought, than a protestor.

As they sat down, Holly said politely, "You were probably expecting to see a Second Lieutenant Nathans today, ma'am, but unfortunately she's unavailable. I'm Second Lieutenant Boland. How may I help?"

Barbara Holton fixed her with steely grey eyes. "Has Nathans told you what it's about?" Her voice was East Coast American. Maybe a touch of something guttural in there, though. German? Austrian?

Holly shook her head. "No, ma'am."

"Or that it took me eight weeks of hassling to get this appointment with her?"

"No, ma'am."

"Well," Barbara Holton said, clearly annoyed. "Moving on." She took a yellow folder from her case and pulled out some papers. "I have here a Freedom of Information enquiry. And this is an affidavit from an attorney. It states that I am an American citizen affiliated to an accredited media organisation under the definition of the 2007 Open Government amendment, and therefore entitled to make such an enquiry and have you respond to it in a timely manner." She slid a card and a letter across the table.

Holly picked them up and read them thoroughly. They showed that Barbara Holton was editor-in-chief of Women Under War, which – from the dot com address – appeared to be some kind of online publication.

Her heart sank. This clearly wasn't going to be as simple as receiving a petition. It was highly unlikely she'd be able to deal with it herself. But equally, she didn't want to have to go and drag Mike out of his briefing unless she absolutely had to.

"Very well," she said, stalling for time. "And the nature of the enquiry?"

Barbara Holton took another document out of her folder. "My questions relate to the period 1993 to 1995—"

"Ma'am, I very much doubt that anyone here—"

"I'm talking about the archives, obviously," Barbara Holton continued as if Holly hadn't spoken. "Which are administrative documents under Chapter 5 of Law Number 241."

"If there is documentation, it may well be classified."

"Second Lieutenant, you have almost two miles of document archives in the tunnels here and at Aviano. Along with the forty-eight nuclear warheads, of course. I very much doubt that even a tenth of them are classified."

Holly sighed. "May I see the questions?"

Barbara Holton slid the papers across the table, the pages fluttering with static on the polished wood. Peeling them off, Holly read:

> As an accredited American media representative I formally request:
>
> 1. Any information held at Camp Ederle relating to visits by General Dragan Korovik, commander of the Croatian Militia, to Camp Ederle to receive training, advice or intelligence in 1993–5.
> 2. Any information or minutes relating to meetings at Camp Ederle between General Dragan Korovik and US intelligence officers in 1993–5.
> 3. Any photographs, including but not limited to aerial reconnaissance, provided to General Dragan Korovik in advance of Operation Storm in 1995.
> 4. Any notes or discussions relating to atrocities against civilians in the former Yugoslavia.
> 5. Any notes, documents or other records discussing the use of systematic rape of females as a weapon of war.
> 6. Any minutes from February to May 1995 relating to the subsequent decision by the Italian government to authorise an expansion of the US Military base at Camp Ederle.

Holly read the document twice. Few of the references meant anything to her. Operation Storm – she vaguely recalled the name from her father's time. From what she recollected, after the fall of communism the country then known as Yugoslavia had descended into a brutal civil war that only ended when NATO organised airstrikes against Kosovo and sent in huge armies of peacekeepers. Storm had been a counter-offensive by the Croats against the Serbs, just another episode in the long and brutal struggle between rival ethnic groups jostling for power and territory. Barbara Holton seemed to believe the US Military had been involved in some way. But how that could possibly relate to the decision to expand Camp Ederle, she had no idea.

Moreover, she knew better than to ask. Over the years she had from time to time come across conspiracy theorists – often reasonable and intelligent people, college graduates or friends of friends – who as soon as they heard she was in line for a minor division of Military Intelligence would tell her with absolute conviction that 9/11 was a CIA plot, that the Apollo moon landings were faked, that President Obama worked for Al Qaeda or that the Chinese were behind the collapse of Lehman Brothers. There was no point in trying to have rational conversations with these people. Because there was no definitive proof their theories weren't true, such evidence as there was would always be dismissed as inconclusive. The fact that there wasn't a shred of proof they *were* true, on the other hand, was simply taken as evidence that those trying to keep the real truth from the public had done their job well.

She said, "Ma'am, I'm going to have to consult as to whether we even have this information."

"You'll see from my correspondence with Nathans why I have good reason to believe it's here."

"That may be so, ma'am, but Second Lieutenant Nathans

is no longer based at this location, and I haven't been able to review that correspondence."

Barbara Holton eyes narrowed. "How long have you been doing this job, Second Lieutenant Boland?"

"It's my first day, ma'am," Holly admitted.

The other woman stared at her. Then she laughed. "Oh, that's terrific. That is just *outstanding*. Your first day. You've got to hand it to the military, haven't you? When they want to stall you, they really stall you."

"Ma'am," Holly said wearily, "I can assure you there is no significance whatsoever attached to the fact that I am new to this post. The army redeploys personnel all the time. I promise you that I will expedite this request just as thoroughly, and just as speedily, as Lieutenant Nathans would have done."

Which wouldn't be hard, she reflected, since Nathans hadn't even bothered to transfer it to someone else before she left. She suspected that the file of correspondence Barbara Holton had referred to was long since consigned to the trash.

"Well, we'll see. Under the Act, you have fifteen days to respond."

"Unless we need extensions or clarifications," Holly said mildly.

The other woman raised her eyebrows. "So you *are* familiar with the legislation?"

"I majored in government and military science. I'm also familiar with Executive Order 13526, which allows the government to retrospectively classify, redact or otherwise restrict any information that it decides should properly have been classified at the time."

Barbara Holton regarded her silently for a moment. It was the first time Holly had challenged her. To her surprise, the other woman seemed almost pleased.

"The government won't classify this," she said.

"May I ask why not?"

"Because the government doesn't know it exists. Let alone what it means."

More conspiracies. Holly said evenly, "Well, if it does exist, and there is no clear reason to redact it, then I will find it and pass it on to you."

"Yes," Barbara Holton said. "I do believe you will." She stood up, leaving the yellow folder on the table. "Fifteen days," she said, nodding at it. "Though I'd appreciate it if it could be quicker. Strange as it may seem, getting these old files is extremely urgent. If you need me, my cell number's on my card." She held out her hand, her eyes holding Holly's, assessing her coolly. "A pleasure to meet you, Second Lieutenant."

"Mike," Holly said when her team leader returned from his briefing. "What's the SOP with Freedom of Information enquiries?"

Breedon shrugged. "You wait fourteen days, you send a polite note saying the information isn't available. Or you ask the applicant to provide the document file number, if you want them to get really pissed at you. What's it about?"

"Something to do with a Croatian general called Dragan Korovik."

"Operation Storm?"

"That's right. You remember it?"

"Negative – that was well before my time. But I read about it. To be honest, that's one of the few wars no one even gives a fuck about any more. The Croatians were clearly the good guys – the Serbs were carrying out ethnic cleansing, bombing Sarajevo, trying to annexe Bosnia, all that shit, despite a UN arms embargo. In the end Bosnia and Croatia both survived and three democracies were born. In geopolitical terms, it's a rare instance of a happy ending."

"She mentioned atrocities."

"Yeah, well. You know how it goes: you say atrocity, I say an unfortunate instance of collateral damage."

While he was speaking she'd been logging onto Intellipedia, the intelligence community's equivalent of Wikipedia. As one of the million or so intelligence professionals around the world cleared to use the global Intelink network, she could access confidential information on hundreds of thousands of subjects in seconds. "Women Under War appears to be a creditable organisation," she said thoughtfully, scrolling through the pages. "It says here they've been involved in making representations to the ICTY."

"Which is...?"

"The International Criminal Tribunal for the former Yugoslavia. It's part of the UN International Court at The Hague." She typed another search. "*That's* interesting."

"What is?"

"General Dragan Korovik is being held at the ICTY right now, pending trial for war crimes committed back in 1995. He was handed over by the Croatian authorities just last year. A few weeks ago his lawyer said he'd be testifying that everything he did was sanctioned by the US government."

"Which of course it wasn't," Mike Breedon said reflectively. "Or we'd have been in breach of that UN resolution."

She scanned the rest of the Intellipedia article. Dragan Korovik had risen from obscurity at the beginning of the war to take command of the fledgling Croat army. Initially on the back foot against the larger Serb forces, he'd then carried out what Intellipedia called a series of brilliantly executed counterstrikes, wresting a large chunk of western Bosnia from Serb control, most notably the heavily-contested region of Krajina. Civilian deaths had been high, however, and after the war Korovik was forced into hiding – although it was rumoured, Intellipedia said, that he'd actually been living quite openly under the protection of the new government. Only when his capture was made a condition of Croatia joining the European Union, a decade later, was he finally "discovered" and arrested.

"Sounds like a field ration of canned worms to me," Mike said, reading over her shoulder. "What do you want to do?"

"I guess I'd better take a look in those archives."

"Really?" His tone said he wouldn't have bothered.

"That's the law, right?"

"In a manner of speaking." She looked up at him. "Aw, this Open Government shit gets my goat." He grimaced. "Every time someone wants to accuse us of something, we end up looking for the evidence for them. Almost like we're being forced to work for the other side. What's the point?"

"Sure," she said. "What's the point? But I'll follow up anyway. Just to keep her off our backs."

"Thanks. Appreciate it, Holly."

Despite what she had just said, it was not purely to keep Barbara Holton off their backs that Holly intended to provide her with such information as she could. *You will embody at all times the integrity and professionalism of the US Military*, Major Forster had said earlier. The law maintained that Barbara Holton was entitled to have her enquiry answered. And that meant Second Lieutenant Holly Boland would do her very best to provide it.

Seven

THE CARABINIERI BOAT bounced at high speed over the waves. Kat, once again freezing, was glad now of the icy spray that slapped her face with every jolting impact. Lunch had encompassed an *antipasto* of baby octopus grilled directly over a gas flame and served with red flakes of chilli and plenty of good olive oil, followed by *spaghetti ai ricci di mare*, pasta tossed in a sweet, fragrant sauce of sea urchin sacs flavoured with fennel, vermouth and saffron, and finally a *tiramisu*, a rich coffee sponge soused with Marsala. During the meal the two of them had shared a bottle of light, smoky Friuli from the mountains. She wasn't used to drinking at lunchtime – well, no more than an *ombra* or two with friends – and she was hoping she'd be fully sober by the time they reached Poveglia.

Neither the wine nor the waves seemed to affect Piola. He was, she had decided, one of the calmest people she had ever met. Purposeful, yet laid back. And – remarkably for a senior officer, in her experience – he seemed genuinely interested in her opinions.

"So why does a woman dress up as a priest?" he'd asked at the restaurant, after the owner had taken their order.

She'd been thinking about this, so she answered immediately. "Not as fancy dress. I already checked – none of the carnival shops in Venice supply such a thing. Besides, our victim is quite small. These priests' robes were real, and they fitted. I think she must have bought them online."

Piola raised an eyebrow. "You can do that?"

She nodded. "I found a couple of sites in the US that ship worldwide. Actually, I think her cassock is a Semi-Jesuit with Cincture, manufactured by an American company called R. J. Toomey." She pulled out a piece of paper. "I printed off the page from their catalogue."

Clearly impressed by her initiative, he took the page and examined it. "OK. Let's say you're right. Our victim is determined enough to get robes sent over from the US. Or maybe she's American, and brought them with her. I return to my original question: why?"

"The other thing I found online..." Kat spoke hesitantly, knowing that she was about to commit the cardinal sin of theorising ahead of the evidence. But Piola nodded for her to continue.

"Yes, Capitano?"

"There are organisations that campaign for women's ordination. You know, for women to be allowed to become priests."

Piola gave her a sideways glance. "A 'grave delict', as Father Cilosi reminded us. Of course, not everyone would agree."

He was fishing, she knew; trying to discover whether he was working with a strident feminist. Just as she couldn't help wondering if, despite all indications to the contrary, she was working for yet another macho misogynist. It had happened too many times for her not to tread carefully.

"The Pope's ruling does seem a bit... extreme," she said.

He smiled. "When I see the naivety of some of the things

the Church does... They really have no idea what ordinary people think, do they?"

"Quite," she said, relieved. "Anyway, it just seemed to me that Father Cilosi dismissed the possibility that the victim had anything to do with the Church very quickly. Maybe we should find someone who takes a different theological view before we accept that he's right."

"It's a good point," he said thoughtfully. "Check it out, will you? And well done, Capitano. That's just the kind of analytical thinking I don't always encounter in those of your rank and experience."

She hoped he thought her flush of pleasure was just because her cheeks were being warmed by the wine.

"Did you notice that he lied?" he added.

"Cilosi?" she said, surprised.

He nodded. "When we showed him those tattoos. He was... discomfited, somehow. And then he gave an equivocal answer about how he could pass us on to someone who was an expert in the occult. It was almost as if he was trying to insinuate that the tattoos had some kind of dark significance, without actually saying so."

"Why would he do that, though, if it wasn't true?"

Piola shrugged. "I don't know. Perhaps he just loves his Church so much that he doesn't like the thought of this woman being associated with it. Or perhaps it's something else completely, something that isn't even relevant. It's one of the things you learn about a murder investigation, Capitano. You don't necessarily have to tie up every loose end. You just get hold of them and pull, see which ones start to unravel."

Their octopus came – a plate for the two of them to share containing about a dozen of the tiny creatures, each one barely bigger than a Brussels sprout and dotted with flakes of chilli. As they speared them with their forks, he said conversationally, "Tell me, what other investigations have you worked on, Captain?"

She told him about her most recent cases – mostly to do with immigration rackets and petty crime. He knew a surprising amount about each one, accurately pinpointing where mistakes had been made, and establishing what her own role had been. She realised he was only trying to build up a picture of how competent she was, what tasks he could safely delegate to her, but she also found herself flattered by his attention. The two of them, sharing a bottle of wine over a good lunch, talking intently across the table – in different circumstances, this would have counted as one of her more successful dates.

She banished the thought from her mind, appalled at herself. *Katerina Tapo, this man is your superior officer. You complain that men don't treat you professionally; so now be professional.*

She sat upright, determined to adopt a more appropriate demeanour. "I'm sorry, sir. What were you saying?"

She asked him about himself, but on that subject he was reticent – again, a refreshing change from most male officers of her acquaintance, particularly since in his case modesty was unwarranted. Amongst her generation of *carabinieri*, Aldo Piola was famous for his part in the so-called Relocation Trials. A few years before, the Italian government had adopted a policy of resettling known Mafia figures from the South in northern Italy, where, it was assumed, they would be cut off from their support systems. The policy had backfired, the resettled *mafiosi* simply setting up new operations in the North instead, using the same techniques of bribery and intimidation of witnesses that had been so effective in their hometowns. Piola had achieved three convictions in seven cases – not a huge number, but a record nevertheless. It was said that his bosses, many of whom had proved curiously less effective, were furious he'd made them look bad, and for this reason alone he was unlikely to rise higher than colonel – a relatively lowly rank in a country where the very slowest train is designated "Express" and the most commercial grade of olive oil "Extra-Virgin".

Emboldened by the wine, she asked him about that, and he laughed.

"Why would I want promotion? You think Carabinieri generals have an easy life? They spend their whole time having meetings and being told off for other people's mistakes." He grew serious. "When I was very young, I thought I wanted to be a priest. But show me a priest who actually gets to make the difference that we do. If you do your job well, there's no more satisfying conclusion than seeing someone who committed a crime go to jail, and know that it was you who put them there." He sighed, suddenly sombre. "Of course, in Italy all too often they don't – go to jail, I mean. And that's the main reason some officers decide they can't be bothered any more."

There was an instance of Piola's unusual approach when he called for the bill. The owner immediately announced that he was always happy to give a free lunch to the Carabinieri, so grateful was he for their work in keeping the streets safe, so much more did he admire them than those lazy good-for-nothings the State Police, et cetera, et cetera. Piola didn't argue. He simply waited patiently for the man to finish, then pulled out two twenty-euro notes and said politely, "I'll need four change." He must have been keeping a tally all along.

And yet, when she'd tried to pay her share, he grunted that he earned more than she did, and besides, it had been his invitation. "When you ask me out, you can pay," he said in a voice that brooked no argument.

"All right. I'll get the next one," she said, and found she was already looking forward to it.

Now, as they approached Poveglia, the boat slowed. There was a rickety old jetty, but it didn't look as if it had been used for years. The driver edged towards an area of crumbling concrete on the shore instead.

The island was tiny: a kilometre or so long, and half as wide, bisected at one end by a sea channel. Trees and vegetation grew wild, pierced only by an ugly brick tower. Presumably that indicated where the old hospital was. It wasn't the only lagoon island to be abandoned, she knew. To the north, Santo Spirito was also deserted, while the octagonal fort to the south had been derelict for as long as she could remember. There was always talk about these smaller islands being turned into fancy hotels, but the plans inevitably foundered on the cost of transporting building materials across the lagoon; not to mention on Venice's byzantine planning regulations, which defeated all but the best-connected.

Piola hoisted himself onto dry land, turning to give her a hand up.

"Someone's been here recently," she said, spotting something on the ground. She picked it up with an evidence bag and showed him. It was a cigarette end, fairly fresh from the look of it.

"Jin Ling again," he said, studying it. "Interesting. Do you believe in coincidences, Capitano?"

"Yes," she said, and he laughed.

"Good answer."

They pushed through the undergrowth in the direction of the tower. "This place was run by nuns, originally," he said conversationally. "I'm old enough to remember it. In fact, one of my first cases brought me here. A suicide, one of the doctors. Turned out he'd been giving himself the patients' drugs. He threw himself off the tower. Of course, people said it was just another instance of the curse of Poveglia."

The abandoned hospital was in front of them now. A four-storey brick-built building about two hundred yards in length, it gave off a palpable sense of decay. At some point it had been partially covered in scaffolding and an attempt made to board up the lower floors, but it hadn't been particularly effective, to judge by the doors hanging off their hinges, discarded window-boards and graffiti.

"Kids," Piola said. "I've heard they come out here as a kind of dare. Who can spend a whole night in the haunted asylum, that kind of thing."

The main door was wide open. Inside, debris littered the hall – lumps of plaster, torn-out electrical wiring, an old wheelchair missing its wheels. Something small and agile scurried into an adjoining room. Kat found herself hoping that Piola didn't suggest they split up.

"We should split up," he said. "I'll go this way."

She kept as close to the windows as she could. The rooms smelt of woodsmoke and burnt paper. A thump upstairs, echoing on bare floorboards, made her jump. Just a pigeon, hopefully. Everywhere there was more debris – almost, she thought, as if the place had been ransacked rather than merely abandoned. Glass crunched under her feet. Strange pieces of electrical equipment, built with the solidity of a different age from Bakelite and brass, lay abandoned in corners.

Then she rounded a doorway, and her heart leapt into her mouth.

Eight

DANIELE BARBO TOOK a *motoscafo*, a water taxi, back to Venice from the mainland. He had said nothing to the small but persistent group of journalists and supporters who'd gathered to see him emerge from court. The verdict was "Guilty", just as he'd expected. Sentencing had been deferred for five weeks, to allow the court to carry out a psychological assessment that would determine whether he was fit to be imprisoned. It was a stalling tactic on the part of his lawyer, no more. If he was deemed incapable of coping with a normal prison, he would be sent to a psychiatric institution instead, from which he would be released only after the doctors pronounced him fit to go to jail. It was a classic Catch 22, an administrative closed loop of the sort in which Italy's legal system excelled. Once embroiled in it, he knew, he would find it all but impossible to extricate himself.

A large fine was, on the face of it, a better option. To the outside world Daniele Barbo appeared to be fantastically wealthy, the sort of person who could pay a million-euro penalty without thinking about it. Few people realised – and none of the journalists who had written profiles on him had ever bothered to discover – that he was actually almost penniless. His father had invested all his money in modern art, then left the artworks to a charitable foundation set up in his name. The shares in the family business, meanwhile, had been diluted by re-issue after re-issue, none of them instigated by Daniele. He was allowed to live in Ca' Barbo, the family *palazzo*, but only under strict conditions: the building itself was entailed to the Foundation. He was only at liberty now because the Foundation's trustees, men he distrusted and loathed, had agreed to stand bail.

That his father had believed this arrangement was for his son's ultimate benefit, Daniele didn't doubt. His troubled teens, and his involvement with the nascent computer hacking scene, had exacerbated the guilt his parents felt about his kidnap and mutilation, convincing them that he was too withdrawn from the world to manage his own affairs. But he also knew his father had been advised that this was the most effective way to ensure Daniele could never sell any of his art. When presented with what was, at heart, a choice between keeping his precious collection intact or passing it on to his son to do with as he wished, Matteo Barbo had chosen the former.

Now, of course, that son was known as an internet entrepreneur, something his parents could never have foreseen. The website Daniele had created, Carnivia.com, actually had considerably more than the number of users Wikipedia claimed. But to call it a business was a misnomer. Unlike Google or Facebook, its data was never used for marketing purposes or sold to big corporations. It downloaded no adware or cookies, surreptitiously, onto your computer, nor did it track which sites you went to when you left. Over the years numerous would-be investors had approached him with proposals for making money out of it. He had always refused.

The boat pulled up at Ca' Barbo's private jetty. As Daniele stepped onto the damp wooden boards he couldn't help glancing upwards at the four floors of Gothic and arabesque splendour soaring above him. The Victorian art critic John Ruskin had called Ca' Barbo "the most extraordinary small palace in Venice". Now, over a century later, the whole of the lowest floor was unusable because of the threat from rising seawater. The recent *acqua alta* had swept inside as casually as an incoming tide breaks into a child's sandcastle. The building was principally stone and marble, so nothing important would rot, but the invasion had left scum marks halfway up the walls and a sour, fetid aroma.

Going upstairs, he went immediately to the palace's old music room. These days it housed four massive NovaScale servers, computers so powerful that even in the depths of winter the room needed to be cooled with portable air-conditioning units. In contrast to the inlaid armoires and velvet curtains that adorned some of the other rooms in Ca' Barbo, this room was furnished with his own choice of furniture – plain desks from Ikea, cheap melamine workstations and wheeled office chairs. Only the technical equipment was the very best and most expensive – massive screens, sleek stylus-and-pen tablets, keyboards that glowed softly in the perpetual dimness. Bar displays that rose and fell in real time, like waves on the lagoon, showed in pulsing backlit increments how many hundreds of thousands of users were crammed into each of the NovaScales' chipsets at any precise moment. You could set your watch by their ebb and flow, just as much as by Venice's tides: the soft surge as the east coast of America woke up, the leap as schoolchildren in California came home from school, the flickering quiescence as Europe went to sleep.

Pulling himself towards a screen, he logged on. They were already waiting for him online. Eric, Anneka, Zara and Max.

Technically, he supposed, they were his employees, but he doubted they thought of themselves that way. They were the Deep Wizards of Carnivia: the programmers who cleaned and disinfected its streets, policed its alleyways and settled its disputes. They were also, he supposed, his friends, although he had still never actually met two of them in person, and had no particular desire to do so.

They didn't need to ask him how it had gone today, having followed the trial via Twitter feeds and blogs.

Bummer, Max wrote.

We'll survive, Daniele replied. *It's a tactic, nothing more. Has anything happened?*

One more attack, Anneka wrote. Her avatar was a Chinese dog, but he knew that she was actually a shaven-headed young Dutch woman, both eyebrows studded with piercings. She'd first come to his notice as the leader of a gang who'd devised a brilliant way of stealing credit card details using fake Windows Security Updates. *Not a particularly sophisticated one. Just your regular zombie Denial-of-Service.*

How many?

Half a million. They ping-flooded the servers, then tried sockstress. Carnivia saw them off easily enough. But the interesting thing is the time they chose.

Which was?

1.04 pm.

?????

The exact same time you were found guilty.

It was another demonstration that whoever was behind this was targeting him personally. Half a million home computers, infected without their owners' knowledge by a tiny piece of dormant software, had suddenly come to life and tried to access Carnivia. Had the people in this forum not been on their guard, the cumulative effect of such a spike in demand could have overwhelmed the servers, the flood of information seeking out weaknesses in their programming like a great wave battering a seawall.

Carnivia's robust, Max observed. *It's you they think is the weak link.*

Thnx. I'd worked that out too.

Yes, but think it through. They're not trying to get to Carnivia to get at you. They're trying to get at you to get to Carnivia. It may seem personal, but it isn't. They've simply decided that you're the most unstable element. It's kind of a compliment to your coding, actually.

Daniele nodded. He had come to that conclusion too, sitting in the cell below the courtroom, but it was good to hear it from someone else.

Zara wrote, *There's something I need to show you.*

You would never have known from her posts that Zara was profoundly deaf. Like him, she was a mathematician by training, and they sometimes collaborated on some of the more arcane projects and puzzles that Carnivia threw up.

She was bringing up his Wikipedia page. *I've seen this,* Daniele wrote.

Sec.

She switched to a view that showed the raw HTML, the code in which the actual content of the page was written. The final section of his profile had been changed yet again, he saw. Now it read:

Barbo is awaiting sentencing.

Carnivia, his website, remains offline.

Automatically, his eyes flickered towards the servers. The second sentence, at least, was untrue. But Zara was underlining the IP address which indicated the source of the information, an eleven-digit number which identified the computer it had come from as accurately as a licence plate identified a car or a cell number a phone.

The number on the screen was his own IP.

That's neat, Eric wrote admiringly. *Really neat. How did they do that?*

Inside job, Max suggested, adding a wry smile to show that he was joking.

Maybe they want you to think *it's an inside job*. That was Anneka. *More messing with your mind.*

It's a distraction, Daniele typed. *Max is right: to work out how to stop them, we need to look at their objective. These people don't want me. They want to get inside Carnivia.*

Because...? Eric challenged.

Because they hate the idea that there are two million people having conversations they can't spy on, Max wrote.

Or perhaps it's more specific than that, Daniele responded. *We have five weeks before I'm sentenced. It isn't long, but we can use it to find out what's happening here. We'll learn something from looking for whoever it is who's doing this. But I have a feeling we'll learn even more if we go looking inside Carnivia itself.*

Nine

"GET THESE MEASURED as well as photographed," Piola instructed.

The room went white as Hapadi's camera captured the scene, fixing Piola, Kat and the hastily-assembled forensic team against the crumbling walls of the old hospital room. All of them were wearing white paper overalls now, and the camera's flash made it seem as if they momentarily disappeared and then reappeared again, like ghosts.

The subjects of the photographs were the symbols daubed on the dilapidated plaster: simple line drawings, sprayed hastily across every blank space, even the broken windows. Some appeared to be similar to the markings on the victim's arm.

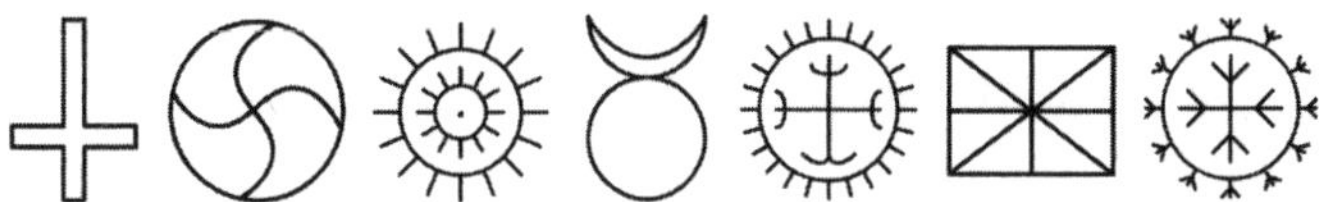

A table had been pushed into the centre of the room: on it, a chalice and an upturned cross showed all too clearly what its intended use had been. But even that was nothing compared to the spray of rusty red that burst like a giant ink-blot against the far wall, or the long smear that showed where the body had been dragged towards some French windows that gave directly onto the lagoon.

"As far as publicity goes, this could be another Beasts of Satan," Piola said quietly.

Kat nodded. The revelation in 2004 that the ritualistic murder of two sixteen-year-olds had been orchestrated by a heavy metal group called the Beasts of Satan had provoked a massive public outcry – the so-called "Satanic Panic". The Vatican had introduced new exorcisms; tarot readers and fortune tellers had been banned from daytime TV; there had even been calls for heavy metal music to be outlawed. She'd been a teenager herself at the time, but she remembered all too well how the media had hysterically blamed the police services for failing to "root out" the "canker of evil" in the first place.

"Which is why we keep this development to ourselves for now," Piola added. "But equally, we'll need to step up the investigation. I'm going to ask for a team of twenty officers. Double shifts, overtime, all the bells and whistles. And I want every single person warned not to speak to the press, or they'll have me to answer to. Would you see to it?"

"Of course." She hesitated. "Does that mean you want me to run the operations room?"

"No," he said thoughtfully. "I think I want you to stick with me."

Once again she hoped he didn't notice how pleased she was. "I'll speak to Allocation."

"Colonel?"

They turned. One of the forensic team was holding up a small leather case. "I think you'll want to see this, sir."

Even though he was already wearing gloves, Piola took the case from the technician by the edges, opening it carefully to avoid disturbing any prints. Inside, in separate compartments clearly designed for the purpose, were wafers and three phials of liquid. The liquid in one phial was red, in the next clear, and in the third golden-green.

"Wine, water, and holy oil," Piola said.

"I believe that's what they do. For a black Mass... they use a consecrated host." Kat couldn't help being shocked. "To defile it."

Piola gazed thoughtfully at the symbols scrawled on the walls. "It certainly looks that way."

"There's this too, sir," the technician added. She held up a credit-card-sized piece of plastic, encased in another evidence bag.

"A hotel room key," Piola said. "Well, well. I think we may be about to find out who our mysterious priestess is, Capitano."

Leaving the technicians to finish scraping samples from the blood spray, Kat and Piola took the boat back to Campo San Zaccaria. Malli, the Carabinieri's lead IT technician, dusted the key card for fingerprints before placing it inside a card-reader.

"Most of the room keys we see here aren't actually used for opening hotel rooms," he explained. "Because the magnetic strip is compatible with credit card readers, thieves use them to store stolen card details. You think your card's still in your pocket, but actually that waiter you handed it to after lunch cloned it to a blank key card at the same time as he debited your bill." He typed some instructions on his keyboard, and some lines of data appeared on the screen. "You're in luck. This is just your standard-issue MagTek room key." He pointed. "The Europa Hotel, in Cannaregio.

Room 73. Key 1 of 2, active from December 22nd through January 18th. In other words, she hasn't checked out yet."

The Europa was a small, inexpensive place not far from Stazione Santa Lucia. It wasn't where Kat would have chosen to stay if she were coming to Venice. The cheap, shiny armchairs in the foyer, and the cheap shiny suits worn by those sitting in them, pecking at laptops or muttering into cell phones, suggested that this was strictly a businessman-on-a-budget place. She guessed most of the guests would only be staying a night or two.

A good place to remain anonymous, she thought.

A female desk clerk, squeezed into a polyester uniform two sizes too small, looked indifferently at their IDs and nodded them upstairs. More polyester underfoot, and a maid who looked considerably more alarmed to see them than the desk clerk had. She was probably an illegal, Kat thought. Most of the cheap labour in Venice was provided by migrants from the former Eastern Bloc these days.

Room 73 was a featureless corporate box identical to a million other featureless corporate boxes around the world. Only the view outside the window would differ – and this window, rather surprisingly, overlooked a quiet *rio*, a pretty backstreet canal about eight feet wide. Opposite, an old warehouse crumbled gracefully into the water, its window ledges colonised by buddleia and moss.

Clothes were piled up on the twin beds. "Looks like she was preparing to leave," Kat said.

Piola pointed to a damp patch on the wall. "What do you suppose that is?"

The patch had a faintly pink tinge. Now that she looked at the room again, Kat realised there was something odd about it. Possessions had been heaped up on every available surface, as if someone had made a desultory attempt to sort them into piles. A laptop power cable was draped over the back of the chair. Suitcases lay in one corner, empty, as though tossed aside. In the small, functional bathroom, two washbags spilled their contents across the sink.

"Capitano?"

She turned. Piola was holding up a pillow from one of the beds. It had a hole right through it.

"We need to talk to the maid," he said. "And the manager. Now."

The manager was younger than Kat, a spotty youth from Slovenia whose name badge identified him as Adrijan. The maid, whose name was Ema, looked even more terrified than before, though whether because of the Carabinieri's presence or her manager's Kat couldn't tell.

Gradually, with Adrijan translating, it became clear what had happened. Just after 3 p.m., Ema had entered the room and found it in a terrible mess. There was blood on one wall, in the shower and on a sheet, and the contents of the drawers had been tipped onto the floor. She'd tidied up as best she could, but she wasn't sure where everything was meant to go.

Piola stared at the two hotel employees with a mixture of disbelief and fury. "She *tidied up*? What did she think the blood was?"

Adrijan passed the question on, and the maid mimed someone clutching their nose. "Perhaps a nose bleed," he said helpfully.

"And this?" Piola demanded, holding up the pillow with a hole in it. The maid shrugged helplessly.

Piola sighed. "Tell her she almost certainly interfered with a crime scene." He turned to Kat. "What do you think?"

"I'm wondering who the crime was against. If our..." She hesitated, not wanting to use the word "priestess" as Piola had done earlier. "If our victim was killed on Poveglia, who was attacked here?"

"Exactly," he agreed. "Two washbags, two suitcases. And according to Malli, two key cards were issued. When they finally get round to printing out the ledger, I'm sure we'll find there were two guests in this room."

"Two women."

Piola raised an interrogative eyebrow. "No male clothes," she explained. "And the washbags both contain make-up remover."

"But how did the killer get the body out?" he mused. Turning back to the hotel employees, he said, "Ask her – when she tidied up, was the window open?"

The maid nodded, keen to be of help now. "*Si*," she said in broken Italian. "I close."

Both *carabinieri* crossed to the window and peered down. Beneath them, the brown waters of the *rio* lapped against the hotel's back wall.

"Call in the divers," Piola said to Kat. "Tell Allocation we need them here right away. And get a second forensic team over here, to search this room."

For the second time that day Kat donned a paper suit and covered her shoes with elasticated bags. The hotel ledger had indeed yielded two names, but better still, the room safe had yielded two passports. One was Croatian, in the name of Jelena Babić. The photograph matched the corpse in Hapadi's morgue. The other was American, in the name of Barbara

Holton. The photograph showed a middle-aged woman with short grey hair.

"Better inform their embassies," Piola said.

"We can't be certain Holton's dead yet, sir."

"I give the divers about five minutes." He grimaced with frustration. "If only we'd got here a few hours sooner."

"Sir?" Kat said hesitantly.

"Yes, Capitano?"

She indicated the laptop power lead. "There's a lead but no laptop. Either our killer took it or—"

"Or it's in the water too? I'll speak to the divers. They won't like it – finding a body in that pool of shit's one thing, but looking for a laptop could take days." He nodded. "Good work, Kat."

As he went off to talk to the divers she found herself noting that it was the first time he'd called her by her first name.

While she waited for Piola to return, Kat looked through the evidence bags the technicians were putting to one side. One caught her eye. It contained a lock of long black hair inside another bag.

"Why's this been double-bagged?" she asked, curious.

The technician shook her head. "It was in that bag when we found it. So we put the whole thing inside one of ours."

"Strange." She held it up to examine the hair more closely. It was a woman's, she guessed from the length, coiled into a loose circle that had partially unwound to fill the sides of the bag. "Both our victims have short hair, according to their passport photographs."

"Want us to run some tests on it?"

"Yes. It can't be usual to take something like this away with you."

Moving along, she found a bag containing pages torn from *La Nuova Venezia*. The pages were all from the back section, where prostitutes' small ads jostled with chat lines, dating agencies and boats for sale. Some of the prostitutes' ads had been crossed out with a biro.

"Also curious," she murmured to herself.

She moved along the line. The problem for the search team was knowing what should be bagged for analysis and what was irrelevant, so to be on the safe side they had bagged almost everything, from the women's sweaters and coats right down to the contents of the wastepaper basket. Kat looked at the latter. It had contained some empty toiletry bottles and a supermarket receipt. According to the receipt, the two women had bought Pop-Tarts, bottled water and tinned chickpeas from Billa on the Strada Nuova two days before, with a credit card. She made a note to ask the card company for all the other transactions they'd made.

The technician brought over a document.

"Looks like she rented a *topetta* while she was here," he commented, showing her a hire form made out in the name of Jelena Babić. "Sure she wasn't suicidal?"

It always amazed Venetians that tourists were allowed to rent small boats by the day, subjecting themselves to the *vaporetti*'s klaxons and the curses of gondoliers as they tried to dodge the goods barges and even cruise liners that plied Venice's cluttered waters. It was, most agreed, a wonder that more weren't killed.

Kat looked at the hire form. "From Sport e Lavoro in Cannaregio. I'll give them a call."

She was still on the phone to the hire company – as she'd expected, their boat had been found drifting in the lagoon by a fisherman and returned to them: no, they hadn't thought of contacting the police, or indeed of calling the number they had for the customer on the rental form – when she heard a shout from outside. She hurried downstairs.

Piola had been right: it had taken the divers only a few minutes to locate the second body. Barbara Holton had also been shot in the head, and quite recently – the wound was still fresh. There was a laptop wedged into the hotel bathrobe she'd died in.

"Don't get your hopes up," the lead diver warned them as they waited for an ambulance boat. "We've retrieved laptops from the canals before. This water isn't kind to them."

"Excuse me for a minute, sir," Kat said, struck by a sudden thought.

She went back inside to the check-in desk, where Adrijan had been replaced by a grown-up in a proper suit, doubtless called in from head office as soon as it became apparent a murder had taken place.

"Do you charge for internet access?" she asked.

The manager nodded warily. "Of course."

"So you make your guests log on via a network?" she persisted. Again he nodded. "That means your rooms are connected via a hub. Which in turn means you can monitor your guests' internet activity. And I'm guessing that, in a corporate chain like this, it's standard policy to do just that."

"We can't discuss—" he began automatically, before remembering who he was dealing with.

"Just get me a printout," she said, turning away before he could argue.

"So now we have two murders," Piola said. "Connected, definitely. But the same killer? Possibly, possibly not."

They were in a little restaurant a hundred yards from the Carabinieri HQ. It was 11 p.m.: they'd been reviewing the evidence for hours in the operations room before her boss had decided that they needed to eat if they were to keep going any longer. When they'd arrived at the restaurant, the owner had exchanged a few quiet words with Piola, then brought them *cicchetti*, small plates piled high with an assortment of tasty morsels to snack on: tiny fried chicken livers; big, fat sardines from the lagoon, served with tangy vinegar-soaked onions; a dish of olives; and some balls of sweet, milky mozzarella; all sharing space on the table with a heap of papers from the investigation.

Kat was almost drunk with exhaustion. Her eyes felt dry and scratchy, as if they'd been sandblasted open. But she was also strangely elated. The last twenty-four hours had thrown more challenges her way than she'd faced in her entire career to date, and she knew that so far she was dealing with them pretty well.

"Father Cilosi called back," she said, chewing on an olive and dropping the stone on the side of her plate. "He's given me the contact details for that expert in the occult he was talking about. A Father Uriel."

Piola raised an eyebrow. "Another priest?"

"Sounds like it. Though the place he works at sounded more like a hospital of some kind. The Institute of Christina Mirabilis, over towards Verona – I've got an appointment with him first thing tomorrow morning."

"So that should confirm whether we're really dealing with some kind of Satanic Mass. But even if we are, it may be tangential to the murders. Both our victims were shot, which doesn't sound like a ritual killing to me. Knives, strangulation, drowning perhaps, but I've never heard of a Satanist using a gun." He drew a sheet of paper out of a file. "The autopsy on the first body – Jelena Babić, that is – has been completed. Seems you were right, Capitano. They found an American manufacturer's label in her robes. R. J. Toomey, just as you predicted. And something else. Ballistics have taken a first look at the bullet. It's a little misshapen from the entry into the skull but they're fairly sure it's a..." He glanced at the page, finding the place, and she noticed how he had to hold the paper away from him to focus on it. So he needed glasses but was too vain to get them, she thought. "A 6.8 millimetre Remington SPC."

"American?"

"Yes. It says here it was developed for US Special Forces. Oh, and it was fired through a Remington silencer. Also developed for Special Forces."

There was a silence as they both considered this information.

"Of course, these American connections may just be a coincidence," he added. "We still believe in those, don't we?"

He poured them both more wine, a light Garganega bottled by the restaurant owner's brother. "What about the printout of internet traffic from the hotel? Anything useful there?"

"Malli wasn't sure." She located the list in her folder. "The hotel doesn't distinguish between websites visited by one guest and another. Mostly they're porn sites, plus a few escort agencies and Google Maps, which is pretty much what you'd expect given the sort of hotel it is. But I think we can assume *this* was accessed from Room 73." She showed him. "When I googled Barbara Holton, this website came up. Womenunderwar.com. And we can see whoever accessed that site went on to access this one, here." She pointed again. "Carnivia.com. After that, nothing."

"Carnivia? That's something to do with the Barbo kid,

isn't it? The boy who got kidnapped by the Red Brigades?"

"Exactly. But I don't understand the connection. From what I've read in the papers, Carnivia's some kind of gossip site. You know, schoolkids saying who's got a crush on who, that kind of thing."

There was another silence. Kat realised she was actually swaying with tiredness.

Piola noticed it too. "Time for you to go home, Captain. There'll be many more late nights over the coming weeks, and I don't need you exhausted."

The owner chose that moment to come over with two glasses of grappa. "For me, definitely," Piola said, taking one. "But she's going."

Kat was too tired to argue, but she took the second grappa from the owner anyway. "Ten more minutes."

It was another hour before she dragged herself away, and then another hour after that before she was back in her apartment. But despite her fatigue, she wasn't ready for sleep.

She felt the irresistible momentum of a big investigation, the thrill – there was no other word for it – of the pursuit. She'd heard senior officers say that the pressure of a homicide, the race to gather evidence while it was still fresh, was as addictive as crack cocaine, and just as destructive of family life, normality, sleep. She could understand that now. Exhaustion and excitement battled in her brain.

And something more, too: there was something nagging at her, something she'd forgotten.

As she took off her make-up, she mentally ran through her to-do list. Chase Malli to see if he could get anything from the soaked laptop. Ditto with Barbara Holton's cell phone. Try to follow the dead women's information trail into Carnivia.

Check their names with Interpol and their respective embassies, to see if either of them had records and to start the task of contacting next-of-kin. See whether the bullet that killed Barbara Holton matched the one from Jelena Babić's autopsy. Go through the statements of the other hotel staff, in case any of them saw anything. Follow up those crossed-out prostitutes' adverts in the paper – what was *that* all about?

And something else, something that was still eluding her.

Piola. She'd told Piola she would do… something. She could see him now, nodding with that thoughtful, engaged expression he had. He wasn't like most senior policemen, abrupt, cynical and sneering. There was something academic about him, but also something a little debonair. Somehow they added up to a quality that made her want to earn his praise.

The pressure she felt, she realised, wasn't just the pressure to gather evidence. It was the pressure to retain Colonel Piola's respect.

Then it came to her. She'd told him she'd find someone who took a different theological position from Father Cilosi on women priests.

Going to her laptop, she typed "women priests" into Google and skimmed quickly through the resulting sites. Some seemed rather sad, filled with lengthy justifications of why the writers would reluctantly accept the Pope's position but continue to speak out against it "from a position of respectful conscience". Some were angry, pointing out that the Bible was full of misogynistic references to the ritual uncleanness of women.

In Leviticus 15:19–30, it says, "When a woman has a discharge of blood, and blood flows from her body,

> the uncleanness of her monthly periods shall last for seven days... Anyone who touches her bed must wash his clothing and wash himself and will be unclean until evening." That's the real reason they don't want us to be priests, and why priests have to be celibate. They hate and fear our genitals.

Others were wistful, citing examples of other faiths which had previously refused to countenance women priests but now accepted them. And through it all ran a recognition that the current Pope was never going to change his mind. A hardliner who had spoken out against the evils of liberalism, who wrote approvingly of the "traditionalism and vigour" of congregations in emerging countries, he quoted time and time again Canon Law 1024: "Only a baptised man validly receives sacred ordination."

On one site she came across a blog post headed "Why illegal ordinations are wrong". The argument was the by-now familiar one, that those who believed in the right of women to be ordained should try to change the Church from within. But the writer went on to add:

> We should not persuade ourselves that it is ever permissible to ordain women under the present arrangement. Those who have been tempted to take this view are in error.

That was interesting: it suggested there were indeed some who thought differently. Had those individuals perhaps gone one step further? Were there, even now, women who somehow considered themselves to be genuine Catholic priests?

She opened up a new email message and wrote a short

note to the blogger, explaining that she was trying to get in touch, in confidence, with people who supported female ordination.

Having sent it, she scanned the rest of her inbox quickly. Her mother had sent a note to her and her brothers reminding them that they'd promised to come to lunch next Sunday. Her mother hadn't copied the email to her sister Clara, she noticed. She'd known Clara wouldn't need reminding.

Kat didn't reply to the email. It was almost 3 a.m. on Tuesday morning, and a lot could have happened by Sunday.

Ten

HOLLY BOLAND HIT her jet-lag with an early-morning run along Ederle's apparently endless perimeter, followed by a light breakfast in the D-FAC, the on-post dining facility. As army chow halls went, it wasn't too bad – someone had tried to brighten it up with a cheery-sounding name, "South of the Alps", and there were brioches and Italian cakes on offer as well as the usual waffles and hash browns. Even so, she longed for the day when she would be living off-base, able to start her mornings with an espresso and a bite of freshly baked *cornetti* or *bomboloni*, instead of these stadium-sized cartons of frothy milk, flavoured with a shot of watery caffeine.

After breakfast, she checked in with Mike Breedon. There still wasn't much for her to do, so she decided to make a start on locating Barbara Holton's papers – or more likely, she thought, establishing that no such papers existed.

After numerous phone calls, she succeeded in tracking down the staff sergeant responsible for the base archives. He directed her first to a voluminous pile of authorisation forms to be written up in duplicate, and then to a small building at the edge of the administration block. As she got there, clutching her forms, she saw that a long line of soldiers was exiting the building. Each was carrying a stack of three cardboard boxes, like ants with crumbs.

"What's going on?" she asked one of them.

He shrugged without stopping. "Guess they need the space, ma'am."

Inside the building an iron stairway, echoing with the stamp of standard-issue Belleville boots, spiralled down into the earth. Fighting her way against the tide of soldiery, she found herself in a long, low access tunnel lit with bare bulbs. Uniformed figures were bringing more boxes from either direction, humping them into piles by the exit.

She found the NCO in charge and repeated her question. He too shrugged. "We're shifting some of this, is all."

"Why?"

His look told her clearly that he rarely searched for any rhyme or reason behind his orders. She tried a different tack. "Where's it going to?"

"Camp Darby is what I heard."

"Know where I'd find the files for 1995?"

"As it happens, I do. Way along there, to the left."

Further down the tunnel the lightbulbs became more intermittent. Dimly lit alcoves contained trestles and pallets piled high with boxes. "Archive" was far too grand a term: this was clearly just a dumping place for papers no one was quite sure they were authorised to throw away. Still, someone had tried to make sense of it: laminated A4 sheets taped to each alcove indicated which year each stack related to. Some years contained bigger piles than others. Presumably those were when the larger military engagements had taken place.

"1995" consisted of a truck-sized heap of boxes. The line of soldier-ants was already about twenty feet away, emptying the alcoves one by one. She had no more than twenty minutes, she estimated, before she would be politely asked to vacate the area so they could clear it.

The first three boxes she opened contained standard stores requisition forms that could be of little interest to anyone. The next two held random collections of administrative memos. The sixth contained aerial reconnaissance photos. One of Barbara Holton's questions had related to such images, she recalled, but how could she possibly know who these photographs had been provided to or what terrain they showed? She decided to move on.

It was time-consuming work, and by the time she was halfway done the first soldiers were hovering at the alcove entrance. She called, "Do the one across the way first, will you? I'm almost through here," knowing that a friendly smile would be more effective than trying to get their orders changed. She turned back to the boxes and pulled out another, thicker file. Some words in a Slavic language jumped out at her. *Siječanj–Ožujak 1995... Medački džep. Planirani unaprijed za glavne SIGINT USAREUR*. She didn't speak Serbo-Croat, but she spoke fluent military acronym, and she knew that SIGINT USAREUR meant Signals Intelligence originating from US Army Europe. She grabbed it. Another file immediately below bore the hand-scrawled title "66th INTERCEPTS BiH". The 66th Brigade was the umbrella organisation for Military Intelligence in Europe, and BiH was presumably Bosnia–Herzegovina. Then there were a couple more that appeared to contain dates and times, all in the same distinctive Slavic language. She grabbed those too, put the files under her arm and called, "All yours, guys."

On an afterthought, she turned to one of the soldiers as they passed her. "These'll need to be reunited with the others someday," she said, holding up the files. "Any idea who I should send them to?"

"Negative, ma'am. Request came in via Intel is all I heard."

She nodded her thanks and hurried away, the files securely under her arm. It meant nothing, she decided, that Barbara Holton's Freedom of Information request had specifically mentioned some kind of three-way involvement between Military Intelligence, Camp Ederle and the Croatian Army. If you started treating such small coincidences as significant, pretty soon you ended up thinking like a loony conspiracy theorist yourself.

Eleven

DANIELE EMPTIED A can of Red Bull energy drink into a half-empty cup of coffee and stirred the mixture with the end of a pencil before downing it in three gulps. He tried not to think what it tasted like.

They'd been up all night, crawling through electronic tunnels and backdoors within Carnivia that only this small band of people knew about, searching. Searching for something they might not even recognise when they saw it.

The reason for his persecution by the authorities, he was certain, lay somewhere inside Carnivia. This wasn't just some random attack on a channel of communication they couldn't control. Someone was looking for something specific, some conversation thread or uploaded titbit of information, and they were prepared to destroy him to get to it.

Which meant that, so far, they hadn't found it.

He wasn't sure exactly what he'd do if he and his programmers found it first. It would almost certainly be encrypted and untraceable, like the majority of Carnivia's traffic. But he hoped that from the size and shape of it, and the pattern of uploads, he might be able at least to figure out what kind of thing he was dealing with.

You know, Max typed from halfway across the world, *there's always a possibility that we're playing right into their hands.*

How so?

They tried to hack into Carnivia themselves and failed, right? Looking for the exact same thing we're looking for. And now here we are, doing it for them.

Daniele ran his hands through his hair, exhausted. Then he typed, *You're right. Plan A sucks. If I had a Plan B, we'd probably go to it. But I don't. So let's keep looking.*

Twelve

HOLLY TOOK THE files from the archive back to the Liaison Office and examined them more carefully. Three files, consisting of about twenty pages of loosely inserted material in all. She tried entering some of the Slavic words into Google Translate, but the inverted circumflexes and other unfamiliar accents easily defeated her US-layout keyboard.

"Mike, do we have any Serbo-Croat translators on base?" she asked her boss.

"NFI. But I could send an email or two if you like. This still your Open Government request?"

"'Fraid so."

"Frankly, I doubt you'll find anyone. The Pentagon won't have seen any point in training interpreters in those languages since Kosovo, and that must have been almost fifteen years ago. World's moved on, right?"

"Right," she said with a sigh. Through a nearby window she could see a dozen soldiers spotting each other over the assault course. It looked fun – or at least, physical and challenging. For a moment, she regretted not fobbing Barbara Holton off with a form letter and some platitudes.

"I do know one person you could try, though," Mike was saying.

She turned her attention back to him. "Yes?"

"Ian Gilroy. He was the local CIA section head before he retired – a real Cold War warrior from the old days. He comes on base once in a while to give lectures." Mike made a face. "I went to one, a while back. Can't say it was riveting. I suspect it just gives him an excuse to use the PX, get his car serviced and chew the fat with the other old-timers. You know how it is with these retirees."

"Sure," she said. "Ian Gilroy. Thanks, I'll try him." A thought suddenly struck her. "Mike," she said slowly, "this isn't all some kind of elaborate snipe hunt, is it?"

"Snipe hunt?" he said innocently.

Postings abroad were notorious for snipe hunts. Newly arrived soldiers were sent to the armoury to ask for a crate of left-handed grenades. Airmen were sent to the stores for tins of camouflage paint. Seamen were ordered to help calibrate the radar by wrapping themselves in tinfoil. The variations were endlessly inventive, whether for duplicate Humvee keys, replacement spirit-level bubbles, copies of gun reports, or any of the hundred-and-one other practical jokes that kept combat-ready troops entertained in long foreign postings. Only now did it occur to Holly that a suspiciously articulate middle-aged American woman brandishing an obscure FOIA request might be something similar.

Mike smiled at the thought. "Wish it was – it would be a pretty good one. But no, not so far as I know. You chose to do this, remember? Only yourself to blame."

The Camp Ederle Education Centre consisted of no fewer than three affiliated colleges: University of Maryland, Central Texas College and University of Phoenix. She looked up the lecture schedules on her computer. Between the three, she could study everything from Criminal Justice to Business, all heavily subsidised by the government. Even so, she knew, most soldiers preferred to spend their free time racking up internal army qualifications.

Ian Gilroy taught two courses: Italian Military History and Roman Civilization. In total he gave only three classes a week, and they seemed not to lead to any particular major. It certainly read more like a retiree's hobby than a serious academic pursuit.

Seeing that his seminar on Italian Military History would be finishing within the next half hour, she caught a bus over to the Education Centre. The place was busy, mostly with women in civilian clothes. There were almost a thousand service spouses living near the base, she knew, and they had to keep busy somehow. Alongside them were a smaller number of older men, also in civvies. These would be the retirees: ex-soldiers or officers who had settled down nearby and were entitled to use the base facilities for as long as they lived. Her own father had talked about doing something similar at Camp Darby.

She felt a sudden pang of heartsickness. Many of these men were about the same age as him. White hair combined with an upright, military bearing – dignified and frail at the same time – always got to her.

She found the right classroom and peered inside. Two men of about seventy were sitting watching another man of a similar age. He was drawing a diagram on the whiteboard as he talked. She guessed that must be Gilroy, and stepped back into the corridor to wait.

After about five minutes the door opened and the two other men came out. Gilroy was cleaning the board down, meticulously scrubbing it clean with methylated spirits.

"Mr Gilroy, sir?"

He turned. He was white haired, and his physique had the slenderness of age, but his firm blue eyes showed no sign of wateriness as they took in her meagre pips. "Yes, Second Lieutenant?"

"I'm here to ask a favour, sir. I'm told you might speak Serbo-Croat – I have some documents I'm looking to translate."

Clearly pleased to be asked, he nodded. "I'll certainly try. But I have to warn you, my skills in that direction are somewhat meagre. Back in the day, it was our Russian we tended to work on. Do you have the documents with you?"

She gave him the papers, and he waved her to a seat. Pulling out a pair of reading glasses tucked discreetly into his shirt pocket, he scrutinised them.

"These are mostly dates, and what appear to be meeting notes," he said after a minute. "At a guess, I'd say they relate to Operation Storm."

"That tallies with my intel, sir. But why would the US Army have archive notes relating to Storm? My understanding is that there was no US involvement in that conflict."

He glanced over the reading glasses with a smile. "What's your name, Second Lieutenant?"

"Boland, sir. Holly Boland."

He stared at her. "Not Ted Boland's daughter? Little Holly who used to make those Italian cookies for barbecues?"

"Affirmative, sir," she confessed.

"Well, I'll be...! Your father and I didn't see each other often, of course – he was down at Pisa and I was up here in Venice, although I took my chain of command from Langley." She nodded at the discreet acknowledgement that he'd been CIA. "But I certainly swung you round on my arms a few times – in the days when I was still capable of such things."

He smiled ruefully. "But you haven't come here today to listen to an old man's reminiscences."

"On the contrary, sir. I'd be honoured to hear your recollections of my father."

"Well, perhaps on another occasion." He turned back to the documents. "May I ask exactly what it is you're looking for?"

"Well, that's the thing – I'm not quite sure. A Freedom of Information request came in. Something to do with a man called Dragan Korovik."

"And who is he, when he's at home?"

"He is, or was, a Croat army general. And he's certainly not at home, not at the present time. He's awaiting trial for alleged war crimes relating to Operation Storm."

Gilroy raised his eyebrows. "Well, it's certainly an intriguing mystery. And I have to confess, I've rather missed those since I retired. Mind if I take these and try to work it out?"

"Please go ahead, sir." As he folded the papers, she added, "That's a copy."

"So not classified?"

"Doesn't appear to be."

"Good. And whether there's anything useful in here or not..." He tapped the folded pages. "I'd like to borrow you for dinner sometime. Been into Venice much yet?"

She shook her head. "I only got here yesterday."

"Then we'll go to a proper Venetian restaurant and you can fill me in. My treat." He paused, then added, "I do get some news, via friends back home. I'd heard that your father's no better. I'm very sorry."

"Thank you, sir," she said. For some reason, this old warrior's calm sympathy was almost harder to bear than her own family's regular updates. She swallowed away the sudden catch in her throat. "I'm sure he'd be glad to know so many people are thinking of him."

"Things like that, they put life into perspective, don't they?" He tapped the papers she'd given him. "But in the meantime, I'd be pleased to help you with your puzzle, Second Lieutenant."

Thirteen

STILL WEARY FROM her late night, Kat drove inland towards Verona for her 9 a.m. appointment with Father Uriel. She got lost several times in the Veneto countryside before she finally located the Institute of Christina Mirabilis, nestled on its own amongst rolling vineyards and quiet woods. To judge from the ancient stone of the buildings, and the stained glass in some of the windows, it had once been a monastery or convent. The area between Venice and Verona was liberally dotted with such places, most of them dating back to the sixteenth and seventeenth centuries when *La Serenissima*, as Venice was known – The Most Peaceful One – provided a safe haven for those of every persecuted religious affiliation. In the modern age many had become hospitals or colleges, often still run by nuns or monks from the original order. Something along those lines was clearly the case here: as Kat parked she observed a number of nurses in grey nuns' habits, hurrying busily from building to building.

The receptionist, another nun, took her to Father Uriel's office and knocked on the door for her.

"Come in," a voice called.

A man in shirtsleeves sat at a desk, typing briskly into a small computer. Apart from the white *collarino* of his shirt, and the small metal cross pinned to his chest, he might have

been any other busy medical man at work. A doctor's couch, complete with a paper hygiene sheet, stood to one side.

Breaking off from his work, he stood and greeted Kat with a handshake. "Pleased to meet you. I'm Father Uriel." His Italian was excellent, but a hint of clipped vowels suggested that it wasn't his first language.

"Thank you for seeing me, Father."

"Not at all. I understand it relates to the abomination at Poveglia?"

"To the murder, yes."

"It was not only the murder I was referring to," Father Uriel said quietly. She must have looked at him questioningly, because he continued, "There are many different ways of allowing evil into our world, Captain."

"You're talking about the occult?" she said cautiously.

"Amongst other things."

"But this is a hospital, isn't it? I suppose I'm a little surprised to hear a medical person talking in such terms."

A hint of a smile creased the corners of his eyes. "The dividing line between the spiritual and the medical is sometimes less clear cut than my purely medically trained colleagues would have you believe. Whether you use the term 'psychosis' or 'possession', for instance, is often more a matter of your training than any real difference in the symptoms you're describing. In earlier times, of course, prayer was often the only remedy for such illnesses. But in the modern age, we have powerful pharmacological treatments too. So here at the Institute we use both approaches – pharmaceutical interventions and spiritual ones, working in combination. Quite literally, the best of both worlds."

"Interesting," Kat said, not wanting to get drawn into a general discussion about the Institute. "But it's your specific

expertise with the occult that brings me here today. I'm told you might be able to identify some of these." Opening her file, she took out Hapadi's photographs showing the symbols daubed around the Poveglia crime scene.

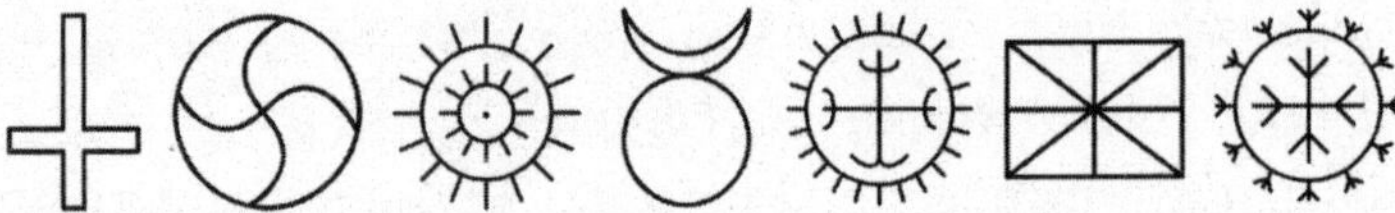

Father Uriel scanned the images one by one. "Yes," he said, nodding. "Some of these are very familiar to me." He pointed. "This one is the upturned cross, obviously. It signals to Satan that he's being welcomed to a blasphemous space." He indicated another. "This is the Horned God, a symbol representing the Evil One. And the entwined double S here represents the Salute and the Scourge, a symbol of obedience to evil."

"So there's absolutely no doubt in your mind that these symbols are sacrilegious?"

"None whatsoever." He handed the photographs back quickly, as if unwilling to handle them any longer than was absolutely necessary.

"What about these?" She pointed to two of the symbols he hadn't mentioned. "They're very similar to some tattoos we found on the victim's body."

A little reluctantly, Father Uriel examined the pictures again. "Sometimes an individual cult or temple will devise its own iconography, deliberately impenetrable to outsiders," he said with a shrug. "To record the various horrors perpetrated by an individual member, for example. In such cases, the symbols do have meanings, but they may be unfathomable to us."

"I see. Well, thank you, Father. You've been very helpful."

As she put the photographs away, he said, "You know, some of the older nuns here worked at Poveglia. When it was still a mental hospital, I mean."

"Why was it closed?" she asked curiously.

"Somewhat unusually, I believe it was at the nuns' own instigation. Many of them had come to believe that it was a place of great evil. According to them, there were apparitions, strange occurrences..." He shook his head. "It had been a *lazzaretto*, of course, a plague island, and there were all sorts of superstitions about it. The diocese, naturally, tried to ignore their complaints at first. Nuns can be terribly superstitious, and it's not healthy to encourage such fears."

"What happened?"

"Eventually, I understand, it was observed that something was affecting the patients – something that seemed to have no medical explanation. So the decision was taken to move them to sites such as this one, where they began to improve almost immediately."

"Can I ask you, Father..." She hesitated, unsure how to word this tactfully.

"You want to know if I actually believe in the occult," he said quietly. "And the answer to that is complicated, because I am both a man of God and a man of science. As a priest, I certainly believe in the Devil. But as a doctor, I believe that the terrible power the Devil exerts over certain minds stems partly from a weakness within our own natures. People embrace evil because it excites them."

"So symbols like the ones I showed you just now – they're not real? Not in a literal sense?"

"Oh, they're real," he assured her. "And just as prayers have an effect, so do they. I couldn't tell you whether Poveglia is actually haunted by evil spirits, Captain. But I can tell you that it's just the kind of place that people who wish to commit the blasphemies we've been discussing would be drawn to."

Fourteen

HOLLY SPENT AN hour phoning different departments at Camp Darby, trying to discover where the archives from the tunnels had been taken. Eventually a staff sergeant told her that two truckloads of papers had just appeared outside his hangar without warning, and he was darned if he knew what to do with them.

"You weren't expecting them?"

"No, ma'am. And I can't find out who ordered them to be brung here, either. That happens plenty, though – stuff just arrives. My bet is, someone up your end wanted the space."

"And what will happen if no one tells you what to do with them?"

"We'll wait a couple of weeks, then recycle. US Army's fully committed to a responsible carbon footprint. And what with all the F-16 runs and the phosphorus bombs, we've got a bit of catching up to do." He chuckled at his own wit.

"Roger that. Look, will you do me a favour, Staff Sergeant? Don't recycle them until I can find out what's going on?"

"Like I say, we generally wait a couple of weeks," he said, the shrug of indifference audible in his voice. "After that, we gotta do something."

*

She sent out emails using her secure *@mail.mil* address to the local CIA sections and Department of Defense stations, enquiring whether they had any interest in the Camp Ederle archives. As an afterthought, she added a request for any unclassified documents relating to Barbara Holton's FOIA application. An auto-reply message indicated that she could expect a response within fifteen working days.

She phoned the cell number Barbara Holton had left her. It went through to voicemail, so she left a message.

"Ma'am, this is Second Lieutenant Boland from Caserma Ederle, updating you on the progress of your Open Government application. I regret that I will need an extension of time, as provided for under the legislation, to establish whether we have the information you requested."

After she put the phone down she knew she should really have wiped the whole question from her mind. There were more pressing matters to deal with now. Child and Youth Services had just sent a request for a translator to assist with a series of presentations to families of service personnel on Saying No to Narcotics. The Soldier's Theatre needed help with local-language posters for their upcoming charity gala. The Dental Clinic was proposing to employ a local assistant and urgently wanted someone to compare Italian dental technician qualifications with American ones.

But being Holly Boland, who was raised to make her bed neatly every morning, and who likewise preferred to square away every topic neatly in her mind before moving on to the next one, she continued to think about Barbara Holton's FOIA request while she was performing those other duties, fascinating and important though they were.

Fifteen

THE SOUND OF ringing cell phones was not uncommon in the operations room, and it took Colonel Piola a few seconds to notice that this particular phone wasn't being answered. He glanced around the room incuriously, since the ringing was somewhere nearby, but soon forgot all about it when it stopped.

A few moments later, however, there was a shrill beep, indicating that the caller had left a voicemail.

That, too, was easy enough to ignore. But whoever owned this particular phone had set it so that it beeped at regular intervals until the voicemail was listened to. Piola was trying to sift through the evidence they'd gathered so far in order to decide on the most urgent avenues of investigation, and the intermittent beeping was distracting. He looked around again, this time with a degree of annoyance at whichever thoughtless subordinate had left their phone behind instead of carrying it in their pocket.

Almost immediately, his eye was caught by a flashing light on the table where the evidence from the hotel room was waiting to be logged. The phone they'd found, still inside its evidence bag, had lit up. That meant there was a message.

Covering the distance to the table in three quick strides, Piola picked up the phone. Without opening the bag, he touched the screen. The words "Voicemail Calling" flashed up. He held it to his ear, listening through the plastic.

"Ma'am, this is Second Lieutenant Boland from Caserma Ederle..."

Reaching for his notebook, he wrote down the name. Then he found his own phone and punched in Kat's number.

"*Pronto*?" her voice replied.

"Kat, how far are you from Vicenza? I need you to talk to someone called Second Lieutenant Boland at Caserma Ederle."

Sixteen

HOLLY BOLAND RECEIVED a call from the guardhouse saying that there was an officer of the Carabinieri asking to see her. While they escorted her unexpected visitor over, she readied a meeting room. This, she had gathered from Mike, was going to be one of her regular duties. Any complaints from the local police about American soldiers getting rowdy in local bars, or committing traffic offences, would be directed to her. It was expected that she would listen sympathetically, in the hope the Italians wouldn't press the matter too hard. Then it could be dealt with internally. If the soldier had recently returned from deployment in a war zone, the penalties were usually light.

She was surprised, therefore, when the officer in question turned out to be a plain-clothes detective – although, in truth, the term "plain clothes" hardly did justice to the casually elegant attire of the raven-haired young woman who now took a seat across from her. She was more surprised still to be asked whether the name Barbara Holton meant anything to her.

She explained that Barbara Holton had come to her with a Freedom of Information request.

"Concerning?"

"I would need her permission before I answer that, ma'am. FOIA requests are confidential."

Kat Tapo raised an elegant eyebrow. "You should know that Barbara Holton is dead. We believe the bullet that killed her may have come from an American-designed weapon. We're treating it as murder."

For a moment the stark word hung in the air.

"Even so, the application is still confidential. Smythson vs State Department, 2009," Holly added, almost apologetically.

Kat considered. "In that case, I'd like to see the information you would have provided to Signora Holton in *response* to her request," she said. "It will help to establish whether the enquiry had any bearing on her murder."

Second Lieutenant Boland looked even more discomfited. "That won't be possible either, ma'am. The archives relating to Ms Holton's request are no longer held on this site."

Again an elegant eyebrow inched upwards. "They've been got rid of?"

"The archives were scheduled for relocation, yes."

"How convenient. Congratulations, Second Lieutenant. You appear to have dealt with Signora Holton's request just as efficiently as the Italian Army would have done." Kat smiled, hoping to build a rapport with the American, but the Second Lieutenant didn't reciprocate.

"The request and the relocation were in no way connected," she said stiffly.

"If you say so. Anyway, how shall we proceed?"

"In what respect?"

"I'm an officer of the Carabinieri, you're an officer of the US Army. We're allies – colleagues – expected by our respective commanders to cooperate as fully as possible. Yes?"

"Of course."

"And I need to establish whether Barbara Holton's visit here had any possible bearing on her murder. Let's say you didn't actually show me that Freedom of Information request, but simply left it on the table here, perhaps while you went to get me some water… I'm very good at reading upside down. Particularly if I'm the only person in the room. And then I could leave here reassured that we're not wasting resources on an irrelevant line of enquiry."

"That would still be a breach of confidentiality, ma'am," Holly said, taken aback.

Kat sighed and crossed one leg over the other. Her foot swung, scything the air with impatience. Both the shoe and the skirt – and the leg that connected them – were immaculate. Holly found herself envying the other woman's dress sense, along with the opportunity she had to display it. The US Army hadn't even gotten around to designing separate fatigues for women, although they were always promising them.

"Of course," Holly added, "if there is any evidence at all that connects your investigation to Caserma Ederle, and you provide us with it, we will investigate it ourselves to the very best of our ability." Determined not to be intimidated, she held the Italian's gaze, although she suspected she wasn't quite matching the scorn that Captain Tapo appeared to be able to convey with a simple curl of her upper lip.

"On my way here today," Kat said, "I had someone look up the record of investigations carried out by the US Army on the Carabinieri's behalf here at Ederle. It was interesting. But hardly encouraging." She leant forward and stabbed the table with the ends of two fingers for emphasis. "In the last five years, there have been twenty-four investigations. And to date, the number of convictions in Italian courts stands at zero. I assume you know about the cable-car deaths at Cermis?"

Wrong-footed by the sudden change of subject, Holly shook her head.

"A US Military jet was flying through the mountains just north of here on a training mission. Except that the pilot of this particular jet had made a bet, on video, that he could fly his plane between the two lines of the cable car that cross the valley. He sliced one of the cables with his wingtip and the car plummeted sixty feet to the ground. The occupants died, all twenty of them. The US Army refused to hand over the aircrew, saying they'd be investigated and tried in a military court. Guess what? They were acquitted, every single one. Even the pilot. Over a decade later, the Italian warrants for their arrest are still outstanding."

Holly couldn't take her eyes off Captain Tapo's hands, which throughout this speech had been conducting a separate, even more bravura performance of their own, as if the Captain were a mime artist juggling a dozen invisible balls at the same time.

"Ma'am, I'm not authorised to comment on that particular—"

"Of course you're not. Or on the sniper with post-traumatic stress disorder who decided to hone his skills on civilians here in Vicenza. Or the man who was beaten to death in a bar in Venice because he dared to challenge three GIs who were hitting on his girlfriend. And you wonder why people object to the fact that you're doubling this base in size! Ten thousand US personnel in the Veneto alone, twenty thousand in all Italy. You know what? In any other country, that would be considered a good size for an army of occupation."

There was silence. Then Holly said, "Ah, getting back to this FOIA request..."

"Forget it," Capitano Tapo said with magnificent disdain.

"You're not going to do anything. Why should you? It's only a dead civilian, after all."

Irked as much by the other woman's clothes as her haughty manner, Holly said, "I can tell you that the FOIA request relates to a General Dragan Korovik and his command during the Bosnian war – a period for which we no longer hold records here. Barbara Holton ran a website called Women Under War. She made the request in that capacity. And that is the total extent of her involvement with this post."

Just for a second there was a glint of triumph in the captain's dark eyes. "That's what I had assumed," Kat said. "Thank you for your help, Lieutenant. It makes things so much easier when we cooperate, doesn't it?"

Seventeen

AS SHE WAS escorted back to the Camp Ederle guardhouse, Kat found herself pleased with the way the interview had gone. She'd achieved rather more than she'd expected to, in that getting any information at all out of the US Army was notoriously difficult. Playing second fiddle to Piola was all very well, but it was nice to handle things herself once in a while.

And it had been satisfying to provoke the little American mouse. She knew that a high proportion of the women in the US Army must be lesbians, but even so she couldn't see why on earth they would put up with wearing those appalling, sexless camouflage suits all the time, even when they were just sitting in an office being unhelpful and there was nothing to be camouflaged against. It would make more sense, she thought, if Second Lieutenant Boland had a desk, a box file and a grey wall printed on her fatigues. Then she'd be almost invisible.

Pleased with this observation, which she was sure would make Colonel Piola smile if she managed to work it into her report later, she turned to the *carabiniere* who was escorting her back to the guardhouse. "Do you always do this?"

"What, ma'am?"

"Escort visitors off and on the site."

The *carabiniere* shrugged gloomily. "At least twenty times a day. It's all part of the pretence that this is still Italian territory. When the truth is, the Yankees do what the hell they like. Our *comandante* is nominally in charge of the whole camp, you know that? And all they use him for is to wheel him out in his dress uniform when they give each other medals. God knows who I offended to get this posting."

A thought struck Kat. "Do you keep records? Of all the visitors, I mean?"

"In a manner of speaking. That is, we write down their names and the time. There's not much else to do, frankly."

"Would you still have the records from 1995?"

"If you'd asked me that a few months ago, I'd have been able to say yes."

"Why? What happened after that?"

"We had a fire at the warehouse where the Carabinieri records are kept. Not just these, but everything relating to the whole province." He shrugged. "People are blaming the Mafia."

"People blame the Mafia for everything."

"True, but who else could it be?"

"Sure," Kat said, remembering what the mouse had said. *A period for which we no longer hold records here.* So now no one at Ederle had any paperwork relating to that period. But perhaps that wasn't surprising, given how long ago it had been.

They'd reached the security barrier. The *carabiniere* saluted a farewell, his elbow mournfully drooped at the thought of his own continuing misfortune.

When the *capitano* had gone, Holly cleared up the room, a little annoyed with herself for having allowed the woman to rile her. But most of her anger was directed at the *carabiniere*. Intelligence work and police detection weren't so different, after all – they both depended on analysing the facts coolly and without prejudice. Yet the Italian had swept in, scattering insinuations and allegations almost at random. "How convenient," she'd said approvingly, when she'd heard about the archives being moved. It had been on the tip of Holly's tongue to retort that if the US Military was as riddled with corruption as the Carabinieri clearly was, they'd never fight a single battle – just like the Italians. But that would hardly have been consistent with the objectives of LNO-3's hearts and minds initiative.

Sighing, Holly shook her head. People like Captain Tapo reminded her that you could speak Italian like a native – could almost think of yourself as one – but there would always remain a gulf between the way your mind worked and theirs.

It occurred to her that now Barbara Holton was dead there was no administrative reason to continue with her FOIA enquiry. She made a mental note to request a copy of the death certificate, so that she could close her file. And she'd better tell Ian Gilroy not to waste his time translating the documents she'd given him.

Back at her desk, she found two emails waiting, both relating to the FOIA. The first was from the CIA section in Milan.

The CIA regrets that it can neither confirm nor deny the existence of documents responsive to your request.

The next was from the Office of the Department of Defense.

> The DoD regrets that it can neither confirm nor deny the existence of documents responsive to your request.

Stonewalled. And with the exact same wording, too. But then, she reminded herself, there was nothing unusual in that. It would have been more unusual if they *had* found something.

Barbara Holton might have been murdered, but there was no reason whatsoever why it should have anything to do with any information she'd been eliciting from Holly.

She shook her head. *Quit thinking like a conspiracy theorist.*

Eighteen

RICCI CASTIGLIONE HESITATED on the threshold of the church of San Giacomo Apostolo in Chioggia. The interior was dark and silent, the air spicy with candle wax and incense. He dipped his fingers in the holy water by the door, crossed himself, and hurried across the echoing space to a side chapel.

Madonnas, dozens upon dozens of them, looked down on him from every height, crowded onto the walls like posters in a teenager's bedroom. Tourists usually took it for a quaint display of devotion to the Virgin Mary, but this was actually another madonna altogether: Madonna della Navicella, Our Lady of the Seas, whose image appeared miraculously on logs and boats washed up from the depths of the lagoon. She was, the fishermen knew, an older and more potent goddess altogether than the Mother of Christ. Along with her likeness, the chapel walls were crammed with *tolele* – little offerings of gratitude for those she'd saved from the waves.

Ricci stood for a moment, his head bowed, struggling to form into words what he wanted to say to her.

This time I've gone too far. But it wasn't my fault. It was the American.

As he turned away, his eyes met those of the old priest, sitting patiently in the confessional across the way. "No customers today, Father?" he called, trying to sound braver than he felt.

It was the old crow's silence that did it. Ricci had committed many bad acts in his life. Once, he'd burnt a rival fisherman's boat. On several occasions, he'd cheated on his wife with prostitutes offered to him for free in return for services rendered. He'd stabbed a man in anger, and still believed it was Our Lady of the Seas who had made sure the man didn't die – a living victim could be silenced with threats, but a dead one meant the police for sure.

His smuggling, and the other errands he ran, he didn't count as sins – they were someone else's misdeeds; all he was doing was shifting them from A to B. But this thing with the woman dressed as a priest gave him a feeling of terror he couldn't shake off. It was wrong – he could feel it, and not just in the leaden sickness that gnawed at his stomach. Every single one of his crab pots had remained stubbornly empty all week. And now there was news of two Carabinieri officers asking questions amongst the fishermen. If only the American had asked him where to dump the body, instead of just tipping it into the water!

Evil had attached itself to him, in the form of the abomination washed up on the steps of La Salute. From there it was just a short step to a drowning in one of the inexplicable storms that sometimes appeared in the lagoon out of nowhere. The Madonna della Navicella – she was female: she wouldn't like such a desecration on her patch.

Like many of the fishermen, Ricci had never learnt to swim, and his relationship with the sea was like that of a man who lives on a volcano: in his bones he knew that it was only a matter of time before it claimed him.

He looked around. There was no one else about. Crossing

quickly to the little booth, he pulled the curtain shut and muttered in the direction of the face half-hidden by the grille, "*Mi benedica, Padre, perchè ho peccato.*"

Bless me, Father, for I have sinned.

Nineteen

IT WAS ALMOST noon by the time Kat got back to Campo San Zaccaria.

"How was the American?" Piola asked.

"Unhelpful. But also irrelevant, at least on the face of it." She explained about Barbara Holton's FOIA request. As she'd hoped, Piola smiled at her description of the by-the-rules American she'd had to wrest the information from.

"Any progress here?" she added.

"Some, from the forensic team who looked at the Poveglia crime scene. You know the symbols on the wall? Some of them were sprayed *over* the peripheral blood spray."

She thought quickly. "So they were added *after* the victim was killed."

His nod told her that he appreciated not having to spell it out. "Exactly. And the way the blood spray was mixed with the ink shows that it was done almost immediately."

"Meaning what?"

He shrugged. "Who knows? Perhaps the killer was making a kind of commentary on what he had done."

"You said 'some of the symbols'. Which ones were there before she was killed?"

Piola drew a sheet of contacts towards him and circled three of the designs.

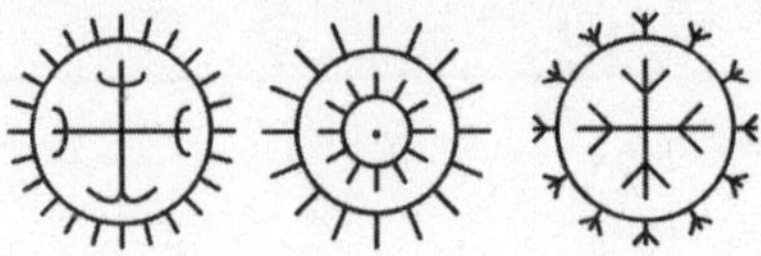

"These. Two that match the tattoos on our corpse, and one that's very similar." He looked up. "What did your expert have to say about these three?"

"Father Uriel?" She thought back. "He never actually gave me an opinion on them," she said slowly. "I mean, some of the others he identified very quickly as having occult meanings – blessings to Satan, that kind of thing. But when I asked him about these, he didn't really say anything."

"He didn't recognise them?"

"That's the strange thing. If you don't recognise something, it's pretty easy just to come right out and say so, isn't it? 'I'm sorry, Captain Tapo, I have no idea what these are.' But he didn't do that. He made a little speech about how occultists sometimes devise their own symbols as badges of rank – he gave me the *impression* they could be something along those lines, but he never actually said so."

"So we have someone who perhaps recognises these symbols, but doesn't want to say so," Piola mused.

"Not just *someone*," she said. "A priest. I think that Father Uriel might be the sort of man who doesn't like to tell an outright lie. So he takes refuge in misdirection instead."

"What could possibly make a priest want to mislead a police investigation?" Piola asked rhetorically.

Kat nodded. "Something that might embarrass the Church. Oh, and he knew about Poveglia. He was trying to tell me what an evil place it was, how it was just the sort of place Satanists might choose to hold their rituals. At the time

I thought it was odd that the conversation had taken a turn in that direction, but with hindsight I think he was trying to nudge me further towards the occult connection."

"Because...?"

"I don't know," she said, frustrated. "But there's something that isn't right here, isn't there?"

"Your first homicide, and you're telling me you already have an instinct for when something's wrong?" She started to apologise, and he cut her off. "For what it's worth, I agree. There are too many contradictory lines of enquiry – which makes me think that some of them must be smokescreens, thrown up to put us off the scent. But let's not jump to conclusions, Captain. Evidence-gathering first. The theories can come later."

Her inbox was full of emails, including one from the website that had published the blog about illegal ordinations.

> Captain Tapo,
>
> In response to your enquiry, I write to inform you that this organisation holds no information whatsoever regarding anyone involved, however tangentially, with attempted ordinations of women. If we did have information that any of our members were involved in such activities, we would immediately cut all links with them and pass the information to the relevant Church authorities.
>
> Sincerely,
>
> The webmaster

"Arse coverer!" she said out loud.

There was another email below it, from an address she didn't recognise.

Dear Captain Tapo,

I understand you want to speak to someone about women priests. I am a woman, and I am also a Catholic priest. There are, to my knowledge, well over a hundred of us, the Church's current position notwithstanding. Exact numbers are hard to establish – many of us don't even know our own Sisters in Christ, having been ordained through catacomb ordinations.

I would be happy to discuss this further with you if we can establish a safe way of doing so. Do you have a Carnivia account? It would be easier if you did.

Forgive me if I don't use my real name.

"Karen"

Piola, hearing her whistle of surprise, looked up.

"An email from a woman priest," she explained. It was curious, she reflected, that despite the wary tone of the first note, it could only have been that writer who'd forwarded her own email to "Karen".

"So they do exist?"

She gestured at the email. "She claims they do. She mentions Carnivia, too. That's the second time that name's come up. I wonder why?"

Piola shrugged. "I'm too old to figure out all this internet stuff. I'm going to leave that part to you and Malli. Make it a priority, though, will you?"

*

Giuseppe Malli occupied a windowless room high in the attic of the Carabinieri headquarters. Long ago, when the building was a nunnery, this had been one of the more austere novice's cells. Now it was crammed with bits of electronic equipment: hard drives, partially disassembled laptops, lengths of cabling and portable monitors.

"Ah, Capitano," Malli greeted her. "I've just been examining your little mermaid." He held up a laptop hard drive in a clear plastic bag. "It's no good, I'm afraid. The waters of Venice have taken everything she knew. Want me to throw her away?"

"Better not," Kat said, taking the bag from him. "Useless or not, it's still evidence. Do you have the paperwork?"

Every item of evidence in the building was accompanied by its own chain-of-custody file. In theory, it should be possible to account for every minute it had spent since coming into the Carabinieri's possession.

Malli waved a hand at the mess on his workbench. "It's here somewhere. I'll send it on."

"Thanks." She found a place to perch. "I'd like to ask you something else, actually. What do you know about a website called Carnivia?"

"No more than anybody else, I suspect. Why?"

She explained about the two links the investigation had thrown up – first, from the victims' hotel room, and secondly in the email from the woman who claimed to be a priest.

Malli considered. "At a guess, they're using Carnivia as a kind of secure communications network. That's pretty clever, actually." Seeing her look of incomprehension, he explained. "Carnivia uses encryption technology to keep its users anonymous. Daniele Barbo wrote the algorithm himself, and amongst hackers it's recognised as being about the best there is. So once you're inside Carnivia, your communications are safe. It's like having your own military-grade communications channel. Better, actually. The US Department of Defense's systems have been hacked in the past. Carnivia never has."

"Didn't I read that Barbo's in some kind of trouble?"

He nodded. "Refusing to allow the government access to monitor website traffic is an offence now. His sentencing's in a few weeks' time. Most people think he'll go to prison rather than let the authorities into Carnivia."

Her mind was working overtime. "So if he were to tell us whatever it was our victim was using Carnivia for before she was killed, it might help him with the judge?"

Malli laughed. "I see where you're going with this, Captain, but I wouldn't hold out much hope if I were you. No one's ever persuaded Daniele Barbo to do anything he didn't want to. And the one thing he really, really doesn't want to do is to give people like you and me access to his website."

She replied to "Karen", saying she'd meet her wherever and whenever was convenient. Then she set about opening a Carnivia account.

It was barely more complicated than registering with an online retailer. First, she had to choose a Carnival mask in the "mask shop". As a Venetian, that took her no time at all: she always wore a Columbina, a smiling half-mask decorated with feathers and lace. Meanwhile, with her permission, the site was searching her computer for information.

After a minute or so, a message appeared.

Good morning, Inspector Katerina Tapo

Current location: Carabinieri Headquarters, Venice

Is the following correct?

There followed a long list of everything Carnivia had learnt about her. She read it, astonished. It had divined not only her job, rank and age but who she worked with, who her friends were, where she lived, what school and college she'd been to... the list went on and on.

It ended with the words:

Don't worry, in Carnivia you will be completely anonymous. Your new identity is Columbina7759.

What would you like to do?

From the options, she selected "Enter Carnivia".

Twenty

AN HOUR LATER, Kat finally logged out. She was aware that her cheeks were burning. Her head was spinning.

Whatever she'd been expecting, it hadn't been this.

To begin with, she'd just walked around, delighting in the fact that the 3D world of Carnivia was an exact replica of the city she knew and loved. Every detail was perfect, right down to the sleepy ginger cats sunning themselves on the windowsills, and the way the water in the canals glittered in the late afternoon sun, rising and falling slowly with the tides. But this was a Venice without grime and without tourists – unless you counted the masked figures who walked the pavements, slipping into doorways and gondolas on business of their own.

Unsure what to do next, she'd followed a stream of people into the Doge's Palace, where they seemed to be consulting huge ledgers laid out on tables. Going over, she saw that each book contained a list of names. As she opened the ledger nearest to her, the names changed. Now they were all of people she knew – names the website had gleaned from her hard drive. Against some were brief notations.

Delfio Cremonesi – four entries.

Francesco Lotti – two entries.

Alida Padovesi – six entries.

Alida Padovesi had been in her year at the Carabinieri training academy. They'd lost touch, although Kat kept meaning to Facebook her. She clicked on the name. Pages riffled.

Alida Padovesi. Body 6/10, face 5/10. Not great in bed – strange since she's had so much practice. I know she's been with at least ten other men since she transferred to Milan...

Alida Padovesi. The other night we were all at a restaurant and she told me she wanted to go to bed with a woman. I think she was hitting on me...

Alida Padovesi. Why is she sleeping with Bruno Corsti? Could it be something to do with the American Express gold card he's given her?

It was horrible – but Kat couldn't tear herself away. She understood now why Carnivia and its creator aroused such strong passions. She hated the fact that she was reading this tittle-tattle, but to stop was almost impossible. Every time she resolved to walk away, she spotted another name she knew, another entry that begged to be read. A part of her simply wanted the names to disappear, so she wouldn't have to summon the willpower to stop reading of her own volition.

Then, in a sudden moment of horror, it occurred to her that there might well be gossip like this about herself as well.

She checked.

Katerina Tapo – eight entries.

When she clicked on her name, though, the website brought up a message.

Are you sure?

She hesitated, then clicked "Cancel".

Twenty-one

DANIELE BARBO LOGGED onto Carnivia, just as he'd done a thousand times before. At the log-on screen, with its picture of a grinning Carnival mask, he typed an administrator password. Nothing changed on the screen, except for a two-line option for administrators only that appeared below the log-on:

Do you wish to be:

a) visible

b) invisible?

He clicked "b", then "Enter".

He was inside a gorgeously marbled Venetian *palazzo* – the exact same *palazzo*, in fact, in which he was sitting in the real world. The main entrance to Carnivia was modelled on Ca' Barbo, although the modernist sculptures and paintings installed by his father had been expunged from the online version. A few pundits had had a field day with that particular detail. In fact, as he'd patiently tried to explain at the time, it was simply easier to model the three-dimensional parts of Carnivia on a place he was familiar with, and removing the

Giacomettis and Picassos avoided problems with the Foundation, which owned the copyrights.

It was a good explanation, but even so, he'd secretly known the pundits had a point.

Around him, figures in seventeenth-century costumes and masks hurried to and fro. In Carnivia, Ca' Barbo was a convenient place to pick up post or catch a gondola to other parts of the city. You could even use a virtual computer here, which meant that when you went on Facebook, for example, your real identity was shrouded behind your Carnivia mask.

The little app that informed a Facebook user "You've got a secret admirer", accompanied by the gift of a virtual rose that gradually shed its petals over the course of the next few days, had been one of the first things to bring Carnivia worldwide attention. Millions of anonymous messages had been sent, particularly after a feature was added that allowed the admired to strike up a private, anonymous dialogue with their admirer.

It hadn't been long, of course, before someone had copied the source code to produce "Someone thinks you suck". In the furore that followed, Facebook had tried to ban all Carnivia applications – only to find that it was powerless to block the coding, so carefully had it been built. It was part of Carnivia lore that it had taken a personal appeal from Mark Zuckerberg to Daniele Barbo before the latter agreed to reveal how it was done.

That controversy, however, was nothing compared to what happened when Daniele allowed Carnivia to scour real-world data from your computer – to "scrape" it, in geek-speak – and use it to build up a picture of who you knew: your colleagues, your family, neighbours, friends, even which celebrities you followed. It was, its detractors said, an inducement to participate in the worst sort of mob behaviour – and yet the numbers visiting Carnivia had quadrupled overnight.

Daniele never answered his critics. He had no great interest in what people used his website for, nor did he see why he should be held responsible for what they posted. Venetians had been wearing masks for almost five centuries – in fact, when they were first introduced, a person was punishable by law if they *didn't* wear a mask when engaging in scandalous behaviour, the intention being that a merchant who lost a fortune on the gambling tables of the *casinò*, or whose wife took a lover, should be able to carry on trading with no loss of confidence in his ability to manage his affairs. Rumour and scandal were as much a part of Venetian life as dance and debauchery. There was even a word, *chiacchiere*, which meant both "to slander" and "to pass the time pleasurably". In his city these were old debates, settled long ago.

Now, invisible amongst the anonymous figures, Daniele took a seat and waited patiently for twelve o'clock.

He had no idea who he was waiting for, or why. He only knew that, in his painstaking trawling of Carnivia's data, he'd spotted one or two tiny anomalies, individual patterns of behaviour he couldn't quite explain. He was here to follow up one of them.

At exactly twelve o'clock each day someone accessed Carnivia, took the same brief walk, posted the same brief encrypted message, then left. And at exactly twelve o'clock the same force or forces that were trying to overwhelm Carnivia's servers threw their weight against its defences. Were the two things connected? He was certain they must be.

But whether the visitor was an accomplice of the would-be intruders, or their intended victim, he had no idea.

At midday a figure materialised in front of him. It was a woman – not that gender had quite the same meaning in Carnivia, being a matter of personal choice rather than of biology. She was wearing a Domino, the carnival mask so called because it was derived from the hoods of priests or "domini", black on the outside and white within.

The woman turned, examining those around her carefully, as if searching for someone. Then she spoke to the whole community – a relatively uncommon thing to do there. Even so, the message was encrypted: only the intended recipient would be able to decipher it.

"*Wrdlyght? Dth reht jerish?*"

There was no reply. After a moment the woman turned and went to the jetty. Stepping over the gondolas, she headed into the city. Daniele followed her. After a hundred yards or so, she turned and slipped into a tiny neighbourhood church, a simulacrum of Santa Maria dei Miracoli.

Once again she called out, "*Wrdlyght? Dth reht jerish?*" Once again, no one answered.

The woman knelt in front of the altar in an attitude of prayer. This, too, was unusual for Carnivia, where people tended to indulge in more profane pleasures. Coming up invisibly beside her, Daniele studied her. The mask and costume were both standard ones, displaying none of the elaborate customisations hard-core Carnivians sometimes indulged in. It could have been the avatar of any one of the hundreds of thousands of users who had, at that moment, chosen to enter the world he'd created.

Suddenly, that world shook. Most people would barely have noticed it, or would have assumed it was just some kind of software glitch. Daniele, who was familiar with every line of his world's code, knew better.

It didn't look like an attack. Fireballs weren't falling from the sky; walls didn't topple their stones into the streets; no blood was spilt into the canals. But the fifteenth-century walls of Santa Maria dei Miracoli shifted and slid in crumpled geodesic patterns, momentarily revealing the electronic wireframes within. The marble underfoot lost its pattern, and the sky was briefly visible through sections of the gilded roof. Daniele had the sense that he was a tiny doll in a doll's house that someone very powerful was picking up and shaking, trying to peer inside.

He waited. Carnivia settled again as the servers responded, taking the strain. The attack had been unsuccessful.

The woman got to her feet and crossed to a dark corner, where an old oak chest stood in the shadows. Daniele recognised it as a repository, one of dozens that he and his programmers had scattered around the city. Despite its medieval appearance, it was as secure a place to leave information as anywhere on the internet.

The woman unlocked the chest with a coded passkey and looked inside. Daniele looked too: it was empty. But he was intrigued to see that the interior had been customised with an unusual design, a kind of hieroglyphic pattern carved into the wooden lid. Although he had created the functionality that made such customisation possible, he had never seen anything exactly like it before.

The woman tossed a message into the chest, then locked it again and left. That message was also encrypted, but Daniele had a hunch that he knew exactly what it said.

I waited, but you never came. Where are you?

Twenty-two

HOLLY LEFT IAN Gilroy a message, standing him down from translating the documents she'd passed on. But to her surprise, when he called her back the old agent sounded hesitant.

"What is it?" she asked.

"Well, as it happens I already took a look at them."

"And? Did you find something?"

"Besides, you promised me dinner," he said, not quite answering her directly. "Are you by any chance free this evening?"

"Certainly."

"I have to make an appearance at an art show that's opening in Venice. Would you accompany me? Then we'll eat after."

"That sounds perfect."

"Good." He gave her directions, and they agreed to meet at eight.

She met him at the gallery, a converted warehouse near the Arsenale that was, he told her, often used for the Venice Biennale art fair.

"You have an interest in modern art?" she said, impressed, looking around. She hadn't taken him to be so cutting-edge in his tastes.

He chuckled. "No, not exactly. The man who set up the art foundation that owns this collection was a good friend of mine – Matteo Barbo, an aristocrat from one of the old Venetian families. Before he died, he asked me to take a non-executive seat on its board. So that's another of my little retirement jobs."

"Barbo," she said, thinking. "I know that name."

"The son, Daniele, was kidnapped when he was a child." Gilroy lowered his voice. "Between you and I, that was how I got to know Matteo. The Company was able to offer some unofficial help to the Italians over the kidnap. Unfortunately, and despite our best efforts, the boy lost his ears and part of his nose. He was an odd child even before that, but afterwards he became increasingly withdrawn. His father blamed himself for not paying the kidnappers what they wanted."

"Will Daniele be here tonight?"

"I doubt it. He tries to have as little as possible to do with any of the Foundation's activities." He glanced at her. "You look wonderful, by the way. I hope Ted knows what a beautiful woman his daughter's grown into."

She blushed. "Thank you."

It was true that she'd made an effort. Meeting Captain Tapo had reminded her how well ordinary Italian women dressed, and she'd decided that if she was going to swap her ACUs for civvies once in a while she really ought to do it properly. In the centre of Vicenza she had discovered several small but impeccable shops whose every item managed to made her look about a thousand times more glamorous than she actually was, and she'd spent the afternoon trying things on, becoming more and more unsure in the process which one to actually buy. A sympathetic assistant in Stefanel had eventually found her a simple cashmere dress, hooped with soft grey stripes. She'd fallen in love with it even before she tried it on, but in fact the seamless tube of wool felt unbelievably caressing against her skin. It was strange to look in the dressing-room mirror and see a woman rather than a soldier – the clinging material even gave her wiry body a hint of curves, although she'd have to eat a lot of pasta before she acquired anything resembling Captain Tapo's sensual hourglass figure. She'd also bought some heels, though she'd given up on those even before she left the base. After army boots, even sneakers felt as insubstantial as ballet shoes.

As they walked round, Gilroy explained that Matteo Barbo's particular obsession had been collecting works from an early twentieth century period known as Italian Futurism. They were colourful, vibrant even, but overly macho for Holly's taste and a little repetitive. Not that most of those present were paying much attention to the pictures, in any case. There was a lot of cheek-kissing going on, many glasses of *prosecco* being drunk and recharged. Acclimatised as she was to the graduated formalities of the military salute, it felt strange to be embraced intimately by so many strangers, both men and women, each time Gilroy introduced her. She must have explained who she was and why she spoke such fluent Italian a dozen times before he finally muttered, "Well, I think we've done our duty here."

He took her to Fiaschetteria Toscana, near the Rialto, where the staff – waiters even older than he, in bow ties and black jackets – teased Gilroy about his new girlfriend's age, ostentatiously recommending various dishes to him for their stamina- and potency-giving properties.

"I hope you don't mind," he said under his breath. "I've known these guys for years."

"Not at all," she said, and she didn't. The fuss they were making was so obviously affectionate that she felt flattered rather than embarrassed. Gilroy spoke Italian as fluently as she did, she noticed, although his banter with the waiters was liberally infused with Venexiàn, the impenetrable dialect of the city that was almost a separate language. Even other Italians were outsiders here.

"So," he said when they'd ordered – sardines followed by calves' liver for him, ravioli and swordfish for her. "I took a look at those documents you gave me. And I've also, I may say, been the recipient of one or two enquiries from my former colleagues. 'Who's this Second Lieutenant Boland who's sending us emails about Open Government requests?' Do we know her?'" His eyes twinkled. "I was pleased to be able to reveal that I had the jump on them."

"I was only following through—" she began, but he cut her off.

"Oh, don't apologise. Tweaking the tails of my former colleagues is one of the few pleasures I have left." He grew serious. "Also, I'm never too happy at discovering that my own side may have been up to something – how shall I put this? – *inappropriate*."

She stared at him. "Is that what the documents show?"

He made a very Italian gesture with his hand. It meant maybe, maybe not. "So far as I can tell, they're just records of meetings held at Camp Ederle between 1993 and 1995 – not minutes of what was actually said, you understand, more like schedules of discussions. But why were those meetings being held at Ederle in the first place? And why were the documents in Croatian?"

"Because someone who spoke only that language needed a record."

"Exactly. And to me that suggests we can only be talking about senior Croatian military."

"Dragan Korovik?"

"Possibly. But this is where I start to get a little antsy. If foreign military commanders were having meetings at a US Army base in my section, how come I knew nothing about it? According to protocol, the Agency should automatically be informed of any contact between our side and non-allies."

"So what do you think was going on?"

"Ever hear of an organisation called Gladio?" he said, answering her question with another.

She shook her head. "Should I have done?"

"Well, it's an interesting story. In 1990 the Italian prime minister, Giulio Andreotti, went before his parliament and made a rather remarkable confession. Turned out that ever since the end of World War II, with the full knowledge of successive Italian prime ministers, NATO had been running its own covert military network within Italy. Ostensibly, you understand, its members were ordinary Italian citizens – doctors, lawyers, politicians, priests. The one thing they had in common was that they were passionate anti-communists. NATO trained them, drilled them, supplied them with arms and paid them – all in secret. It was a guerrilla army in waiting. And no one knew a thing about it."

"My God," she said, amazed. "But... why?"

"After the war, when the Russians were tightening their grip on Eastern Europe, NATO thought they were eyeing Italy as well. And the democratic communists were having a surprising amount of success in the Italian polls. Originally, the idea was that if Russia invaded, or the communists got into power, Gladio would rise up, ready to become the official resistance."

He paused to snap a *crostini* between his fingers. "But that wasn't all Prime Minister Andreotti had to confess. It seems that, as the years passed and the Russians stayed behind the Iron Curtain, some of the gladiators began using their expertise – and their NATO-supplied high explosives – to manipulate domestic Italian politics. Over a dozen assassinations, bombings and other atrocities were laid at Gladio's door. Even, it seems, the assassination of another prime minister, Aldo Moro, who was kidnapped, tortured and killed just days before he was due to announce a power-sharing deal with the communists."

"The *anni di piombo*," she said.

"Exactly."

Every Italian knew the term for the political chaos of the seventies and eighties, dubbed the "Years of Lead" after all the bullets that had flown, when the police all but lost control of the streets and it was a brave lawyer who appeared for a prosecution.

"They called it a 'strategy of tension'," Gilroy went on. "Basically, it was about provoking reprisals as much as eliminating opponents. But the point is, Gladio was NATO's responsibility. The CIA knew nothing about it. At least, not officially."

"But unofficially?"

"Oh, we heard rumours. Speculation, little bits of information that didn't make sense; operations that seemed too well planned to be the work of amateurs. And of course the Iran–Contra scandal had shown us just what some of these guys were capable of. But that was all it was – rumour and speculation. So we dismissed it as the usual crackpot nonsense. Made us look pretty stupid when it all turned out to be true."

Conspiracy theories that turned out not to be nonsense after all. Shocked by the implications, she said, "What happened to the network?"

"When Andreotti made the announcement, he said Gladio had already been disbanded, on his orders. No one was to be arrested, no one charged."

"Convenient."

"Very." Gilroy's eyes took on a far-away look. "And of course it already seemed like something that belonged to the past, because the communist regimes were toppling in any case. I guess you're too young to remember all that – the end of the Cold War."

"I remember the Berlin Wall coming down," she said. "I was at a neighbour's, and it came on TV... People were climbing on the Wall and cheering. Then my dad came home early. He said everyone at the base was celebrating. He said..." She paused, her voice catching. "He said, 'Maybe we can all go home now.'"

Gilroy nodded. "That was what we all thought, back then. Communism defeated. NATO's job was done. Most of us really believed it was all over. And instead..."

"Instead?"

"Within a few years Yugoslavia had exploded into civil war. At first it was just a local conflict, but it soon turned brutal. Sarajevo, Bosnia, Kosovo... conflicts of such appalling barbarity, right on Europe's doorstep, that the whole world was clamouring for NATO to get involved. Which it did – not just with airstrikes, but with peacekeeping operations and protection forces. We're still in Kosovo to this day. Post-Cold War NATO's gotten bigger, not smaller." He paused. "I always wondered exactly how that happened."

It took her a moment to catch his meaning. "Wait a

minute," she said incredulously. "Are you suggesting that NATO may have deliberately stoked the war in Yugoslavia, in order to guarantee its own survival as an organisation?"

"I've got no proof of any such thing, Holly. But I simply can't think of any other reason why there should be documents written in Serbo-Croat in the tunnels under Camp Ederle." The blue eyes looked into hers, level and calm. "No one was ever disciplined for Gladio, much less arrested. What did those people do next? Did the network really disband, or did those guys all keep in touch with each other, hatching other plots under the radar? You know, after Gladio was revealed, the police were sent to retrieve its caches of arms and explosives. They'd been hidden in church crypts, catacombs, remote farms... and without exception, they'd vanished by the time the police got round to digging them up. Around a year later, the first bombs were used against civilians in Bosnia. For years I've been asking myself if the Company wasn't made fools of a second time."

She heard the passion in his voice, and knew he was talking about something that still mattered to him very deeply.

"So," he said with a smile, "I guess you have a decision to make, Holly. The person who asked for the information is dead—"

She looked at him quickly. "You think because of this?"

He shrugged. "My information is that the Italian police don't see any connection." She didn't ask him where his information came from, or point out that he hadn't actually answered her question. "The point is, you have no obligation to do anything at all with this information, let alone to go digging for more. No *legal* obligation, that is."

"NATO's basically the US," she said slowly. "If I tried to find out any more, I'd be looking for evidence against my own side. I'd be a… a *whistleblower.*"

He nodded, conceding the point. "On the other hand, I'd know who to go to with whatever you found. We could keep all this in-house."

"We? You'd help me?"

"Of course. I owe your father that much, at least."

It took her a second to register what he'd just said. "My father? What's it got to do with him?"

He looked her squarely in the eye. "Back in the day, Ted Boland was one of those who raised concerns about what we now know as Gladio. He tried to pass them up the line. Hell, he even mentioned them to me. Not knowing any better at the time, I assured him there was nothing to worry about. But by then he'd been identified as a troublemaker. He stayed in post, but I think it blighted the rest of his time at Camp Darby."

"I didn't realise," she said slowly. But it all fitted. There'd been an intangible feeling of failure in those later years, a sense that in some way mysterious to her he'd blotted his copybook. And then the drinking had started, followed a little later by the first of his strokes.

"If I *were* to pursue this," she said, "how would I do it?"

"Just follow the evidence. It seems likely to me that it was quite a small group of people taking policy-making into their own hands. They wouldn't have trusted the usual channels of communication – there would have to have been face-to-face meetings, like the ones you've already identified. And that means there must be some kind of evidence trail."

"Mr Gilroy, sir – Ian – I need to think about this."

"Of course you do. It's a big decision." He paused. "I should tell you, it's been a while since I ran an active operation, Holly. But whatever expertise or advice an old spy can still offer, it's yours."

Twenty-three

SHE COULDN'T GO to bed. She was still too psyched by her conversation with Ian Gilroy, too disturbed by the implications of what he'd said. It was after midnight when she got back to the base, but she heard the distant throb of rock music pumping from the direction of Joe Dugan's bar.

Outstanding, was how Private Billy Lewtas had described it.

It was Saturday night. She started walking in the direction of the music.

Billy Lewtas had been right: Joe Dugan's was a pretty cool bar. In fact, if your idea of a good bar was a dimly lit, spacious blues shack somewhere in the Texas countryside, crammed with physically fit young men, where the music was so loud the bass lines flipped in your chest and groin like a second heartbeat – and frankly, Holly didn't know many people for whom that wouldn't describe a pretty good bar – then you were going to love it.

Still in the woollen Stefanel dress she'd worn to her meeting with Gilroy, she was a little overdressed for her surroundings, but it was better than fatigues. She texted Billy, to see if by any chance he was here.

He was. Within minutes she had a beer in her hand and was surrounded by a crowd of eager young men. Males outnumbered females here by about three to one. It was one of the things you just got used to in the army. Coming from a family where she'd been the only girl amongst three brothers, she often wondered if that was one reason she was so comfortable with military life. If you had a problem with men en masse – or indeed with buckish high spirits, hollering, cheering, being splashed with beer or with a general overabundance of testosterone all around you – this was not the place to be.

She soon discovered that one reason the testosterone level was particularly high was because three companies of Marines had just flown in from Afghanistan. This was their first R&R since being shot at. Cameras and phones were being passed around, displaying films and photographs. She gathered that their mission had been incredibly hot and incredibly dangerous. She saw pictures of village elders with extravagant beards; women in burkas with glittering eyes; grinning Afghan children in brightly coloured woollen hats, holding packets of M&Ms in one hand and giving a big thumbs-up with the other.

She saw a picture of a Taliban fighter with his throat cut, and another in which a soldier clowned around, holding a severed head in front of his own like a mask. Mostly, though, she saw an awful lot of brown houses and brown fields and suntanned Marines in sunglasses and no shirts.

A second lieutenant called Jonny Wright bought her a beer. It irked her slightly that he assumed he had the right to monopolise her, just because he and she were level-pegging junior officers, but when he told her he was going outside for a smoke she went too.

By "smoke", it turned out, he meant dope. "Finest Afghan black," he said with a grin.

"You brought this stuff back with you?"

"Hell, no. We have to unpack our bags and pass them by the sniffer dogs before we even get on the plane. I get this in Vicenza."

They went round the back of the block to smoke it. It was strong and sweet and she loved the way her head seemed to fill up and expand softly like a helium balloon at the very first toke.

"You going to give me a blow job now?" he asked, taking another puff.

"Am I fuck!" she laughed.

He passed her the reefer, and as she took it he held her wrist, put his foot round behind her knee and forced her to the ground, swiftly and deftly. "No, I mean I really need a blow job. Right now."

"Fuck you," she spat, suddenly aware that he was serious.

"I shared my dope with you, I bought you a beer. I haven't had a BJ in six weeks, and it ain't going to suck itself. Now open that pretty little mouth."

He was strong, and he had her arm twisted in such a way that he could control her with one hand. With the other he flipped his penis out.

She tried to stay calm. "This will end your career in the military, Jonny. Think about it. Then do the smart thing and put that away. Do it now and I won't tell anyone."

He laughed at her. "End *my* career? But you're not telling anyone about this, Second Lieutenant. Not unless you want to fail a drugs test."

She'd been an idiot, she realised.

"Just do it," he breathed, taking her silence for assent. He leant back against the wall and put his hands over her ears, steering her head towards his now-erect penis. "Don't make me give you a slap."

"OK," she said quickly. "OK, all right? Just ease up, will you?"

"Good girl. No tricks now."

His hands relaxed. She got one foot underneath her, so that she was crouched like a runner at the starting block.

Go.

She powered up at him, her head lowered so that the top of it rammed up into his groin with the force of a quarterback's charge, directly at his balls. With the wall behind him, his body had nowhere to go. She felt him fold around the area of impact like a book.

He slumped to the ground, his breath wheezing, as she stood up.

"See you around, Jonny Wright," she said sweetly.

Twenty-four

KAT WOKE ON Sunday morning and registered a faint sense of disappointment. What was it? She glanced across at the empty side of the bed. No, it wasn't that. Although it had been a while since a Saturday night had gone by without her enjoying some male company at the end of it, she could live without it – in fact, it was usually round about now that she would be wondering how she could tactfully suggest to Ricardo or Quinzio or whoever it might be that it was time he had a shower and got going.

No, she realised that the reason she felt disappointed was precisely because it was a Sunday, and thus a day off work.

She looked at the clock. Half past nine. She'd slept late, but then she hadn't got home until after two. She and Piola had worked until midnight, then eaten *risotto all'Amarone* – the classic Veronese recipe, the rice cooked in red wine made from partially dried grapes – at the little *osteria* round the corner from Campo San Zaccaria, talking about the case until exhaustion overcame them.

She got up, made some espresso in her Bialetti, then headed towards the shower. En route, she booted up her laptop. There was still some background searching to be done – she'd made a list, in fact, of all the things she wanted to double-check when she had time.

Opening her notepad, she found her notes from the interview with the American army officer. She typed "Dragan Korovik" into a search engine and hit "Enter".

An hour later the coffee pot was empty, and she still hadn't had that shower.

Daniele Barbo hadn't yet been to bed. He'd been walking the streets and alleyways of Carnivia, invisible as an angel, looking for women in Domino masks. Several times he'd followed one, only to see her disappear into one of the gambling halls or cyber-brothels that were Carnivia's main places of recreation. He was fairly certain that none of these were the woman he was looking for.

He checked back at the church of Santa Maria dei Miracoli, as he'd done repeatedly over the last few days. As he approached it he saw two figures slipping through the tall oak doors, and quickened his pace.

Inside, a curious sight met his eyes. The pews were full. Around thirty figures in matching Domino masks and black costumes sat facing the altar, motionless, their heads bowed. A stream of encryption filled the air. It would be intelligible to all those who shared a passkey: he'd bet that meant every person present except himself.

At the front, facing the group, was a lone figure. It, too, was wearing a Domino mask. It was also, somewhat incongruously, wearing a chasuble and stole.

As Daniele watched, the figure spoke. "*Freg mkil yrt ortinariop?*"

As one, the congregation replied, "*Kptry iplf dwsta.*"

He was watching a priest take a service, he was in no doubt about that. At any other time, he would have been amused as well as intrigued to discover that Carnivia was being used for such an unexpected purpose. But now, given all the events of the last week, his first thought was "Why?"

Holly woke up in her bare, functional room at the Ederle Inn Hotel that smelt of air conditioning and boot polish and remembered it was Sunday.

She'd slept badly, unable to rid herself of the anger she'd felt at the Marine officer's attempt to force himself on her. Anger at him, yes, but also at herself. She'd walked into a trap, sharing that reefer. Not that she'd have reported him anyway – or at any rate, not unless she'd been unable to fight him off. In the army, it wasn't the culture to complain about any but the most serious transgressions. You were expected to fight your own battles.

Just like it wasn't the culture to be a whistleblower.

Outside, the sounds of the base were much as they were on any other day. A platoon of grunts was jogging past her window, egged on by a staff sergeant. As the soldiers ran, they chanted a Jody, in time-honoured fashion.

Used to love a beauty queen
Now I love my M-16.

Tomorrow, perhaps, they'd be deploying to Afghanistan, where they'd be shot at by an enemy who didn't wear a uniform and who improvised bombs out of clothes pegs and cell phones. Perhaps it was no surprise some came back a little crazy.

She wondered how long it would be before she herself saw combat. Several years, probably, by which time the Afghan war would in all likelihood be over and a new conflict risen to take its place. Some people were predicting a Cold War in

Africa, with China as the new enemy. Others said there'd be a conflict with a resurgent Islamic alliance led by Iran. The only thing certain was that, somewhere in the world, the United States would always be fighting.

Could it really be, as Gilroy had suggested, that some of those wars were being stoked by the military itself? It wasn't beyond the realms of possibility, she knew. Even within the army, there were plenty of people who thought that the claims about weapons of mass destruction in Iraq had been cooked up and given to the British in order to provide the Pentagon with a compelling, but arm's-length, pretext for invasion. But she couldn't shake her conviction that the people who did such things had betrayed the deepest-held principles of the service.

Pulling on her own PTs, she headed outside, easily keeping pace a couple of hundred yards behind the grunts, their chanting so familiar to her that it barely registered until it turned profane.

See that lady all in black?
Makes her living on her back.
See that lady from the South?
Makes her living with her mouth.

She thought about Second Lieutenant Jonny Wright. Was he capable of taking part in an operation like the one Gilroy had described – an operation that ran counter to everything that the US Army was supposed to stand for? Of course he was, if someone else planned it and told him what to do. And who would stop people like that, if not her and Gilroy?

Do not presume to think that because this mission is easy and safe it is unimportant or without valour, Major Forster had said to her. Well, now she was being offered a mission that was surely more important to the honour of the military than any task she had ever been given.

I'll do it, Dad.

She recalled something Gilroy had said, just before they parted. She'd asked him why he cared so much about these secrets of the past. Surely he should be enjoying his retirement now?

It was just as they were leaving the restaurant. Venice was foggy and the lights along the canals were fuzzy with mist. At their feet, the black waters stretched away like a gently rocking dark mirror.

"I've realised that there are three things I care about, Holly Boland," he'd said at last. "One is my country, which I served for thirty years. The second is my former Agency – its probity and its reputation. And the third – well, the third is this place. It gets under your skin, Italy, doesn't it? Hell, I've lived here so long, I've probably gone a little bit native by now. If some of our people were screwing with this country, and they did it on my watch, I want to know about it. And if I can, I want to put it right." He laughed, and patted her shoulder. "Or maybe it's just more interesting than giving lectures on Roman military history."

Despite the difference in their ages, she'd recognised in him a fellow outsider, one who could, like her, see this situation from a broader perspective. But now, thinking the evening over, she realised how cleverly he'd hooked her. He'd said he'd help her – made it look as if he was agreeing to be enlisted by her. But a part of her acknowledged that it might have been the other way round: that it was actually her who'd just been recruited, and to a cause she still didn't fully understand.

Twenty-five

"LOOK AT HIM! Such an adorable *bambino*! He gives her such pleasure, doesn't he?"

Kat sighed. Much as she loved her mother, she sometimes wished she could be just a little more subtle. When every sentence came freighted with innuendo like this, it made a family lunch exhausting.

Mamma was talking about Kat's thirteen-month-old nephew Gabriele, who at that moment was sitting on the lap of Kat's grandmother, Nonna Renata. Gabriele clutched a teaspoon in a pudgy fist that was already greasy with *ragù*. His fat little face was also liberally plastered with it, like a lipstick that had gone horribly wrong. In addition he wore a huge, delighted smile, as Nonna Renata combined feeding him with jiggling him on her knees.

"Eighty-nine years old, and she's lived to see her great-grandchildren," her mother said. "Well, her first great-grandchild. Of course, she'd had me *and* all your uncles by the time she was your age. *And* she'd taken four years out before that to fight in the war."

The subtext, of course, was that Kat's sister Clara had succeeded in producing a baby, whereas Kat had not. And Clara's perfectly round watermelon of a bump, not to mention a radiant smile to match little Gabriele's, was a constant reminder that another was on the way. Despite being the older sister, Kat was a disappointment. She hadn't so much as brought a boyfriend home since college, let alone produced a child. Her mother had been uneasy about her career choice from the start, and the continuing lack of anyone permanent in Kat's life only reinforced her fears.

For her parents' generation, the Carabinieri were simply the butt of jokes. Even now, her mother would happily trot them out after a grappa or two... A farmer sees a Carabinieri car driving backwards up a mountain. "Why are you driving backwards?" he asks. "We're not sure there'll be anywhere to turn round," comes the answer. A little later the farmer sees the same car driving backwards down the mountain. "Why are you driving backwards now?" he asks. "We found somewhere to turn round after all," the *carabiniere* replies.

How do you burn a *carabiniere*'s ear? Phone him while he's ironing.

A motorist asks a *carabiniere* if the indicators on his car are working. "Yes they are," comes the answer. "No they're not. Yes they are. No they're not..."

To escape, Kat went and sat next to Nonna Renata, whom she liked. She'd long suspected that her grandmother wasn't quite as keen on babies as her mother assumed, and she wasn't surprised when Gabriele was quickly handed to her because he was "getting a bit heavy". So she took over the feeding and the wiping of sticky fingers while they talked. Nonna Renata loved to tell stories of her days amongst the Garibaldini, the partisans who decamped to the mountains when the Germans occupied Italy, and for her part Kat never tired of hearing them.

"We couldn't get married, of course," Nonna Renata said with a cackle. "There were no priests – they'd all run away.

So we lived like people who were married, even those of us who weren't. But no babies, not if we could help it. It was a time for fighting, not for wiping bottoms."

"And which did you like better," Kat asked slyly, "the war, or wiping Mamma's bottom?"

Nonna Renata's eyes darted to check her daughter wasn't listening. "The war! It was the best time of my whole life. Afterwards, we thought everything was going to continue like that, but of course the priests and the other men wanted things the way they were before. So it was back to babies and baking after all."

"I think I'd have liked the war."

Nonna Renata nodded. "You take after me, I've always thought so. Now tell me, how's *your* war going?"

"I'm doing my first murder," Kat confessed proudly.

Just for a moment the old woman looked confused. "You're going to kill someone? I didn't think that was allowed any more."

"Sorry, Nonna – I meant, I'm on my first murder investigation. I'm under a really good colonel, someone who's done at least a dozen homicide investigations—"

Later, as she was helping carry the dirty dishes into the kitchen, her mother commented, "So, when will we get to meet this Aldo Piola?"

"You were listening?"

"I could hardly help it – you talked about nothing else for twenty minutes. He's good-looking, I hope?"

Kat groaned. "Mamma, he's my boss."

"The two aren't always mutually exclusive, are they?"

"And he's married."

"Married!" Her mother looked shocked, as if she'd caught out Piola in some terrible crime.

"Of course. Why wouldn't he be?"

Her mother didn't answer directly. "I remember a time when the Carabinieri didn't allow women officers," she said tartly.

"That was over ten years ago. And before you say anything, no, he's a perfect gentleman. Not a lech, not a grabber. And very respectful of my work." Even before the words had left her mouth she knew her mother would make that face, the face that said Kat was still twelve years old and knew nothing about the real world. She wanted to shout, *I'm an officer of the Carabinieri, Mamma! I see dead bodies that have been shot and then dumped in canals! I deal with gangsters and criminals! I think I know how to look after myself!*

But instead she just sighed and said, "I'll go and chat to Papà, shall I, before he falls asleep?"

Twenty-six

SHE'D MEANT TO go straight home from her parents' apartment in Sant'Elena, but the conversation with her mother had left a residual irritation that Kat knew from experience couldn't be fixed by an evening of TV and Facebook. So she took a detour.

She told herself she was just going for a walk. It was true that she loved Venice on these winter afternoons, when the *bora*, the cold north wind, whisked tiny flakes of snow down from the mountains and the air seemed to sparkle as if filled with specks of gold. This was the empty month, the brief low season when the city's sixty thousand residents were for a short time not hopelessly outnumbered by the six million tourists who filled its narrow pavements the rest of the year, and Kat took full advantage, striding purposefully towards Campo San Zaccaria without even realising at first that was where she was heading.

She made her way up to the operations room, expecting to find it empty. She'd spend a couple of hours catching up on paperwork, she decided, writing up her reports from the previous week, so she'd be ready to face the new week unencumbered.

To her surprise, there was a woman in Piola's glassed-off office. As the woman stood up, nervously examining her surroundings, Kat saw she was wearing a low-cut top under her leather jacket.

Piola re-entered with a bottle of wine and two plastic cups. He set them down on the table, and the woman touched his shoulder and said something. He smiled in acknowledgement. Although Kat tried not to leap to conclusions, there was no mistaking the intention with which the woman was arching her breasts towards his gaze.

Just then he looked up and saw Kat. He waved for her to come and join them.

"This is Spira," he explained as she entered. "It seemed like a good day to bring her in for a chat. Spira's a little shy."

Spira laughed dutifully. Her sly dark eyes darted across to Kat's face, assessing her. Now that Kat was closer, she could see how much make-up the other woman was wearing, how cheap the leather jacket was. Of course. A prostitute.

"On Sundays her boyfriend goes to church, followed by lunch with his mother, so Spira gets a few hours' rest," Piola went on. Spira nodded, apparently happy with this description of her pimp's schedule. "I was curious about this," he added, holding up the page torn from the back of *La Nuova Venezia* that had been found in the hotel room shared by Jelena Babić and Barbara Holton.

"I know some of these girls," Spira interjected, pointing at the small ads that had been crossed out. Her accent was thick – probably East European, Kat thought; like hotel chambermaids, the majority of the sex workers in Venice were also illegals from across the Adriatic.

"Is there anything you can tell us about them?" Piola asked.

"*Da*. This one's blonde, this one's brunette. This one, her pimp's got her on smack—"

"I meant, anything about this group of girls in particular. Anything they have in common."

Spira scrutinised the page more closely. "They're all Croats," she announced.

"You're sure?" Kat asked.

Believe me or not, it's all the same to me, Spira's shrug implied.

"What about these two women? Have you seen them before?" Piola asked, placing photos of Jelena Babić and Barbara Holton in front of her.

"*Da*. This one." Spira tapped Jelena's picture.

"When?"

"She was looking for a girl. Round Santa Lucia."

"She tried to pick you up?"

"*Ne*. I mean she had a picture of a girl. She wanted to know if we'd seen her."

"What was the girl like?"

"Dark hair, dark eyes. Also *Ustasha*," Spira said, using the Serbs' derogatory term for a Croat.

"Get someone to take a look through the possessions we bagged from the hotel room," Piola suggested quietly to Kat. "See if the picture's there." To Spira he said, "And had you? Seen her, that is?"

Spira regarded him as if he were an idiot. "It was on the street. You think I want to end up in a canal with my throat cut?"

"But if you *did* see her again... Would you recognise her?"

Spira shrugged. "People all look the same on the street. The dicks look the same. The money looks the same. After a while the faces look the same as well."

Piola sighed. "If you like, we could arrange for you to go from here to an organisation that rehabilitates girls like you. They'd help you get clean, arrange for you to go home..."

"If I go home now, my family will throw me out. And the people who brought me here will find me. At least in Venice I'm working. I'm paying off my debt. And my pimp looks after me."

Piola said nothing, giving her the chance to change her mind. Eventually she said, "Can I go now?"

"Yes," he replied, just as Kat said, "One more thing."

"What?"

Kat went to her desk and found the sheet of symbols from Poveglia. "Do you recognise any of these?" she asked, putting them in front of the prostitute.

"These, no," Spira said, pointing at the symbols Father Uriel had already identified. Her finger moved along to the ones that matched the tattoos on Jelena Babić's body. "But these are *Ustasha*."

"Croatian? You're sure?"

Spira nodded. "The old women have them. It's a Catholic thing. You don't see it so much now."

Kat and Piola exchanged a glance. "Thank you, Spira," Piola said, getting to his feet. "You've been very helpful. I'll show you out."

By the time he returned, Kat had already trawled through Google Images. Using the keywords "Croatian", "Catholic" and "tattoo", she'd found some pictures that confirmed what the prostitute had told them.

"Look," she said, spinning her screen to show Piola. "They're called *stećak* symbols. According to this, Catholics in Bosnia originally tattooed their children with these markings in the hope that the Turks wouldn't take them as slaves – they couldn't be forcibly converted to Islam if they had Christian symbols on their skin. After the fall of the Ottomans, the tattoos remained as symbols of the underground Church in Croatia."

"Interesting," he said. "I wonder what it means."

But she already knew. She felt a rush of exhilaration as everything slotted into place.

"The reason those particular symbols were *under* the blood spray, unlike the others, was because Jelena Babić drew them on the hospital wall herself, before she celebrated Mass. They're symbols of her faith. The killer couldn't erase them, and he knew they might lead us to the truth, so he added the other designs himself, to throw us off the scent. Jelena was no Satanist. She was, or believed herself to be, the real deal – a woman, a Croatian, and a Catholic priest." She shook her head. "The misdirection nearly worked, too. I assumed that Barbara Holton's contact with the Americans at Caserma Ederle had no bearing on her death, because there was no connection with priests or the occult. But there *was* a link to Croatia. She was asking for information about a Croatian general called Dragan Korovik, who just happens to be facing trial at The Hague for war crimes. If the US Military thought he might reveal something they'd rather was kept hidden, it would explain why they're trying to cover their tracks."

"But why was Jelena Babić on Poveglia in the first place?" Piola asked. "Why was she saying a Mass there? Why did the killer murder Barbara Holton when she didn't even have the information she'd requested – and according to the officer you spoke to, didn't have much chance of getting it, either? There are more questions than answers here, Capitano."

"I think we need to lean on the Americans at Caserma Ederle. We need to establish exactly what the answers to

Barbara Holton's questions would have been."

"OK." Piola got to his feet. "But in that case, this may get political. We'd better talk to our prosecutor first."

"We've had one assigned?"

"As of last Friday. Benito Marcello. Know him?"

She shook her head.

"Me neither. Meet me at the court offices at eight o'clock tomorrow morning, and we'll see if he's in agreement."

He took a coat from behind the door – Armani, she noticed, in lightweight dark blue cashmere, and hung on a proper hanger rather than just the coat hook. "And now it's time to get out of here," he added unnecessarily. "Coming?"

There was a pause. She found herself hoping that he'd suggest getting a drink and perhaps some food before they went to their respective homes.

Then she mentally kicked herself. It was Sunday, and the poor man had barely seen his family all week. "I'm going to catch up with some paperwork," she said. "See you in the morning, sir."

Twenty-seven

PROSECUTOR BENITO MARCELLO was young, good-looking, well dressed, and frankly incredulous.

"You think this is some kind of American conspiracy?" he said disbelievingly. "You're crazy."

"Many of the indications do point to a multi-national dimension, sir," Piola said judiciously.

"Oh, please," Marcello scoffed. "You've failed to gather any hard evidence whatsoever, Colonel, so you've simply filled the gaps with ridiculous speculation. And now you want to subpoena the US Army!" He shook his head. "You Carabinieri. I don't know how you do it."

The reference to the stereotype of institutional stupidity was subtle, but no less effective for that. Kat felt her cheeks burn.

To his credit, her boss seemed unfazed. "We're not advancing any one theory more than another at the moment, sir. But we think it's important to follow every lead before the preliminary hearing."

Kat waited. She knew only too well that the prosecutor had the power to direct their investigations in whichever way he chose. Marcello would then lay the results of their investigations before a court; only if the court agreed with him that there was enough *prima facie* evidence to charge someone could she and Piola *officially* begin gathering evidence. Which meant that, in theory, any investigative work done before that point would then have to be repeated. It was a crazily complex system and didn't inspire confidence: for one thing, many cases never resulted in prosecutions, even though they had already taken up a great deal of court time, and secondly, it was effectively up to the individual prosecutor which cases were pursued and which were not.

"Let me propose an alternative scenario," Marcello said crisply. "We have two female foreigners, one American and one Croatian, sharing a hotel room in our beautiful city. We have an obscene ceremony in a remote location, decorated with sacrilegious and occult symbols. We have the ultimate desecration of the Mass by one of them, wearing a priest's robes. All thoroughly unsavoury, but no doubt a thrill to those of a certain disposition – and when we ask what kind of disposition these two women had, we learn that they were the sort of people who pursue elaborate conspiracy theories. We learn that they frequent dubious websites and choose to lurk in dark corners of the internet, where such things grow unfettered. And then we discover, too, that they were seen looking for a prostitute – a very specific prostitute; no doubt one who shares their particular tastes."

He paused, and with a sinking feeling Kat realised where he was heading with this.

"Perhaps they have a row, these two women, between lovers. Perhaps one of them decides she isn't keen on sharing their bed with a prostitute after all. There was a ceremony, sexual in nature; exciting and illicit, yes, but perhaps the participants were not equally willing… The American, let's say, kills the Croatian. Later, filled with remorse, she kills herself in the room they shared, toppling out of the window as she does so. This, it seems to me, is far more plausible than the conspiracy story that you have dreamt up, and leaves far fewer loose ends." Marcello knitted his fingers together and placed his hands on his desk, nodding with the satisfaction of a man who is rather impressed – not for the first time – by his own brilliance.

"Two beds," Kat said.

Marcello looked surprised that she'd had the temerity to speak. "I beg your pardon, Capitano?"

"You said 'their bed'. But these women didn't share a bed. There were twin beds in the hotel room, and both of them had been used. There was nothing at all, in fact, to suggest that they were lesbians."

The prosecutor made a dismissive gesture. "Beds can be pushed together."

Another criticism sometimes levelled at the Italian legal system is that it encourages prosecutors to devise preposterously lurid theories, since at the time of devising them they are not required to back them up with hard evidence – indeed, the more lurid the better, since it helps to ensure that they can proceed to the next stage. The prosecutors at the trial of the American student Amanda Knox, whom they alleged had forced her flatmate Meredith Kercher into a violent and deadly sex game, had attracted just such criticisms from the international media.

"Besides," Marcello added, "even if they hadn't been intending to share a bed, they may have done so in a mood of experimentation. Women are more fluid about such things than men, I believe. Perhaps being in Venice persuaded them to try something out, possibly for the first time..."

Kat stared at him, unable to believe what she was hearing. Fury flushed her cheeks. She was, she knew, about to blow her own career before it had barely begun, by telling Avvocato Marcello just what she thought of his theory.

"If it happened as you say, she managed to shoot herself in the shower, then walk to the window and shoot herself again," Piola said quickly. "Using a pillow as a silencer. And weighing her own body down with her laptop in the process, to make sure it didn't float."

"Stranger things have happened."

"Indeed. So I take it, Avvocato, that you would like us to re-dredge the canal to see if we can find the gun, the presence of which below the hotel window is essential to your theory?"

Marcello paused. "Not *essential*, Colonel. It is perfectly possible that the *acqua alta* has swept the gun along the canal bed and out to sea. But yes, you should certainly concentrate your efforts on looking for the weapon. And not, repeat not, on any supposed internet aspects, conspiracy theories, or – heaven forbid – unauthorised approaches to the US Military."

Piola nodded. "Indeed, that's very clear. Thank you for your time, Avvocato."

Twenty-eight

THE VENETIAN DIALECT is rich in words of scatological abuse, and Kat managed to employ about four of them even before they'd reached the street.

Piola was more sanguine. "It's a useful test. If he thinks his ridiculous sex-game scenario is plausible, so might a jury. We'll look for his weapon. If nothing else, it'll help to rule it out. Set up a briefing for the divers, will you?"

Back at Campo San Zaccaria, however, they received the news that someone was waiting for them. "He won't give his name," Francesco Lotti told them. "Said he'd talked to you before. I've put him in Room Two."

In the interview room they found the young fisherman from Chioggia who'd told them about the lights on Poveglia. He was looking nervous.

"Lucio, isn't it?" Piola greeted him. "How can we help you?"

The fisherman kneaded his fingers. "There's something I didn't mention last time," he said anxiously.

"Yes?"

"When I told you about Poveglia... I didn't tell you that I saw a boat as well."

"A boat? Did you recognise it?"

Lucio nodded. "Of course. I know all the boats. And I've seen this one round there before."

"Go on."

"It belongs to Ricci Castiglione. But you must swear not to tell anyone it was me who told you." He hesitated. "He goes there a lot, if you see what I mean. And not just to fish."

"Cigarettes?" Piola asked shrewdly.

Lucio nodded again.

"Is he the source of those Jin Ling you smoke?"

"Yes, he is," Lucio said, clearly surprised.

"And what else does he bring in?"

A shrug.

"Is he connected? You know what I'm talking about, Lucio."

Reluctantly, Lucio nodded his head. "I believe so."

"Why have you come forward now? You must know it could put you in danger."

"I know Mareta, his wife," Lucio said awkwardly. "She's not a bad woman – she has nothing to do with what he does. But now he's gone missing. And she knows enough to know she isn't meant to call the police. So she asked me if I'd speak to you for her." His eyes went to the door, suddenly fearful. "In Chioggia everyone knows when someone goes to the police station. She thinks it will be safer here in Venice."

That made sense. Chioggia was a notoriously close-knit community, a fact reflected in the number of families with identical surnames.

"And does Mareta have any idea where her husband might have disappeared to?"

"No. But I do. He has a *cavana*, a lock-up boatshed, just out of town. I've been there to buy cigarettes."

"Show us on a map," Piola said. "And, Lucio – we do have to take an official statement. But we won't tell anyone in Chioggia that it was you who told us."

*

When Lucio had gone, Kat and Piola looked at each other.

"An organised crime connection," Piola said. "This gets murkier and murkier, Capitano."

"But if there *is* such a connection – if we choose to pursue it – it doesn't fit with Avvocato Marcello's lovers'-tiff theory," she pointed out. "We'd be doing the exact opposite of what he told us to do, in fact, which is to look for the gun with which Barbara Holton supposedly killed herself."

Piola nodded.

"Screw it," he said at last. "One of the sergeants can brief the diving team. They're not going to find anything, anyway. Let's get down to Chioggia."

Ricci's *cavana* was the last in a row of a tumbledown boatsheds just to the south of town. It looked more like a marine scrapyard, Kat thought to herself, than a storage area. Half-rotted fishing boats, scraps of nylon fishing-net, old crab pots and rusting fish tanks littered the spaces between the sheds. The whole place stank of spilt diesel and fish guts, and the ground underfoot was iridescent with scales.

Although it wasn't yet lunchtime, there wasn't a soul to be seen around any of the neighbouring lock-ups.

"Were they expecting us?" Piola wondered aloud. "And if so – now, specifically, or just in general?"

Ricci's shed had once been painted a cheery dark blue. Now, rust poked through the peeling paint. Piola rapped on the steel door. There was no answer. Carefully, he slid the door back, wincing as it scraped on the concrete floor.

Inside, it was just as messy as outside. They edged past a skiff raised up on trestles and found themselves in a dimly lit area Ricci had clearly used for storing the crabs he caught. Four large steel tanks, each about five feet square and four high, gave off a stench of brackish seawater.

"Dear God," Piola said suddenly, crossing himself. Kat followed his gaze.

Sticking upright out of one of the tanks were a man's feet, still clad in fishermen's rubber shoes. Kat went to see where the rest of him was, ignoring Piola's words of warning. For a moment she couldn't make sense of it – the crab tank had to be deeper than it was, or those stones somehow had to have been piled on top of the body, or—

Then the stones moved, and she realised what she was looking at. She gave a cry and stepped back just in time; as the bile reached her throat, she was able to turn her head away and avoid contaminating the tank with her vomit. But the image of those crabs would stay with her forever: dozens of them, like tiny, implacable Hermann tanks, shifting uneasily, trying to nudge and pull each other out of the way, their feathery claws buried deep in flesh, ripping it apart, as if the man's face had exploded from within. One eye socket had been picked clean as an eggcup, right down to the bone; and the throat was now no more than a few pieces of skin flapping around grey vertebrae. She'd seen, too, the way one of the larger crabs had lifted its thick right claw towards its mouth, a morsel of ragged white meat held delicately in its pinchers...

For a second time her vomit splashed on the concrete. "Sorry," she gasped.

"Don't be. That's... I've never seen anything myself..." Piola put his arm round her shoulders, his olive complexion now pale. "Let's get you outside."

He made her sit on a wooden breaker right by the sea,

where the cold wind from the mountains filled her lungs with clean air.

"Stay here," he instructed, once he was sure she wasn't going to faint. He went back inside. She heard sluicing sounds, the noise of a brush on wet concrete.

After a few minutes he re-joined her. "I've cleaned up. No one will know. And don't worry – there's absolutely no chance that there was any useful DNA on that floor. We haven't done any damage to the evidence."

"Thank you," she said, as grateful for that "we" as for the cleaning up.

He shrugged off her words. "Forget it. Let's call it in now. The place will need to be taken apart. There's what looks like a couple of crates of Jing Lin cigarettes in there, still wrapped up in plastic, so that fits with what Lucio told us about the smuggling. And there's a room at the back with an old mattress in it. I found ropes, too – fishing ropes, but with slipknots in them. It looks to me like someone's been tied up in there."

"The victim?"

"Maybe. Or maybe one of *his* victims. Whatever it is, I don't think Marcello's going to be able to make his stupid lesbian-witch theory stand up now."

It took hours to get the pathologist and scene-of-crime technicians to the site, during which time Piola packed Kat off to a bar for some restorative grappas. It took more time still to work out how best to remove what was left of the body. When at last Ricci's remains had been bagged up and signed over to the pathology team, Piola went over to have a word with them.

"What will happen to the crabs?"

The head technician looked over at the tanks and shrugged. "They're no use to us."

"Do me a favour, will you? Put them back in the sea. If we leave them here, sooner or later they'll find their way to the market, and this case is ghoulish enough already."

After that the two of them went to inform the widow, Mareta, of her husband's death. It was clear to them, however, that she already knew, or at least had had her suspicions. She had obviously asked Lucio to speak to the police as much to get it over with as because she'd nurtured any real hope he might be found alive. Nor would she answer any questions. Fear of the Mafia ran deep here, and she could expect a widow's pension if she kept her mouth shut.

Even when she was shown some of the hundreds of packets of Jin Ling her husband had been storing, she still maintained that he was only a poor fisherman.

"What about girls?" Piola asked. "Did he ever bring any women in via the lagoon?"

Mareta's eyes flashed with anger, and she muttered something under her breath. But she only shook her head. It was clear they'd be getting nothing out of her.

"We'd better update Avvocato Marcello," Piola said as they left her house. "But that can wait until tomorrow. He's probably poncing about at the opera by now."

It was dark, and they had to wait for the ferry back to Venice. Kat suddenly felt desperately tired. Once the boat arrived she collapsed into one of the hard plastic seats on deck. Neither of them spoke much as the lights of Venice gradually neared across the lagoon.

"Come on," Piola said when they reached the city. "I'll drop you off. It's Mestre, isn't it?"

She tried to protest, but he was having none of it. Together they retrieved his car – a surprisingly elderly Fiat – from the multi-storey. Like most commuters who drove into the city each day, Piola used the car parks at Piazzale Roma or on the manmade island of Tronchetto, located next to the docks at Venice's western edge.

"Did you hear about the scam some of those car parks were running?" he said conversationally as they turned onto the Ponte della Libertà.

"What scam?"

"There was a spate of thefts from the cars. Often nothing very valuable was taken, but it's a nuisance to get back from a day in Venice to find your car's been broken into and a window smashed. So they introduced a 'Left Valuables' facility. For five euros a day you hand your camera, bags and so on to a man who locks them in a strong room." He paused. "Have you guessed the scam?"

"He steals them anyway?"

"Better than that. The original break-ins were done by the same mob that runs the car parks. Not only did they get what they'd stolen, they created a business out of something no one had bothered to pay for before."

There was a part of her – an old Venetian part – that couldn't help but be impressed by the sheer mercantile cunning of it. "How were they caught?"

"They weren't. Every time demand drops off, they just smash a few more windows."

"We'll get them one day."

"Perhaps," he said, and for the first time that day she thought that he, too, looked weary.

"This is me up ahead," she said as they neared her apartment. "But you can drop me at the corner."

He pulled over. "Goodnight then, Kat."

"Goodnight, sir."

He looked at her as if about to say something. She had a strong sense that he was going to tell her not to call him sir when they were alone.

"Kat... I want you to know that you're a good officer," he said quietly. "One of the best I've ever worked with. Today was a tough day. Tomorrow won't be."

On an impulse, she leant across to kiss him on the cheek. Not understanding, perhaps, he turned his head towards her. She stopped, her mouth a couple of inches from his.

Hesitantly, he kissed her on the lips.

She felt vertiginous, as if she'd jumped off a very high bridge and was now falling; falling through the air. She knew the moment of hitting the water must come, that the kiss must end, and that there would follow apologies and awkwardness and regret, but while she was still falling she couldn't think about all that. She could only think about the feelings that had been blossoming in her ever since she'd been given this assignment.

The feelings she had for Aldo Piola.

She went on kissing him back. While she was kissing him, everything was all right.

"Kat," he whispered, breaking off but holding her head with both hands, as if he couldn't bear to let her go completely. "Tell me to stop. Tell me to stop and I swear this will never have happened."

"I don't want it to stop," she said, and she kissed him again, more fiercely.

A part of her was still lost in the moment, in the sensations inside her mouth and the sudden furnace of longing that had ignited in her belly, but another part of her knew that it was up to her to choose: leave it here or ask him up.

"Come up," she said.

"Are you sure?"

"I'm sure."

He locked the car and followed her up the stairs to her apartment. As she put the key into her door she thought of all the other times she'd done this, the men she'd brought here when she was drunk or sober, happy or lonely, when she'd needed company or just decided that she liked the look of whoever was chatting her up. This felt different.

She needed this more.

Inside, she turned to him again. This time their embrace was more leisurely: the unhurried, frankly sexual embrace of two people who knew how this was going to end and could take their time getting there.

Even so, he broke away to say, "You can still change your mind, you know."

"Are you crazy? I want this as much as you do. Or do *you* want to change your mind? It's OK, you can."

Mutely, he shook his head. She went and found a bottle of *prosecco*, some ham, olives. The sofa felt too formal, so they sat on the floor, hip to hip, sipping the crisp, sparkling wine.

She rested her head on his chest. "When did you...?"

"The first time I saw you. At Santa Maria della Salute. Walking through the freezing water in those bare legs." He ran a hand down her leg, as if unable to believe that he could. "*These* legs."

She shifted position, opening her knees so that his hand could slip between them. It travelled up the inside of her thigh, lighting a fuse of pleasure along the way. "And you?" he said, taking the hand away. She smiled. It was a good sign: a man who knew when to hold back.

"I don't know. At the mortuary, perhaps. Or when you took me to lunch that first time, at Chioggia, and you made the owner take your money." She shivered. "Or maybe today."

He drank some more *prosecco* and turned to her. She felt the bubbles dancing in her mouth as they kissed, the sweetness of the grapes. His end-of-day stubble was rough under her palm.

"Come to bed," she whispered.

Then there was the surprise of undressing, of being naked in front of him for the first time, and the astonishment of the pleasure as he touched her. He went slowly, methodically even, calmly bringing her almost to the brink with his caresses before she'd even got his shirt off. And then – at last! – she'd undone his belt, and had him in her hands, and it was his turn to groan with pleasure.

Naked, there were swirls of dark hair over his chest and stomach, like rosettes. His body was thick and hard, as if he were a medieval count in his armour; the rounded breastplate and cuirass of an older man's body.

"Now," she said, unable to wait any longer. "*Now*."

He slid inside her, and she wanted to scream with how good it felt.

He paused. "You can still change your mind, you know."

She banged his chest with the side of her fist. "Now you're just teasing me, you bastard."

He laughed. But after that there was no more teasing.

Afterwards, still overwhelmed, it was all she could do to say, "My God. My *God*. How did on earth did this happen?"

"I have absolutely no idea."

She turned to look at him. "Do I call you Aldo now we're in bed, or do I go on calling you sir?" she said mischievously.

"Actually, I rather like the idea of being called sir in bed." He reached up to cup her breast, smoothing his thumb over the nipple. "It makes it sound as if I could do anything I wanted."

She was always surprised how, in bed, each relationship was different – how *she* was different, with different people. There were some men she was relaxed with, others with whom she was shy. She could be prim, or wild, or wary; with some men she wasn't comfortable unless she was in control, whereas others somehow prompted total sexual abandon. And yet she'd discovered that you could never quite predict, until you got into this strange, naked arena of the bed, which it would turn out to be. The one thing certain was that, once it was fixed in the very first coupling, it was fixed for ever.

She said, "But, *sir*, you can." As she said it she felt a little thrill, and knew that this was going to be the dynamic of their relationship – one that she'd never experienced before, or expected to: that she was going to be, in some as-yet indefinable, tongue-in-cheek way, subservient to him.

"Good," he said. His hand continued to explore her body – delicately, not with the focused intent to arouse with which he'd touched her earlier, but as if he simply wanted to commit every inch of her to memory; as if she were a keyboard on which his fingers played a tune audible only to him.

She reached for him and found he was getting hard again. The second time, their lovemaking was slower, more considered. She concentrated on giving him pleasure, and found herself deeply satisfied to discover that she could do this to him, that she had the power to bring him to the very edge of ecstasy.

It was only much later, after she'd gone to get the wine and the olives again – discovering in the process that he was a man she enjoyed being naked in front of; which, again, was not something that happened with everyone – that he said quietly, "Of course, you know I'm married."

"Of course," she said neutrally.

"Kat, I can't justify this. I can't defend myself. I have children..."

"I know," she said. "Let's not talk about it. Not ever."

The word, with its implied promise, hung between them for a long time.

They slept, and then sometime in the night she woke to find him dressing. She pretended to be asleep – because this, too, was something that couldn't be acknowledged: where he would go now, what lies he might have to tell. The furtive shower, perhaps the welcoming kiss.

What had happened in this room had taken place in a bubble, a separate world; one that had no connection with the world outside the investigation.

Or so she told herself.

Twenty-nine

OH, SHIT.

Kat woke up and knew, instantly, that she'd done something stupid the night before. She cursed herself. *Why do I have to be so damn impulsive?*

There was no time to think about that now, though. The important thing was to look as if nothing had happened. The Carabinieri headquarters was a cauldron of gossip, particularly about sexual matters. It was one of the reasons she made it a rule never to sleep with colleagues, and why she told casual pickups she was a travel agent.

Oh well: two rules broken in one night. But deep down, she knew it was rather more serious than that.

The second reason for discretion was that she wasn't sure how Aldo was going to feel about what had happened. In the cold light of day, having gone home to his wife and children, he would almost certainly be regretting the whole thing. Better for her to pretend it was no big deal.

As she walked into the operations room she steeled herself to meet his eye with nothing more than a nod and a polite "Good morning, sir." But in the event she didn't need to. He was already in his glass-walled office, and she knew him well enough by now to understand that the expression of studied politeness on his face actually meant he was furious. With him was Prosecutor Marcello – sitting in Piola's chair, she noticed. There was also a female *carabiniere*, and a woman whom Kat recognised from somewhere.

Of course: the chambermaid from the Europa Hotel.

Piola beckoned for her to join them. "Avvocato Marcello has been busy," he said neutrally. "You remember Ema?"

"Indeed." Kat nodded to the chambermaid, who looked terrified.

Marcello said, "Going through this lady's statement, it struck me that it was somewhat patchy. I had an insight that she might be an illegal worker seeking to avoid drawing attention to herself. So I exercised my right to summon her before me personally, and suggested a favourable recommendation to the Office of Immigration if she gave a more complete account." He held up a plastic-sheeted document. "I have it here."

Kat took it from him and scanned it.

On one occasion I entered the room and found the two women kissing... On another occasion it was clear from the bedsheets that they had been making love... I believe on one occasion I heard the sound of a violent fight coming from their room...

She glanced at the maid, who kept her eyes on the floor. "Ema? Is this true?"

The girl nodded, a little reluctantly it seemed to Kat.

"Well, this piece of paper certainly appears to corroborate your hypothesis, Avvocato," Piola said with withering disinterest, as the female *carabiniere* took Ema away.

"Correction, Colonel. This *evidence*..." Marcello gave the word a determined inflection, "is the first hard proof of motive in the case. And it also explains why the forensic material at the second crime scene is inconsistent. The maid was desperate to avoid the appearance of a crime, knowing that it would draw the attention of the police, so she cleaned up more thoroughly than you realised."

"On the other hand, sir, we have the link to organised crime offered by the body of Ricci Castiglione—" Piola began.

Marcello cut him off. "It's not a link, Colonel, because there is no proof of causality. A criminal has been killed by – you maintain – other criminals. The fact that he may also have been involved tangentially in your investigation is neither here nor there."

"We have a witness statement linking him to the crime scene."

Marcello frowned. "From who?"

"A fisherman. He saw Ricci Castiglione's boat at Poveglia on the night of the murder."

"But not Castiglione himself?"

"No," Piola admitted.

"Then it's hardly conclusive. Visiting the island may make him a potential witness, but it doesn't turn our lovers into mobsters." Marcello thought for a moment, then snapped his fingers. "But let's say you're right, and he is involved. Castiglione was visiting the island to meet a smuggling contact. Naturally, he was less than happy to discover that his rendezvous had been invaded by a couple of gay tourists intent on a secret ritual. Perhaps he was even offended by the priest's robes – some of these fishermen can be very superstitious. So he shot one of them. Later, he realised that the other one might identify him. So he followed her to her hotel and shot her, too."

"Weighing down her body with her laptop...?"

"... in order to make it look like a robbery," Marcello concluded. "So you see, Colonel, the fact there was no weapon found beneath her hotel room yesterday also proves nothing – he might have taken it with him, and disposed of it later."

"We do, however, know that the weapon that killed both women was in all probability designed for US Special Forces."

Marcello shrugged. "Doubtless he trafficked it in from Bosnia or Croatia, along with the cigarettes and the drugs. There were many weapons left behind after the war."

"Well, let's see if our forensic team find any evidence in the boatshed to support this new theory of yours," Piola said calmly.

Marcello shook his head. "They've been stood down."

"Stood down?" Piola said incredulously. "By whom?"

"By the *commissario* in charge of the investigation. I've reassigned that case to the Polizia di Stato, who are already investigating a number of murders relating to smuggling and organised crime. Of course, I've told them to be sure to share any relevant findings with you."

"I see," Piola said icily. "That's very kind."

Marcello got to his feet. "Well, Colonel, I shall leave you. I'm sure you have plenty to do wrapping up the few loose ends that still remain. But it's good news that we're now making such excellent progress." Was there just a hint of irony, Kat wondered, the slightest inflection of emphasis on that "now"? "And good day to you too, Capitano." The lawyer's eyes swept over her. "You are looking, if I may say so, particularly beautiful this morning. Colonel Piola is a very lucky man."

"Sir?" she said, horrified. Had Piola said something?

He waved his hand. "To get to spend so much time with you, I mean."

She couldn't help it: she blushed, although Marcello seemed to assume that it was prompted by his compliment rather than her own guilty conscience. His chest visibly puffed up inside his suit, he sauntered from the room.

"Prick," she said when he'd gone.

Piola smiled wearily. "What's the betting that Avvocato Marcello's generous offer of intervention with the Immigration authorities, far from making it possible for Ema to stay in this country, somehow has the exact opposite effect and she's hastened back to Eastern Europe before the ink is dry on this bullshit?" He picked up the maid's statement and tossed it back onto the desk. "Anyway, there's no point in questioning her again now. She knows what Marcello wants to hear, and she'll keep on saying it. You know," he added bitterly, "the problem is that he's actually quite good at this. Sooner or later he'll come up with some ludicrous theory that explains away everything – every scrap of evidence there is. And there won't be a single thing we can do about it."

"Except collect more evidence."

"Except collect more evidence," he agreed.

She leant over his computer and typed in "Benito Marcello". "Interesting," she commented.

"What is?"

"Our prosecutor appears to be one of the most successful lawyers in the Venetian judiciary. *La Nuova Venezia* calls him 'a rising star'."

"I hope there's a 'but'."

"He doesn't appear ever to have prosecuted a case against

organised crime. It isn't that he fights them and doesn't win. He just never seems to get them."

"Or when he does, he makes sure they go away," Piola said. "I thought he looked like he was covered in something slippery. But I assumed it was just his greasy hair gel."

Kat smiled. Even though on the face of it nothing had been said – even though both of them had been careful not to betray themselves by so much as an unguarded look – something, nevertheless, was different. That last remark, for example, was one that he wouldn't have made to her twenty-four hours before.

He came to stand by her, looking down at the computer screen. Impulsively, she touched the back of his hand briefly with her own. Equally briefly, he squeezed her fingers, and she felt her pulse quicken. *Ridiculous*, she thought, *ridiculous*, but she darted him the quickest of smiles, and a wave of happiness washed over her when he smiled back, the lines around his eyes crinkling.

"So," he said, stepping back. "Where were we? Oh yes – they found the photograph Spira was talking about, the one the victims were showing to the working girls. It was with the other possessions from the hotel room that were waiting to be logged."

He passed it to her. It showed a pretty, dark-haired girl, no more than sixteen or seventeen years old.

"There were several copies. And," he said, holding up an evidence bag, "when they were found, they were tucked inside *this*." The bag contained a book. On the cover were the words *Svetom Pismu*.

"Is that the Bible?"

He nodded. "In Croatian. And no, it hasn't been defaced with occult symbols, upside-down crosses or any of that nonsense."

"I'd bet the lock of hair we found also belongs to the girl in this photograph. We should run the DNA through the records. And we should start showing the photograph around ourselves. It's way too early now, but I could check out the streets around Santa Lucia this evening."

Later that day a huge bunch of flowers arrived for her at the office. There was no note, but she found an email from her boss in her inbox.

Thought I'd better send you some before the prick does.

She smiled to herself, and sent a two-word reply.

It's appreciated.

She would be careful. She would be careful, and what happened inside the bubble would stay inside the bubble.

So it happened that when she left Campo San Zaccaria at about four o'clock to go home and change into clothes more appropriate for a long, cold evening hanging out in the seedy bars round the train station, she was also carrying a large bunch of flowers. The combination of an attractive officer of the Carabinieri and blossoms proved irresistible to the waiting photographer, who snapped her twice before she'd even realised that it was her he was pointing his camera at.

There was a journalist too, walking alongside her when she didn't stop, asking question after question but barely pausing to hear an answer. "Are you part of the investigation into the black magic murders, Capitano? Can you confirm that the women were lovers? Is it true the murders were linked to the Carnivia website?"

She muttered "No comment" and kept walking. It was ridiculous – the journalist must have known she wouldn't speak to the press, and besides, anyone after a scoop wouldn't do it like this, in full public view: they'd call discreetly by phone, or arrange a quiet word in one of the bars round the back of Fondamenta San Severo.

Which meant, perhaps, that he already had his scoop, and what he wanted from her was precisely that "No comment".

She got out her phone and called Piola.

"The press are outside headquarters," she said without preamble. "They're calling it 'the Black Magic Murders'."

He swore softly. "The prick doesn't waste any time, I'll give him that. OK, thanks for the warning."

By half past six she was in position near the train station, wearing jeans and an old leather jacket. It was still quiet: at this hour you mostly got the girls who sat quietly with their pimps, toying with drinks and not saying much while the men shouted and jostled and brandished phones and money at each other. Occasionally, when the men went to piss or the girls stepped outside for a cigarette, she'd be able to get one on her own for a moment. Then she'd show the photograph. "Ever seen this girl?" The reaction was mostly the same: a disinterested glance, a shrug, then a slyer, second glance at Kat as they realised she was a cop. After that they simply turned their backs on her.

Her next question, as she pulled out her ID, was: "Has anyone asked you this before?" She was lucky if she even got a shrug.

Sometimes, if she was fortunate, the girl would be high.

Coke was the best: it made them talkative. A few women said they'd been shown her photograph before, "by a Croatian woman".

All the girls she spoke to were East European – Croatian, Bosnian, Slovenian, Serbian, Macedonian, Albanian, Montenegrin: a roll-call of bloody, half-formed countries that together made up Italy's mirror-image across the Adriatic. All were dead behind the eyes. Many had tiny pustules and burns round the mouth that even too much scarlet lipstick couldn't disguise: the legacy of chronic solvent abuse.

One said to her, "Two Croat women showed me this."

"Two? Are you sure?"

"But one spoke with an American accent."

Something fell into place in Kat's mind. So Barbara Holton, despite the American-sounding name, spoke Serbo-Croat. A second-generation American, perhaps, with parental links to the old country.

Another girl looked at the photo, chewed her gum twice, and said blankly, "A man showed it to me."

"What sort of man?"

"An American. But he wasn't buying."

"What did he look like?"

The girl shrugged. "Like a john. He was big, you know? Strong-looking."

Twice Kat was threatened by pimps with flick-knives. Producing her police ID made the pimps back off a little, but they didn't put the knives away. She got out of those bars fast.

And then there was one girl, lucid and articulate, with a pimp nowhere in sight, who said she'd talk if Kat paid her for her time. Kat gave her the fifty euros she asked for. No, she hadn't seen the girl, or the Croatian-speaking women looking for her, but she'd heard stories about an American man looking for one particular Croat girl, so maybe they were with him.

The girl seemed happy to keep talking, so Kat asked her what her background was. Her Italian was better than most, but she still spoke with an East European accent.

The girl, who had earlier said she was called Maria but now said her real name was Nevena, was from Bosnia. Her family had lost their house and all their savings in the civil war. As a result, when a family friend suggested Nevena could earn good money working as a nanny in Italy, her parents had encouraged her to go. For her part, she'd hoped to send enough money back for her younger sisters to get an education. She'd known, of course, that it would mean being trafficked into Italy illegally, but that hadn't seemed such a great crime when there were, according to the friend, people in Italy who couldn't get nannies and babysitters because Italian girls were greedy and wanted too much money.

She hadn't worried when the trafficker took her passport, or when she was separated from the group of would-be migrants and taken in a different vehicle. The man who was driving her took her to a remote farmhouse and raped her, violently, although he took care not to mark her. The worst thing, she said, was the feeling of powerlessness: knowing that he could do whatever he wanted and there was absolutely nothing she could do about it; no one she could report him to. She'd hated him so much that when he passed her onto another man she was relieved rather than frightened, although it had scared her when she'd seen money changing hands.

The second man put her in a van with three other girls and took them to a tiny fishing port, where they were put on a boat and brought across to Italy at night. After they landed, they were taken to a place where some other girls were already waiting. One of them explained how it worked: they were being sold along a supply chain that ended up in the big Italian cities, where they would have to earn back the money that whoever eventually bought them had paid for them. Because they didn't have their passports, they couldn't run away, and if they somehow escaped and went to the police their families back home would be targeted.

She'd asked how they could ever earn enough as nannies to pay back the traffickers. It was the other girl's silence that finally made her realise what was going to happen to her.

There was another remote farmhouse, in the Italian countryside this time, where the girls were "trained". Those who resisted were raped until they stopped resisting. Those who didn't resist were shown pornographic videos and instructed to "do it like that". All the girls were filmed having sex, and were told that if they stepped out of line the films would be sent to their families.

By that time Nevena had made a decision. She was going to survive, so she did what she had to do. After a while, she said, you got used to it. Men didn't hurt you if you knew what you were doing and made it look as if you wanted to please them. When she finally got to Venice she was sold to a pimp for 1,500 euros, and told that once she'd earned it back her passport would be returned.

It turned out to be even harder than it seemed. The cost of the room where she serviced her customers was taken out of her earnings, as was the *pizzo* due to the Mafia. She had to pay for her food, and a deduction was made for lighting, heating, laundry and medical check-ups. Even so, she'd nearly made it, after a year of having sex with as many as six men a night. But not long before she reached the magic figure, her pimp sold her to someone else. Now she had to start all over again. But she was going to do it; she wasn't going to let herself give up hope.

Nevena spread the money Kat had given her on the table. She pushed ten euros to one side. "That's the *pizzo* – what Romano has to give the Mafia." She took another ten and put it on top. "That's for my upkeep." There were three tens left. "He gets that, and I get that," she said, putting two on the pile and leaving one out for herself.

Kat gave Nevena her card. "There are organisations that can help you," she said, just as she always did. "They can take you away from this work, send you back home..."

For a moment the girl looked as if she was tempted. Then she pushed the card back across the table. "Thanks, but if I do that I'll lose everything I've saved, and they'll still come after me. It's better to do it their way. Then when I go home there'll be no video in the post, no attacks on my family, and I'll be able to pretend I've just been a nanny, like they thought."

"What if your pimp sells you again?" Kat said gently. "Have you thought of that?"

"I don't think he will," she said. "I don't think he's as bad as the others."

"Keep the card, anyway," Kat said, leaving it on the table. "Keep it somewhere safe."

Around eleven, as the bars were getting noisier and the pimps more threatening, Piola came to find her.

"I thought you might want some company. If only to watch your back."

"What I want," she said wearily, "is to get the hell out of here."

"Shall we eat?"

She shook her head. "Let's go home."

In her apartment she kissed him, feeling the solid warmth of his body. She started to undress him – only to stop, suddenly, at the thought of a girl from Bosnia who'd thought she was going to be a nanny, who was shown pornographic videos and told to copy what she saw in them.

She said, "I can't do this."

"I understand," he said gently. "Come on, let's get you to bed."

He got her under the shower, then took her out and dried her, making her kneel between his legs so he could rub her hair with a towel. It was how her *papà* used to do it when she was a child.

He put her to bed and pulled the covers up over her. "Shall I go?"

"No," she said. "Stay for a bit."

He climbed in, fully dressed, and held her. But sleep still wouldn't come.

She told him about Nevena. "And what does the law say about Nevena?" she said furiously into the dark. "That she's a criminal. That she isn't even one of our citizens. That she doesn't have any rights. And so she has to keep screwing for money, because we won't help her."

"And all the time the Mafia takes its cut."

"Just like everything else in this city."

"You know, when I started, it wasn't this bad. But now... I know for a fact that every single gondolier has to pay the *pizzo*. Every croupier in the municipal casino is a Mafia placeman. Half the hotels are laundering drugs money, and a kid straight out of school can set himself up with a handgun and a kilo of cocaine on easy credit. And what do the police do? We say: let's focus on the important stuff, the murders and the crimes against property. The prosecutors look the other way, jury service is like winning the lottery, and the judges go along with it or get blown up. And that isn't the important stuff?" He was silent a moment. "The thing I keep asking myself is, why Italy?"

"What do you mean?"

"Why is it that our country is so especially corrupt, when others aren't? Spain, Greece, Portugal, France... Poorer countries, some of them, yet none of them have an organised crime problem like ours. What's so unique about Italy, that we haven't been able to root it out?"

"Maybe it's just one of those things."

"Maybe. Or perhaps it's something about us. Our national character. Perhaps we'll never be free of it."

"Don't be a pessimist. Even Nevena has hope."

"Nevena was fed hope," he said. "That's what makes it worse. They've got it down to a fine art, haven't they? They used to give the girls a little bit of smack to keep them docile. But hope is cheaper, and just as effective. The most obedient whore is the one who thinks she's working her way out of whoring. Capitalism, the pimp's best friend."

"You think she'll be sold on again before she can pay off her debt?"

"I'd bet my life on it. Sorry."

They both dozed a little. Later she woke him up and they made love in the dark, slowly and gently, and she thought how extraordinary it was that this act could be so wonderful and yet at the same time so terrible; that it could keep women like Nevena in debt bondage and yet, between her and Aldo, mean so much, and comfort so profoundly.

Thirty

FROM THE MORNING edition of *La Nuova Venezia*:

"BLACK MAGIC MURDERS" SNARE FOREIGN TOURISTS

- **Woman's body was "dressed in Catholic robes"**
- **Prosecutor warns of "depraved world of occult"**
- **"Illegal" website implicated in deaths**

The body of an East European woman found near Santa Maria della Salute during La Befana was dressed in the robes of a Catholic priest, prosecutors confirmed yesterday.

The woman was believed to have been killed while trespassing on Poveglia, an island declared unsafe for visitors by the Commissary of the Lagoon. A second body, belonging to an American woman of East European extraction, was later found in the *rio* below the hotel room they shared. A hotel chambermaid has said she heard the couple arguing violently on at least one occasion.

It is believed that the women were accompanied to the island by local fisherman Ricci Castiglione, 37, also found dead on Monday in circumstances that a source close to the investigation described as being "consistent with suicide".

The prosecutor, Marcello Benito – widely regarded as one of the city's most effective – said yesterday in a statement,

"It's much too early to draw any definite conclusions. However, I can confirm that occult symbols were found at the first murder scene. Of course, such matters were for a long time considered extremely dangerous, and even from our modern perspective we can see that there may be good reasons for that."

He added, "If a local person has been drawn into this unpleasant affair, and has taken his own life as a result, then that only underlines just how real these dangers still are."

Asked if there were indications that the two women were lovers, a Carabinieri spokesperson said "No comment".

In a further twist, it appears that the pair may have bragged of their activities on a controversial website. Carnivia.com, which is based in Venice but attracts online visitors from across the world, allows users to exchange messages and even video material anonymously. Amid concerns that it could be used by pornographers and occultists, the Italian government recently applied for access to Carnivia's servers under anti-secrecy laws. The site's owner, Daniele Barbo, is currently awaiting sentencing for refusing to cooperate.

Barbo had not responded to requests for a comment as this edition went to press.

"So Ricci Castiglione committed suicide," Kat said disgustedly.

"Apparently," Piola said. "Drowned himself in a tank full of his own crabs in remorse at having murdered two gay East European witches. Impressive."

"You said yourself, Marcello's good at this. There's almost nothing in this account that doesn't fit the evidence, with a little shoehorning."

"Until you know what it leaves out," Piola agreed.

It was mid-morning, but the operations room was quiet.

Overnight, half of the officers on their investigation had been reassigned to other cases.

Piola sighed. "The trouble is, we don't have anything concrete to offer as an alternative. There are so many elements that seem suggestive – but when we chase them, they turn into will-o'-the-wisps."

"Don't worry," she told him. "We'll get there. Something will give, I'm sure of it."

After the discovery that the tattoos on Jelena's body were Catholic in origin, Kat had sent a second email to "Karen", the woman who'd called herself a priest. She'd heard nothing back at the time, but now, out of the blue, there was a message waiting in her inbox.

> Log on to Carnivia now. Meet me in Campo San Zaccaria. Come alone.

She did as she was told, except for one small thing: while in Carnivia her avatar appeared to be alone, in reality Piola was standing next to her at the computer, fascinated but confused.

"So this is a kind of computer game?" he asked, as she hurried through the virtual equivalent of Venice to Campo San Zaccaria.

"Malli tells me it's technically a mirror world, which in turn is a kind of MUSE – a multi-user simulated environment. They're huge in cyberspace. Second Life, World of Warcraft… there are tens of millions of users on those sites alone. My brother used to be obsessed with a mirror world called Twinity. He spent hours every day interacting with it. Niche players like Carnivia are tiny by comparison."

"So they're mainly for teenagers?"

"Some are. But Carnivia's a bit different, because everyone wears masks. Your Carnivia persona can effectively be used to shield all your activities on the internet, if you want it to."

As Columbina7759, she crossed a perfect simulacrum of Piazza San Marco, walked along the Riva degli Schiavoni, and turned north into Campo San Zaccaria.

"Here we are."

It was strange, to be both sitting in a building and seeing a perfect replica of it on the screen, right down to the slight crack in the pediment above the door.

"Remarkable," Piola breathed.

In front of the Carabinieri headquarters a figure in a Domino mask was waiting. As Kat hurried towards it, a pop-up screen appeared above its head.

Domino67980 wants to chat to you. Accept?

She clicked "Yes".

Thank you. Your chat will be encrypted.

A balloon appeared from the figure's mouth.

– *Follow me.*

She followed. The figure led her to a quiet corner of the square.

– *What do you want to know?*

Kat typed:

– *Are you a priest? A real one, I mean?*

– *You've started with a difficult one.*

There was a pause. Then Domino67980 wrote:

– *According to the Pope, I'm not. But the theology is actually on our side. It's bishops who choose priests, not popes. And if a bishop decides to ordain a woman, then as soon as that woman has received the Sacrament of Holy Orders she is a priest, in the eyes of God. A heretic one, perhaps; even an abomination. The Church can excommunicate her. It can try her in an ecclesiastical court and defrock her. But according to the basic tenets of Catholicism, she has the "indelible mark" of priesthood on her forever, and there's no reason why her sacraments and prayers, although illicit, are any less valid than any other priest's.*

– Is that why you won't give me your real name or location?

– Exactly. The Church knows, or at least suspects, that we exist. It's spending vast resources trying to track us down. And when it finds us, it persecutes us.

– In what way?

– It varies. There was a woman priest in Chicago, for example, called Janine Denomme. It was only after she died, in 2010, that the diocese found out she'd been ordained. It refused to let her funeral take place in a Catholic church, or for her to be buried in consecrated ground.

– Why do you do it? If there's such a risk, I mean?

There was another long pause. Then:

– I can't answer for the others. But all Christians believe that receiving the Sacrament of Holy Orders changes a person – it leaves an indelible mark on their soul. That means it's something you feel at the very deepest level of your being. If you're called to the priesthood, as I was, then you don't feel complete without it.

– And the Church's position?

– Is simply wrong. Yes, canon law says that only a validly ordained man can administer the sacraments. But it's long

been accepted in legal circles that a phrase specifying the male gender can include the female. A "manmade disaster" is a disaster caused by the whole human race, not just the male half. When Christ said "No man is without sin", he didn't mean to imply that women are. The ban on women is simply misogyny and semantics. The whim of man, dressed up as the will of God.

– In your last email you mentioned "catacomb ordinations". What are they?

– A catacomb priest is one ordained in secret, without Vatican approval. The term was used mainly of priests in communist Eastern Europe. Things were much more flexible there – it was accepted, for example, that a catacomb priest might be married, in order to deflect suspicion. There were a small number of female priests, too, before the Vatican woke up to the controversy they might cause. Some of those women eventually became bishops, and in turn ordained other women. It's from them that the present "line" of women priests receives its Apostolic Succession.

"Eastern Europe again," Kat commented. "Everything leads back behind the iron curtain."

"Ask her about Poveglia," Piola said.

– Do you know anything about a Venetian island called Poveglia?

– Yes. It's a place of historic significance for our movement.

Surprised, Kat typed:

– Why's that?

– Because of Martina Duvnjak.

– Who's she?

– Martina Duvnjak was a catacomb priest in the 1950s in what was then communist Yugoslavia. So far as we know,

she was one of the very first women priests to be ordained. Martina ran great risks, deliberately getting herself arrested so she could minister to women in the communist regime's prisons – lawless places where it was all too easy to disappear without trace. She heard confessions, celebrated Mass, gave Extreme Unction – all the duties any priest might administer to her flock.

– What happened to her?

– To begin with, the Vatican turned a blind eye to her work. But then it sent word via her bishop that she had to stop. Duvnjak questioned the decision, and in the 1960s the Vatican invited her to Rome to discuss her case. The journey, of course, was fraught with difficulty, since it involved crossing into the West. As a convicted criminal, she could never hope to get a visa, so she was smuggled into Italy via Croatia.

– And?

– Forgive me, I'm typing this in an internet café and occasionally I have to stop if someone passes too close. She got as far as one of the islands in the Venetian lagoon – Poveglia – where she was met by a delegation of clerics. When she refused to recant, they took her to a nearby mental hospital, where she remained locked up for the rest of her life.

– That was the old hospital on Poveglia? She was imprisoned there?

– Effectively. She had no rights, no passport... hardly anyone in the West even knew she existed. She was just an inconvenience. It suited them all to pretend she was mad. Eventually she died there, completely forgotten by the outside world. But to us she is a martyr; even one day perhaps, a saint.

– Can you explain why a female priest might want to celebrate Mass there today?

– Of course. For us, the place where she was incarcerated has become a place of pilgrimage. The priest was almost certainly saying a Missa Pro Defunctis, a Mass for the repose of Martina Duvnjak's soul.

"And Carnivia?" Piola said quietly.

– Another woman, an associate of the female priest I mentioned, frequently visited Carnivia. Do you know why she might have done that?

– Perhaps she was also part of our community.

– Community?

– We are very few in number, and spread all over the world. Most of us, of course, are active in the global movement to persuade the Vatican to legitimise female ordinations, but even amongst our fellow activists we have to be circumspect. To the outside world, therefore, we are altar servers, lay workers... But here in Carnivia, we can lay down the burden of our secrecy.

– Do you mean that this is how you communicate with each other? Privately, as we're doing now?

– I mean much more than that. This is how we communicate with God.

– I'm sorry, you're going to have to explain.

– Come with me. I'll show you.

Domino67980 turned and led Kat into the church adjacent to the Carabinieri headquarters, the Chiesa di San Zaccaria. A fifteenth-century fusion of Gothic and Renaissance styles, it was, to Kat's mind, one of the finest churches in Venice. And yet such was the surfeit of beautiful buildings in the city, it rarely attracted even a single tourist into its dark, echoing interior.

The replica in Carnivia was identical, except for one thing. The church she stepped into was full. Masked figures stood facing the altar, where a figure in priest's robes was holding aloft a golden chalice. The air was filled with the sound of singing – an all-female choir, as if the massed rows of avatars had themselves broken into song.

– *This is how we worship.*

"Of course," Kat breathed. Her fingers danced over the keys.

– *And this is valid? Theologically, I mean?*

– *Indeed. Amongst our number we have some of the most respected theologians in the world. They're agreed that since the Holy Spirit is universal, a Mass held here is just as "real" as any other. So long as, somewhere, one of the participants is holding a physical host and physical wine that become the body and blood of Christ.*

– *That's ingenious.*

– *The Vatican won't be happy when they find out.*

– *Why?*

– *Think about it. In here, you only know someone's gender if they choose to reveal it to you. If a woman inhabits a male avatar, does that mean she can celebrate a virtual Mass legitimately? It makes a nonsense of all their rules.*

– *Do you think you might be in danger from them?*

– *Physically? I doubt it, not from the Vatican. But bear in mind that in the old days of the Inquisition, it was never the Vatican itself that burnt witches at the stake. It was the civil authorities, to whom they were handed over. Indeed, it was customary for the Church to make a formal, hypocritical request for mercy, knowing it would be refused. Women priests who reveal themselves have been spat on, burnt out of their homes, ostracised from their communities and congregations, you name it. It wouldn't surprise me if we were at risk of even greater physical harm from those who thought they were doing God's work.*

– I'm sorry to have to tell you that the two women I've been asking about were both killed – murdered, that is.

There was a long pause. Then:

– How terrible. I will pray for them.

– Have you any idea who might do such a thing?

– There are over a billion Catholics in the world, and all but a handful of them accept the Pope's edicts without question. Doubtless some of them would kill on his behalf as well, but I can't help you work out which ones.

The figure in front of Kat flickered, then vanished.

"She's logged off," Piola said.

"Fascinating," Kat said, sitting back. "At the very least, it completely destroys the hypothesis that Jelena Babić wasn't a real priest. In her own eyes, she was just as valid as any man. And it gives us an explanation for what she was doing on Poveglia."

"None of this can be corroborated," Piola warned.

"I think it can – some of it, anyway. When I spoke to Father Uriel, he mentioned that some of the older nuns at the Institute of Christina Mirabilis worked on Poveglia when it was a lunatic asylum. I'll see if any of them can confirm the parts about Martina Duvnjak. I want to go back to the Institute anyway – I'd like Father Uriel to know that I didn't take his brush-off at face value."

"OK. But not let's get distracted. At its heart, this is still a story about organised crime."

"We can't be sure of that," she protested.

He shook his head. "The cigarettes, the death of that fisherman... I agree with you that Marcello's story of quarrelling lesbians is nonsense, but at least it's simple. My thinking is that this may be nothing more than an instance of two worlds colliding. Suppose we accept that Jelena Babić was on Poveglia to say a Mass at the spot where this other priest had been locked up. And that whatever Ricci Castiglione was doing there, it was connected with the Mafia in some way – let's say, picking up contraband. So far, so clear, yes?"

Kat nodded.

"He finds someone else there, so he kills her – and yes, perhaps Marcello's suggestion that the gun was his, smuggled in over the Adriatic, isn't such a bad one. After he's killed Jelena, Ricci tries to make the murder scene look like a black Mass, both to cover his tracks and to reinforce Poveglia's reputation as somewhere people should stay away from. When the body gets washed into Venice, and the murder starts to attract attention, his masters decide to have him killed before he can spill their secrets."

It sounded plausible, but she was reluctant to accept that the persecution of the women priests wasn't somehow relevant to the murder. "As a fisherman, wouldn't Ricci know better than anybody not to dump the body off Poveglia?" she protested. "He'd be aware that the currents would wash it into Venice. And what about the Freedom of Information request to the US Army? The questions about Dragan Korovik? Are you saying none of that matters?"

Piola shrugged. "Since we're not allowed to talk to the Americans, we'd better hope it doesn't. As for the Church... I certainly wouldn't object if we were able to wrap this up without dragging His Holiness into it. I have a feeling Avvocato Marcello isn't going to want to go there either."

"Jelena Babić and Barbara Holton were killed because of their beliefs. I'm sure of it," Kat said stubbornly.

"Is that statement based on evidence?" Piola said quietly. "Or your own beliefs?"

"What do you mean?"

"I mean that perhaps you relate to these women." He gestured at the computer. "Women who are persecuted by men. You feel angry with the persecutors, so you want to be able to bring them to justice. But that's not the case we're investigating here."

His logic stung her, not least because she knew that on some level at least, he was right.

"That's bullshit!" she exclaimed. Piola had the grace not to press his point.

"You know, there's one participant in all this we haven't yet spoken to," he said. "Daniele Barbo. If he'll give us access to the material Barbara Holton uploaded onto Carnivia, it could tell us whether you're right in thinking that the women's deaths were connected to their faith."

"That's a big 'if'. My understanding is that he doesn't cooperate with the authorities."

"It's worth a try. You should see him, anyway."

"You don't want to come along?"

"He may respond better to you on your own."

"You mean, I should flirt with him?" she asked, astonished.

"There won't be any need to. A woman like you only has to walk into a room and any man in it wants to please you, even if he doesn't realise it. Barbo's some reclusive computer nerd, isn't he? I doubt he's ever seen a woman like you, at least not in the flesh."

"I think perhaps now you're the one seeing this from a personal perspective," she said, unsure whether to be offended or flattered.

"Believe me, I'm not." He looked at her, amazed. "Is it

really possible that you don't understand how beautiful you are?"

"Aldo, this is making me uncomfortable. We left all that stuff behind twenty years ago."

He shrugged. "Well, I'll let you decide how best to handle it. But I still have a hunch it'll be better coming from you."

Thirty-one

HOLLY BOLAND SPED down the A13 *autostrada* in her new Fiat Cinquecento, a car so tiny it felt like a child's toy and as a result was strangely exhilarating to drive. The day was sunny, the crisp winter air shrinking distances and expanding panoramas. One by one she passed towns and cities that shimmered on the horizon like images from Renaissance paintings. Padua, Ferrara, Bologna... Then through the mountains to Florence, the multi-coloured domes and towers of the historic centre rising like a mirage above the urban sprawl. She'd have liked to have stopped off in Pisa, to see how many of her old friends and neighbours were still living on the same street – most of them, she'd bet – but her first destination had to be Camp Darby.

She'd crossed Italy from coast to coast in just under four hours. Now she turned south along a flat strip of wooded land about twenty miles wide, squeezed between the Tyrrhenian Sea and the mountains. Camp Darby sprawled for about fifteen miles among the pine woods, all the way down to the US Navy dockyard at Livorno. Despite its size, she knew there were relatively few military personnel stationed here. These days, Darby was primarily a missile store and recreation centre. Every year, around fifty thousand soldiers and their families came from other bases in Italy and Germany to spend their vacations in the area, their children playing just yards from the nuclear bunkers. In theory, there are no private beaches in Italy. In practice, the Italian government never complained about the secure double-fencing, multiple ID checks and security cameras.

At the guardhouse she handed over her CAC card to be swiped and asked for directions to the recycling facility. She drove two miles within the base before she reached a huge hangar, situated near the concrete domes that marked, like giant white mushrooms, the lids of the underground missile silos.

In the hangar, sitting at a desk, she found the man she'd spoken to on the phone. She knew the type at once: late fifties, well tanned, the bulging belly squeezed into a uniform two sizes too small that doubled as a corset. Staff Sergeant Kassapian was about two years off retirement, and didn't much care how he spent the time until then.

"I'm looking for the old archives from Camp Ederle that were sent down here," Holly told him. "You said I could take a look, remember?"

"Sure, you can look. Don't suppose it'll help you much." He stumped over to where a six-foot high mound of shredded paper stood in one corner. "That's them."

She stared at the pile, aghast. "They've been shredded?"

"Seems that way," he agreed.

"When did this happen?"

"Yesterday. Orders finally came through. Shred 'em all, just in case. Took forever, I can tell you, and we've got a pretty big shredder. Fact is, we ain't even done."

"There's more?"

He gestured with his thumb towards a heap of boxes in another corner. "Over there."

"Mind if I go through those ones, at least?"

"Well, I guess you can," he said doubtfully. "Seeing as how they sent you all the way down here. Just don't take anything. 'Cause my orders now is to shred them, see? If you take any, I can't complete my orders."

"Thanks," she said gratefully.

Her first task was to try to find any boxes that related to the years of Barbara Holton's request, from 1993 to 1995. Unfortunately, it seemed those had already been shredded.

"Darn it," she said aloud.

"Got what you need?" Kassapian asked, wandering over. His paunch was so large that he leant forward slightly when he walked, like a dog that had raised itself onto its hind legs.

"Not exactly, no."

"So what are you going to do?"

"Well," she said, gesturing at the pile, "I'm going to look through every one of these boxes to see if I can find any documents written in Serbo-Croat."

He made a chewing gesture with his lips, as if he were rolling an imaginary cigar into the corner of his mouth while he thought about what she had just said. "Then what you going to do? Take them away?"

"No, Staff Sergeant, absolutely not. Because you have orders to destroy them, right?" He nodded emphatically. "So, once I have them, if you'll direct me to a photocopier, I'll copy them. And then you'll destroy the originals, and everyone will be happy."

"Sounds fair to me," he said. "You go right ahead. It's not often we get visitors in here, tell you the truth."

She realised that his gruff demeanour was simply a disguise to hide his loneliness. "Thank you, Staff. How about I start with this pile here?" And then, "You know, I pretty much grew up on this base. My father's Ted Boland."

As she'd expected, his eyes lit up. "Ted Boland! Well, I never did. I've been here fifteen years myself..."

He talked non-stop for two hours, by which time she'd pulled about a dozen further documents in Serbo-Croat. There was a photocopier in the office, so she made two copies of each of them, one set for her and one for Ian Gilroy, before handing the originals back to Staff Sergeant Kassapian to destroy, as per his orders.

Thirty-two

LIKE MOST OLD *palazzi*, Ca' Barbo's grand main entrance gave onto the canal, designed to make an impression on those arriving by boat. The street door at the side, by contrast, was virtually anonymous – old, and made of weather-beaten carved oak, but with little about it to announce that within lay one of Venice's greatest houses. Only the carved lion's head set into the wall nearby, its open mouth a dark hole the size of Kat's fist, indicated what manner of dwelling this was.

She pressed the brass bell push, and while she was waiting examined the lion's head more closely. There were no more than half a dozen of these *bocca di leone* left in the city, she knew, relics of an age when the greatest maritime republic on earth had found it necessary to spy on its own citizens. Bending down, she put her ear to its mouth. From within the beast's dark throat came a faint whisper; a resonance like the inside of a cavern, or the roar of far-off oceans inside a conch's shell.

"What do you want?"

She jumped. Standing at the now-open door was a man of about forty. He was casually dressed in T-shirt and chinos, despite the chill of the north-east wind that was whistling up the narrow *rio*. His eyes were bright and piercing, and his hair reached well down his neck, hiding his ears. But it was his nose, inevitably, that caught the attention. Where the nostrils should have been there was a smooth stump of scar tissue, a swirl of flesh like a second belly button.

"Capitano Kat Tapo, Carabinieri." She reached for her wallet, but he cut her short.

"There's no need to show me ID, Captain. It makes no difference to me whether you're who you say you are or not."

"I sent you several emails—" she began.

"I know."

"But you didn't reply."

"I decided I didn't want to see you."

"Even so, I need half an hour of your time," she said firmly. She recalled reading in his Wikipedia profile that he had some kind of Social Avoidance Disorder, and decided to go in hard. "We can do it the official way if you'd prefer, with a warrant and a trip down to the Carabinieri headquarters. But it will take a lot longer, and you may have to wait in the holding cells for a while. We get quite a backlog at this time of day."

A flicker of distaste crossed Daniele Barbo's sensitive features. "Very well," he said abruptly. "Half an hour. No more. I'm busy."

His voice, she noted, was curiously accented – not quite American, but devoid of the usual sing-song inflections of Venetian. Perhaps that was something to do with being partially deaf. "Thank you," she said, softening her insistence with a smile. Barbo only grunted.

The hall he led her into was dark and bare. This didn't surprise her – the ground floors of these palaces were built for trade and storage; the grand reception rooms would be on the *piano nobile* above. There was a noticeable taint of damp in the air. "May I see the inside of the *bocca*?" she asked.

"Why?"

"I'm curious, that's all. One doesn't often get the chance."

He seemed about to say no, then shrugged. "It's your half hour. So long as you're gone at the end of it, you can spend it how you like." He led her to a door at the end of the hallway. "Down there," he said, gesturing.

I'm not flirting, she told herself. *Just building a rapport with a difficult interviewee.*

She stepped down into a long, low room lined with leather volumes. A counter ran along the length of one wall. The only light came from grilles set into the walls, a little above the counter but at foot height for those walking on the *fondamenta*. Everything glistened with damp.

She knew roughly how it worked. Citizens would post their notes – anonymous denunciations of fellow Venetians, morsels of information, gossip, whatever – into the lion's mouth outside, from where they would fall down a chute to this room below. Down here, a dozen spy-masters would have worked night and day by the light of candles, analysing and collating them, building up a secret file on every citizen.

"And thus did the ten great families of Venice maintain the so-called serenity of their so-called Republic," Daniele Barbo's voice said laconically behind her. He reached past her to one of the pigeonholes and tugged: the wood came away in his hand, rotten. "Now it won't last another decade, let alone another three hundred years."

"The damp's from the *acqua alta*, I take it?"

"Not exactly." Again he hesitated, then said abruptly, "Come, if you're so interested. I'll show you." He went to another door and pulled it open. The oak shuddered and protested on the stone floor where it had warped.

Cold, dank air hit her – cellar air. Darkness, and the sloshing of a sea-cave. He flicked a switch and stood back from the door. Stone steps led down to another, even bigger room. Sturdy columns reached up to the roof – supporting all that marble above, she supposed. But where the floor should have been there was nothing but brown water, rippling uneasily, as if the whole room were a tray being tilted in some giant's hands.

"Twice a day this is under water. Although it generally dries up in summer." He pointed to the wall, where, as if to record the height of a growing child, dates had been scrawled in charcoal. High-water marks. "These go back to 1776. Some of the oldest have already been washed away. When Ruskin wrote that Venice was melting into the sea like a cube of sugar in a teacup, it was Ca' Barbo he was talking about – his name's in the visitors' book."

She could just reach the nearest shelf without stepping down into the water. Pulling out a brown folder, she saw that the pages were covered in handwriting, the ink now fuzzy with damp and mould. "Shouldn't these be moved?"

Daniele Barbo shrugged. "Who's interested in them now? They're just old secrets. Shall we go upstairs? You're wasting your thirty minutes."

He led her up the main stairs. The transformation couldn't have been greater – here, the floors and walls were delicately marbled, lit by Gothic arched windows as intricately carved as barley-sugar twists. But she couldn't forget that it was all perched precariously on top of that sloshing seawater, those rotting, stagnant offices for spies. But that was Venice for you: beauty built on filth; brackish water overlaid with gorgeous perfume; cut-throat commerce jostling for space with the greatest glories of Italian civilisation.

"What an amazing place," she said conversationally. "You

must feel very privileged to live here." He didn't bother to reply.

He led her along the *portego*, the main upstairs hallway, into a salon. The carved cabinets and elaborate glassworks one might expect in such a room were conspicuous by their absence. Instead, it had the feel of a college seminar room. The furniture was cheap and functional, and there was a large whiteboard covered in what looked like mathematical equations.

"So," he said, taking a seat. "What did you want to ask?"

"I need to access some conversations that I believe took place on your website." Sitting down opposite him, she pulled out the list from the hotel. "The person who logged on at these times was killed soon afterwards. We want to know who she was contacting on Carnivia, and why."

He barely glanced at it. "This is one of the women the newspaper claims were Satanists?"

"We believe the media speculation is unhelpful."

His eyebrows flickered, as if she had finally said something he hadn't expected.

"If you were able to assist us in our inquiry," she added, "we could provide a character reference. It might influence the sentencing in your trial."

His upper lip curled. "I doubt that."

"I could write to the judge—"

But he had already interrupted her. "I'm afraid you've had a wasted journey, Captain. I can no more access a conversation that took place in Carnivia than you can. Everything that's said there is encrypted."

"But you could tell how often she was going online, and for how long," Kat persisted. "You could tell whether she was communicating with one individual or many. And then there's all the data you scrape from your users' computers – that's the correct term, isn't it, 'scrape'? Email addresses, geographical locations, shopping habits, who her friends were... that information could be incredibly useful to us."

"Even if I could give you that information, if I did so without a warrant valid in her home jurisdiction I'd be in violation of international privacy laws. You'd be better off trying the hard drive of her own computer."

"We did. It was found in the canal, where it had been lying in salt water. There was nothing on it we could retrieve."

"Hmm," Barbo said non-committally.

"In addition," she continued after a moment, "I've discovered that women priests – that is, Catholic women who say they've taken Holy Orders – are using Carnivia to hold Masses. Do you know anything about that?"

He shrugged. "What people do in Carnivia is up to them."

"But you don't seem surprised."

"Not everyone who needs privacy is a criminal, despite what the government would have us believe."

I'm getting nowhere. She leant forward a little, pulling her shoulders back while simultaneously opening her eyes a little wider. The effect she was after was eager awestruck disciple rather than raging nymphomaniac, but it was possibly a finer distinction than she would have liked.

"Daniele," she said, "your help would really mean a lot. To me personally, I mean."

He looked at her stonily. "Do you really think *that* will make a difference?" he said witheringly.

It wasn't just her words, she knew, that he was referring to. She felt a little ridiculous. Not for the first time in her life, a sense that she was at fault turned into a sudden flash of temper.

"Oh, fuck this," she said. "Why am I even trying to be nice to you? You're a sad geek who's going to prison. Where, by the way, I hope you rot. I'll solve this case without you."

He blinked. "Are you done?"

"It appears so." She stood up. "Thank you for your time."

"I didn't say I wouldn't help you," he said calmly. "Only that it couldn't be done in the way you suggested. It so happens that our interests coincide, Captain. I'll get you the data. But not from Carnivia. I'll retrieve it from the laptop."

She frowned. "I told you, we already tried that. It's useless."

"You're mistaken."

"What makes you so sure?" she said, curious.

"I've done it before."

When Daniele was ten years old, his parents had given him a computer – a Commodore 64, one of the very first mass-market devices with a hard drive. Its processing power was eight bytes, less than a thousandth of the capacity of a modern credit card. But by the time he was twelve, he was as fluent in the programming language BASIC as he was in Italian, his father's tongue, and American, his mother's. What was more, he felt infinitely more at home in the world in which that language was spoken than he did in what others called the "real" world. In this new universe, everything obeyed a set of rigid, predictable laws. Everything was programmed, and if it didn't behave the way you wanted it to, you reprogrammed it until it did.

That summer, the family transferred to their villa in the Veneto countryside, just as they did every year when the heat and the stench in Venice got too bad to bear. Daniele had insisted on taking his computer. His father had been carrying it to the launch outside when he slipped, and it fell into the canal. To his parents' consternation, Daniele had immediately dived in to retrieve it. He developed a fever from the polluted water, but as soon as he was better, he set about salvaging what data he could from the hard drive. It was painstaking work, like rebuilding a smashed vase that had been crushed almost to dust. But eventually he had succeeded.

He still wondered whether his father had really slipped, or whether his parents had simply decided their son was spending too much time with only a keyboard for company.

None of this he felt inclined to share with Captain Tapo, of course, although he was aware that she was watching him curiously.

"That hard drive is evidence," she said. "If it were to leave police custody at all – let alone to be placed with a convicted criminal – it would no longer be of any use in court."

"It's of no use in court as it is," he pointed out. "What do you have to lose?"

She hesitated. She still had the hard drive, after all, and it was true that Malli had said it might as well be thrown away. What was the difference between disposing of it and giving it to Barbo?

But, she reminded herself, if there *were* something on it, and Barbo could retrieve it, she had no guarantee as to what he would do with that information. He could just as easily steal it for his own ends, and then say it had been irretrievable. Piola, she knew, would regard this proposal as utterly unfeasible.

"I'm sorry," she said, shaking her head. "I can't do that."

He shrugged, as if that were the answer he had been expecting. "I understand. But will you do something for me?"

"What?"

"When your investigation becomes stalled by people you

can't even identify; when evidence goes missing, or witnesses are silenced; when you and Colonel Piola are prevented from following leads you know are promising – then, will you reconsider?"

She didn't say that most of those things were already happening. Instead she nodded. "Perhaps."

"In that case, Captain," he said, standing up, "I'll be expecting your call." The interview was over. She glanced at her watch. It had taken exactly twenty-nine minutes.

As she left she saw that he had gone to the whiteboard and was studying it intently, tracing the mathematical formulae on it with his pen, as if reading a page of music that only he could hear.

Thirty-three

KAT DROVE OUT to the Institute of Christina Mirabilis, where Father Uriel had grudgingly agreed she could speak to one of the older nuns about Poveglia. But her mind wasn't on the forthcoming interview so much as her conversation with Daniele Barbo.

She tried not to make snap judgements about people. Detective work had taught her that the smiling father who proudly showed you pictures of his children might turn out to be abusing them. The likeable old rogue who spent most of his time tending his vegetable patch might turn out to be a killer for the Mafia. Young professionals, to all intents and purposes no different from her, might be slaves to their cocaine habits, or beat up their partners.

But she'd formed a strong opinion about Daniele, which was that he could be useful to this investigation. She wouldn't go so far as to say that she trusted him – but whatever her feelings about his website, his stand on not allowing the government access to it at least pointed to someone who could be principled when he chose to be.

Piola, she knew, would say the decision wasn't theirs to make. When police officers started making their own rules, they became part of the problem. And the logic she was employing – that Daniele was trustworthy precisely because he had refused to cooperate with a lawful request by the government – was hardly one she would be able to defend in court.

She was no nearer resolving her dilemma by the time she was shown into Father Uriel's office. Sitting in a leather armchair, and almost dwarfed by it, was a woman so tiny she looked barely more substantial than a child, although a slight stoop to her neck betrayed her real age. She was wearing the grey habit and white wimple of a nun.

Father Uriel obviously intended to stay and listen to their conversation; Kat was equally adamant that he wouldn't. Once she'd persuaded him to leave, she asked a few introductory questions to put the nun at her ease. She quickly realised it was hardly necessary: Sister Anna was only too keen to talk.

She was, she said at once, one of the longest-serving nurses in the hospital. "That's the advantage of being a nun," she exclaimed. "There's no one making you retire."

"So you worked in the hospital on Poveglia before this?"

"I did. And a horrible place it was too. Oh, not the hospital, that was fine enough. But the island had a bad feel to it." The nun lowered her voice. "They did say it was haunted. And although I'm not saying I ever saw anything myself, it definitely had an atmosphere. Those poor plague victims, you know. None of us would eat the fish." She nodded significantly, as if to say that not eating the fish was all the proof that could be required.

"What sort of people were the patients?"

"Oh, it wasn't like now," Sister Anna assured her. "Most of the Reverend Fathers we treat here... well, they seem quite normal, don't they, until you know what they've been up to. In those days we had more what you might call mad people.

People who weren't right in the head," she added, as if Kat might not understand what mad meant.

Kat noted the indiscreet aside about the Institute's current clientele and stored it away for future reference. Priests who required Father Uriel's personal combination of prayer and pharmaceuticals... Perhaps the Institute was one of those shadowy places one heard of where those who had disgraced the Church were quietly sent for treatment. That might explain why Father Uriel seemed so evasive. "Were there any women at the asylum?" she asked.

The bird-like face nodded vigorously. "Oh yes. Almost as many as men, I'd say. Poor creatures, you wouldn't believe—"

Kat cut across her. "Do you remember a woman called Martina Duvnjak?"

Sister Anna blinked rapidly. Then she said, "Oh, dear, yes. They called her the abomination."

It was the same word Father Uriel had used. "Why?"

"Well," Sister Anna pursed her lips, "she was deluded, the poor woman. She thought she was..." She shook her head at the awfulness of it. "A priest," she whispered.

"And was she?" Kat asked baldly.

The old nun looked shocked. "Of course not."

"But she believed she was?" Kat persisted.

"The patients believed all sorts of things, poor dears," Sister Anna said primly. "But yes, that was her particular fixation. It wasn't one I was likely to forget. "

"And the doctors treated her how?"

"In the usual way. With drugs and prayers and electric shocks."

"Successfully?"

Sister Anna considered. "I would say that she was calmer at certain times than others. When she first came, I understand, she was in a terrible state. She would talk about how His Holiness had summoned her to Rome, how she was going to show the world that women could be in orders. They had to restrain her on occasions, I heard."

Kat tried to imagine what it must have been like for Martina Duvnjak – smuggled into a foreign country, only to be imprisoned in a mental hospital where no one believed, or wanted to believe, that she was what she said she was. Where those whom she had trusted most betrayed her most profoundly.

"And yet you say she was called the abomination?" she said.

Sister Anna nodded. "Indeed."

"Why would they call her that," Kat asked, "if she wasn't one?"

For the first time in their conversation, she had the satisfaction of seeing the other woman rendered speechless.

Father Uriel was loitering in the corridor. "I trust that was useful," he said, bustling forward.

"Sister Anna was very informative," she assured him.

"Good. Well, unless there's anything else, I'll walk you back to your car."

As he steered her towards the main entrance, she said, "Incidentally, we identified the remaining wall markings at the Poveglia crime scene. The ones you didn't recognise."

He turned his face towards her, professionally curious. "Yes?"

He was just a little too good, she thought. He was working so hard at keeping his face impassive that he'd neglected to convey the normal interest that anyone, surely, would show on being told such a puzzle had been solved.

"They're called *stećak* markings. They're Catholic, not occult. From Bosnia and Croatia."

Again, his face gave nothing away. "That's one less mystery, then, isn't it? Although I should point out that religious symbols can also be appropriated and abused by occultists."

"I'm sure. But in fact these markings were drawn on the wall before the other symbols were added. Before the priest was killed, even."

Involuntarily, he flinched.

"Sorry," she added, "I should have said, 'the woman dressed as a priest'. Tell me, Father, if you had a woman as a patient today who genuinely believed she was a priest, how would you treat her?"

He considered. "Well, every treatment programme is different. The individual circumstances would determine—"

"But you *would* treat her?" she persisted. "You'd say she was deluded, just as Martina Duvnjak was?"

Father Uriel didn't react to her mention of Martina's name. "Medicine has moved on a great deal since those days."

"But the Church hasn't. The position on women priests has, if anything, hardened."

He didn't reply.

"Last time I was here," she said on an impulse, "you offered to show me round."

He frowned. "Did I?"

"I've a few minutes to spare now. Would you give me a tour of the premises, please?"

She could see him calculating, then deciding that the easiest thing was to go along with her lie, bare-faced though it was. "Of course. We've nothing to hide here, Capitano."

Abruptly he turned, barely waiting for her to follow.

"These are all treatment rooms," he said, gesturing at the rooms on their left without breaking stride. "We can't interrupt the patients' therapies, I'm afraid."

"When you say 'patients', Father, I take it you mean 'priests'?"

If he was annoyed that Sister Anna had divulged this information, he didn't show it. "The Institute is a privately funded charitable facility, working under the auspices of the Catholic Church. As such, we prioritise those from within the ecclesiastical community."

"Fallen priests."

"Sick priests," he corrected. "As I think I said to you, the approach we use here combines the medical and the spiritual. That's a greater overlap than many people imagine. Cognitive behavioural therapy and the rigorous self-examination of a monastic rule, for example, have many similarities. Prayer and visualisation therapy... Confession and non-directive psychoanalysis... Even concepts as apparently old-fashioned as penance and penitence have their parallels in the twelve steps of an addiction programme."

"And the drugs you use?"

"Help to manage symptoms and make the patient more receptive to therapy."

"More suggestible, you mean?" she said, hoping to provoke him, but Father Uriel was on familiar territory now and his phrases had the well-polished tone of ones that had been trotted out many times before.

"If only curing the sick were as simple as suggesting to them that they've been cured," he said mildly. "It worked for our Lord, of course, but here our miracles are rather more uncertain."

From behind one of the closed doors she heard – faintly

but unmistakeably – a woman moaning in simulated ecstasy. "Is that *pornography* I can hear?"

Without stopping, he tilted his head. "It's possible. Flooding, or confronting an addict with the object of their craving, is standard treatment for certain forms of sex addiction."

He led her through a high-ceilinged refectory into a kitchen. Men in brown habits with knotted cinctures at their waists were preparing food at long counters. A few looked up. She felt their stares burn into her briefly, before their eyes dropped back to their work.

"We are a community here, as well as a hospital," Father Uriel was saying. "While they're with us, patients observe the monastic rules."

It was eerily quiet. "Including the vow of silence?"

"Yes. Except in the treatment rooms and other specially designated areas. We find it helps to focus their minds on their treatment."

A tall, thickset man wearing, rather incongruously, a black woollen hat as well as his monk's habit, came in with a dead deer across his shoulders. He hefted it down onto a counter and reached for a knife. Blood dripped from a neat hole between the stumpy antlers.

"That deer's been shot," Kat said, surprised.

Father Uriel nodded. "Indeed. We're almost self-sufficient here – there are two hundred acres of farm and woodland surrounding the buildings. The majority of our patients work the land in some way."

"Very admirable. I'm just surprised you let psychiatric patients use firearms."

"We're very careful, I can assure you. But trust and rehabilitation are fundamental to what we do here. Except for those undergoing a specific intervention, no door is ever locked."

"I'll need a list of all your weapons, and the calibre of bullets each one uses."

"Of course," he said stiffly. "Though I assure you, you'll find no irregularities."

He took her out of the kitchen by a different door, into a long passageway. This was clearly part of the original monastery. Above her head, massive stone arches scalloped the ceiling. Father Uriel walked on, quickly.

On her right she glimpsed a room with a bare stone floor. Painted in flowing script over the door were the words *Il celibato è la fornace in cui si forgia la fede.* Celibacy is the furnace in which faith is forged. She held back for a closer look. The room was empty apart from a row of wooden pegs. Knotted leather cords hung from some of them. A brass tap jutted from the wall. In the floor, a depression in the stone was clearly some kind of drain.

Father Uriel reappeared at her side. "This is a scourging room, isn't it?" she said accusingly.

"Yes. It's not in use, of course, and hasn't been for decades." He smiled faintly. "What was once spoken of approvingly by the Church as 'self-discipline' is now called 'self-harm' and treated accordingly. Proof, if you like, that we have indeed moved on."

She crouched down. The wall was discoloured and crumbling, but even so she could make out several rust-coloured spots a few inches above the ground.

"These bloodstains don't look that old to me, Father."

"The room has been used for butchering pigs, I believe. The drain makes it convenient for such things."

She stood up, feeling a little foolish. "Oh."

"Was there anything else...?"

"Yes. I'd like to see a complete list of the patients who were here in the first week of January, please, together with their passport details," she said, all pretence that this was not an interrogation abandoned.

He spread his hands apologetically. "I'm afraid that won't be possible, unless you bring a warrant. We want to cooperate with the police, naturally, but we also have a duty to preserve our patients' confidentiality."

There was no chance whatsoever that Marcello would give her a warrant without any further evidence to support it, she knew. She suspected Father Uriel knew it too.

"You seem suspicious, Captain Tapo," he said gently. "Can I ask what it is that you suspect us of?"

Caution, and the desire to provoke him, battled briefly. She said, "I think you lied to me about those *stećak* markings. I think you recognised them from the start."

"Ah." Father Uriel had the grace to look a little shamefaced. "It's true that it did occur to me they might be Croatian in origin. Although," he added quickly, "I don't think I actually lied. It was stupid of me not to tell you what I suspected, though. I should have realised that you would identify them sooner or later."

"Why didn't you want to tell me what they were?"

"These are difficult times for the Church. With respect, Captain, your own hostility and willingness to assume the very worst of us is mirrored, on a larger scale, in the wider world. I feared that if you drew an erroneous connection between what happened on Poveglia and the Church, this Institute might get dragged into your investigation. And it's essential for our work that we keep a low profile."

"Many of your patients have committed criminal offences

in their own countries," she guessed. "Having the police wandering around might frighten them away."

"Perhaps," he agreed.

"In fact, let's take that a step further. Many of the priests you treat here are women-haters of one sort or another. None of them would exactly be in favour of female priests, would they? You can see why I've good reason to be suspicious."

He looked her directly in the eye. "Captain, I accept that your victim may have been on Poveglia because she felt some misguided affinity with a previous patient of ours. But that's as far as the connection goes. You've seen how remote we are here – there's simply no way that a patient could go missing and commit a crime without our being aware of it. As a man of God, I promise you that if I had any evidence at all that linked a patient here, past or present, with your murders, I'd save you the trouble of a warrant and tell you. But I don't."

Thirty-four

ALDO PIOLA DROVE down to Chioggia, taking care to park some distance from the house he intended to visit. When Mareta Castiglione opened the door she recognised him and froze.

"Can I come in?" he said quietly. After a moment she nodded and let him past. He noted that before closing the door she checked to see if any neighbours were watching.

"No one saw me," he said. "I just want to ask you some more questions about your husband."

"What about him?"

"Let's sit down, shall we?"

Back at headquarters, Kat did some internet searches on the Institute of Christina Mirabilis. As she'd expected, information was scant. There was a bland, uninformative website – with no map, she noticed, no contact details other than an email address, and no explanation of what the hospital actually did.

She clicked on a tab titled "Who we are" and read:

> The Institute is a privately funded charitable organisation generously supported by donors at home and abroad. We acknowledge in particular the longstanding support of the Companions of the Order of Melchizedek.

That was all. She ran another search, this time for the "Order of Melchizedek". There were a number of links, mostly to pages pointing out that Melchizedek was the first priest mentioned in the Old Testament, and that all priests were thus sometimes said to belong to his Order. There were several organisations with similar-sounding names, but most seemed distinctly amateur. None had links to the Institute of Christina Mirabilis.

Then she came across a website that, though light on content, had clearly been professionally designed. A symbol at the top caught her eye. The upper half was a conventional Christian cross, but the lower half resembled a sword, the down-beam transformed into a short, stubby blade. She'd noticed a pin of a similar design in Father Uriel's lapel.

> The Companions of the Order of Melchizedek are dedicated to promoting and defending the highest personal and moral standards amongst the priesthood. "The Lord has sworn, and He shall not repent: thou art a priest for ever, according to the order of Melchizedek" – Psalms 110:4.
>
> Admission to the Order is by invitation only. There are twelve degrees, each of which must be fulfilled before the candidate progresses to the next.
>
> "He beareth not the sword in vain: for he is God's minister, an avenger to execute wrath upon him that doth evil" – Romans 13:4

That was all. She tried clicking on individual words, but none contained links. A "Contact us" button looked hopeful, but led only to a blank page and the words "Under Construction".

If the Companions of the Order of Melchizedek were funding an entire private asylum, their resources must be vast. That wasn't in itself suspicious – quasi-religious organisations such as the Knights of Malta and the Red Cross of Constantine were, she knew, able to raise huge amounts from those attracted to their particular blend of ceremony, snobbery and charity. But those organisations – she checked, to be certain – had thousands of individual webpages devoted to their work.

Even so, there was nothing here which implicated the Institute in any wrongdoing. Perhaps Father Uriel had been right: she was inherently hostile towards the Church, and as a consequence was willing evidence into existence rather than following a genuine trail.

Piola hated doing it, but he had no choice.

"But I think you knew, Mareta," he persisted. "I think you knew about the girls he brought in on his boat. A woman always knows, doesn't she? I think you knew that was how he got paid sometimes. That he went with the girls for nothing."

She was already crying, but now she squeezed her eyes shut and shook her head so violently that tears flew through the air, like a dog shaking water from its fur.

"What I'm looking for is proof," he went on relentlessly. "Something I can show a prosecutor."

"There's nothing," she gasped.

"Nothing? Or nothing you can tell me? Mareta, I understand there are some things it's not safe to talk about. But girls who go with other women's husbands? They're nothing but sluts. Why protect *them*?"

"I found a film," she said.

The instant she said it, he knew that this was it, this was the breakthrough he'd been looking for. He tried to keep the excitement out of his voice. "What sort of film?"

"A disc. Him. With one of those... those *creatures*."

"What creatures, Mareta?"

"My husband. And a... a whore."

"How much did you watch?"

"A few seconds. It was enough."

"Did you tell him you'd seen it?"

Mutely, she shook her head.

"So what happened to the film? What did you do with it, Mareta?"

"I put it back."

"Yes? Where?" If she'd returned it to its hiding place and never told her husband she'd seen it, there was a slim chance it might still be there.

Her eyes went to the floor.

Piola pushed back the rug with the edge of his shoe. One floorboard had no nails in it. He got down on his knees and pulled it up. It was stiff; he had to get out his car keys to lever it free.

In a cavity under the board were two fat bags of white powder. And a disc. No markings, no title.

He left the drugs where they were and stood up with the disc in his hand, careful to hold it by the edges. "Well done, Mareta. You've done the right thing."

"Don't tell anyone," she said in a dull voice. "Please, Colonel. It's too dangerous. Ricci always kept his mouth shut. He wouldn't even talk to a priest usually, and then look what happened..."

"I'll have to write this up, just like any other evidence. But only the prosecutor will see my report."

She shook her head and moaned. "No..."

"Mareta, I have to take it."

"I'm not letting you have it. Give it back." She made a sudden grab for the disc.

"Mareta, listen to me," he said, taking an evidence bag from his pocket and slipping the disc inside. "I'm taking this film because I think it could be evidence of a crime. I think the girl you saw your husband having sex with may have been unwilling. That's why, legally, I'm entitled to take it. It's called 'reasonable grounds'. Do you understand?"

"No, no, no," she keened. She began to slap her own face, whether in grief or rage at her own stupidity in telling him about the disc he couldn't say. "You mustn't take it. They'll kill me."

"I'll keep it safe."

"I know what you want." She stared at him, wide eyed. "Of course you do. Take the drugs. Just not the film. I'll..."

"You'll what, Mareta?"

"I'll go upstairs with you," she whispered. "That's better than any film, isn't it? The real thing."

He felt an unbearable sadness. Standing up, he said gently, "I have to go now. I promise I'll keep it safe."

She pushed her hands over her eyes and let out a terrible wail. As he left the room, all he could see of her was black hair cascading over her face and those two hands, beating a savage rhythm against her own flesh.

At Campo San Zaccaria he went straight to his office and put the film into his computer, ignoring Kat, who was trying to catch his eye through the glass.

For a moment the metal whirred uselessly in the disc drive and he thought he was going to have to call a technician to come and make it work. Then it started. He forced himself to watch for several minutes with the sound turned down.

Kat knocked and entered all in one movement and he jumped to pause it.

"What's that?" she asked curiously.

"Don't look. Please, Kat. I don't want you to watch it."

"Why not?"

He made a hopeless gesture. "It's Ricci Castiglione. With a girl." He took a breath. "I thought maybe he'd filmed himself with one of them. But it's worse than that."

"What is it?"

"It's one of the videos they use to... keep the girls docile."

"Let me see."

He shook his head. "I can't."

"Because I'm a woman, or because I'm your lover?" she said, her voice low but furious.

"Because I want to protect you from filth like this," he muttered.

"Filth is our job." Without waiting for him to answer, she reached past him and pressed "Play", swivelling the screen so they could both see.

"Oh my God," she said after a few moments. "This is clearly rape."

He nodded. "Mareta must have known that. But maybe he was the same with her. Some men... they end up thinking this is the way it's meant to be. Some women too, when it's all they've ever had."

She reached out and paused the image again. "You were right. I probably didn't need to see it. But now that I *have* seen it, I'm going to watch it all, with the sound up, to see if there are any clues, anything at all, that could help us identify the girl or the place where it happened."

"Kat, you realise what this means, don't you? I think we've found a pipeline. Poveglia's how they bring the stuff in – cigarettes, drugs, guns, even girls. I'll bet they use a number of fishermen like Ricci for the last leg, to avoid suspicion. If we play this carefully, we may be able to roll it up section by section – first this end, then back to Eastern Europe. We might even get to some of the big players at last, the money men who sit in their nice houses and never get their hands dirty."

"It's not a new pipeline, either," she said slowly. "Remember Martina Duvnjak? She was smuggled into Italy from Croatia, on her way to the Vatican. Her journey ended on Poveglia."

"That would make sense. Though in those days organised crime was all about trafficking goods *into* Eastern Europe, of course, not out of it. Back then a pair of Levi's or a Sony Walkman changed hands in Moscow for five times its Western price."

"Walkmans – they were a bit like iPods, weren't they?" she said mischievously, glancing at him. "Only not as good?"

"So let's say the supply chain operates in both directions," he continued, getting to his feet and pacing. "And that it's been running for decades. My God!" He stopped. "I wonder..."

"What?"

"You remember I told you that one of my very first investigations was a death on Poveglia? A young doctor. His body was found at the foot of the clock tower, full of drugs. But it didn't really make sense – he had no history of drug taking, and it seemed strange that he'd have injected himself with hallucinogens. At the time people were saying he must have gone mad. But what if he'd simply seen something he shouldn't have, and was silenced?" He shook his head. "Poor devil."

"Where does this leave Jelena Babić and Barbara Holton?"

"I'm still of the view that they wandered into something on Poveglia they couldn't possibly have anticipated, and paid the price."

"And I still think there's more to it than that." She told him about her visit that morning to the Institute. "If it was the Order of Melchizedek who locked Martina Duvnjak up on Poveglia, maybe they're somehow connected to the pipeline too," she concluded.

"The Catholic Church working with organised crime? That's a little far-fetched, surely?"

They were splitting along gender lines, she realised. To him, the Mafia connection was the bigger prize. To her, proving that the Church had in some way sanctioned the murder of a female priest was more important.

"Let's not argue," he said softly.

She shook her head. "No. Let's not."

"We'll leave early and eat near your place – somewhere we don't have to think about work."

"I've got a better idea," she said. "I'll cook. Perhaps some *bigoli* with *ragù*? But it may not be early." She ejected Ricci's disc from Piola's computer. "I still intend to go through this video frame by frame."

Later Piola looked up and saw Kat make a note, carefully, as she peered at something on the screen.

She's tougher than I am, he realised. *Less romantic, less likely to get carried away.*

Why she was sharing her bed with him he had no idea. He still didn't know whether he dared tell her how deeply he was falling in love with her.

One reason he'd gone back to tackle Mareta Castiglione on

his own that afternoon, without Kat as backup, was that he'd known he'd have to lean on the widow, go in hard about Ricci screwing other women. He wasn't sure he could have done that in front of Kat. He'd have hated for her to see him being a bully. Not to mention a hypocrite. What was it he'd said to Mareta? *Girls who go with other women's husbands? They're nothing but sluts.* He hadn't meant it, of course, but he doubted he could have uttered those words in Kat's hearing.

He caught her eye through the glass wall of his office. *Not long now*, he told her silently in his head. *A few more hours, and we'll be in bed together.*

Thirty-five

HOLLY BOLAND APPROACHED the Education Centre with a box file stashed neatly under her arm. Once inside, she went to the room where Ian Gilroy taught his class on Italian Military History.

There were no other attendees. Gilroy had made sure of that. It was the perfect way to make contact with him: anyone looking through the glass panel in the door would see only a teacher in civilian clothes, and a solitary student seated in the first row.

"I can teach you how to do by-the-book dead-letter drops if you'd prefer," he'd joked. "But if a US Army base isn't a secure debriefing venue, where is?"

Now she had to tell him that the US Army base was itself part of the trail.

"I went down to Camp Darby, as you suggested," she said, opening up her file. "Most of the documents from 1995 had already been destroyed, but I found these older ones – this is a set for you."

"Thank you," he said, taking them and spreading them on the desk. It could have been any academic receiving a student's paper.

"Looking through, I noticed that one name kept cropping up. *Here*, for example, and *here*." She pointed. "Villem Bakerom."

"That name's not familiar to me."

"Nor me. And when I ran it through Intellipedia, it didn't ring any bells either. Then I thought, why not try putting it into Google Translate? Turns out it's the same as this name that's already in the file in English – *here.*" She showed him.

"William Baker?"

"Exactly."

"And who exactly do we think this William Baker might be?"

"That's the problem – I've no idea," she confessed. "I've checked all the databases I can think of – Inprocessing, the dental centre, even the auto repair shop. There's no record of any military personnel of that name. No civilian employee, either. But whoever he was, he was at Camp Ederle a lot – look at all these dates. He seems to have organised one large meeting in particular – it's here in the documents, *Srpanj 1–4 Devetnaest Devedeset Tri.* That is, July 1st to 4th 1993. The location is given in the Croatian documents as *Kamp Ederle, Italija.* But after that, I draw a blank. I can only assume William Baker was his cover name."

"Unless he isn't a person at all," Gilroy said slowly.

"What do you mean?"

"You're probably too young to remember the old phonetic alphabets—"

"We use phonetic all the time. Alpha, Bravo, Charlie..."

He nodded. "That's the standard US-NATO set. But before that was introduced, every service had its own, slightly different version. The Navy alphabet started with 'apples' and 'butter', for example. The British Royal Air Force said 'ack' for A and 'beer' for B, so 'anti-aircraft fire' became 'ack-ack'. And in the old US Army alphabet, the phonetics for W and B were William and Baker."

She stared at him. “Of course. Why didn’t I think of that? But we still don’t know what WB stands for.”

“Perhaps not, but we do know that the military at that time had a penchant for codenaming operations using the old service alphabets. Operation Victor Charlie was an offensive by the US against the Viet Cong in Vietnam. Able Archer was an A-bomb simulation back in the 1980s.”

“So ‘Operation William Baker’ might have been a codename for—” She stopped, staggered by the implications.

“Exactly. ‘Operation War in Bosnia’.”

Thirty-six

AT THE TRONCHETTO car park, Aldo Piola climbed into his car with a weary sigh. It was well after ten o'clock. Only the fact that Kat had made him promise to be at her apartment by eleven at the latest had made him leave when he did. The results of the forensic tests from the crime scenes, which always took a week or so to process, had come through. Most simply told him what he already knew, but even so the reports, which were written in a dry scientific language that often required the use of a dictionary, had to be gone through line by line in case he missed something.

The traffic, which would have been light if he'd made the journey a little earlier in the evening, was dense again now. A new production of *Rigoletto* had recently opened at La Fenice, and many of the drivers heading back to their homes on the mainland were in black tie. Once over the Ponte della Libertà he indicated right for his turning, glancing automatically into his rear-view mirror as he did so.

A carnival mask, a blank white Bauta, loomed up from the back seat like a ghost. For a moment he couldn't process what was happening, thought it must be some kind of joke. Then he felt a leather belt slipping round his neck, the reek of sour food as a gruff voice spat into his right ear. "That's it, Colonnello. Keep driving. I'll tell you when you can turn off."

The accent was Venetian, working class. Piola steered back onto the carriageway. It was difficult – his head was being wrenched back and up by the tightness of the belt, making it hard to see the road.

"What do—" he croaked, but the belt jerked impatiently against his windpipe.

"No talking."

After five hundred yards his assailant said, "Turn here."

He took the exit the man indicated. It led off the dual carriageway to an industrial estate. There were several open patches of ground where developments hadn't yet taken place – roundabouts with access roads that petered out into wasteland, where one day warehouses or light industrial units would be built.

The man pointed. "That one."

When the road ran out, Piola had no option but to slow down.

"Turn off the engine."

He was aware that his heart was pounding. He focused on the fact that his assailant was wearing a mask. Why do that if he was going to kill him? To his left, he saw a single headlight approaching across the rough ground. *Thank God.* Then he realised that of course the man would have brought an accomplice. Hit-men always used motorbikes to escape.

The man wrapped the belt around his fist, tightening it further, the edges biting painfully into Piola's windpipe. Piola could hear his captor breathing as he worked it tight. Something metallic and very solid tapped his head, just behind his right ear. A gun.

"You should keep your nose out of other people's business," the man's voice said.

The gun came into his field of vision, the barrel turning so that it was pointing directly into Piola's forehead. He fought to breathe. Was he going to die after all? Here, on a piece of wasteland, like so many policemen before him? Involuntarily, he flashed on all the bodies he'd seen that were found exactly like this. Two bullets in the head. Bloodspray on the driver's side window, away from the gunman's clothes. No witnesses.

He held his breath, waiting for it to happen.

There was a click.

Relief flooded his limbs. *Not dead. Not dead after all. Mock—*

"Next time," the voice said, "it'll be loaded."

Pain exploded through his skull. He jerked forward, only to jerk back again as his neck tightened against the belt. Not a bullet into his brain, he thought, but a pistol-whipping. The gun smashed into his head again – the man was using the pistol like a club, hammering him with the heavy grip. *God, the pain.* More blows rained onto his skull, each one threatening to shatter it like a walnut. His vision closed into a long, dark tunnel as consciousness slipped away. Another blow, this time to his forehead. He felt the skin splitting open like a laddered stocking, the numb sting as air met blood.

A final blow to the back of his head, and everything went black.

Kat liked to cook, although she didn't own a single cookbook and had little interest in learning new recipes. To her, the pleasure lay in doing what she'd done a thousand times before; processes learnt as a child in her mother's kitchen, requiring absolutely no thought. To make duck *ragù* she first sliced an onion, softened it for five minutes in oil while she chopped the duck giblets and liver, and then, while those were frying too, chopped the rest of the duck. A glass of red wine was added to the sauce and allowed to evaporate. Meanwhile she boiled water for the *bigoli*, the fat tubes of buckwheat-and-duck-egg pasta that are to Venetian cuisine what spaghetti is to the South. Finally, a couple of bay leaves and some chopped tomatoes went into the sauce. Then she washed two lovely whole radicchio from the neighbouring town of Treviso marbled with red veins and perfect at this time of year, and put them to one side, ready to sauté as soon as Aldo arrived.

She wasn't surprised that he was late, and in any case the *ragù* would only improve with more simmering. She opened a bottle of Valpolicella, a nice *ripasso*, hearty enough to pair with the duck but not as overwhelmingly heavy as the more traditional Amarone, and poured herself a glass.

While she was waiting she booted up her laptop. And then, because she thought it would amuse him when he arrived, she went to Carnivia and typed in his name.

Aldo Piola, Colonnello di Carabinieri, Venezia – three entries.

"Only three?" she said out loud. "Aldo, you disappoint me." She clicked again, and stopped short.

Aldo Piola. The word is that he had an affair with Augusta Baresi.

Aldo Piola. Currently pursuing the forensic technician, Gerardina Rossi...

Aldo Piola. So, have he and Alida Conti slept together yet? There's certainly been a lot of flirting going on...

Kat stared at the entries. Two of the names meant nothing to her, but she knew and liked Gerardina, a dark-haired, pretty forensic technician. Piola had worked a case with her, over a year ago.

She'd known about his wife, of course, but this was different. Somehow, discovering that she wasn't his first affair disturbed her.

No, admit it, she thought to herself. *Be honest.*

It hurts.

She tried to analyse why she felt this way. Surely it was crazy to be jealous of previous lovers, but not of the wife he went home to every evening? She'd be outraged if a man got upset about her own former partners. So why did these past affairs, or possible past affairs, make any difference?

Because, she realised ruefully, she'd been flattered to think that his feelings for her were so overwhelming that he'd broken his marriage vows for her sake, and hers alone. She'd known absolutely that what they had wasn't a *fling* or a *liaison* or any of those other casual, throwaway words. Not that she'd expected it to be permanent – far from it – but it was somehow a thing apart, bound up with the incredible intensity of the murder investigation.

She'd read somewhere that in the armies of Ancient Greece and Sparta, a male fighter took a younger warrior to be his lover for the duration of the campaign. The two would train together, sleep together, fight together, and ultimately die together. In some strange way, her relationship with Piola felt more like that than an *affair.*

"Fuck you, Aldo," she said aloud.

She'd told herself that she wasn't going to look up what other people had said about *her* on Carnivia. But now, a little bitter, and with the wine making her reckless, she did.

Katerina Tapo – nine entries.

She clicked.

Are you sure?

Yes.

They'd left him his car keys, at least. He could only have been unconscious for a few minutes – he could see light bouncing off to his right, as the gunman's motorbike careered away over the rough ground.

He felt for his phone. Also still there. So he could call for an ambulance. Or go straight to the Ospedale dell'Angelo, less than twenty minutes away. He knew he shouldn't really drive with possible concussion, but he was damned if he was going to sit and wait for some paramedic to tell him so.

He started the engine. The cut on his temple was bleeding into his right eye, so he angled his head to one side. That was better.

He drove up to the main road and turned left, away from the hospital, in the direction of Kat's apartment.

She read the entries with a mixture of horror and detachment. *So this is what people think of me.*

"Slut" figured more than once, as did "manipulative", "ambitious", "self-centred" and "bitch".

Prick tease... Has all the men wrapped round her little finger... Led me on... Thinks she's something special...

And one that almost made her smile:

I thought she was way too hot for a travel agent.

Then there were the ones like:

Called her back three times, she never answered.
Lousy lay anyway, didn't even want to see her again.

You didn't need to be a detective to spot the inconsistency in *that*.

What came across with horrible clarity was the way people resented her. Women resented her because men were attracted to her. Men who were attracted to her resented her because she hadn't slept with them. Men she *had* slept with resented her because she hadn't called them back for a second date.

Once, when she was at the Training Academy, she'd seen something similar about herself written on a cubicle wall in the toilets. For days she'd been miserable. She'd even tried being extra nice to everyone, in an effort to make herself more liked. All that happened was that she despised herself. And finally, after a few days, she'd thought, *Oh, fuck it.*

What am I meant to do? How am I meant *to behave?*

Whatever people thought, she never used her looks to get favours or promotions. OK, so maybe asking Francesco Lotti, who clearly had a soft spot for her, to swing her a homicide allocation could be construed as taking advantage. But what was the alternative? Stop trying to get ahead, just because she looked a certain way?

Irritably, she pushed the thought aside. She looked a little further down the list of entries. It was all pretty much the same, a litany of bitchiness and envy mixed with a few names. Nothing that actually mattered.

Apart from the last one.

> Kat Tapo. How long before suave Colonel Piola falls for her charms? They've been seen enjoying late night risotti at the Osteria San Zaccaria on more than one occasion. I don't suppose his wife and kids have seen much of him recently...

Her blood ran cold. That changed everything. If the anonymous gossips were this vile about men she'd had casual hookups with, imagine what they'd make of an affair with her boss.

The doorbell rang.

As she stood up she looked at her kitchen with fresh eyes. The duck *ragù* simmering on the stove. The pan of water waiting for the *bigoli*. The sauté pan ready with its little pool of golden-green olive oil for the radicchio. *How sad is this?*

She decided that the only sensible course was to break it off. Tonight, while her resolve was still strong. They'd have the talk, and then it would be over.

The doorbell rang again.

She composed her features into the neutral expression appropriate for someone about to end a relationship and opened the door.

He fell inside. "Oh my God," she gasped, all her thoughts immediately forgotten. "What happened?"

"Gunman," he croaked. He touched his throat. "Can't talk."

"I'll get some grappa."

She got him a glass of grape spirit and went to run hot water for his cuts. "Come here. And lie down."

He wouldn't lie down, but she got him into a chair so she could sponge his temple. "What have they done to you?" she whispered, horrified.

He closed his eyes. "Nothing much. I'll live."

"Nothing much!" A thought struck her. "You *are* going to report it, aren't you? Get forensics to examine your car, have a proper investigation..."

He shook his head.

"You're crazy! Why not?"

"Because I was on my way here," he said quietly. "How could I explain that, without people finding out about us?"

She hesitated. It was her cue, she knew. She would never have a better opening. *Aldo, they're already starting to gossip. We need to talk...*

She said nothing. She knew, in that moment, that she didn't want this to end. Some day, yes, but not here. Not now.

His bloodshot eyes opened, looked up at hers.

"Kat, I'm falling in love with you," he said wearily, as if he was breaking the worst news in the world; as if he wished it wasn't so.

Thirty-seven

AVVOCATO MARCELLO LOOKED appalled. His eyes kept straying, with a kind of horrified fascination, to Piola's face, now sporting a number of livid red-black bruises. Once Kat thought she saw the prosecutor actually flinch, as if imagining the pistol smashing into his own smooth-skinned, well-shaven face.

"And those were the only words he said? 'You should keep your nose out of other people's business,'" he persisted. "You're sure?"

Piola nodded. "Quite sure."

Marcello's expression attempted sympathy and alarm at the same time. "This is terrible," he said for the third or fourth time. "Truly terrible."

It wasn't clear, Kat reflected, whether he meant specifically terrible for Piola, or for anyone tangentially attached to the investigation.

"And do you have any idea," the prosecutor continued, "why this might have happened?"

Piola passed over a copy of Mareta's disc.

"You want me to watch this?" Marcello said nervously.

"Please."

Marcello managed about two minutes before reaching out to eject it from his computer. "Terrible," he repeated, as if in shock.

"The link to organised crime is now incontrovertible."

"Indeed." Marcello picked up an old-fashioned-looking fountain pen and rolled it back and forth anxiously in his fingers, as a man might toy with a cigar he isn't allowed to smoke until later. "And you had the disc why?" he asked after a few moments.

"Mareta Castiglione chose to give it to the Carabinieri, rather than the Polizia di Stato," Piola said. He didn't think it worth antagonising the prosecutor by mentioning that he'd shaken Mareta down to get it.

Kat found herself looking at the pen in Avvocato Marcello's hand. It was an Aurora, the oldest and most prestigious Milanese pen makers. The best ones cost up to a thousand euros.

"So in a sense," Marcello said thoughtfully, "the gunman was right."

"Sir?" Piola said, clearly surprised.

"I don't mean to criticise, Colonel, or to make light of your injuries. But the proper course of action would have been to pass the film, and the person who gave it to you, straight on to the *commissario* with responsibility for investigating the organised crime aspects of this case."

Piola said nothing.

Marcello kept building on his riff. "Indeed, this unfortunate affair illustrates precisely the dangers of not following such a course. An investigation into organised crime requires special measures to protect the safety of the investigators. It becomes almost foolhardy, in a sense, to try to follow such leads without proper precautions."

"Sir," Piola said. "If I may... We think we've lifted the stone on a major pipeline out of Eastern Europe—"

"Exactly," Marcello said, nodding. "Organised crime. It

should be handed over to the Polizia in the first instance, and then to the proper international authorities."

"We believe the girl in the film is an Eastern European, forced into prostitution in Italy against her will. Before they died, Jelena Babić and Barbara Holton were seen questioning Eastern European prostitutes around Stazione Santa Lucia. They were looking for a particular girl, a Croatian. Their deaths and the organised crime aspect of this case are inseparable." Piola stopped, aware that he was starting to raise his voice.

Marcello barely glanced at him. "I'm just not sure your investigation is going to tell us very much more, Colonnello. You don't know who the girl in the video is, or who the girl the two women were seeking was, or even why they were looking for her in the first place. And while of course I'm glad you've dropped the ridiculous suggestion that the United States Army was somehow implicated in the murders, it does seem that we've come to the end of the line as far as collecting evidence is concerned."

Piola sighed. "At least let us try to resolve why the murder victims were talking to the prostitutes."

Marcello considered. "Very well," he conceded. "I suppose that is still a valid line of enquiry. But I'm going to set a time limit on it. Let's say three days. After that, we'll agree that Barbara Holton and Jelena Babić were two foolish foreigners, killed by Ricci Castiglione when they trespassed on a derelict island where he was carrying out criminal activities. There are plenty of other cases far more worthy of your attention, Colonel." He glanced at Kat. "Many of which would offer the *capitano* here far greater opportunities to display her talents. None of us wants to get bogged down in something murky and ultimately unproductive, do we?"

His words were addressed to Piola, but his eyes remained on Kat, so it was she who eventually broke the silence that ensued. "Indeed, sir."

Marcello nodded. "Well, thank you both for coming."

When they had gone, Marcello swivelled his chair towards the window and thought some more, rolling the Aurora in his fingers, taking pleasure from the weight of the fat, cold metal.

Then, with a sigh, he lifted his desk phone and dialled a number.

"Sir?" he said respectfully. "You asked to be kept informed of progress on the Poveglia investigation... Of course. There have been some developments, but nothing I think to be alarmed about."

He spoke for three more minutes, then put down the phone.

Thirty-eight

"I WON'T GIVE UP."

"I know you won't."

They were in bed, the two of them, their noses almost touching. Lying under him like this, Kat could see every pore and laughter line around his eyes, like some rough landscape marked by watercourses. And above it, the bruised and scabbed crater of his wound.

"They'll have to drag me off this case. Until then, I follow the evidence. And fuck Marcello."

Aldo might be zealous when it came to refusing favours and attempts at petty corruption, but he had an exhilarating disregard for commands from his superiors, however clear-cut. He also had an ability – one she'd not come across in other men she'd slept with – to slow his lovemaking temporarily in order to talk about whatever was on his mind, as he was doing now. She found she rather liked these conversational intermissions, with him inside her but not quite motionless; pleasure deferred but balanced with another kind of intimacy, the physical and the verbal in temporary equilibrium.

She resisted the urge to say that it wasn't Avvocato Marcello he should fuck right now. Instead she said, "Be careful, won't you?"

"The more evidence we have, the safer we'll be. They want to frighten us, that's all. But yes, I'll be careful."

She kissed him and he started to move, rocking her gently.

Suddenly she knew that she didn't care about the other affairs. She didn't care about the wife. She'd rather have a small part of Aldo Piola than all of some shallow ambitious boy her own age.

"I love you," she said. It felt like jumping off a cliff, like the first time they kissed. "Aldo, I love you."

"I love you, *sir*," he joked. And then, "Kat, I love you too."

Thirty-nine

HOLLY SAT IN a quiet corner of the Ederle Inn bar, nursing a glass of Californian chardonnay. Despite the fact that Camp Ederle was surrounded by vineyards – the Veneto being one of the biggest wine-producing areas of Italy – even the beverages were imported from the US.

Since her encounter with Second Lieutenant Jonny Wright, she'd avoided the busier bars on base. Not that she was avoiding Wright himself, not exactly. She'd checked: his unit would be shipping back to Pendleton within a couple of weeks. In the meantime, she had plenty of other stuff to think about.

Like how she was going to find any proof of the theory that between the 1st and the 4th of July 1993, a group of renegade NATO officers had met with a Croatian general at Camp Ederle, to plan exactly how to draw NATO into a brutal new conflict.

More than anything else, she needed names. It was frustrating that Ederle's guardhouse records had been destroyed in a warehouse fire. Once, she would have scoffed at any suggestion that the fire and Dragan Korovik's trial were somehow connected. Now, she couldn't help wondering if the moment Korovik was arrested, someone had given orders that any evidence linking his activities to the US should be found and erased. She had a horrible feeling that if so, the clean-up had been all too successful, and she and Gilroy were just a few weeks too late.

"Can I buy you another one of those?"

She looked up warily. The speaker was a young captain with a staff officer's insignia on his lapel. He seemed innocuous enough, but even so she hesitated.

"I'm still on US time, and I fly straight back tomorrow," he added. "Don't think I'm going to get much in the way of sleep tonight." He extended his hand. "Tom Haslam."

"Pleased to meet you, Tom. I was just going, but..."

"Maybe one more?"

He seemed pleasant and a little lonely, so she nodded. "Why not?"

He tapped the edge of his credit card on the bar to get the Italian barman's attention. "*Due bicchieri di vino bianco, per favore.*" His Italian was terrible, but she liked that he'd bothered to try. It was a rare courtesy here.

"Room number?" the barman asked in English.

"Seventeen."

The barman, whose name was Christofero, checked his computer. "You don't have a tab yet. I'll need your passport or military ID, please."

Haslam frowned, patting his pockets. "I left my ID in my room."

"Let me get these," she offered.

"No, I'll go get it. Jeez, the hoops they make you jump through just to get a drink," he grumbled, turning towards the door. "It's not like they don't know who I am – I practically had to send them my life history just to get a room."

She wasn't listening. She was staring at the bartender, struck by a sudden thought.

"Christofero, when was the Ederle Inn constructed?"

He shrugged. "About twenty years ago, I guess. I've been here ten years, and Massimo was here before I was."

"Do you always ask for ID before you set up a room tab?"

"Of course. That's the system."

"Why?"

He shrugged again. His job was to put out pretzels and pour beers, not to question military bureaucracy.

"And can you search the bar bills by date?"

"*Si*, I guess so. But why would I want to?"

She got up and went round the bar to inspect the till. It was ancient, like the till computers you saw in bookshops or opticians. If she wasn't mistaken, that wasn't even Windows she was looking at, but old-fashioned keyboard-based DOS.

"Type in a date for me, would you?" she said. She watched his fingers lift over the grimy old keys, waiting.

"Type in July 1st, 1993," she said.

If a group of people were travelling to Camp Ederle for a three-day meeting in the summer of 1993, they'd need accommodation. The Ederle Inn Hotel was the only short-term accommodation on base. And thanks to military bureaucracy, the names and addresses of every person who stayed that night had been meticulously logged against their bar bills.

The rickety old inkjet printer chattered and stuttered as it disgorged them, line by line, from somewhere deep within the depths of the geriatric computer's memory.

Excusing herself from the drink with Tom Haslam – slightly guiltily: she felt she owed him better – Holly took the printout back to her room. There were five Croatian names. Three had military rank – a general, a colonel and a major.

The general was Dragan Korovik. The two Croats without ranks had "Fra" in front of their names.

A quick search of the internet confirmed what she'd immediately suspected: "Fra" meant "Father" in Croatian.

Even so, she stared at her laptop in disbelief. *This wasn't just the military. Somehow, the Church was involved as well.*

Then came a couple of American names without ranks: John R. Jones and Kevin B. Killick. They sounded obviously fake to Holly. Sure enough, their Washington addresses turned out to be non-existent too.

They had to be spooks of some kind.

Colonel Robin Millar, Staff Officer, NATO Supreme Headquarters, Casteau, hadn't troubled to take any such precautions. An apparently gregarious man, he'd stood several large rounds in the bar, and charged them to his room tab.

Could he represent the Gladio network Gilroy had talked about?

She started methodically checking out the other names in the group. Bruce Gould, Senior Vice President, MCI, Virginia. Another quick search revealed that this was a company called Military Capabilities International. According to their website they provided "leadership resources, personnel and executive expertise for communities, companies and nations around the world". The home page was decorated with pictures of smiling ethnic children clustered around armed Americans wearing military fatigues, aviator sunglasses and bad moustaches.

She typed "Croatia" into the site's own search box, and a new page appeared. "MCI provides time-sensitive strategic security services to emerging democracies. Our on-site teams have played vital roles in Kuwait, Nigeria, Iraq and Bosnia/ Croatia." No explanation of what that actually meant, but she was pretty sure MCI were a quasi-corporate private army, one of several that hoovered up trained servicemen and put them to work in the private sector.

Thomas Hudson from General Atomics Aeronautical in California – she soon established that their main interest was the manufacture of Predator drones. Stewart Portas, from Portas Public Relations in New York. Antonino Giuffrè, no address given. Intellipedia had nothing on him, but according to Wikipedia, someone of that name was currently serving a ten-year prison sentence in Italy for organised crime.

The Church, NATO, arms manufacturers... and now the mob.

Dr Paul Doherty, whose address was listed as Department of Psychiatry and Behavioral Sciences, Stanford University.

They even had a psychiatrist on board.

She went over to the Liaison Office and raided the stationery cupboard for supplies – Post-it notes, marker pens in three different colours, a flipchart pad. Lugging them up to her room, she took down the bland print of the Grand Canyon that hung on one wall and started constructing a spider chart, mapping the connections between the various institutions with arrows and dotted lines.

She had thirteen names, but Robin Millar had stood drinks for sixteen people. That meant there were at least three attendees who hadn't needed to book accommodation. Either they were already on base, or they lived near enough not to have to stay the night. She took three Post-its, put question marks on each of them for now, and stuck them to one side.

Next to each person she had a name for she added details of what that person was doing now. Several had become senior executives of their companies. Robin Millar, she discovered, was currently working for MCI. Dragan Korovik, of course, was in a prison cell in The Hague, but the other Croatians appeared to have important positions in the new government, or, in the case of the priests, the diocese – one was credited with having organised the Pope's visit in 2011.

A link man between the Croatian Catholic Church and the Vatican.

According to newspaper articles she found on the internet, when the Communists first took control of Croatia, the Croatian Church managed to get all its gold and cash reserves out of the country and into the Vatican bank, where the money had stayed, accumulating interest, for over fifty years. The Vatican had never made any secret of the fact that it regarded those funds as earmarked for re-establishing Croatia as a Catholic nation.

Under the Post-it marked "Vatican" she added "The money?".

Standing back, she realised there was one name that still had no details attached to it. She'd established that Dr Paul Doherty had left Stanford in 1995, aged twenty-seven; after that, she could find absolutely nothing about him. Which was odd – a young academic, if he was regularly publishing his work, should be easy enough to track down.

Wondering if he could have been whisked off into some obscure Pentagon research department, she tried Intellipedia and the even more restricted SIPRNet. Still nothing.

Going back to the regular internet, she switched from Google to a number of other, less well-known search engines – Bing, Blekko, Slikk and Sphider. Lastly, she tried a program called Resurrection, which trawled through the internet's "dark pages" – cached material from long-defunct search engines such as Lycos and Magellan that no longer corresponded to any existing sites.

Gotcha.

The material she found was dated from 1992, and appeared to come from an obscure academic journal, *The Journal of Behavioral Science.* When a journal like that published a paper, she knew, it first put out a short précis or abstract so people could decide if they wanted to read the whole thing. She had found the abstract for the only paper Paul Doherty had ever published.

Of the article itself there was still no sign, but what she read in the abstract was enough to have her reaching for a memory stick.

It was time to share what she'd learnt with Ian Gilroy.

Forty

THEY FOLLOWED THEIR orders. They went out amongst the prostitutes and the drug addicts of Santa Lucia and showed them the photographs. Barbara, Jelena, and the unnamed young woman who looked Croatian. They even showed a picture of Ricci Castiglione, in the days before the crabs had feasted on his eyes.

Because even with his damaged face Aldo looked like a policeman, it was Kat who went into the seediest bars, the taxi-cab offices and the backstreet poker games where Italian was rarely heard. Sometimes she dressed like a whore, to get past the owners. Sometimes she arrested the pimps before bringing their girls in for a quiet chat.

She always told the women there was a way out, an outreach programme or a refuge where they'd be safe. She'd said it so often, and been disbelieved so many times, that now she barely believed it herself.

Piola had been right when he'd said that crime had taken over Venice. It was like a parasite, the sort that feeds on its host and weakens it without ever quite killing it. It slid its tentacles under doors and through windows, along canals and beneath the grand palaces. It was a sea monster wrapped around the city, sharing its life blood, feeding off its nutrients. Most of the time it was invisible, but if you knew how to see it, it was there. It was there in the way the girls and their pimps were never more than a hundred yards from a hotel where they could take their punters, no questions asked. It was there in the nods between the boatmen, the weary smiles of waiters thanking diners for a tip they'd never get to keep.

Marcello's three-day deadline came and went, and still the two of them immersed themselves in the filth of Venice, in the dark fetid waters that had been getting slowly darker and more fetid for centuries.

And, finally, they found Bob Findlater.

Or, strictly speaking, Bob Findlater found them. A courteous phone call to Campo San Zaccaria, asking for an appointment "as soon as was practicable". There were some difficulties because he spoke very little Italian. Piola's English wasn't great, but Kat was fairly fluent. They had a translator on standby, just in case.

He came in with no lawyer, just his passport and an apologetic smile.

"My name is Robert Findlater," he began. "Though people call me Bob. I'm an American citizen, and I believe I can explain why Barbara Holton and Jelena Babić were killed."

He was a tall man, quite broad, in his early forties, crew-cut. When he took off his jacket, his biceps bulged against an expensive T-shirt.

He placed an A4 photograph on the table. It showed a dark-haired girl of about seventeen or eighteen. It was the same photograph Kat had been touting round the bars of Santa Lucia.

"This is my daughter," he said. "Melina Kovačević. She's missing."

"Go on," Kat said.

He hesitated. "It's quite a lengthy story."

"That's OK. Just tell us in your own words."

That was the way it worked with questioning: the first time you let them get it all out, without interrupting. The second time, you took them back over it, asking for more details, probing and challenging. Then you went through it one more time, making sure you'd understood, that there was nothing else the interviewee could add.

If there was a fourth time, it was because you thought they were lying.

"I spent eight years in the military," he began. "Fought in the Gulf War, was just about to get out in 1990 when I had the chance of an assignment to UNPROFOR – that's the United Nations Protection Force. We were the first peacekeeping unit to go into Krajina. These days, of course, it's in Croatia, but back then it was part of what had been known as Yugoslavia."

It was, he said, an extraordinary period. Despite having seen action in Iraq, nothing could have prepared him for the barbarity of Yugoslavia's civil war.

"People were bayoneting their neighbours, then torching their houses. The Serbs had set up concentration camps and were rounding up anyone they didn't like the look of. Both sides were preaching ethnic hatred from their pulpits. The men were torn between going off to join one of the liberation armies, or staying to protect their families. No one had any food, but everyone seemed to have weapons and explosives."

The UN had designated a number of safe-haven enclaves in Krajina, he said, enforced by peacekeepers. "Problem was, we weren't allowed to open fire unless our own safety was threatened. The locals soon realised they could pretty much do whatever they wanted to each other, and there wasn't a whole lot we could do about it."

One day his unit was tasked to evacuate civilians from an area that was coming under heavy bombardment. "And that's where I found Soraya – Melina's mom. She was hiding in a cellar, covered in dirt and dust, but I could see straight away how beautiful she was. She was a Bosniak – a Muslim Bosnian, the only grouping with no army to back them up. It was a miracle she'd survived so long, really. I told her she could come back to our base to clean up, but really I knew it was the only place she'd be safe. And things just started from there."

"What sort of relationship did it become?" Kat asked. "Were you married?"

Bob Findlater looked rueful. "I was, at the time. But not to Soraya. I didn't even know we'd had a child together until after I'd gone back home. A neighbour who knew I cared for Soraya wrote me to say she'd had a baby girl. I wrote back, but I never heard anything."

Eventually his marriage broke up. Childless, he then decided to try and track Soraya and Melina down.

"Turned out Soraya had died towards the end of the war, and Melina was brought up in an orphanage. Well, of course that just made me even more determined to find her. She'd be almost eighteen by now – not too late to go to college. I thought I could offer to pay for that." He took a breath. "Then I found out she came to Italy to work as a nanny."

Piola and Kat exchanged glances.

Findlater nodded. "I realised fairly quickly that if you try to enter this country illegally, you pass through the hands of some pretty unpleasant characters. It's my belief she was forced into prostitution instead."

"So you're still looking for her?"

"Not personally – my Italian's patchy, as I said. No, I found some good people and paid them to do the job for me."

"That would be Barbara Holton and Jelena Babić?"

"That's right. Barbara ran a small organisation that had been doing good work in Croatia, reuniting victims of the war with their families. I found her online, did some background checks. She seemed very competent. I knew she'd be able to do a better job than I had, and it tied in with her own work on the long-term consequences of war.

"She recruited a friend from Croatia to help – that was Jelena, of course. To begin with I tried to tag along, but I soon realised they were more effective on their own, so I went back to the US for the Christmas holidays and left them to it. It was only when I checked into their hotel yesterday that I heard the terrible news from the desk clerk."

Kat thought hard. It all made sense, but the first rule was to look for whatever could be corroborated or verified and double-check it. With both Barbara and Jelena dead, that might be difficult. "How did you pay them?"

"In cash, initially. Two thousand dollars, plus a thousand for expenses, with another three thousand to come if they found her."

Kat saw Piola make a note. There hadn't been any cash in the women's hotel room, but then again, the killer might have stolen it.

"Did she give you a receipt?"

"Yes. But I'm sorry to say I haven't kept it."

"How did you contact Barbara when you needed to speak to her?" The numbers retrieved from the woman's European cell phone had mostly been of local shops and bars.

"By email, mainly."

"Do you still have the emails?"

"Some – the ones that are stored on my laptop."

"What about the letter from the neighbour saying you had a daughter? Do you have that?"

"Sure, back home."

"And your UNPROFOR documentation?"

"Likewise."

Piola said, "We found a lock of hair in the hotel room Jelena and Barbara were sharing. Do you know anything about that?"

For the first time Bob Findlater looked puzzled. "I guess they must have taken hair from one of Melina's relatives," he said slowly. "To match the DNA, in case there was any doubt when they found her."

"They didn't tell you?"

Findlater shook his head. "As I said, I left that side of things to Barbara. Maybe that was naive of me."

"What do you mean?"

"Before I left, I saw how fearless the two of them were – questioning prostitutes and pimps, getting physically threatened but never taking no for an answer. I assume that's why they were killed."

Neither Kat nor Piola responded.

"Well?" he said. "That *is* the most likely explanation, isn't it?"

"It's one possibility," Kat said at last. "At the moment we're not ruling anything out."

"Have you considered," Piola said carefully, "that the child may not be yours? The UN peacekeeping mission was, as I recall, ultimately unsuccessful. The war escalated, and many of the Bosniaks were driven out of Krajina. Life for civilians was... difficult. Particularly for the women."

"You mean Soraya might have been raped?" Findlater shook his head. "From what I know of the timings, that doesn't seem possible. But even if it turns out that Melina isn't my natural daughter, she's definitely Soraya's. If I wasn't there to protect Soraya, and the worst *did* happen, Melina's doubly my responsibility."

"Melina's fortunate that you're wealthy enough to take on a dependent," Kat said. "What do you do, incidentally?"

"After I left the army, I went to work for a private contractor. We provide security and training packages to multi-national companies, that kind of thing. I do all right."

They ran over the interview one more time. Bob Findlater was completely consistent in his answers.

"We'll need you to stay in Venice for a week or so," Kat said at last. "We may have some more questions."

"No problem. It'll give me a chance to keep looking for Melina."

"I'm not sure that's a good idea."

"Don't worry. I can take care of myself."

"I thought the same," Piola said. "The one who got me had a gun."

Findlater stared at Piola, only now connecting the colonel's ravaged face with his own situation. "Jeez. These guys mean business, huh?"

"It appears so. You must assure us that you won't continue looking for your daughter. It may not be safe."

Findlater nodded reluctantly. "I guess."

"The fact is," Kat added, "we don't even have any reason to believe she's still in Venice. If events happened as you suggest, the traffickers would almost certainly have moved her on after they'd killed Barbara and Jelena."

The American sighed. "That's what I figured. It's just hard to give up, you know?"

"We'll take a DNA sample from you, just in case. That way if we do find her, we'll be able to link her to you immediately." Kat took a disposable swab kit out of the drawer and pulled on the gloves. "I'm sure you're familiar with these. We just need to rub this bud round the inside of your mouth."

Findlater hesitated. "Will it really help? As you said, she may not even be my biological daughter."

"It'll speed things up if she is, though."

He leant forward so that Kat could rub the swab around the inside of his mouth. As she did so, her face only inches from his, she became aware that his blue eyes were locked intently on hers. Disturbed, she forced herself to concentrate on what she was doing.

As she put the bud into the paper sleeve and sealed it, he gave her the ghost of a smile. *He fancies me*, she thought.

"Thanks," she said, peeling off the gloves and extending her hand formally to shake his. "We'll be in touch, Mr Findlater."

"Amazing," Piola said when the American had gone.

"Extraordinary," she agreed.

"After all this time, we finally have answers to almost every question we've been asking ourselves. It all fits. The photograph, the hair..."

"What about the approach Barbara Holton made to the Americans at Caserma Ederle?" she objected.

Piola shrugged. "As he said, finding Melina tied in with Barbara's own work."

There was a long silence as both of them thought through

the interview, looking for inconsistencies.

"It can be hard, sometimes," Piola said slowly, "when the correct answer finally presents itself, to acknowledge that it *is* the correct answer. Psychologically, I mean. When there have been so many false positives, it's easy to treat a breakthrough as just another one."

She nodded.

"On the other hand," he added, "we have to be sceptical. It's our job."

She looked at him. "You don't believe him either, do you?"

"Something's not right," Piola said. He got to his feet, unable to sit still any longer. "I don't know what it is. But somewhere in all that Disney-movie crap about his long-lost daughter and how he just wants to change her life, there's a nasty little lie. I'm sure of it."

"It's the lack of phone records that bothers me. If Barbara was working for him, why isn't there some kind of evidence trail? The only thing that definitely links them is that we know some of the prostitutes reported an American man asking questions about a Croatian girl."

"We should show his picture to some of them. His passport photo will do – we can get that off the immigration guys at the Guardia di Finanza. And while we're at it, let's check he really left and entered the country when he said he did."

She nodded. "I'll take care of it."

"Did you notice," he said thoughtfully, "that he was a little strange about having his DNA taken?"

She blushed.

"Oh," Piola said. "I see." He rubbed his jaw. "Although I don't, actually. I mean, certainly, a beautiful woman swabbing the inside of your mouth isn't something that happens every day. But it started before that, when you first told him you'd need DNA. He seemed... angry, somehow."

"Why might that be?"

"I don't know. But there have been cases where a killer involves himself in a murder investigation, apparently just as a witness to help the police, only for his DNA to trip him up."

"We don't have DNA from the crime scene, though."

"No," Piola agreed. "But he may not know that." He sighed. "You know, Avvocato Marcello is going to love this. Every last loose end tied neatly into a bow. It'll all be handed over to Interpol and the organised crime team before the ink's dry on our reports."

"OK," she said. "Let's hypothesise for a minute. Say Findlater *isn't* telling the whole truth. Where does that take us?"

"It means..." Piola said. He took a breath. "It means this is even bigger than we thought. It means that whatever or whoever we're on the trail of, they're the kind of people who can whistle up a plausible ex-military American with solutions to all our questions any time they want to."

"More than that," she said. "It means they know what the questions *are*. They know where we've got to with the investigation."

"Marcello?"

"Who else?"

There was another long silence.

"So," he said at last. "Just suppose we were foolhardy enough to continue investigating in the face of possible corruption from our own side, Mafia death threats and American ex-soldiers bearing lies. What would we do next?"

She said, "We'd take the fight to them. We'd tell Marcello we don't believe a word of it. Then we'd go back to Findlater and tell him the same. Hell, maybe we even arrest him for the murders. We'd rattle their cages, and wait for them to panic."

Forty-one

HOLLY INTERCEPTED GILROY on his next visit to the Education Centre, following him into his classroom. Shutting the door, she explained what she'd learnt.

"This is remarkable, Holly," he said when she'd finished. "Well done."

She flushed with pleasure.

"There's an old Venetian saying," he added. "'A fish stinks first from the head.' And this stinks plenty. I think you may have just found those responsible for putting together Dragan Korovik's military strategy."

"Not just his military strategy, either." She handed him the abstract. "Read this."

Pulling his glasses out of his shirt pocket, Gilroy read the title aloud. "*From 'God on Our Side' to Genocide: Libidinal Frenzy as a Precursor to Mass Psychosis*. Sounds pretty dry."

"It gets less so, believe me."

He put it on the arm of the chair and read.

Abstract

A number of psychological studies have explored the circumstances in which individuals can be induced to harm others. In *Obedience to Authority: An Experimental View* (1974), Professor Stanley

Milgram describes persuading volunteers to give electric shocks to strangers, merely by using verbal prompts such as "It is absolutely essential that you continue", a process that has come to be known as "moral authorisation".

In the Stanford Prison Experiment (1971), Professor Philip Zimbardo examined the behaviour of twelve students assigned the role of "guards" over twelve "prisoners". The latter were deliberately "dehumanised" by being given numbers instead of names. This experiment was, notoriously, abandoned because of the increasingly sadistic behaviour of the "guards".

This paper looks at a number of twentieth-century conflicts in which extreme acts of violence have taken place. In addition to "moral authorisation" and "dehumanisation", it identifies a number of other possible precursors to violence. These include "ethnic otherness", "historical inevitability", "blaming the victim" and "collective paranoia".

The author uses Freud's concept of "libidinal frenzy" to describe how a combination of such factors may induce a kind of mass psychosis in which whole populations can only be satisfied by each other's extermination.

Keywords: collective psychosis, crimes against humanity, mass rape, religious hatred.

"My God," Gilroy breathed. "It's like he's describing a step-by-step guide to creating a genocide."

"Exactly."

"And the full paper?"

"Even more curious. Usually you can get hold of academic papers pretty easily – that's what the internet was originally built for, after all. But when you enter these details into a service such as PubMed, it comes back with 'No results found'. Doherty's article is never cited, never referred to by other psychiatrists, never linked to... Either it wasn't published after all, or it was somehow redacted – erased from the collective memory of every search engine and website on the net."

Gilroy thought a moment. "So," he said at last. "What do we do with this remarkable trove of information, Holly Boland?"

"I was hoping you might have some ideas on that."

"Who else knows about this?"

"No one."

"Let's keep it that way for now. I need to think it through."

She opened her mouth, then closed it again. Noticing, he said, "Yes, Holly?"

"Is it possible this was all a perfectly legitimate psy-ops operation? After all, destabilising foreign countries is hardly new territory for the US. We did it in Nicaragua, in Panama, Iraq..."

"Sure. But in those countries we were either legitimately at war, or had presidential approval. And anyone stoking a conflict in the Balkans was doing it in the face of a United Nations resolution that actively forbade other states from getting involved. No, it seems to me that when you put all this together, you've got a kind of ad-hoc coalition of vested interests – private military, arms manufacturers, rogue NATO officers, even the Mafia – all working together to make sure the powder keg ignited."

"The thing I still can't get my head round," she said, "is what those priests were doing there."

"Presumably their role was to provide the 'moral authorisation' Doherty talks about. Preaching ethnic hatred in their sermons, and so on."

"But they must have known, if they'd read Doherty's paper, that they'd be helping to tip their country into the most appalling violence."

"Perhaps they thought it was a price worth paying. Or maybe they'd simply convinced themselves that they were doing God's work. If so, it wouldn't be the first time religion has got mixed up with war. Voltaire put it well, Holly: 'To make a man commit atrocities, first make him believe absurdities.'"

Forty-two

"HEY," TRENT WOLFE said. "Daniele, right? I'm Trent, the President of Rocaville, and this is my VP in charge of Mergers and Acquisitions, Jim Khalifi."

Neither man was older than twenty-six, and both were wearing shorts, sandals and faded hoodies. Daniele shook their hands, then took a seat.

They were meeting in the lobby of the Cipriani, one of Venice's finest and grandest old hotels, where the Americans were staying. Daniele wondered whether the Cipriani would try to enforce its notoriously strict dress code – gentlemen eating in the restaurant were expected to wear a tie, even in the humid summer months – or whether the fact that Trent had taken the Palladio Suite, a ten-thousand-dollar-a-night glass box suspended over the lagoon with its own private entrance and launch, had persuaded them to make an exception.

All three ordered Cokes. Trent leant forward. "Listen, Dan, I'm going to jump straight to it. We think what you've done with Carnivia is just great. It's so rare in these asshole marketing-led times to find a site where someone actually cares about the coding, right? Most of the kids we see today are only starting dotcoms in the hope they'll do an IPO by the time they're in college and sell out to Google before they graduate."

He spoke like a veteran from another age – which, in a sense, he was. Back in 2005, Rocaville.com had passed its one-million-user mark in just three months. On the back of that success, Trent Wolfe had gone around the world buying up internet businesses with a keen eye for what would be successful, and an almost total disregard for stock market valuations.

"I never thought of Carnivia as a dotcom, actually," Daniele said. "More as a kind of experiment."

"Exactly." Trent pointed the straw of his Coke at him. "Which is why it doesn't make money. Carnivia has *integrity*. That's why I flew over. The way I see it, this is your hour of need."

Daniele nodded.

"The bottom line is, we'll give you help in whatever form you want it. We'll invest in Carnivia outright or a chunk of it – minority or majority share, that's your call. Or we'll put you on the payroll and pay your legal bills."

"That's very generous," Daniele said.

Trent smiled. "I just think us 2.0 guys should stick together. One day you'll do the same for me."

"To be frank," Daniele added, "I've been expecting this."

"You have?" Trent shot his VP an amazed look. "We didn't even discuss this ourselves until last weekend. We were having a hackathon and someone said, 'What about Carnivia? We need to reach out to those guys.'"

"I meant," Daniele explained, "that I'd been expecting *someone* to make an offer for Carnivia. After all, what's the use of putting pressure on me personally if it doesn't net the site itself? So I assumed that at some point before my sentencing, someone would come along and try to buy it, on terms apparently so generous that I'd be a fool not to accept."

"Not buy. *Invest*," Jim Khalifi murmured. His boss shot him a warning look.

"And because I knew that those making the offer would somehow be linked to those who engineered the false charges against me, I've taken the trouble to investigate your company more thoroughly than perhaps you thought possible," Daniele added.

Trent blinked. "Hey. Everyone knows me. I blog, I tweet... My life's an open book, right?"

"Is it, though?" Daniele said. "For example, everyone knows, or thinks they know, that Rocaville are a bunch of fresh-faced Silicon Valley techies who are currently giving Facebook a run for its money. But how many people know that your three biggest investors are actually defence contractors?"

Trent looked puzzled. "Our seed capital came from gaming companies..."

"Which, if you follow the ownership trail far enough back, turn out to be controlled by arms manufacturers. The US government is the biggest purchaser of high-end 3D graphics systems in the world. Only they call them Visual and Sensor Simulation Training systems. And the defence industry is currently the single biggest investor in high-tech R&D in the US. That cool, funky software company which took a thirty per cent stake in you at start-up, for example, had itself recently been acquired by General Dynamics, the government's biggest cyber warfare contractor. You're a front man for military interests, Trent."

Trent's smile barely slipped. "That's like saying I'm bankrolled by the Kremlin just because some Russian dude's got his pension invested in our stock."

"Without your three biggest investors, you'd be nothing," Daniele said calmly. "I'm betting that a few days ago, you got a call from one of them, setting up a meeting. There probably weren't any last names, just some mumbo-jumbo about national security and how they were giving you a chance to prove that, despite the tattoo and the sandals, you're a loyal American. Am I right?"

There was a long silence.

"If you're so paranoid," Jim Khalifi said suddenly, "why did you agree to meet with us?"

"I want to know who's behind the attacks on me, and why. I don't flatter myself it's for my coding – I may have created the algorithms, but anyone reasonably smart could copy those. I think it's much more likely your friends want access to Carnivia so they can bypass the encryption – in other words, they want to be able to eavesdrop on someone who currently thinks Carnivia is secure. But who?"

"If we're who you say we are, we'd hardly tell you," Trent Wolfe said.

"Perhaps. But my bet is, you're thinking back to your meeting with those guys and wondering if *they* were really who they said they were. There's a big difference between being asked to help your country and betraying your principles for a bunch of arms manufacturers, right?"

There was another long silence.

"Look at MCI," Trent Wolfe said suddenly. "That's all I'm saying. Jesus, Dan, that's all I'm saying and it's way too much."

"Who are MCI?"

"Military Capabilities International. Private armies, government contracts – you name it, they provide it."

"And who's paying them?"

Trent shook his head. "I don't know, I swear, and if I did I wouldn't tell you. These fuckers don't fuck around. As far as they're concerned, this conversation never took place, OK?"

Forty-three

KAT MADE HER way unobtrusively to the front desk of the Hotel Europa. She waited until there were no guests around, then flipped her ID under the clerk's nose. "Remember me?"

Startled, the young man nodded.

"I've got a warrant to look at one of your rooms," she lied calmly. "Only I've left the paperwork back at the station. I'm going to have to examine the room first, and fax the documents to you later."

He frowned. "This would be the room where the murder happened?"

"No. It's the room belonging to a guest. Mr Findlater."

"I need to check with my—"

"No, you don't. I don't care what your company policy is, and I don't have time to deal with your head office. I just need ten minutes in his room, then I'll be out of your hair."

She could see corporate caution battling with the ingrained desire to say yes to a confident-sounding officer of the Carabinieri. After a moment's hesitation, he opened a drawer and pulled out a stack of key cards. A swipe through the machine, some typing on his computer keyboard, and he handed her a card. "Room 244. He's not there."

As she walked to the lift she checked she had phone signal. Piola would text if she needed to get out quickly, although she was confident that wasn't likely. Findlater had been asked back to Campo San Zaccaria with the emails between him and Barbara Holton he'd referred to. Piola would keep him busy for at least forty minutes.

They'd debated the merits of this excursion late into the night. Obviously, any evidence Kat found without a search warrant would be inadmissible. Even if she found something, and somehow managed to get a warrant after the event, it was a high-risk strategy – if it became known she'd already been into the room, it would discredit not only the evidence, but potentially the whole investigation.

So this was purely a fishing expedition, to see if their hunch was correct; a prelude to announcing to Prosecutor Marcello that they didn't believe Findlater's story.

The maid hadn't cleaned Room 244 yet – there was a breakfast tray outside, waiting to be collected, and a "Do Not Disturb" card over the door handle. That was curious, Kat thought, since Findlater wasn't inside. Just in case, she knocked. No answer.

She pushed the card into the lock and waited for the light to go green. Checking the corridor one last time to make sure no one was watching, she slipped inside.

The bed was already neatly made. The reflexes of a career in the military, no doubt – that part of his story had undoubtedly been true. Beside the bed, a canvas holdall sat on a trestle. Inside were some casual but expensive clothes: T-shirts, polo shirts and chinos, all neatly folded.

In the bathroom were a few toiletries. By the bed, a bottle of water. There were no books, she noticed: no personal items of any sort, only an empty laptop sleeve and an ID card from a company called Military Capabilities International in the name of Robert Findlater. Dirty laundry was already stowed neatly in a hotel laundry bag. The room was so bare, it was almost as if it hadn't been occupied at all.

Or, she thought, as if it had been carefully tidied in readiness for just such an inspection.

Under the window was a small desk. Its surface was also bare, except for a sheaf of paper slips weighed down by another water bottle. She moved the bottle and examined them. They were his receipts – simple meals in cafés, a *panino* at the airport, room service dockets, an ATM slip for five hundred euros. Since landing at Marco Polo two days before, Bob Findlater appeared to have done nothing more untoward than have the occasional beer.

Accepting that she'd drawn a blank, she headed for the door. As she reached it, she heard voices in the corridor beyond – a male guest wishing the maid a cheery "*Arrivederci*" as he departed.

She drew back, waiting. The man's footsteps, and the squeak of his luggage wheels, passed down the corridor. She heard a "ping" as the lift arrived.

That was when she noticed a bent toothpick lying on the carpet, just inside the door.

She retraced her steps. In the bathroom she found another toothpick, similarly bent, also just inside the door.

"Shit," she said under her breath, recalling the "Do Not Disturb" sign. Not knowing exactly where in the door jamb he'd placed the toothpicks, there was no way she could now disguise from Bob Findlater the fact that his room had been searched.

Back at Campo San Zaccaria, she met up with a gloomy Piola.

"His emails checked out," he said. "That is, he *appears* to have sent about a dozen messages to Barbara Holton, and she *appears* to have replied with updates on the progress she and Jelena were making in tracking down his darling daughter. How did you get on?"

She told him about the toothpicks.

"It's not illegal to want to know if your room's been searched," he pointed out. "After all, it was us who told him to be extra careful. Nothing else?"

"Actually, there was one thing," she said slowly.

"What?"

"It's a tiny detail – in fact, I didn't think anything of it at the time. But I found a pile of receipts in his room."

"And?"

"Don't you think that's curious? If a man goes looking for his long-lost daughter, why would he keep the receipts – who would he claim the money back from? In fact, Findlater specifically said that he *didn't* keep Barbara Holton's receipt for the three thousand US he gave her. So why's he keeping a record of his expenses for this trip, unless someone's paying him?" She looked at him. "Findlater's not looking for his daughter at all, Aldo. Or if he is, it's only because someone's told him to."

"Or," he said gently, "he's just a man of habit. Was the bedroom very neat?"

"Extremely," she admitted.

"So he makes a tidy pile of his credit card slips, too. I'm not disagreeing with you, Kat. But it's hardly a smoking gun."

"It's all we've got."

"It's all we've got," he agreed. "So. Time to face Marcello."

*

The meeting with the prosecutor was short and to the point. He was not prepared to listen to any more crazy speculation, whether about Americans, Croatians, priests or anyone else. They were to write up their reports and close down the investigation.

"I don't get it, Colonnello," he said sarcastically. "What is it with this case? Murders are committed in this city all the time. Most are wrapped up within a few days, a few weeks at the most. Why do you want to waste so much time on this particular investigation?" He paused, still looking at Piola, and then, quite deliberately, let his gaze travel across to Kat.

"There must be *something* about this case that's affecting your judgement and causing you to prolong the investigation, Colonel," he continued. "I'm just wondering what it can be."

Kat forced herself not to react, not to flinch or blush under the prosecutor's gaze as he looked from her to Piola and back, one eyebrow raised interrogatively.

After a few moments he nodded, satisfied he'd teased the two of them enough. "Very well. I'll expect your final report in the next few days."

"He doesn't know anything," she said as they left the prosecutor's offices. "He's just trying to rile you."

"I know," Piola said. "Don't worry. I can't be put off so easily."

They walked back to Campo San Zaccaria. It was almost as quick as waiting for a *vaporetto*, so long as one made a detour north of Piazza San Marco, crowded with tourists even at this time of year

"When I went to see Daniele Barbo," she said hesitantly, "he suggested he might be able to get the data off Barbara

Holton's laptop. He's done something similar before, apparently."

"Yes?"

"I said no, of course. But he said the offer would remain open. It strikes me that we've actually got something concrete for him to look for now – we could ask him to establish whether Barbara Holton really sent those emails, or if Findlater was fabricating them."

"Yes, except that giving her machine to a convicted hacker who's awaiting sentencing for breaking internet privacy laws would be an insane thing to do."

"Granted. But it might help..."

"We need evidence we can *use*, Kat. Evidence that will convince people like Marcello. Nothing else is going to get him off our back."

The two of them were the only ones based in the operations room now. It had the feel, Kat admitted to herself, of a case that had long since come to an end.

Her mobile rang. "*Pronto*?"

"Kat, it's Francesco. There's a case Allocation need to assign quickly – a big one. A politician who's strangled a rent boy, says it was an accident but there's evidence the *feno* was blackmailing him. Your name's been suggested."

"Who's in charge?"

"You, if you want it. Your own investigation. The prosecutor asked for you personally."

"Which prosecutor?" she said, although she'd already guessed the answer.

"Avvocato Marcello."

Through the glass wall of Piola's office she watched him pick up a brown envelope that was lying on his desk. He pulled out the contents and looked at them. For a moment he froze. Then his eyes turned towards her.

She knew she would never forget the expression in those eyes – something far worse than horror or despair. "I've got to go," she said into the phone.

"Allocation need an answer—"

"Tell them I'm too busy." She hung up. "What is it?" she called across to Piola.

He didn't reply. She hurried into his office and took the photograph from his hand. The print was grainy – it had been taken at night, with a long lens – but the subject was clear enough.

Piola. And Kat. Entering her apartment, his arm around her. His head was turned towards her. She was laughing.

Just in case there was any doubt, there was a second photo as well. It showed the window of her apartment. She was lowering the blinds. Aldo was also in the shot, behind her, his hand reaching out for her. She was wearing a bathrobe.

There was a note, a sheet of A4 printer paper on which someone had typed the words:

`These have been sent to your wife.`

Forty-four

"THEY MAY NOT have gone through with it," she said. "Perhaps it's just a threat."

He shook his head. "I have to go home. She'll have opened it by now." Carefully he gathered his coat and hung it over his arm.

"What are you going to say to her?"

"I don't know." He sounded dazed.

"Aldo, we have to talk."

"Yes. Later. First I need to go home and talk to my wife."

He left the room like a sleepwalker. "Will you phone me?" she called after him.

He didn't reply.

She looked at the top photo again. It had obviously been taken some time ago, since it showed Piola before he'd been beaten up. So whoever employed the photographer had known about the two of them almost from their first night together – had probably used the knowledge, in fact, to plan Piola's beating and the mock execution.

Her blood ran cold.

And now... she tried to imagine the conversation Piola would be having when he got home. But she couldn't. It was completely outside her experience, never having been in that kind of relationship herself.

She felt like a schoolgirl caught doing something terrible, something so bad that you were simply left alone while the grown-ups went to talk about it amongst themselves.

The wife will blame me, she thought. *Of course she will. Because, after all, I am to blame.*

Without even meaning to, she found herself logging onto Carnivia. Under her name it said "fourteen entries".

She clicked on the most recent.

So it's true! The Ice Captain and The Terribly Serious Colonel have been investigating each other! Can't imagine what they talk about in bed!

"Oh, for God's sake," she said, disgusted. She logged out. Then, to take her mind off what Piola and his wife might be saying to each other, she started on some paperwork.

The desk phone rang, the caller's number not one she recognised. She grabbed it, thinking it must be him.

"Is that Colonel Piola?" a man's voice said, clearly distressed.

"He's not here. Who is this?"

"I came to see you. I'm Lucio the fisherman – the one from Chioggia, remember?"

"Yes, I remember. How can I help you?"

"It's Ricci's widow, Mareta. She's in hospital. She was beaten up last night. The doctors say she nearly died."

"Who did it?"

"She's not saying – she can't, she's got a broken jaw. They say she may never talk properly again." The young man sounded hysterical. "You couldn't keep it to yourself, could you? You had to let it leak."

"I'll come over."

"No! Stay away from her! Stay away from all of us! Why should we bother with you lot? We might as well just shoot ourselves, and save them the bother."

It was three hours before Piola came back. He couldn't meet her eye. She followed him into his office.

"Is she OK?" she asked.

"Of course not."

"What about you?"

"That's not really the point, is it?"

"What did you say to each other?"

"That's... private," he said quietly, and she flinched. "Kat, look... Obviously I've promised her that it's all over between you and me."

Foolishly, in her hurt she tried to make a joke of it. "Well, I've been dumped many times, and that probably wins the prize for the most direct."

"'Dumped'? You make it sound as if we were teenagers, dating," he muttered.

"Well, what was it, then?" She was desperate for him to talk to her, but he seemed to have retreated from her. It was as if a barrier had been abruptly brought down on his feelings.

"It was a stupid, wrong, inconsiderate affair," he said coldly. "I was an idiot to let myself get tangled up in it."

Tangled. She heard in his words an echo of the conversations he'd already had that afternoon: the ones that really mattered, with the woman he was married to.

What about me? she wanted to shout. *What about my feelings? Who got me tangled up in this?* But of course she couldn't. Because she wasn't married to him. She was the wrong-doer, not the wronged.

"Mareta Castiglione's in hospital," she said.

Piola swore. "What happened?"

"A punishment beating, from the sound of it. They broke her jaw."

"I'd better get over there."

"Lucio said not to. But if you're going, I'll come too."

"Kat..." He shook his head. "Perhaps I'm not being clear enough. I promised Gilda that it's over."

"Yes, I understand that."

"I mean, I can't go on working with you."

She stared at him.

"It would be impossible," he said gently. "You do see that, don't you?"

"What are you saying?"

"I'll ask for one of the male captains to assist me for the remainder of the investigation."

"What!"

"Anything else wouldn't be fair."

"How exactly is *this* fair?" she demanded.

"I meant, fair on my wife. You can hardly expect her to be happy about the situation if I go on sharing an office with you."

She couldn't believe she was hearing this. "This morning I turned down a murder investigation of my own to stay on this case."

"I'm sorry. But there'll be others."

"That's not really the point, is it? We should be able to work alongside each other as professionals, whatever our personal feelings."

He sighed, and rubbed his head with both hands. She could read, only too clearly, what was going through his mind. *First a furious wife, now an angry mistress.*

"If you'd said to me, before we went to bed, that once it was over between us you'd be kicking me off the case," she added, "do you imagine for one moment that I'd have gone ahead?"

"I'm just trying to find a solution that works," he said wearily. "The present situation has clearly become impossible, for reasons which I accept are entirely my fault. The only answer, so far as I can see, is for you to be transferred to another investigation. That case you mentioned – I happen to know it's gone to Zito. I spoke to him on the way in. He'd be happy to have you on his team."

"Oh, great." She could imagine it already – the sniggers, the glances, the whispers behind her back. *That's the captain who screwed Aldo Piola, and had to be shunted off the case when the wife found out!*

"Let me make one thing clear," she said. "I'm really, really sorry about your wife. I realise now that sleeping with you was a stupid, irresponsible thing to do. But I'm not moving. I was put on this investigation, and I'm staying on it until we either find the killer, or Marcello drags us out of here and turns off the lights himself."

"And what do I tell my wife?" he said hopelessly.

"That's your problem. But you could start by telling her that you don't actually have the right to get rid of me, just because I was foolish enough to go to bed with you."

Forty-five

DANIELE PUSHED BACK his chair and looked at the clock. It was 4 a.m.

He'd been investigating MCI relentlessly, unable to sleep or eat until he'd finished. Their official website had told him very little, but from within the reams of bland corporate jargon he'd filleted the names of half a dozen senior employees.

Knowing that senior executives would almost certainly have the latest smartphones, Daniele had taken the names and cross-referenced them against the records of the four largest American cell phone companies. Then he sent a text to each phone. It simply said: *Are you out of your meeting yet? I need to catch up.* When the owner of the phone opened the text, assuming it was from a colleague, it downloaded a tiny piece of software which immediately began running a password algorithm on the executive's remote access email account, also stored on the phone. In hacking terms, it was relatively simple – what was known as a "brute-force attack". Chinese hackers used a similar technique when they hacked into Google in 2010.

Once he had access to the employees' email accounts, Daniele arranged for each of them to receive an internal email. In every company, he knew, there were dozens of banal messages flying around – emails to say that the air conditioning needed to be repaired, or that the company had won some obscure award, or announcing some baffling corporate restructuring. In many cases, the recipients would click on them anyway, to stop them appearing in their inboxes as "unread".

In this case, Daniele simply created a flyer to say that another MCI employee was about to run a marathon in aid of a good cause, and was looking for sponsorship. When the recipients clicked on the flyer at their desk computers, it sent details of their system user names and passwords straight back to Daniele. Within a few hours he was inside the company network, trawling through the thousands of emails that flew back and forth every day.

MCI were pretty good – they used codenames as well as encryption for the most sensitive messages, and at other times they deliberately used elliptical language that mirrored the US Military's brevity codes. But he learnt enough to discover that Carnivia was "the target", and that the overall objective was to "delete the vapour trail". In plain English, it was a clean-up operation.

He could hack them all he liked, but without more pieces of the puzzle, he couldn't work out what it was they were trying to scrub themselves clean of. Not for the first time, he wondered how he could persuade Captain Tapo to give him Barbara Holton's hard drive. The answers were in that machine somewhere, he was certain of it, but every day that passed meant that the hard drive's platters would be rusting further from the salt water it had been immersed in.

Whenever Daniele was stressed or frustrated, he focused on a mathematical equation. It was a practice he had begun during the long, terrifying days of his kidnap, when he'd set himself simple exercises in mental arithmetic to take his mind off the things his kidnappers were saying they would do to him if his parents failed to pay the ransom. Gradually, the numbers in his head had taken on substance – the mathematical world revealing itself to him as a series of tangible patterns, so that he began to glimpse in the bare bricks of the room he was imprisoned in, or the arrangement of leaves on the tree outside the barred window, a reality far purer and more satisfying than that in which he was forced to spend the rest of his waking hours. He retreated even further into the world of mathematics after his mutilation, to escape the pain, and again after he'd watched in terror the brutal, botched assault on his captors by Italian Special Forces. Even as the outside world was celebrating his return home, he had been withdrawing deeper and deeper into that other reality, the reality where everything made perfect sense.

He stepped inside just such a world now. "Monstrous moonshine" was the name given by mathematicians to an extraordinary number pattern. In order to perceive it, you had to imagine a 24-dimensional torus generated by a Leech lattice, and apply it to a number progression known as *M*, the Monster module – a series not unlike pi, but rather harder to calculate. He gazed on it with awe, and felt some of his anxiety seep away.

If he was sent to prison, this world would, he knew, be his only retreat. But he doubted, frankly, whether it would be enough to keep him sane.

He had to find some way of turning the tables on MCI. But how, he currently had no idea.

Forty-six

HOLLY MET UP with Ian Gilroy in Vicenza. As requested, she was sitting at a café table slightly off the main *piazza* when he dropped into a chair opposite her.

"I've been thinking about that package of yours," he said without further preamble. "I think you should take it to my ward, Daniele Barbo."

"A civilian?" she said, surprised. "I thought we wanted to deal with this in-house?"

"Yes... but I don't think we have quite enough to go to the authorities with yet. When you pull up a weed, you need to get the roots – all of them, even the smallest, deepest tendrils, or else the damn thing just grows back even stronger. We need the names of everyone who knew about WB, chains of command, outcomes – all the detail. Plus we need to know what Barbara Holton had found out, and who she was sharing it with online. And the Doherty paper. If anyone can track down a document that's somehow been erased from the internet, it's Daniele." He hesitated. "I should warn you, though, that he's not an easy individual to deal with. He may also be somewhat wary about my involvement. He blames me, along with the other trustees of the Barbo Foundation, for certain decisions his father made about his upbringing. The truth is that we tried to exert a positive influence behind the scenes, but his father only ever heeded advice that fitted with his own inclinations... A bit like Daniele, in fact. Extreme stubbornness runs in the family."

"Would it be better if I didn't mention your name at all?"

"Perhaps say that I reluctantly provided an introduction, rather than that it was my idea. If I'm right, he'll see this as a possible solution to some pressing problems of his own."

"Such as?"

"I think I'll let him tell you about that. The less you know before you meet him, the better. And one other thing, Holly. If you get the chance, encourage Daniele to involve the Italian police. That Carabinieri officer you mentioned, the one who came to see you about Barbara Holton... She and her superior officer have been forbidden from contacting you directly. I suspect they'll jump at the chance of doing it at second hand, through Daniele."

"Doesn't giving our information to the police increase the risk of it becoming public?"

"A small risk, yes. But I think it's a manageable one. And at the end of the day the police can be prevailed upon to be discreet. That's the way it works in Italy."

Forty-seven

KAT SHUT THE door to her apartment and leant against it, fighting the tears. She'd held it together all day. Now, finally, she was looking forward to a good cry.

The bedroom still bore traces of Aldo's presence. Only last night they'd made love here. He'd lain in her bed, showered in her bathroom. The bottle of grappa he'd drunk from sat on her kitchen table, half empty. The glasses they'd used were in the sink, unwashed.

Fuck you, she thought angrily, and then: *I love you.*

But did she really, she wondered. Was love this overwhelming intensity of physical desire and yearning, or was it more like what Aldo and his wife must have – the long years of occupying the same space, children, the pain of betrayal, the possibility of forgiveness? That was the question she hadn't asked him that afternoon, she realised: *do you love her?* She hadn't needed to. She'd already known the answer from the look of desolation in his eyes when he saw the photographs.

Kat, you've been a fool. A marriage-wrecking fool.

She poured herself a large tumbler of grappa and booted up her laptop. As if scratching an itch, her fingers wandered almost of their own accord towards the Carnivia log-on.

Katerina Tapo – twenty-one entries.

...Turns out she only got the Black Magic Murders because Piola had already told Allocation he wanted to work with her. Francesco Lotti tried to make her think it was him who'd swung it. Poor lovesick Lotti!

... I heard Madam isn't happy about the wife finding out, and now Piola's getting it in the neck from both sides...

...This is what happens when you bring women into a military organisation. You can't blame the men...

"Oh, for God's sake," she said wearily. She clicked the window closed, determined never to go near that damned website ever again.

It was ironic, therefore, that the very top email in her inbox bore the address *DanieleBarbo@carnivia.com*.

Dear Captain Tapo,

Can we meet? I have something for you.

Regards,

Daniele Barbo

PS You should bring that hard drive.

Muttering an expletive, she deleted it.

The next email was from the Guardia di Finanza, the police department with responsibility for Italy's borders. Earlier, when she'd been doing her paperwork, she'd followed up on Piola's request to get hold of the scan of Findlater's passport, together with the dates he'd entered and left the country. According to the email, the dates corroborated Findlater's story. Wearily, she clicked on the attachment. Findlater's smiling face, ten years younger, filled her screen. It was as if the smug bastard was jeering at her.

She peered forward. In his passport photo Findlater was wearing a sports jacket and an open-neck shirt. There was something in the lapel – some kind of tiepin.

It was hard to be sure, because the resolution of the image wasn't great, but it looked to her like a cross. The downpiece of the cross widened, then narrowed to a point. Like the blade of a short, stubby sword.

If she wasn't mistaken, it was identical to the tiepin she'd seen Father Uriel wearing. And to the logo on the home page of the Companions of the Order of Melchizedek.

She went into her "Deleted Items" folder, moved Daniele Barbo's message back to her inbox, and re-read it.

She did still have the hard drive. And Malli, predictably, had never got round to dealing with the chain-of-custody paperwork. If by some miracle anyone ever followed the paper trail, it would indicate that the drive was still sitting somewhere amongst all the other clutter on his workbench.

Kat Tapo never did cry that night. She came close – there was sleeplessness, regret and a sickening, unaccustomed feeling in the pit of her stomach caused by the knowledge that she'd done wrong; but mostly what she felt was a hardening, icy sensation that she recognised as resolve.

Forty-eight

THEY MET IN the drawing room at Ca' Barbo, with its eclectic mixture of Renaissance frescoes, modern paintings and cheap dorm-room seating. Daniele Barbo, Holly Boland and Kat Tapo.

The room, Kat thought as she looked around, reflected the oddities of its owner. Occasionally you could see the Venetian aristocrat in him, politely offering them *spritz* – the classic Venetian drink of Campari, white wine and sparkling water – in exquisite eighteenth-century goblets. Then, abruptly, he'd start talking about TCP protocols and packet-switching logarithms, the aperitif forgotten as he whisked through incomprehensible explanations, absent-mindedly pulling open a can of Diet Coke as he did so.

Most of the time, however, he seemed almost disinterested in the two women's presence, his eyes drifting towards the whiteboards covered with mathematical notations that lined the walls.

Kat looked across at Holly Boland. She had to concede that she might have misjudged the American a little. She'd written Holly off as a desk-bound bureaucrat with zero imagination and no balls, but the woman exuded an air of calm confidence as she explained why she'd brought them together. Of course, Kat thought, as a soldier Second Lieutenant Boland was more used to taking orders than taking the initiative. But her account of how she'd tracked down the names of those attending the Ederle conference, if true, showed impressive investigative skills.

If true. Kat was all too aware that in addition to the sin of sleeping with a senior officer, she was now contemplating handing over evidence to a convicted criminal and revealing details of a Carabinieri investigation to a foreign intelligence operative. If found out, she'd be court-martialled at the very least. For that reason, even Piola didn't know she was here yet.

"We're none of us here by choice," Holly was saying. "And it wouldn't suit any of us if other people got to hear about it. The reason we're meeting is that all of us, separately, have been investigating evidence trails that now appear to be linked. My proposal is that we pool what we've learnt and see where the overlaps are. Agreed?"

Kat nodded. Daniele examined his nails.

"I'll go first," Holly said with a sigh. "Daniele, may I use one of these whiteboards?"

He shrugged. "If you wish."

"So," she said, getting up and uncapping a marker pen. She had worn civilian clothes for this meeting, presumably to avoid drawing attention to herself in Venice, but to Kat's way of thinking the clothes she'd chosen – a hoodie, jeans and trainers – simply made her look like a teenage boy. "I have a conference in 1993 at Camp Ederle involving General Dragan Korovik, the Italian Mafia, a private security company called MCI, a psychologist, the Church..." One by one she listed the known protagonists at William Baker, then laid down her marker. "Kat, what do you have?"

"I have a murder involving Croatia, Camp Ederle, the Church, a mental hospital, an MCI employee, the Mafia..."

Kat got up and listed the connections. Point for point, the two lists were almost identical. "Daniele, your turn."

He waved away the marker. "The only concrete thing I have is MCI."

Kat wrote it down for him. "Then that's the start point. We have to follow the links between MCI and these other players." She hesitated. "Daniele, that means I'm letting you try Barbara Holton's hard drive. Amongst other things, I need to know if you can reconstruct her emails to and from Bob Findlater."

He nodded. "I can get on with that while the two of you look for overlaps elsewhere."

"No," Kat said, shaking her head.

"Why not?"

"While you're working on that hard drive, either Holly or I will watch you at all times." She held up a hand to forestall his objections. "I know, I know – I'm sure if you wanted to you could lift the information from it without my even noticing. The point is, I'm crossing a line just by letting you touch it. I need to limit my culpability from 'insanely trusting' to 'criminally negligent'. Which brings me to my second point. You're still refusing, as far as I can see, to actually delve inside Carnivia and tell us what's going on there. So I'm going to ask you one more time, with no judges or lawyers present: is there anything that you can do to trace that information that you haven't already done?"

He met her gaze calmly. "There is one thing."

"Go on."

"When I followed one of the women priests on Carnivia, I came across a chest with a *stećak* marking on it, similar in design to the ones you found at Poveglia. I realised that the chest was a repository – a way of transferring large amounts of data between individuals."

"And?" Kat said.

"I discovered that several repositories in Carnivia were customised with the same symbol. They were clearly being used to transfer files relating to a specific project. It seems a reasonable hypothesis that it might be something to do with your murders, since in at least one case whoever was expecting the information never received it."

"Who was the recipient?"

"I don't know. I need the algorithm – the encryption key – that Barbara Holton used to log on with, which would have been automatically saved to her hard drive along with her other personal information. If I can retrieve that, I'll know who she was really working for. But I'm willing to bet it wasn't Bob Findlater."

Forty-nine

KEEPING AN EYE on Daniele while he worked on the hard drive turned out to be rather more complicated than Kat had anticipated. Naively, she'd imagined he'd simply hook the drive up to a computer and run some tests on it. In fact, it turned out, the first thing he needed was a clean room in which to work.

And a "clean room", it transpired, didn't mean going over Ca' Barbo with a Hoover.

"In order to restore the drive, I need to take it apart and physically clean the seawater residue off the platters," he explained, sighing at their ignorance. "Computer hard drives are sealed units for a very good reason. Ordinary air contains microscopic dust particles that would scour them like sandpaper. I need a closed environment, with a filtered recirculating airflow."

Using materials from a hardware store, Daniele set about constructing a sealed booth with its own air-conditioning unit, lined with carbon-fibre material to reduce the possibility of static. He turned out to be a methodical, painstaking craftsman, never cutting corners and making sure each stage was perfect before going onto the next.

When it was built, the booth was given a separate power supply, to minimise electrical surges, and an ioniser to dissipate any charges that built up. Special plastic-coated tools were cleaned and demagnetised before being installed on the carbon-fibre-lined workbench. Only then did he put on a forensic suit and enter the booth with the drive.

The booth had to be sealed while he was working, but he'd reluctantly agreed to a video link so that the two professionals could observe him. In practice, however, Kat soon became impatient with the slow pace of the work, and left Holly to supervise Daniele while she went off to continue showing Bob Findlater's picture to the prostitutes around Santa Lucia.

"So how come the Carabinieri's IT guy didn't do any of this?" Holly asked over the link as Daniele began dismantling the hard drive. Evidently it wasn't a completely stupid question: instead of snarling, he actually honoured her with an answer.

"Most computer experts are actually just experts in which specialist software to use," he said. "To inspect a hard drive, for example, you'd rig it up to a program like Helix or IXimager. That tells you what's in the slack space – the bits of data that have been deleted but not actually wiped from the machine. For ninety per cent of investigations, that's perfectly sufficient."

He broke off to place the hard drive covers to one side. "For more advanced stuff, like the Madrid bombing or the Shuttle disaster, almost every government agency in the world uses an outfit called Kroll Ontrack. In fact, if I had a fire-damaged hard drive in one of my own computers, that's probably who I'd go to as well. Seawater's a bit more specialist, though. The problem isn't so much the water itself – the actual data is stored magnetically – as what it leaves behind when it dries. When someone like Malli starts the drive up to copy it, the residue on the spinning disc scours into the surface, corrupting the data. I'm hoping that Malli didn't try too hard, in fact, because the less he did, the better my chances are."

He donned a surgical mask, powder-free latex gloves and a static-dispersing wrist-strap as he began the delicate operation of freeing the platters.

"We're in luck," his muffled voice said over the feed. "There's still moisture in here."

"That's good?"

"It's like the wooden pilings that hold up these Venetian houses. So long as they stay wet, they don't corrode."

He placed the platters in a bowl of purified water. "There. Now I need to leave them to soak."

He exited the booth and stripped off the mask and forensic suit. She saw his eyes go to the whiteboards covered with mathematical notations at the back of the room.

"What are those?" she asked curiously.

He grunted. "A maths problem."

"I gathered that. Is it something to do with computing?"

"In a manner of speaking." He glanced at her. "I doubt you'll understand."

"So do I, but tell me anyway."

He picked up a marker and went over to the board, tracing a path through the formulae. "The problem is called *P versus NP.* Effectively, it boils down to a simple question: if a computer can be programmed to verify the answer to a theorem, why can't it be programmed to solve the theorem in the first place? It's one of the seven Millennium Prize problems in mathematics. Only one has been solved so far."

"And you think you can solve it?"

"I used to think so. But now I doubt that anyone can."

"So why keep trying?"

"Why?" he echoed, surprised. "Because it's beautiful. Like a piece of music, or a sculpture. The problem itself, I mean – it says more about the condition of being human than any symphony or portrait ever could."

"You mean you just like to look at it?"

"Look at it, listen to it... these aren't adequate words. Here..." He crossed to where another whiteboard stood by a wall and slid it to one side. Behind it was an abstract painting. "That's a De Chirico. My father thought it one of the most sublime things in his collection. And here..." He slid the whiteboard back so that it covered the painting again. On it was the notation $e^{i\pi} + 1 = 0$.

"That's Euler's Identity. Any serious mathematician will tell you that it's one of the most profound works of art ever created – more beautiful than the Sistine Chapel, more elegant than the Parthenon, purer than the Requiem Mass. In just three simple steps it answers one of the most fundamental questions of existence."

"Which is...?"

"Oh – 'Why are circles round?'"

While Holly was still mentally scratching her head about that one, Daniele led her to the next room. In the corner was an elongated sculpture that looked to her like a Giacometti. Incongruously, it had been given Ray-Bans and a trapper's hat to wear. But it was the fresco on the wall, a landscape, to which he was pointing. Over it he'd stuck a Post-it on which he'd written the numbers 6, 28 and 496.

"Those are what's called 'perfect numbers'. That means if you take all the numbers they can be divided by, and add them together, you get the same number you started with. So the number 6, for example, can be divided by 1, 2 and 3. Add 1, 2 and 3 together, and you also get 6. The Ancient Greeks thought the perfect number pattern was proof of the inherent harmony of nature."

"So the fresco is a painting of a landscape," she said slowly, "and the other is the... the..." She struggled to find the right word.

"The essence of the landscape," he finished for her. "Exactly."

She began to understand now. What had appeared to be a casual defacing of the palace's artworks – his father's hated legacy – now looked like a reinterpretation of them. Several times after that she pointed to a Post-it stuck on a priceless work of art and asked him what it meant. A seascape bore the notation $X_0(N)$. "The modularity theorem," he explained. And a still life of flowers and fruits was plastered with what he told her were Mandelbrot equations. The actual mathematics might be far too advanced for her, but she knew enough to comprehend that Daniele Barbo had a mind unlike that of any other person she had ever met.

At last Daniele returned to the booth, removed the hard drive platters from the bowl in which they had been soaking, and opened a crate of aerosols.

"Those are air dusters, presumably?" Holly said.

"Pretty much. Canned air isn't actually air – it's a cocktail of gases like trifluoroethane that compress easily. The problem is that to stop kids from sniffing it, manufacturers add another chemical to make it bitter, and the bittering agent can leave a residue. This is NASA-grade canned air."

It was as he was painstakingly drying off the platters that she was struck by a thought.

"Daniele, I think I've worked out why you built Carnivia."

He didn't reply, but over the video link she saw him stiffen.

Too late, she realised she was blundering into a minefield. *Oh well: there's no backing out now.*

"Everyone calls it a social networking site," she said. "And I've been puzzled by that, because it seems like a contradiction – you're the least social person I've ever met. But I've been thinking about those maths problems of yours. You see the world as a series of equations, don't you? Yet the truth is that the world isn't quite like that – it's untidy, and unpredictable, and various random factors keep messing up the picture."

"Which leads you to what conclusion, Second Lieutenant?" he said softly.

"I think the real world turned out to be too random a place in which to try to solve puzzles like *P versus NP*, or whatever you called it. So you built your own, neater version instead, one where you could limit the variables. All those people who join Carnivia... unwittingly, they're all just part of a giant mathematics simulation. Like a glass-sided ants' nest in a laboratory. And that's why you care about Carnivia so much, isn't it? Not because of the four million users, or however many it is. It's because the puzzle you built it to process isn't solved yet."

"Hmm," he said non-committally. There was a long silence, followed only by the hiss of air as he applied another air duster to the hard drive.

In the circumstances, she thought, that was as good an answer as she was likely to get.

When the hard drive was finally dry, Daniele emerged from his booth with a black box the size of a cigarette packet in his hand

"It's fixed," he said simply. "Or at least, enough to give it a try."

He hooked the hard drive up to a computer, plugging it into a USB port just as if it were a memory stick.

"I'm not going to try to run it with Windows," he said, "just in case it's programmed to erase itself. And this way I don't need to know Barbara Holton's username or password."

"How do you know what you're looking for?"

"I don't. But Carnivia saves user information to a very specific location. I'll start there and work backwards."

Fifty

THEY GATHERED AT the Foundation's latest art exhibition. Four men, all in their sixties, none of whom had any interest in art. Each positioned himself in front of a different picture. Should a tourist turn up – an unlikely occurrence, since the pictures in this room had been carefully selected from the most unfashionable, unappealing items in the late Matteo Barbo's collection – the receptionist would turn them away, explaining that as it was almost lunchtime no more visitors were being admitted. The tourist would shrug, and reflect that this kind of thing happened all the time in Italy.

"I'm not sure it was wise to send Findlater himself," Ian Gilroy said reflectively to the picture in front of him.

"We had forty-eight hours' notice. There was no one else who understood the gravity of the situation," a voice responded to his right.

Gilroy turned, and walked across the room to where Balla's *The Car Has Passed* hung against a plain red background.

"My understanding is that the Carabinieri investigation is now closed," the third man said. "The prosecutor has informed me that the final report will be circulated within days."

"Correction," Gilroy said. "The investigation may be closed. But the Carabinieri are still investigating."

"Once the general's trial is under way, it will be too late to submit further evidence in any case," the second man pointed out.

"Perhaps. But I for one would like to know exactly what evidence remains to be found." Gilroy peered at the painting. "These are actually quite good, you know. The sense of movement... He really captures the way the viewer gets left behind, wondering what just happened."

"Every event leaves traces," the third voice said.

"But not every trace incriminates." Gilroy bent to read the card next to the painting. On it were some excerpts from the Futurists' manifesto. "'We will glorify war – the world's only hygiene,'" he read aloud. "'Militarism, patriotism, the destructive gesture of freedom-bringers, beautiful ideas worth dying for, and scorn for woman.'" He sighed. "They weren't the most appealing bunch, were they?"

"What do you have in mind?" The voice to his left was straining not to sound impatient.

"I have a terrier," Gilroy said, stepping back again so that he could look at the painting properly. "Do you know about hunting with terriers? The little terrier goes bravely into the fox's earth, and even though it's much too small to kill the fox itself, it pins the fox down. And that gives the huntsman time to dig out the earth, and send in his hounds."

"What happens to the terrier?"

"It depends. Sometimes the fox kills it. Sometimes the hounds get it, along with the fox. Sometimes it manages to limp back to its owner."

"I have a feeling I might have met your terrier. Here, in fact, at the gala opening."

"Possibly. But just to be clear – hands off. She's my property. Not to be targeted or killed in the excitement of the hunt."

"Very well. If you really think she's worth it."

"She discovered details about William Baker that even I hadn't known. Your hounds are two a penny, my friend. But a good terrier's hard to find." He turned to the fourth man, the one wearing a clerical collar who had so far kept quiet. "And as for *your* lot, Father, I think it's time this was left to the professionals, don't you?"

Fifty-one

DANIELE MIGHT HAVE described the hard drive as "fixed", but it soon became clear that didn't mean the information on it was now readily accessible. The data was so corrupted, he explained, that it had effectively been reduced to tiny, unconnected pieces. He would have to pick through thousands of fragments, trying to fit them together byte by byte.

After a day of work he had only succeeded in reconstructing a few isolated portions of the messages Barbara Holton had exchanged with her contacts on Carnivia.

> ... held in a camp known as the Birds' Nest in the Krajina region...

> ... testimony supports the allegations made by Jelena B...

> ... came up to the Birds' Nest every day, sometimes four or five truckloads of soldiers at a time...

"These look as if they relate to Operation Storm," Holly said. "She must have been gathering reports of atrocities against civilians."

While Daniele continued to work on the drive, Kat and Holly researched the words "Birds' Nest Camp". Even translated into Croatian, there was nothing on the internet – or if there was, it was buried amongst a million photographs of songbirds rearing their chicks, and recipes for Chinese soup.

"We need to narrow the search terms," Holly said. "Daniele, can you give us anything else?"

"A little."

> "We knew the rapes would begin when 'Marš na Drinu' was played over the loudspeaker of the mosque. While the song was playing, all the women had to strip and soldiers entered the homes, taking the ones they wanted. Frequently the soldiers would seek out mothers and daughters. Many of us were severely beaten during the rapes..."

"Several of Barbara Holton's questions related to 'rape as a weapon of war'," Holly said quietly.

"*Marš na Drinu* is a Serbian drinking song," Kat reported from her laptop. "From the reference to a mosque, I'd say this is testimony from a Bosniak girl about an attack by Serb soldiers."

Daniele said, "There's this, too."

> "I was playing dead after a hand grenade was thrown into my front room. As I was lying there I heard foreign voices outside and an interpreter translating the words into Croatian. He was saying, 'Nothing must remain, not even the cats, not even the children.'"

"So this one relates to a *Croat* offensive," Kat said.

"Which involved foreigners," Holly added. "Barbara appears to have been collecting evidence to show that both Serbs and Croats were committing similar atrocities."

Without comment, Daniele brought them another fragment.

> "Sometimes they would bring in a new recruit. He would be ordered to choose a girl, rape her and then kill her. Or, as a game, the girl would be offered a choice – submit to rape by the soldier, or be killed by him. It was a great joke for the other soldiers if she chose death, because the soldier was perceived to have been humiliated. So he would be ribbed and teased even as he tried to earn his manhood back by killing her in the most brutal way imaginable."

"My God," Kat said, outraged. "This is appalling."

> "The camps had innocuous, feminine names, like 'Coffeehouse Sonja', 'Nymphs' Tresses' or 'The Birds' Nest'."

The new names gave them enough to do a more detailed search. What they found was even more horrifying. Even in the first three years of the Balkan war, when these things were still being counted, an estimated twenty thousand women were raped, many in special places of detention set up for just that purpose. Each side blamed the other for being the first to use such tactics.

For an hour or more there was silence as the two women read through the official reports. As early as 1994, the United Nations had analysed "tens of thousands" of allegations of rape, concluding:

> Rape and sexual assault are reported to have been committed by all of the warring factions. Some of the reported rape and sexual assault cases are clearly the result of individual or

> small group conduct without evidence of command direction or an overall policy. However, many more cases seem to be part of an overall pattern. These patterns strongly suggest that a systematic rape and sexual assault policy exists...

And yet little seemed to have been done about it at the time. Indeed, as the country spiralled deeper into violence, and UN observers were pulled out for their own safety, the issue was apparently almost forgotten in the general confusion.

Kat felt her cheeks burning with anger. All this had been happening less than two hundred miles away, just across the Adriatic Sea, yet so accustomed had Europe become to thinking of the Communist Bloc as a separate entity that even today, people didn't talk about what had happened. Unable to sit still any longer, she jumped to her feet and strode to the big, barley-twist windows for some air, just as Daniele said quietly, "Aha."

She turned. He was pointing at his screen.

"This is who Barbara Holton was contacting in Carnivia."

They crowded round his computer. *rcarlito@icty.org.*

"ICTY is the International Criminal Tribunal for the former Yugoslavia," Kat said. "Based in The Hague. Barbara Holton's website mentioned that she'd done some work for them in the past."

Holly was typing the email address into a search engine. "And R. Carlito is Roberta Carlito," she informed them. "Her official title is 'legal analyst'. She reports directly to the chief prosecutor. Unofficially, I'd say she's some kind of paralegal investigator."

"So maybe Barbara Holton was supplying her with evidence for Dragan Korovik's trial."

"But what did that have to do with Findlater?"

"Barbara Holton thought there had been American complicity in the conflict," Holly said. "Operation William Baker confirms it. Maybe Findlater was tasked with making sure that evidence never reached the Hague."

"Deleting the vapour trail," Daniele murmured from behind his computer.

"That would explain why Findlater was looking for Barbara Holton and Jelena Babić," Holly said. "But it doesn't explain why they were all looking for Findlater's daughter."

The same idea struck both women at the same time. They looked at each other, understanding flickering between them.

"Barbara Holton wasn't just looking for Melina Kovačević," Kat said slowly. "She was looking for proof of a war crime."

"Because the two are one and the same thing," Holly agreed.

"I don't get it," Daniele objected. "How?"

"That lock of hair Kat found in the women's hotel room – if it came from Soraya Kovačević, it would contain DNA that, when compared with DNA from Findlater and DNA from Melina, would prove they were Melina's biological parents."

"Piola always said that Hollywood story about finding his daughter so he could give her a college education was bullshit," Kat exclaimed. "Holly's right – Findlater wasn't using Barbara and Jelena to find Melina. He was trying to find her before they did."

"But why?" Daniele repeated.

"To kill her. To destroy the evidence. That's what this is

all about. It's Melina herself who's the smoking gun. Her DNA is living proof of a war crime."

Whichever way they looked at it, they kept coming back to the same hypothesis.

Findlater had claimed he'd found Melina's mother cowering in a cellar whilst on duty in Krajina as a UN peacekeeper, and that they'd fallen in love. "But if the truth was a bit different," Kat said. "If, say, he was in Croatia as an MCI operative, one of those stirring up the conflict by any means possible, including sexual violence against women..."

"'Libidinal frenzy,'" Holly said. "Rape as a weapon of war. One of Paul Doherty's precursors to genocide."

"... then he might well have committed rape himself, on Soraya. Melina was the result."

"We need to get in touch with this Roberta Carlito." Holly looked at Daniele. "Can we email her? Is that secure?"

"Absolutely not. But you don't have to email her. You can contact her the same way Barbara did, on Carnivia."

They logged onto Carnivia, sent Roberta Carlito an encrypted message, and waited. Within half an hour they got a message back asking them to meet her in Piazza San Marco.

For Holly, this was her first experience of assuming a Carnivia identity. Strolling with Kat and Daniele's avatars along a beautiful canalside pavement, the canals themselves mercifully free of tourists and stinking diesel-engined *vaporetti*, she couldn't see what all the fuss was about. "It's so beautiful," she kept saying, surprised.

"Beautiful but rotten," Kat said tersely. "Just like the real thing."

Daniele shrugged. "It's a place. People live in it. Some are good, some are bad. Most are a mixture of the two."

They arrived in the Piazza San Marco and found a woman in a Domino mask waiting in front of the Doge's Palace. Daniele supplied the encryption code from Barbara's computer, and Kat typed:

– Good afternoon, Ms Carlito. We're friends of Barbara Holton. I believe you've been looking for her?

– Is she all right?

– I'm afraid not. She's been murdered.

There was a long silence. Then:

– I was afraid it must be something like that.

They walked along the Riva degli Schiavoni as Roberta Carlito explained how she first came across Barbara Holton.

– Barbara was one of a dozen unpaid volunteers collecting evidence of crimes committed during the war in the former Yugoslavia. Specifically, crimes against women. Affidavits from victims, witness statements, timelines of events – without its own executive arm, the ICTY doesn't have the resources to gather these things, and local police are often implicated in the original crimes themselves and have no wish to help us. So we rely on a network of pro-bono lawyers and activists.

– Jelena Babić was another one of those, presumably.

– No. *Jelena was a witness – one of the first Barbara found. But they became friends, and Jelena used her contacts to introduce Barbara to other victims.*

– Victims of what, exactly?

– Ah... How much do you know about places like Coffeehouse Sonja?

– A little, now. They were rape camps, we understand.

– Yes. The rapes served several purposes. They helped to demoralise and terrorise the population, of course. They

brutalised the soldiers, making it easier for their commanders to order them to commit even more violent acts in the future. But there was another purpose too, in that the women would often become pregnant. The lack of birth control was quite deliberate. Effectively they were turned into breeding machines for their captors, to fill the area with children of the victors' ethnic type – the mother's ethnicity being seen as less important than the father's. It was a way of making the issues of race and religion even more toxic than they already were.

Kat wrote:

– What if we told you these tactics were being planned even before the war in Bosnia? And that a small number of NATO officers had a hand in it, along with a private military contractor with links to the US government?

– I'd ask you for the proof. That's what's always held us back – actually proving there was more to this than the usual brutality of war. About a month ago Barbara thought she'd finally found a "golden thread", as she called it. She had an affidavit from a Bosniak woman called Soraya Kovačević who'd been imprisoned in the Birds' Nest camp. Soraya alleged that one of her rapists was an American military contractor attached to the Croatian forces as an advisor. Even after all this time, she could still identify him. It's the perfect test case for us – if we can make it stand up, we'll have linked every stage of a known atrocity, from planning through to commission, back to US proxies.

– What do you need to make it stick?

– An affidavit from Soraya Kovačević, together with valid chain-of-evidence documentation so that its authenticity is beyond question. Some maps and photographs of the area would be a bonus, too. But most of all, we need corroborating DNA proving that the American is the father of Soraya's child.

"In other words," Holly said out loud, "we not only need to find the mother, we need to succeed where Barbara Holton and Jelena Babić failed, and find the daughter as well."

– *Where do we begin?*

– *Jelena's evidence should help. She identified the Birds' Nest camp as being in the Krajina region, near a town called Brezic. I should add that time isn't on our side, though. Korovik's trial begins in just under two weeks, and full disclosure requires that we submit any evidence to the defence in advance. Once the hearing starts it'll be too late for any of this.*

Sensing that Daniele had had enough of their presence in Ca' Barbo, the two women removed themselves to a nearby *bacaro.*

"You know," Holly said thoughtfully, once the two of them were sitting at a table in the back of the bar, with a couple of spritzes in front of them. "There are plenty of people who'd say stirring this stuff up now is a waste of time. History moves on, people forgive and forget. Croatia's joining the European Union, it's starting to have a tourist trade... What's the point in raking up a crime that took place almost twenty years ago, in a war that most people couldn't even find on a map?"

"That's right," Kat agreed. "Most people would probably say that."

Holly gave her a sideways glance. "Not you?"

Kat shook her head. "You?"

"Nope," Holly admitted.

"A crime is a crime," Kat said. "People should know about it. And crimes like these... Yes, they involved civilians. But many were directed specifically against *women*. I'm not sure that's an area where we *have* moved on, not altogether. Women are still being trafficked, women are still being treated as second-class citizens. Things are better than they used to be. But that war isn't over."

"As Jelena found out to her cost."

"Yes." Kat sighed. "You ever meet any discrimination in the military?"

"As a woman, you mean? I've no complaints."

Kat glanced at her. "Meaning, 'some'?"

"I guess. It's like anything: in the army, respect has to be earned. Everyone has something about them that could be construed as a weakness. It's up to you to make sure it isn't what people define you by."

Not for the first time, Kat found herself wondering if Holly Boland might be gay. It wasn't a question you could ask American soldiers, she knew. Don't Ask, Don't Tell still ran deep.

"When I first started in the Carabinieri," she said, "women hadn't been admitted as officers for long. There was still quite a bit of, shall we say, *resistance* to the idea. They used to put pictures from porn magazines in my locker. Once I found someone had masturbated over my uniform. Another time I went to put on my shoe and it was full of piss. Everyone said I should just ignore it."

"And did you?"

"Kind of. That is, I went and pissed in the shoes of the men I thought were doing it, when *they* weren't around. How about you?"

"Nothing in that league," Holly said, slightly in awe of the matter-of-fact way Kat had just delivered that last sentence. "Although I did have someone try to force me into giving him oral sex recently."

"You deal with it?"

"I guess so. I head-butted him in the groin."

Kat nodded, equally impressed. "But for just that reason," Holly added, "it makes me angry to think there were people prepared to drag the US Military into the Bosnian war for their own ends. We serve with honour. That means we fight according to the rules of war, and we seek out and punish those who break the rules."

"So we do this?" Kat said.

Holly nodded. "We do this."

As they left the bar, Kat noticed a couple from a nearby table, a man and a woman, get up to pay their bill.

"That's odd," she said quietly.

"What is?"

"See those two? The woman in the grey coat and the man in brown? They came in soon after us."

Holly glanced over. "That's not so surprising, is it? There must be a dozen people in here who did the same."

"Sure."

But when they reached the corner she hung back, watching.

"Something else about those two," she said as she and Holly walked back towards Ca' Barbo. "They're carrying a guidebook. In Italian. But they're speaking to each other in American."

Fifty-two

BACK AT CA' BARBO, they discussed the possibility that the couple in the bar had been following them. Here in Venice it wasn't so much of a problem, but if they were to go to Croatia it would be better to travel undetected.

"I've had some basic anti-surveillance training," Holly said. "There's not much we can do at airports, obviously, but after that we may be able to give them the slip."

"I'm thinking you should avoid airports altogether," Daniele said. "It's only four or five hours to drive to eastern Croatia from here. But no hire car – the records are all computerised. And you'll need to leave your phones."

"Why?" Kat asked. "Croatia uses the same system, doesn't it?"

"Daniele means that our phones can be used to trace us, through the transmitter masts," Holly explained. "We'll buy pay-as-you-go phones, and turn them off when we're not using them."

"Your credit cards too," Daniele added. "They'll be tracing those for certain."

"We'll take cash. If we're careful, we won't leave an electronic trail at all."

*

While Holly researched their route to Brezic, Kat went back to Campo San Zaccaria. She found Piola alone in the deserted operations room, typing up his report.

"You might want to add that Findlater was lying," she told him. "He was never in love with Soraya Kovačević. He raped her, and now, almost twenty years later, he's trying to get rid of the evidence."

Piola looked at her stonily. "How do you know?"

"I took the hard drive to Daniele Barbo. I've been working with the American, too – the officer from Caserma Ederle. Findlater wasn't just doing this on his own. There was a whole group of them plotting how to make the war in Bosnia so terrible that NATO would have to get involved."

A sigh escaped his lips, as if he couldn't believe how foolhardy she had been. He rubbed his face in his hands. He hadn't shaved, she noticed, and his stubble was flecked with grey. There was an open packet of cigarettes next to his keyboard.

"Have I taught you nothing?" he demanded quietly.

"What do you mean?"

"Let's suppose you succeed in gathering some proof of these... these allegations. Then what? Don't you see – you're already fatally compromised, because of all the rules you've broken to get to this point. Any Italian court would take one look at the case and throw it out."

"What if it isn't an Italian court we take it to? We've been in touch with the ICTY."

"The ICTY are trying Dragan Korovik, not Bob Findlater," he said wearily. "What about justice for the murders of Jelena Babić and Barbara Holton? What about the principle of making sure that crimes committed in Italy are brought to trial in Italy? Anyway, it's not going to happen. I'm standing you down."

"Now you sound like Marcello."

"Perhaps. But as your superior officer, this is my decision to make, not yours. You're not to take this any further. That's an order."

"Then it's an order I'm going to ignore." She hesitated. "You might as well know that I'm going to Croatia with the American officer, to find Melina's mother."

"Kat," he groaned, "Kat... Just think what you're doing. Listen to yourself. This is the Carabinieri. We don't work like this."

"From what I've seen, we barely work at all," she exclaimed. "Don't you see? This is my chance to get something done."

"Hasn't it occurred to you that the reason I'm ordering you not to pursue this is that I'm thinking of *you*?" he said quietly.

"What do you mean?"

He pointed to the bruises on his face. "Why do you think they gave me these?"

"To shut you up."

"And what makes you think they're not going to shut *you* up? Don't you see – if what you're saying is true, then Barbara Holton, Jelena Babić and Ricci Castiglione all died because they knew too much. And each of them knew a lot less than you do."

"We know what Findlater looks like. We'll be on our guard."

"Findlater had help – a lot of help." He was silent a moment. "There was something Mareta Castiglione mentioned... I didn't think anything of it at the time. Ricci went to confession shortly before he was killed."

"You think that was why they killed him? Because they thought he might be spilling his secrets to a priest?"

"Perhaps. But what if it was more than that – what if it was the priest himself who reported that Ricci was leaky?" He shook his head. "If your American's right, you're up against an extraordinary alliance. You think those people are just going to stand by and watch while you dig up the evidence?"

She said stubbornly, "It's got to be done."

He stood up. "Kat... Please. I've messed everything up. My marriage, this investigation... The one thing I won't add to that list is you. Leave the others to pursue this madness if they want to. I don't care about them."

She couldn't think what to say.

"I love you," he said hoarsely. "Just because..." He took a breath. "The decision I made, to go back to my wife... I had to. I hope you understand that. It's my duty. But my heart's with you."

"You wanted me off the investigation. Even before today."

"I can't ever work with you, Kat. But that's *because* of how I feel, not because my feelings have changed."

She was still turning this over in her mind when he kissed her. For a moment she let him, and for a moment more she kissed him back, remembering how good it was, how protected and safe she felt in his arms. Then she pushed him away.

"This isn't fair, Aldo. You're doing bad things and saying they're for good reasons. If I was a man, you wouldn't be trying to protect me like this. And that's why I have to ignore you. I'm going to Croatia to find Soraya Kovačević. Then I'm coming back here to find her daughter. I'll keep you informed of my progress, but I won't let you get in my way."

Fifty-three

AS WELL AS the paper-strewn drawing room at Ca' Barbo, and the almost deserted office at Campo San Zaccaria, there was another operations room that had been set up to deal with the case.

It was small and neat, and it occupied a glass-walled office four thousand miles away, on the fourth floor of an anonymous building in Norfolk, Virginia.

Despite the fact that none of the people in the room were on the payroll of the US Department of Defense, most wore US combat fatigues, complete with badges of rank.

"Their next move is Croatia," a sergeant reported, easing off his headphones and speaking over his shoulder. "They mean to go and find the mother."

"Excellent." The comment came from the only man in the room not in uniform. His dark suit and crisp white shirt were, however, pressed with military precision. "We have good friends in Croatia, for obvious reasons. When do they fly?"

"Hermes' understanding is that they'll be driving."

"So we find the mother before they do," one of the men in uniform suggested.

"That would be a short-term answer," the man in the suit said thoughtfully. "I think we should aim to find a more lasting solution. This has taken up enough of our attention already."

The other men waited for orders. If their opinion was wanted, it would be asked for.

"We'll ask our friends in the Croatian Army to organise a field exercise," the man in the suit said at last. "An emergency drill to test their combat readiness, as per the terms of our on-going training contract with them. Fortunately the Croatian media is still reasonably grateful to their military. A small but tragic accident involving two foreign nationals will simply be taken as proof that more such training is needed."

"Crixus is keen no harm comes to his agent."

The man in the dark suit nodded. "All the more reason that it looks like an accident, then. Crixus will get over it."

Fifty-four

THEY SET OFF before dawn the following day, driving northeast from Venice in Holly's tiny car, with the mountains ahead of them and the sea on their right. At Palmanova, the very tip of the Adriatic, the road arced east and then south, following the great curve of the Laguna di Marano. Few tourists came to these eerily empty marshlands, fewer still at first light, but the road was full of thundering lorries with Slavic names on their sides.

When they'd left Venice, the interior of Holly's car had been military-neat. But the floor was soon strewn with Kat's chocolate wrappers and empty drinks cans. She saw Holly glance at them and twitch, but with her hands on the wheel there wasn't a whole lot she could do about it.

Beyond Trieste they passed into tiny Slovenia. Although part of the former Yugoslavia, Slovenia had been a member of the EU since 2004, and as a result it seemed little different to being in Italy. Half an hour later, though, they crossed into Croatia, and it was as if they were driving into a different century as well as a different country. In the fields, farmers with gnarled, leathery faces slapped at the haunches of oxen yoked to ploughs. Women wore headscarves and jerkins made of some thick, indistinguishable material. Yet some of the houses had satellite dishes on their walls, and they occasionally glimpsed BMWs and other luxury cars.

It felt like a country still being born: a country that hadn't finished changing.

Holly said calmly, "I think we've got company. A dark blue Audi saloon. Italian plates."

Kat glanced in the passenger mirror. "Shall we try to shake them?"

"You bet."

"Might be tricky, given that they're driving a faster car."

"Actually," Holly said, "in car chases, you *always* assume the other guy has a faster car."

"Meaning what?"

"That you don't try to outrace them." As she spoke she was filtering off the carriageway. The other car followed, maintaining its distance. "What we're looking for is a nice patch of suburbia. Just like this, in fact." Abruptly, without using her indicators, she took a right. Immediately she'd done so, she accelerated, then allowed her speed to drop again as the Audi turned into the street behind them.

"And another right," she said, turning again. Again she accelerated briefly before slowing as the other car appeared. She'd now opened up a hundred yard lead.

The street ended at a junction. The lights were red. Without stopping or indicating, Holly jumped the light and turned right into the traffic. There was a blaring of horns, and she waved. "Sorry." Fifty yards later she took a left.

"I can't see them," Kat said, looking back.

"Even so..." Once again she took a series of turns without indicating, this time all to the left.

"I get it," Kat said admiringly. "You're counting the left turns, so that you always come back to the direction in which you were first travelling. Then you do the same with the rights."

"Exactly. It's the automobile equivalent of spinning someone round and round with a blindfold on. Most people simply forget to count. And once they have to make more than one fifty–fifty call on which way to follow us, the odds on them guessing right go down exponentially."

She turned right once more. "Now we're heading back out of town, on a road roughly parallel to the one we came in on. Hopefully, they'll still be wasting time looking for us back there."

"Very neat. But I do have one question."

"Which is?"

"You learnt this in the US Army, right?"

"Of course."

"What happens if they were trained the exact same way?"

"Let's hope they weren't paying attention that day."

They got back on the main road and continued south. Eventually they turned off and began to climb up into the hills. Almost immediately, they began to see signs of damage left behind by the war. Nearly every village still contained at least one house that had been ruined. In some cases, shell holes pockmarked their façades.

"We're entering the Krajina region now. This was one of the most disputed areas," Holly said. "Originally it was part of Bosnia. The Serbs took it, then the Bosnians took it back, then the Serbs got it again, and finally the Croats took it from both of them."

Kat shivered. "It still has a bad feel, doesn't it?" She noticed that, whereas in areas they'd driven through previously the locals had looked at the car quite openly, here no one would meet their eyes.

They drove onwards, towards the coast. "I think we just

crossed the old front line," Holly reported. There was nothing to mark the spot except for a concrete water tower that had been shelled from both directions until parts of it had almost turned to lace. Now it loomed over the road like a modernist sculpture, metal rods poking out of the crumbling concrete, too solid to demolish but too expensive to repair.

Brezic was about fifteen miles beyond. As they drove, Holly pointed out features of the countryside – sightlines, cover, patches of high terrain. She could read the landscape tactically in a way that was completely unfamiliar to Kat. Listening to her, it was as if the last fifteen years had rolled away and the war was still being fought, the ghosts of the soldiers and their victims still patrolling these country lanes.

It was an impression only reinforced when they had to give way at a junction to a convoy of troop lorries. The soldiers in the back of the trucks stared down at the two women with the hungry but resigned look of men who knew it would be a long time before they got any female company.

"Must be an exercise," Holly commented.

Eventually they came to Brezic. It was little bigger than a village, with a small central square, a grocer, a café-cum-bar and a church. As they parked, a few old men glanced up from the tables outside the café. By the time the two women had walked over, they had all shuffled off.

"Seems they're not keen on strangers," Holly said.

Inside the café they found a man washing glasses. Kat took out the picture of Melina Kovačević and said in Italian, "We're looking for this girl's mother, Soraya Kovačević. Do you know her?"

The man barely glanced at the photo before shaking his head. Kat tried again in English. This time he didn't respond at all.

A woman carrying a mop and a bucket came in. When Kat tried to show her the photograph the woman pushed it away forcibly, unleashing a torrent of Croatian that, for all neither Kat nor Holly could understand it, clearly meant they should get out. As the woman gesticulated, Kat noticed the *stećak* tattoos on her forearm.

"This may be more difficult than we anticipated," she said.

"Let's try the church."

As they crossed the square another truck full of soldiers thundered through. It was towing a small trailer-mounted mortar. "American-made weapons," Holly commented. "New ones, too. That's a 4.2 inch A85, same as we use."

"I guess arming a whole new country must be a contract worth winning."

In the church they found a young priest carefully melting together the stubs of old altar candles. "Good afternoon," Kat said politely. "Do you speak any Italian? English?"

"English, yes, a little. My name is Father Pavic. How can I help?" he said with a smile.

"We're looking for this woman's mother." Kat produced the picture. "We'd also appreciate speaking to anyone who knew *this* woman." She added Jelena Babić's photograph.

The young priest studied them. "I don't know either of them. But I've only been here four years. Would you like to come into the office? It may be that Father Brkic knows more."

He led them to a small back room, where an elderly priest sat with his feet near an ancient electric fire, a blanket over his knees. The young man spoke to him respectfully in Croatian, then handed him the pictures.

Father Brkic spoke briefly but emphatically, his gnarled old finger stabbing the photograph of Melina Kovačević.

"He knows this girl," Father Pavic reported. "She grew up in an orphanage just outside the village. But she was a bad girl. She was told to leave because the nuns couldn't stop her drinking and talking to men."

"And the woman?" Kat pointed to Jelena Babić's picture.

The old man hesitated. *He recognises her*, Kat thought.

"*Ne.*" The old priest handed it back to the younger man. Almost surreptitiously, he crossed himself.

"Well, thank you anyway. We'd appreciate directions to the orphanage."

As they were leaving, the older priest suddenly said something else. His eyes were fastened on the fire, but Kat could tell from the way the younger priest stopped and listened that it related to Holly and her.

"*Reci im da treba biti oprezan. Ljudi ovdje ne vole pričati o ratu.*"

"He says you should be careful. People around here are still very sensitive about the war," Father Pavic translated.

"Please thank him for his help," Kat said. She thought to herself *and how exactly did Father Brkic know those photographs had anything to do with the war?*

In the square, parked a little distance away from their own car but with a good view of all the exit roads, was a dark blue Audi.

Fifty-five

THEY DROVE THE mile or so to the orphanage. There was no opportunity on the tiny roads to repeat the manoeuvres that had shaken off their tail before, and when they arrived at the nondescript institution the Audi was still following.

They were shown into an office, where they were met by a stern-looking woman of about sixty. She was wearing a grey habit and white wimple, together with the heavy pectoral cross of a Mother Superior. Once again Kat explained why they were there and produced the photographs. The other woman nodded.

"Yes, Melina was one of our children here," she said in good Italian. "Unfortunately when she reached the age of fifteen she became unruly. Eventually we had no choice but to expel her."

"The thing that puzzles me," Kat said, "is that she wasn't actually an orphan. So far as we know, her mother is still alive. Why did you take her in the first place?"

The Mother Superior hesitated. "It's true her mother is alive, but she was also unmarried. In this country it's still hard for a woman to raise a child in that situation. Often, such children are given to the Church, to be brought up in a more morally appropriate environment."

Kat chose not to challenge that last remark. "So she had no contact with her natural mother at all?"

"To begin with her mother stayed away, but then she got in touch. It was after her mother made contact, in fact, that Melina started to become unruly. I think the girl had built up in her mind an idea of what her parents might be like, and where she herself had come from... It would have been kinder, in my opinion, to leave her in ignorance. But unfortunately we don't have the right to prevent such meetings. And her mother thought she deserved to know the true story." She touched the picture of Jelena Babić. "I believe it was Jelena Babić who put that idea in her head."

"You knew Jelena too?" Kat said, surprised.

"Oh, yes. She used to do charitable work with the children here. She was a good person, but her judgements weren't always sound. We had to ask her to leave, too, after—" She stopped.

"After you discovered that she believed herself to be a priest," Kat said quietly.

The Mother Superior sighed. "Please understand. I myself was called by God – I know how powerful that sense of vocation can be. But Jelena wanted more. And she was convinced that her ordination, as she insisted on calling it, was valid, despite the fact that His Holiness expressly ruled that it couldn't be.

"I told her that no good would come of speaking out. But I think she felt that what had happened to her and to Melina's mother during the war somehow made a difference to their position; that if only people knew about it they'd understand. That was when she decided Soraya should tell her daughter how she came to be born."

"As the result of rape."

The Mother Superior gave them a sharp look and folded her hands in her lap. "We had a great many children here, the same age as Melina, who came from similarly difficult backgrounds. We thought it best not to go into detail about the circumstances that had brought them into the world. How could we? At what age would they be able to cope with such a thing? How could we even know for certain which among them were the result of these crimes and which were not? It seemed fairer not to dwell on the past. Once Melina knew, of course, she told the others... Some became angry, some didn't want to talk about it. It was a very divisive period."

"Which you resolved by getting rid of her."

Steel glinted in the Mother Superior's grey eyes. "As I said, it was her own behaviour that forced us to do that. She had plenty of warnings."

"Did you know she became a prostitute?"

The Mother Superior sucked in her breath sharply. "I didn't, no. How terrible. I will pray for her."

"We believe she was forced into it against her will, by traffickers. Perhaps because she had no one else to turn to after she left here."

"We had no choice," the Mother Superior said firmly.

"What's your understanding of what happened in the rape camp?" Kat asked curiously. "What was it exactly that Jelena and Soraya told Melina?"

The Mother Superior shook her head. "You would have to talk to Soraya about that, not me."

"She still lives round here?"

"Yes. About fifteen miles away, in a village called Krisk. There's one thing you should know, though. Don't look for Soraya Kovačević. That's a Croat surname we gave Melina to help her fit in. Ask for Soraya Imamović. She's a Bosniak."

*

As they got back in the car, the Audi reappeared.

"We're going to have to lose them," Holly commented. "It could be dangerous for Soraya if we lead them to her."

"Understood."

They drove away, following a circuitous route. Kat said, "It's crazy, isn't it? The name Kovačević is acceptable, but the name Imamović marks you out as some kind of alien."

Holly nodded. "What was that phrase in the title of Doherty's paper? 'Libidinal frenzy'? I can see what he means – it's like everyone went psycho for a few years, and when they woke up discovered they'd been raping and killing their next-door neighbours."

A farmer walked into the road and held up his hand for them to stop. Holly pushed her foot down on the accelerator, making him jump out of the way and scattering in all directions the geese his wife had been about to herd across the road. The geese honked indignantly, and the farmer yelled.

"That should hold the Audi up for a few minutes," Holly said, looking in her mirror. "Let's try to put some distance between us. We turn off in a couple of miles anyway."

After two miles they got to the main road.

"Looks like we lost them," Kat said thankfully.

"Looks that way," Holly said. But Kat noticed that she kept checking her mirror anyway.

Following the directions the Mother Superior had given them, they eventually came to a small bungalow set apart from the other houses. A young woman answered the door.

"We're looking for Soraya Imamović," Kat said, producing her Italian ID.

"That's me," the woman said in broken Italian.

Kat did a double-take. She'd been expecting someone much older. This pretty, dark-haired woman couldn't have been much older than she was.

Seeing her confusion, Soraya looked wary. "What do you want?"

"We want to talk to you about your daughter. And about Jelena Babić and Barbara Holton."

For a moment she thought Soraya might be going to close the door in their faces. Then, grudgingly, she held it open.

"You can come in for ten minutes. Then I have to cook."

She sliced vegetables as they talked – more, Kat suspected, so that she didn't have to look at them than because the vegetables needed chopping. That was fine: whatever got her to open up.

"I need to talk to you about the Birds' Nest camp," Kat said, as gently as she could. "I know it's hard for you, but I believe it may help us to understand what happened to Barbara and Jelena."

"They are dead?" Soraya asked.

"I'm afraid so."

"I'm sorry. They were good people."

Kat waited for her to go on.

"Yes, I was with Jelena in the Birds' Nest," she said eventually. "It was after the Croats had to retreat. When the Serbs took this area, they were angry. They went from house to house, looking for the men. They took them to a sports ground and beat them until they'd decided who were the fighters. Then they took them into the woods and shot them. My father was there, and my brother."

Her shoulders sagged, but she continued quietly. "Then they came back for the women. We were ordered out into the street, to line up for them. They were playing a song on their truck – a Serbian marching song. We had to take off our clothes before the song finished, they said, or they would kill us.

"When we were all naked, they made their choices. I was one. They raped us, right there in the street, with all our neighbours watching. Some who tried to resist, or who told them to stop, were killed."

She stopped, remembering. "Afterwards I thought, at least it's over. I would rather be dead but at least I can choose how and when I kill myself. But they put some of us into the trucks and took us to a farmhouse, up on a hill. That was why they called it the Birds' Nest – because it was high up. A long way from anywhere."

She was silent for a moment, chopping carrots. Kat saw that Holly was writing it all down as they'd agreed, the lengthy pauses giving her a chance to catch up.

"There were eighteen of us. Some were Croats, some Bosniaks," Soraya said at last. "Serb soldiers came every day, in trucks. Also policemen, firemen, town officials... They said, 'We will turn you into a good Chetnik girl. You will have strong Serbian babies for us.' But sometimes they killed a woman if they didn't like her. So I think the babies were not as important as they said. I think it was just to... to..." She searched for the word.

"Justify what they were doing?"

"*Da*. Justify. Of course we all wanted to die. We were all good women, before."

"How old were you then, Soraya?"

"Fourteen," Soraya said matter-of-factly.

Fourteen. Dear God. Trying not to let her horror show, Kat said gently, "And Jelena was there too."

"Yes. She was like our mother – the one who helped us. She said she had met a woman once, and that woman had made her a priest. So she blessed people and said prayers for them. When babies were born she baptised them. Even as a Muslim, I let her pray for me. We all did."

"How long did this go on for, Soraya?"

"I told all this to the American woman."

"I know you did. I need you to say it again, so that we can use it as evidence."

Soraya reached for a cabbage and began to strip off the outer leaves. "It felt like my whole life. But it was only a few months. Then the Croatian Army came back and drove the Serbs away. There was a week of fighting – many people died. The Croats came into the camp and said..." She stopped, her hands motionless, remembering.

"Yes, Soraya? What did they say?"

"They said 'All you Croat women, you can go home now.'"

"What about you? Did *you* go home?"

She shook her head. "I was a Bosniak," she said quietly. "Muslim."

"They made you stay?"

"*Da*. Different army, different uniforms. But every other way, the same."

"The Croatians raped you, just as the Serbs had done?"

"*Da*," she whispered. Her shell of composure was close to cracking, Kat could tell. After that, things would go one of two ways. Either she would be unable to talk through her tears, or she'd tell them to leave.

"And what about men who were neither Serb or Croat?" Kat asked quietly. "Were there any of those?"

Soraya nodded. "Not many, but enough. They would tell the soldiers they were too nice to us. They'd say, 'No, not like that. Are you soldiers or children? Do you think the Serbs would treat your women this way? Do it like this.'" Tears began to rain down Soraya's cheeks. Angrily, she brushed them away. "You have to go now. My husband will be home soon. He doesn't like me to talk about this."

"Soraya, could you identify any of the foreigners you saw? Could you identify this man, for example?" Kat held out a photograph.

Soraya looked at it. "Sergeant Findlater," she said in a flat, expressionless voice.

"He raped you?"

"*Da*."

"And you became pregnant? How can you be sure the baby was his?"

"At the time I wasn't sure. But later, yes. She looked just like him."

"What happened after you fell pregnant?"

"Jelena came back. She spoke to the people in charge. She made a deal for me."

"What kind of deal?"

Silently, Soraya pulled up the sleeve of her sweater. On her forearm was a *stećak* tattoo.

"If I became Catholic," she said. "The baby, too. If I was baptised, if the baby was baptised, she could go to an orphanage."

"Jelena converted you?"

"She *helped* me. It was the only way."

"And you agreed?"

"*Da.* Jelena, she baptised us both. Then I was a Catholic. When people said, 'You are a dirty Muslim pig', I say, 'No, I am a dirty Catholic pig'. So everyone was happy." She wiped her eyes in the crook of her elbow. "Eventually, the war was over. I kept my side of the deal. Every week, I knelt down in church. No one could take my little girl away from the orphanage or say I was lying. I even meet Droboslav. A Catholic." From the way a faint smile tried to fight the tears, Kat gathered that Droboslav was her husband, and a good man. Thank heaven for that.

"And Jelena? You still saw her?"

"She brought me news. How Melina was doing. Some photographs. She was beautiful, my little girl. I couldn't go and see her but it was OK. Terrible but OK."

"Until Jelena got angry."

"She wanted to tell Melina who she was. Where she came from. Maybe she was right. Maybe not. Melina got angry. When she left the orphanage, she started seeing a man. A *kazneno*."

"A gangster?"

She nodded. "There were stories about girls who disappeared… I told her, be careful. She said I had abandoned her, I had no right to tell her what to do. After she was gone, I went to the police. They said, 'She is not a proper Croatian. A good Croatian girl would not have done these things. It must be her bad Bosniak blood.' They were happy to be rid of her."

"What did Jelena say about that?"

"Jelena said she would try to find her. She said our story would make people understand what really happened here in Croatia. But I think she was wrong. People just want to forget." She glanced at the clock. "Please, I want you to go now."

"May we take some of your hair? It's for—"

"I know. DNA. I already gave some to the American woman. But you can take more if you want. It's only hair."

Fifty-six

AS THEY LEFT Soraya's house a small van pulled up. A man in mechanics' overalls jumped out, looked at them suspiciously, and strode into the house. Through the window Kat saw a tearful Soraya collapsing into his arms. He caught Kat's eye over her shoulder and scowled.

"Time to move," she told Holly.

Their next destination was the Birds' Nest itself, to take the photographs Roberta Carlito had asked for. The road wound upwards through chestnut woods. Apart from the occasional farmer working his tiny fields by hand, and a few plumes of smoke rising from distant fires, the countryside seemed eerily deserted.

At one of the bends they paused and looked back down towards the valley. There were no cars following them up the hill.

Holly still seemed unusually preoccupied. Kat glanced across at her as they drove on. "You think they were wrong to tell Melina where she came from, don't you?"

"I guess I do, yes," Holly admitted. "I appreciate it's a tricky situation, but to be told that your father was a rapist and that your mother gave you up to be raised in a different faith... That's pretty tough at any age. Personally I'd rather start with a clean slate."

"I'd agree if it didn't affect anyone else. But if telling Melina means that Findlater can be caught, I'd say that changes things."

"It comes down to a judgement call, doesn't it?" Holly said. "Is one girl's welfare more or less important than justice for something that happened before she was even born?"

"I think both are important. Getting the evidence about Findlater and the William Baker conference to the ICTY is only half the job. Once we've done that, we have to do everything in our power to help Melina too."

Soraya had told them that the Birds' Nest was situated on an abandoned farm, the only one up on the ridge. Even so, it took them a good half hour of investigating the numerous little tracks running into the woods before they spotted a ragged metal fence.

They left the car and went closer on foot. The farm consisted of a derelict cottage and four or five dilapidated animal sheds. A small barn to one side had been gutted by fire.

"Not a lot to see," Holly commented. She raised her camera anyway, firing off some pictures.

Kat took a step and felt something small and round turn under her foot. Pushing aside the ivy with her toe, she saw something glint. Bullet casings. A little further on, she almost tripped on the edge of a rusty chain. She pulled it free of the undergrowth. The other end was fastened to a tree.

Kat shivered. Perhaps it was simply the power of suggestion – knowing what terrible things had happened here – but there was something about the place that spooked her. It was a similar feeling to the one she'd had walking round the old asylum at Poveglia.

"Let's go round the other side," Holly said.

From the back, the dilapidation was even more apparent. Old farm equipment rusted into the weeds. A pile of tangled iron struts showed where another building had collapsed into the forest floor.

"A few more shots. Then let's go," she said, just as Holly raised a hand.

"What was that?"

They listened. It came again. A woman's voice, coming from the direction of the derelict cottage.

Hairs rose on the back of Kat's neck and along her forearms. For a moment she thought: *a ghost*. Then she heard a male voice, the sound of an engine. She exchanged a look with Holly. They crept to the corner of the gutted barn.

Parked in front of the cottage was a van. Two men were escorting a young woman towards one of the sheds. The door closed behind her.

The men got back into the van. Holly raised the camera and took a series of pictures as it drove off. Then the two of them turned back to the shed. There were small, high windows along one side.

Peering in through the gloom of the late-afternoon light, they saw five young women sitting on an upturned animal trough, waiting. On the concrete floor next to them were five suitcases.

They pulled back to the woods to confer.

"It's the pipeline," Kat said. "The one that trafficked Melina from Brezic all the way to Italy. This must be part of it."

"I guess the factors that made this an appealing location in wartime still apply. It's remote and secure. And I bet local people still know to stay away."

"Melina could have been kept in the very same place her mother was," Kat said, struck by the horrific coincidence.

"What do we do?"

"For them? I'm not sure there's much we can do, right now. If they're like the girls I spoke to in Venice, they'll have been spun some story about working as nannies or cleaners. They'll trust the traffickers, not two foreign women who turn up telling them it's all lies. And if they warn the traffickers about us, things could get nasty."

They got back to the car and reversed along the track.

"This is why it matters," Kat said suddenly.

Holly looked at her. "Why what matters?"

"This is why old crimes have to be pursued just as much as new ones. Otherwise, they just repeat themselves."

When they reached the road, Holly turned the car round. Kat leant forward, pointing. "Wait. What's that?"

A mile or so below them, troops were jumping down from three trucks and spreading out into the fields. There was a flash, and a dull "crump" echoed from the woods.

"Must be the army exercise we saw earlier," Holly said.

"Holly," Kat said slowly, "could they be here because of us?"

"I don't see how. But just to be safe, let's avoid them. There was a turning about a mile down the hill. We'll take that, then double back to the main road."

Fifty-seven

US AIR FORCE pilot Major Peter Bower edged the joystick further forward, the instruments in front of him reacting immediately as his aircraft straightened. He had another forty minutes of flying left. After that, even if the flight wasn't over, he'd get up from his seat, stretch, and hand the controls to another pilot. Then, putting on his sunglasses against the glare of the early-morning sun, he'd stroll out of the air-conditioned Flight Centre into the dry heat of the Nevada desert and get himself some breakfast at the BX, which he would eat while reading his emails and surfing the net on his tablet computer. After an hour and a half he'd come back on shift and be assigned a different flight, perhaps one over Afghanistan. He preferred the Afghan flights. Everybody did: you knew that the drone you were piloting was involved in a real mission, as opposed to the endless exercises that characterised NATO's European operations.

Like this one. "I have the target," he reported, his voice professionally calm. "One pale small Fiat automobile. One Predator, four missiles. Awaiting orders."

"Copy that," Linda Jessop said to his right. She was operating the sensors – the various cameras, satellite links and imaging systems that were their drone's eyes and ears.

Although like many sensor operators Linda was technically employed by a private contractor rather than the Air Force, the two of them had flown together for about four years. In all that time they hadn't left the ground once.

Nor had they actually set eyes on the aircraft they were flying today, although they were very familiar with the model. The Pentagon had purchased over three hundred and sixty Predator UAVs – Unmanned Aerial Vehicles, usually known as drones – and was currently using them in conflicts all over the world. Peter and Linda flew live missions almost every day. Together with their colleagues, they had been responsible for the deaths of over 2,500 people since the start of the so-called War on Terror.

The Predator they were piloting this morning had been launched from Aviano Air Base in Italy, before flying a few hundred miles to Croatia to take part in a small-scale evade-and-resist exercise. The Hellfire missiles were therefore disarmed: any instruction to fire them would result in a simulated laser strike, a "kill" in name only.

Mistakes using Predators were vanishingly rare. At every step of the way orders were checked and double-checked. It was, Major Bower liked to boast to his friends, the safest and most accurate way to wage warfare ever invented – at least, for the aircrew.

"Targets acquired," Linda confirmed.

The voice of his controller filled his headphones. "Pilot, Sensor: you are cleared to engage."

Even though it was only an exercise, Peter Bower felt the familiar small jolt of adrenalin that came from being given the command to fire. Despite what some people claimed, you never treated it as a video game. He had flown too many conventional airborne sorties and seen too many targets disappear under his crosshairs not to appreciate what his orders meant for those on the receiving end.

Quickly the two of them ran through the pre-launch checklist. On a good day they could do this in twenty-one seconds: coding the weapons, confirming their status, arming the laser and locking on to the target.

Today was a pretty good day: twenty-one and a half.

"Three, two, one," he counted. "Rifle." Next to him, Linda pressed a red button on the side of her joystick. "Three, two, one. Impact."

And, a split-second later, "*Holy shit.*"

On the screen, smoke and debris spread like an ink-blot from his crosshairs. "Live ammunition," he reported urgently. "I repeat, we have fired live ammunition. Confirm target status."

"Copy that," the voice in his ear said. "Cease firing." And then, a few seconds later, "Pete, we need to check this out. We may have a blue on blue. Stand by."

Peter Bower sat back. Despite the chill of the air conditioning, a cold sweat had broken out on his forehead. *Blue on blue.* The words no pilot, airborne or not, ever wanted to hear. The words denoting that you had just fired a lethal missile at a friendly target.

Then, abruptly, he craned forward. As the smoke cleared he could see on his screen that the target, the small Fiat, must have started making a turn just as he fired. The Hellfire, coming from a height of two thousand feet, had taken a few seconds to reach the ground, and despite the laser-guided aiming system had exploded ten feet or so away. The strike had brushed the car off the road and smashed it into the trees, but it looked as if a figure was even now struggling out of the front passenger door.

"Switch to thermal," he instructed Linda. Colours blossomed on the screen. Yes, at least one occupant was definitely alive.

"Continue to observe," the voice in his earphones said. "Pete, we're trying to find out what just happened here. Must have been some kind of error at the arming stage... Don't worry, we'll get to the bottom of it."

Peter Bower exhaled. *Thank you, Lord.*

Fifty-eight

KAT HAD NO idea what had just happened. Something had hit them. The car had blown up. Holly had lost control... Competing explanations jostled in her head.

Her ears ringing, she lifted her head from the airbag and saw blood. That explained the multiple bangs inside the car, she realised: it had been the sound of the airbags inflating. One had hit her face with sufficient force to make her nose bleed.

Or, to look at it another way, her face had travelled towards the windscreen with so much force that the intervention of the airbag had almost certainly saved her life.

She looked around. The car had spun through almost 180 degrees and was now facing back the way it had come. The driver's side was caved in where they'd sideswiped an oak tree. There was broken glass everywhere – she could feel it in her own hair, and her lap was full of it – and ribbons of mangled metal behind Holly's head. But – thank God – Holly was stirring.

Kat pulled at her seatbelt, which had bruised her chest as it tightened and locked. As she fumbled with the catch she looked through the cracked windscreen. It took her a moment to realise that where the car had been seconds before there was now a smoking crater six feet wide.

The belt finally came free and she pulled at the door handle. After another tussle, it opened reluctantly, the frame bent and buckled. She ran around and heaved Holly onto the road.

"It's OK," Holly gasped, getting to her feet. "I'm just dazed. Are you all right?"

"I think so. What happened here?" Something Holly had said earlier came back to her. "My God! They were using live ammunition..."

"Mortars, yes. But that wasn't a mortar." Holly leant against a tree, catching her breath. "That was a mine, or some kind of missile." She hobbled to the edge of the crater. "At a guess, a Hellfire. You can see how it exploded against the ground, not below it."

"Meaning what?"

Holly looked upwards, then pointed. "There. See it?"

High above them a tiny speck circled in the darkening sky. It seemed impossible that something so distant could have wreaked such devastation.

"Drone," Holly said. "Probably a Predator. If so, it has at least three more missiles in its payload."

"Can they still see us?"

"For sure. We need to get into the trees, quickly. They'll have infra-red sensors, but the canopy's pretty high. We should be able to evade detection, at least until it gets dark." She went to the trunk and pulled it open. The hatch had lost its spring and she had to hold it up with one hand.

"What are you doing?"

"We have to take everything we need. We can't come back here. It's too dangerous."

*

They trudged into the wood. Fortunately Holly had brought her things in an army field pack. Kat slung her own sports bag over her shoulder, and concentrated on trying to match Holly's practised military stride. But she found she was shaking with adrenalin.

"Kat?" Holly said. "I've been thinking. Maybe that exercise we saw was actually cover."

"Cover for what?"

"For striking at us. Say they organise some evade-and-resist training with some sort of multi-national component to it. Mortars are fired, there's a bit of confusion... Meanwhile they hit us with a Predator. When it's announced that a US second lieutenant and an Italian captain of the Carabinieri have been tragically killed, most people will assume we were part of the exercise. And those who *do* know better are unlikely to kick up much of a fuss."

"So the Audi was a feint?"

"Maybe. Or maybe they've had eyes on us all the time. One team on the ground, one in the air."

Kat felt fear gripping her insides. If Holly was right, the force ranged against them was overwhelming. "What will they do now?"

"I doubt they'll risk another missile attack. More likely they'll use the drone as recon, get the guys on the ground to pick us off."

"Great."

"On the plus side, I've done this before. Evade-and-resist was part of our training."

"How long did you last?"

"About twelve hours," Holly admitted. "And from the look of those trucks we saw, there are an awful lot of those guys. This may be tough."

Fifty-nine

DANIELE BARBO PRESSED a button on his computer and watched another dozen or so files from Barbara Holton's hard drive reconstitute themselves before his eyes. Enough were readable now to piece together much of the work the American had been doing before her death. Dozens of victim and witness statements, from men as well as women, all relating to atrocities during the break-up of Yugoslavia.

> "It was a group of some ten boys from Posavska Mahala and the surrounding villages who called themselves 'horses of fire'. I knew most of them personally. In particular, Marijan Brnic. I begged him to let me go, reminding him of his past neighbourly relations with my family. He told me to be glad that he was alone since the procedure was different with others, five or six on one girl. They pulled my friend B. N. (19) by the hair, beat her and put a knife to her throat when she tried to break free. She was raped by two of the group."

> "In the interrogation centre our captors beat us every day. One sergeant liked to show off a technique that he had of extracting teeth with the barrel of a revolver. I lost four teeth that way..."

> "When the guards were bored they invented games. They ordered us to carry bags full of sand from one side of the

camp to the other, then beat us for trying to steal sand without permission and told us to take it back. When we took it back we were beaten for not obeying the first order. This went on for hours."

"They made us lie on our backs and then they jumped from a table on to our stomachs. They were trying to give us hernias. One man had a hernia the size of a human head..."

"We women were stripped naked. Male prisoners were made to masturbate in front of us while being verbally abused by the guards. Then the guards took the women away. Sometimes male and female prisoners were made to dance with each other to music while a female prisoner was being raped..."

"They told my friend, 'Here is a riddle. How is it possible to hold both your ears in one hand?' When he said he didn't know, they cut off his ears, put them in his hand and said, 'There, it is possible to do anything if you are us.' They made him clean his blood off the knife by licking it..."

He found a file simply entitled "Why?" and opened it. It contained Barbara Holton's own notes.

– The curious thing is that Bosnia wasn't a particularly divided country before the war. Twelve per cent of marriages were inter-racial. In the west, north and east, most areas consisted of Croat, Bosniak and Serb communities existing peacefully side by side.
– The flashpoint appears to have come in the early 1990s. Suddenly, the newspapers and radio reports were full of ethnically charged speeches and

accusations. Were they the cause of the violence? Or was it something else? How did those inciting the hatred know which buttons to press? How come they were so consistent in their message?
– Both armies, Croat and Serb, employed translators. Who for? Jelena says she knew a girl who was raped in the Birds' Nest by an American. Check it out?

She'd clearly got as far as working out that there was some kind of pattern, and that military contractors might have been involved, but only at the very end had she gathered any hard evidence that they'd given the orders.

Even so, she'd been killed because of what she knew.

Picking up his phone, he dialled Kat's pay-as-you-go number, hoping to check on her progress. As he'd half-expected, it went straight through to voicemail.

Ending the call, he looked at the handset and frowned. After his kidnap, he'd been diagnosed as having a form of autism which amongst other things made him incapable of empathising with other people. He himself had always refused to accept the label, believing that he had simply chosen to turn away from the world in order to pursue a higher calling. But he was aware that there was something missing within him; some music other people heard in human voices that was lost to him, some warmth they found in human friendships that was as invisible to him as daylight was to a bat.

It surprised him, therefore, when he caught himself hoping that Holly and Kat were safe.

But then, he reminded himself, both women were useful to him at present. If he was to evade prison and save Carnivia he had to come up with something far more game-changing than the feeble "character reference" Kat had offered him.

Far better to get something on those who had tried to destroy him, enough to constitute a really valuable bargaining chip, and then trade it for his website and his freedom.

Holly and Kat, he reflected, might have a different agenda. He'd have to deal with that when the time came.

In the meantime, there was undoubtedly more to be found on Barbara Holton's laptop, and then there was Dr Doherty's paper to be tracked down – the full paper, not just the abstract. He had absolutely no intention of honouring his promise to Kat not to discover any information without sharing it with the other two. Daniele Barbo operated alone, and always had done.

Sixty

IT WAS ALMOST midnight. The two women lay huddled together under a single survival blanket from Holly's field pack, in a rudimentary concealment shelter constructed from branches.

Holly had taken charge, rightly assuming that enemy-territory evasion techniques lay outside Kat's field of expertise. As night fell, they lit small fires in different areas to confuse the Predator's thermal imaging cameras, moving on quickly before the fires took hold. Their shelter, by contrast, had no heat source at all. They were relying on the insulating layer of leaves, and the survival blanket, to mask their body heat from the air.

Plus, Kat reflected, the fact that they had almost no body heat left to detect. She was now wrapped around Holly as intimately as she'd ever been with a lover, every possible inch of their bodies pressed against each other to preserve what little warmth they had left. And she was still shivering.

Occasionally they heard distant shouts from the woods below them, the far-off growl of trucks labouring up and down the hill. Kat found herself repeating the words of the Hail Mary in her head, something she hadn't done for years. When she got to the end she instinctively reached to cross herself.

"Keep still," Holly whispered. "We'll move just before dawn, when they're resting."

They'd eaten nothing all night but a bar of chocolate Holly had found in her field pack. But despite her hunger, and the cold numbing her hip where it was pressed into the ground, Kat felt herself drifting off.

Suddenly the air erupted, lifting them both off the ground as casually as if they were being tossed in a blanket. Stones and earth rained down on them. Kat's ears rang. Within moments a second explosion followed, even closer this time.

"Run! Now!" Holly gasped.

They'd already agreed that if they had to make a run for it, the best direction to take would be directly uphill. That way they'd avoid going round in circles or losing their bearings. Now, grabbing her bag, Kat stumbled after Holly.

A third projectile whistled as it fell. Debris pattered on the leaves around them like hail. Kat waited for the shouts and the running boots that must surely follow. None came. *Are we running into a trap?* It certainly didn't seem that way, but she was so disorientated, she didn't trust her own ability to think straight.

Eventually Holly called a halt. Kat collapsed, her lungs heaving. She'd thought herself reasonably fit, but Holly was clearly in a different league.

The woods were once again eerily quiet.

"What's that?" Holly whispered, cocking her head.

On the night breeze Kat caught the sound of truck engines. But they seemed to be getting fainter, not louder. "Are they leaving?"

"I think so." Holly sounded worried. "There's something I don't like about this. I think we should speak to Daniele."

"Why him?"

"I suspect he'll know more about the technology they're using than I do. Those last explosions – I'm fairly sure they were mortars. But mortars shouldn't be that accurate, at least not without being zeroed in by a spotter."

They turned on one of the pay-as-you-go cell phones and dialled. Daniele answered straight away. "What's up?"

Briefly, Holly explained.

"And you've had both phones turned off?"

"All the time."

There was silence as Daniele thought about this. "Hold on," he said. "I'm just going to check something online."

After a minute he came back on. "Those mortars – were they 120 mm?"

"Sounds about right."

"I think they were GPS-guided. The very latest models, only just on the market. It says here they have a CEP of ten metres. Does that mean anything to you?"

"CEP stands for Circular Error Probability – what used to be called the approximate area of impact," Holly said. "A CEP of ten metres means fifty per cent of rounds fired will land within ten metres of the target, which is dramatically better than the traditional kind. But I still don't understand. How could they have our GPS coordinates?"

"Has anyone given you anything electronic? A calculator, alarm clock...?"

"Negative." A thought struck her. "Oh, Jeez."

"What is it?"

"My CAC – my military identity card. It contains a tracking device."

"Holly," Daniele said urgently, "you need to move. *Now.* If they're tracking you..."

"I know. I'd just worked that out too." Clamping the

phone to her ear, she picked up her field pack and began to run back downhill, gesticulating to Kat to follow her.

"What's going on?" Kat panted.

"Daniele, what do we do?" Holly said into the phone. "We need to come up with something fast."

Above them, a projectile whistled through the trees, and a mortar buried itself in the soft earth just yards from where they had been standing a brief while before. The explosion reverberated from the woods like a struck gong. Moments later, another mortar exploded next to the first.

"Holly, stop running!" Daniele shouted into the phone.

"What?" she bellowed, unable to hear a thing.

"I SAID STOP! I have an idea."

"As long as they see the CAC card tracker moving on their screens, they know we're alive," Holly explained as she took the things she needed out of the field pack.

"OK, I get that. But how does chocolate help?"

"By itself, it doesn't. Although we could both use the energy." She broke the bar in half and handed one piece to Kat. "What definitely helps, though, is silver foil."

She pulled her CAC card out of her fleece by the lanyard round her neck. Unclipping it, she slipped it inside the foil wrapper from the chocolate bar, which she folded over it twice. "Pass me the survival blanket, will you?"

She wrapped the survival blanket around the chocolate foil as tightly as she could, then tied the whole package up with the lanyard. "That should do it. As far as the tracker's concerned, my GPS gave up the ghost a few minutes after the latest mortar strike."

"In other words, consistent with a direct hit."

Holly nodded. "Hopefully, they'll assume we're dead.

We should take the batteries out of our phones, too, just in case."

"OK," Kat said, following Holly's lead and springing the battery from her phone. "So what's next?"

"We'll put a click or so between us and here, in case they come looking. Then we'll get some rest and wait for daybreak. After that, I don't know." She hesitated. "Kat, if they were tracking us through my CAC, that means they could have been following my movements ever since I checked in at Ederle. Camp Darby, Ca' Barbo, Brezic... They've simply been biding their time. What's more, they'll be able to spot us as soon as we resurface. If we're to get out of this, we're going to have to find a way of getting back to Italy that doesn't require a car, a credit card or going through Passport Control."

Sixty-one

DANIELE CAUGHT A train out of Venice, then took a taxi. He had never learnt to drive, partly because as a Venetian he rarely needed to, and partly because his brain struggled to process the thousands upon thousands of tiny unstated conventions and interactions that constituted normal behaviour on the road. He understood the rules – but the fact that some rules were habitually broken, while others were not, produced in him a deep sense of perplexity.

Luckily, he wasn't going far – only to the Institute of Christina Mirabilis. The nun on reception checked her appointment screen. "Ah yes. Nine o'clock, to see Father Uriel. I'll tell him you're here."

A few minutes later he was shown into the psychiatrist's office. "Pleased to meet you, Daniele," Father Uriel said, shaking his hand with a friendly smile. "I understand you want me to carry out a review of your medical condition for the courts. I'd be glad to, but I should tell you that it's a little outside my usual field."

"I came across a paper you published, a few years back," Daniele explained. "As I recall, you drew a link between treating those with Social Avoidance Syndrome and certain kinds of psychopathology."

Father Uriel nodded. "Yes, I remember it. I must say, I'm

surprised you came across it. The journal it was published in had a very limited circulation."

"You used a phrase that caught my attention," Daniele said. "Or rather, the attention of the search engine I was using. 'Libidinal frenzy.'"

"Yes?" Father Uriel shrugged. "Well, I may have done. It's a development of Freud's thinking on group psychology and the ego—"

"I know what it refers to, Father Uriel. Or should I say, Dr Doherty. Dr *Paul* Doherty."

Father Uriel didn't reply, but his eyes narrowed fractionally.

"I was scouring old internet caches for that exact phrase," Daniele said. "After all, it's an unusual combination of words... There was the original paper by Dr Doherty, the one that was comprehensively redacted from the web over a decade ago. And then one brief reference in the paper authored by Father Uriel, five years later. You put the letters MRCPsych after your name, indicating a member of the Royal College of Psychiatrists in Britain. I checked – the College had no record of a Father Uriel. But they did have records of a Dr Paul Doherty.

"I remembered that priests, when they're ordained, sometimes take a new name – something personal to them, the name of a saint or biblical figure who inspired them. Such as Uriel. I looked him up, too. He used to be known as the patron saint of repentance. But he's better known as the archangel who stands guardian at the Gate of Eden with a fiery sword."

"'He who watches over thunder and terror,'" the priest quoted quietly.

"I haven't come here for an assessment, Father. I've come here for an *explanation*. I want to know about this conference that was held at Camp Ederle. Operation William Baker."

"For many years I've lived in fear of someone asking me that question," Father Uriel said quietly. "I must admit, after all this time, I was starting to let myself believe that perhaps it would never happen." He sighed. "I had no prior knowledge of what they were planning, you understand. It was soon after I published that paper you referred to, the one about genocide. You must understand: I meant it only as a *warning*. An analysis of the psychological factors that had led apparently stable societies to erupt suddenly into the most appalling violence. Nazi Germany, Rwanda, Cambodia, Northern Ireland, Kurdistan, East Timor... So many tragedies, and yet almost no one had tried to look at them dispassionately and work out what had happened, and why."

He crossed to the window and looked out. "I realised there were certain factors all those situations had in common – the danger signs, if you like. My belief was that, just as an experienced psychiatrist should be able to spot psychosis in a patient before they get to the point of harming someone, so you should be able to diagnose and prevent psychosis in a population. Though I say it myself, it was ground-breaking work.

"I thought the conference would be a chance to disseminate my ideas – after all, why else had they invited me? It was only on about the third day I realised they weren't using my paper to prevent a war. They were using it as a blueprint, to plan one."

"What did you do?"

"Oh, I protested, of course. But they were very clever. They said, we only want to make sure it doesn't escalate. Now we understand how civil conflict works, we'll be able to control it – move populations around, ease the tensions before they turn into genocide...

"Someone used the phrase 'ethnic cleansing'. The man from the PR company, I think. It all sounded so reasonable, so *pragmatic*. And I thought, well, the ideas were already there, in my paper. What good would walking out have achieved? By staying I could at least influence the outcome. To try to make sure that this war, which they assured me was inevitable, was as swift and clean as it possibly could be."

"Instead of which, it turned into one of the most barbaric conflicts of the twentieth century."

Father Uriel nodded. "Blood on my hands. So much blood. It destroyed Paul Doherty – utterly destroyed him. For years he was a patient in one of the same psychiatric institutions he'd previously trained in. And then, at last, he found a cure. Or rather, it found him."

"What was that?"

"God," the priest said simply. "God called me. He told me I had a purpose – a divine purpose – and explained how I was to fulfil it by serving others. Those who had committed acts so terrible that none but God could forgive them – they would be my flock.

"It started with some who'd fought in the very war I'd helped to create – people who had done things so evil they couldn't bring themselves to speak of them even in the confessional. Amongst them there were even priests – men of God – who had incited the very worst, the most appalling acts... I began to focus on them. It grew from there."

"And this place?"

"By then I was well on the way to taking Holy Orders myself. But I knew that my calling was to continue my psychiatric work amongst the fallen. I was certain that many of those involved in Operation William Baker hadn't realised their seed would bear such poisonous fruit... I suggested they might like to fund a facility for those who, like them, had looked into their own souls and discovered there only the most terrible evil."

"You *blackmailed* them?"

Uriel shook his head. "It was more in the nature of asking for what was rightfully owed. After all, the various groups involved in William Baker did very well out of that war. I was simply offering to help clear up some of the debris."

"And the Companions of the Order of Melchizedek? Who are they, exactly?"

Father Uriel frowned. "A benevolent organisation through which the funds for the Institute are channelled, no more."

"I'll need a list of names," Daniele said. "All the details you can remember."

The other man sighed again. "Ask yourself something, Daniele. What good can it possibly do to bring all this to light? That paper of mine... Once it's known about, you must see that others – *many* others – will find it, just as you did. The ideas it contains, the tools by which civil unrest is turned into genocide, will become everyday currency. People like you – the generation that grew up with the internet – like to believe that openness is always good; secrecy always evil. But the reverse can also be true. Sometimes, it's secrecy that prevents evil people from learning how to do more evil."

"My secrecy may have a price."

"Ah." Father Uriel put the tips of his fingers together and looked at him thoughtfully. "You intend to negotiate with those who hold your future in their hands."

"Perhaps. After all, you did."

"Then let me make you a slightly different offer. I realise the reason you gave for coming here today was only a pretext. But as a matter of fact, I *do* believe I can help you. Treatments for your condition have come a long way in recent years."

"I don't need treating."

"Have you ever had a meaningful relationship with another human being?" Father Uriel asked quietly.

Daniele didn't reply.

"Daniele, you don't have to live the way you do, cut off from the rest of the world. You can learn to form connections, friendships... Perhaps, at first, you won't experience them in quite the same way others do. Becoming fully human takes practice. And guidance. Unless you allow someone to help you, you'll never begin."

"If I want a shrink, I can look in the phone book."

"Yes. But if you were going to do that, you'd have done it years ago. Besides, my success rate is well above the norm. I can show you the numbers, if you like."

"Would you medicate me?"

Father Uriel shrugged. "Possibly. But the main work would be a course of cognitive behavioural therapy. Is there someone in particular you'd like to have an emotional relationship with?"

Daniele said nothing.

"Well, think about it." The priest got to his feet.

"How do you know the other parties at the conference will agree?" Daniele asked.

"Oh, they'll agree. You'll understand better when you see the list of names." Father Uriel wrote something down and showed it to him. "This is the person who organised the conference, Daniele. The former head of the CIA's Venice section. Your guardian, Ian Gilroy."

Sixty-two

IT WAS A plan so risky that if there had been any alternative, any alternative at all, they would never even have considered it.

Under cover of darkness, the two women made their way back to the ridge, where the Birds' Nest sat amidst the silent woods. Satisfied there was still no guard, they crept to the shed where the girls were being kept.

As they'd anticipated, the door was unbolted. These women were being held by lies, not locks.

One by one they woke the sleeping girls, asking if they spoke Italian and getting those who could to translate for the others. Then they explained why they were there.

The girls stared at them with a mixture of disbelief and amazement as Kat and Holly told them that, far from being smuggled into Italy to work as nannies and maids, they were actually being trafficked into a life of prostitution. Only when Kat produced a photograph of Melina Kovačević did one of them finally say, "That's Melina. I know her. She went to Italy to work."

Kat shook her head. "She was forced to become a prostitute. Most likely by the exact same people you're entrusting your lives to today."

The girls went off into a huddle, whispering together and shooting occasional glances at Kat and Holly. Then a girl called Živka, who seemed to be the group's unofficial leader, spoke up. "Let's say you're telling the truth. What do you want us to do?"

Kat pointed at two of the girls, one blonde and one dark. "I want you and you to swap clothes, luggage and passports with my friend and I. Hide in the woods until we've been collected, then make your way back to your homes. The rest of you, just play along with it for now."

They didn't have long to wait. Before noon, a van drew up and the door to the shed was thrown open. A burly figure, silhouetted against the light, called the women out.

Holly and Kat were gambling that the trafficker who took them on the next stage of the journey wouldn't know the girls individually, or bother checking their identities so long as the overall number was right. They were right – although the man studied the women as they climbed into the back of the windowless van, where a couple of old mattresses provided rudimentary seating, it was their figures he was paying attention to, not their faces. During the time when this building had been a cattle shed, Kat thought, he'd have looked at his animals with much the same expression as they went off to be sold at market.

Holly and Kat were the last to leave the shed. "*Čekaj*," he called suddenly, just as Holly was about to get into the van. They might not speak the language, but the tone of his voice was clear. *Wait*.

They froze. Stepping forward, he lifted Holly's suitcase into the van and held out a hand to help her up. "*Hvala*," she muttered, keeping her eyes down. He nodded, pleased to have been of help.

"Looks like you've got an admirer," Kat whispered as the

others made room for them. "So gentlemen *do* prefer blondes."

"If he tries anything, that gentleman is dead."

"Seriously, Holly, we need to be ready. At some point this is going to turn nasty."

"Maybe not until we reach Italy, though. Remember that tape you told me about, the one with the smuggler forcing himself on the girl... That was filmed in Italy, wasn't it? I reckon there's a good reason for that. They won't want the girls to be scared of their captors until the last possible moment, in case they try to run away. I bet they're under orders not to touch the merchandise until they're safely over the border."

"Let's hope you're right. But I don't think we should count on it."

"We'll look out for anything we can improvise weapons from. Whatever happens, we should be ready."

They were driven down quiet back roads towards the coast before turning north. Eventually they pulled into another remote farm. The farmer and his wife ignored the girls as they were ushered out of the van and into a barn. There were calves at one end, eyeing them curiously, but at least the animals kept the place warm, and the sheaves of straw were soft and dry.

After another long night, and a rudimentary breakfast of cheese and bread, a different van came to pick them up. The driver took them another fifty miles or so before turning down towards a small harbour.

Again they waited, this time in a boat shed. For the rest of the day, nothing happened.

"It's deliberate," Kat whispered to Holly. "They want the girls weak and tired before they finally start to break them."

None of the girls spoke much. Even Holly was uncharacteristically quiet. Kat was concerned – Holly hadn't seemed to be someone who was easily frightened.

"Are you OK?" she asked when Holly had been staring at the same spot on the wall for thirty minutes.

"What?" Holly roused herself. "Yes. It's just… I keep thinking about my CAC card. The fact that they were tracking it."

"What about it?"

"You can't pick up a signal from those things just by turning on your sat-nav. It was designed for rescuing soldiers from behind enemy lines, so you can imagine how powerful the encryption has to be. The only way my coordinates could have been inputted into those missiles and the mortars is if whoever did it had access to the Pentagon computer network."

"Meaning that whoever's trying to kill us has some powerful connections."

Holly said slowly, "I'm wondering if I've been too trusting."

"In what way? Trusting of who?"

Holly didn't reply.

Leaving her friend to her thoughts, Kat made a fingertip search of the shed. As she'd hoped, it yielded a number of potential weapons: six rusty nails, two lengths of thin-bore steel plumbing pipe, and best of all, a paint scraper and roller. Once the paint-encrusted cylinder had been removed from the roller she had a sharp-ended hook, while the scraper, once sharpened, was almost as lethal as a knife. She distributed her finds amongst the girls, warning them to keep them hidden for the time being.

When she sat down again, Holly said in a low voice, "They won't fight, you know."

"The girls? Why not, if it's for their freedom?"

"Violence doesn't come naturally to girls like that – to most women, for that matter, but particularly this lot. They're pretty and feminine and all their lives they've discovered that they can usually get what they want out of men by being nice to them."

"Meaning?"

"We're going to have to do this on our own – just you and me. Any help from them will be a bonus."

"Do you think that's possible?"

"Could be. There's a saying in the military: plan the fight, and fight the plan. We need to devise a strategy and stick to it."

They talked for several hours, by which time it was still only early afternoon. The traffickers would move them at night, they guessed, when the chance of detection was lowest. They settled down to wait.

Sixty-three

IAN GILROY ACCEPTED the video call, nodding politely at the face that appeared on his screen. "Good morning, General," he said, although it was late afternoon in Italy, and the face on the screen belonged to someone who was no longer a serving officer.

"That terrier of yours has been killed," the other man said without delay. "The other bitch with her, too. I wanted to give you my apologies personally. I know you were fond of those dogs."

Gilroy barely blinked. "May I ask what happened?"

"Both dogs were out in the field, hunting. Unfortunately there was a pack of hounds nearby."

The room Gilroy was in, inside the sumptuous Villa Barbo, a Palladian villa near the town of Treviso, was full of priceless works of art. But his attention remained fixed on his screen.

"Has the terrier's body been recovered?" he asked.

Was it his imagination, or did the other man hesitate? "It was deep in the woods, at night. She may have crawled away to die. Little dogs do that, sometimes."

"Indeed. And sometimes they just go off to lick their wounds."

"Negative. We've had people searching the woods for

days, looking for her. My condolences. But at least it solves the problem of all those bones she was so keen on digging up."

Gilroy stared at the face on his screen. Even across thousands of miles of cyberspace, his fury was self-evident. "What you've failed to grasp, General, is that we needed those bones."

The other man's confident tone faltered. "What do you mean?"

"They were the bait to catch a bear."

"I don't follow you."

"Of course you don't. Planning isn't your strong point, is it? But if by any remote chance you hear one of my dogs barking in the woods in future, you'd better make damn sure there are no more accidents."

Before the other man could respond, Gilroy reached out and disconnected the link.

Sixty-four

AS DUSK FELL two more traffickers came to put the girls onto a speedboat. The speedboat took them a mile out to sea, where they were transferred to a fishing vessel. Still wet and freezing from the speedboat's spray, the women were made to climb down into the hold, where they crouched amongst boxes of wriggling mullet and mackerel. As the fish around them slowly expired, the boat chugged westwards, the smell of diesel, fish guts and engine fumes choking in the confined space.

The girls sat on their luggage or on discarded fishing nets, resting their heads against the shuddering hull, trying to doze as best they could. Every few hours the hatch opened and a crew member in blue waders and rubber overalls jumped down to unload another catch, using a short-handled boathook to steer the nets over the storage crates, before emptying them in a slithering, silvery torrent of fish. He gave the girls a curious glance or two, no more. He showed far more interest when the nets revealed an octopus caught up with the fish. Deftly he flipped it inside out so he could rip away the beak, brain and stomach, tossing them into a box which he took back on deck to empty over the side.

He left his boathook behind.

With a sharp point as well as that lethal hook, it was their best weapon so far. Kat slipped it into her bag, then scoured the hold looking for anything else they could use.

When dawn was still just a faint glimmer over the sea behind them, the girls were taken on deck to transfer to another speedboat. The new boat, an inflatable rib, turned away from the fishing vessel and headed for the darkness ahead at full throttle, reaching land after about twenty minutes. From the shape of the coastline Kat thought they must be landing in Le Marche, south of Ancona, an area almost deserted at this time of year.

This, clearly, was the part of the journey that should pose the greatest danger to the smugglers. Any passing coastguard or plane would spot them straight away. The boat headed into a rocky cove, driving right up onto the shingle, the driver exuding the confident air of someone who knew that all the necessary arrangements had been made and he wouldn't be getting any trouble.

From the beach the girls trudged with their luggage up to where yet another van waited for them by the side of the road. The inside of the van was warm and smelt of cigarettes, sweat and cheap grappa. A couple of empty bottles rolled on the floor. Kat guessed that a group of men had been travelling in it very recently.

Twenty minutes later they pulled into a remote farmyard. Lights burned in the house. The exhausted women were ushered inside.

Sixty-five

DANIELE WATCHED DAWN break over Venice. It had been a long night, and a difficult decision.

Father Uriel's words came back to him. *Is there someone in particular you'd like to have an emotional relationship with?*

There was. She was blonde, practical, and like him she'd grown up with one foot in the Italian culture and one in the American one. While he'd ended up despising the privilege and power that was his birthright, she'd been raised in the shadow of the American military, yet had ended up returning to it.

And now she was his best – indeed, his only – bargaining chip in the negotiation to save Carnivia.

And then there was Kat. Daniele Barbo had a low opinion of his fellow men and women generally. Kat Tapo had many qualities he disdained. She was fiery, impetuous, emotional and energetic. She tended to act first and think through the reasons for action later. And yet he surprised himself by wondering what she thought of him.

Was it possible that Kat was his friend?

It was another cold, grey day, and the pipes were forecasting another surge of *acqua alta*. As the sky turned the same colour as the sea, he made a decision.

Picking up his phone, he sent a text message.

Mr Gilroy, this is Daniele Barbo. I'm on my way to see you.

Sixty-six

THERE WERE SIX men sprawled around the sitting room of the little farmhouse. Seven including the driver, who had followed them in. The men's eyes lit up when they saw the women.

They've been waiting for us, Kat thought.

Around the room, ashtrays and more empty bottles. On the TV, a porn movie. The girls looked at it, then looked away again, trying to ignore what was happening on the screen. The men watched their reactions hungrily.

One of the men held up a bottle of grappa and shook it from side to side. "Here ladies, have a drink," he said in Italian. He had a pronounced Marchigiano accent. So they had landed well to the south, just as she'd thought. These must be local footsoldiers: breaking in a new consignment would be their reward for whatever else they did.

She'd spoken to an undercover officer once, a man who'd infiltrated an organised crime gang. He said the hardest thing about it was overcoming the instinct to arrest people. She realised now what he meant. Without her uniform and badge she felt strangely naked.

Tumblers of grappa were being poured and pressed on the girls. Kat accepted one and swallowed down half in one go. Not enough to get drunk, but enough to give her a little Dutch courage.

There's no way out now but this.

The man who'd driven the van spoke to one of the others, keeping his voice low. "Is everything set up?"

"Upstairs. You get first choice, like we agreed. But don't take too long. The boys are getting impatient, and there's only one camera."

Kat was aware of the driver's gaze raking over them, assessing them one by one. His eyes lingered on her, then moved to Holly. "That one," he said.

The other man grunted. "Get on with it, then."

"You." The driver pointed at Holly. "You, come with me. I need to check your documents." One of the other men laughed.

Kat gave Holly the tiniest of nods. *Plan the fight, fight the plan.* Whatever happened, they were committed now.

As the driver led Holly out of the room, one of the others turned up the volume of the panting actress on the TV. *To muffle any sounds from upstairs*, Kat thought. But it should help her and Holly too. *If the plan works.*

The man patted his lap and smiled at the nearest girl. "Come and sit here, darling. I won't bite."

Frightened, the girl looked at Kat to see what she should do.

"What's it got to do with her?" the man demanded, intercepting the glance. He looked from one to the other of them suspiciously. "What's going on?"

Our best weapon is surprise. And any moment now, they were going to lose that advantage. "I need a drink," Kat said. She grabbed a bottle of grappa from the table and tipped some into her mouth. "And my cigarettes." Bending down to her case, she pulled out the fishing net she'd stuffed inside it, back on the boat.

Hit the enemy with a closed fist, not with open fingers, Holly had told her.

Kat threw the net over three of the seated men, hit another one across the temple with the upended grappa bottle, then began clubbing the struggling figures under the net, aiming for their heads. "Now!" she shouted at the girls.

Terrified, they didn't move. She didn't blame them: she was shaking with fear herself. *No time for second thoughts.* The door crashed open. For a moment she thought the plan was collapsing around her. Then, turning, she saw to her relief that it was Holly.

"X-ray secured," Holly said matter-of-factly. It was not the moment, Kat decided, to tell her friend that she had absolutely no idea what she was talking about. Bending down to her bag, she pulled out the boathook and tossed it over.

No broken bottles or knives – too much blood gets in the way.

No prisoners except the driver.

Maximum incapacitation in minimum time is our objective.

The men under the net were struggling to their feet, but were impeded by the furniture. Holly and Kat were blocking the approach to the only door, and Holly was now lashing out two-handed with the boathook as if it were a baseball bat, connecting with heads and arms every time one came within range, and using the sharp point to jab at the struggling men under the net.

"Out!" Kat bellowed again at the girls. At last, they moved. One of the men, meanwhile, with slightly more presence of mind than the rest, had worked out that it made sense to extricate himself from the net first, out of range of

Holly and Kat's swinging weapons, and then come at them unimpeded. From somewhere down his back he produced a knife.

Holly tossed Kat the keys she'd taken from the driver. "You're next. Go."

Kat hesitated. "It's ready?"

"Ready," Holly confirmed. "Get out of here."

The man chose that moment to launch himself at Holly, knocking the arm that held the boathook against the wall. Holly gave a gasp of desperation as she dropped it.

Kat didn't hesitate. Reaching into her bag, her hand closed around the first weapon it made contact with and pulled it out. The paint roller. As the man drew back his hand to slash Holly in the face, Kat speared his throat from behind and yanked. He collapsed to the ground, clutching at his throat where air and blood bubbled through the puncture. She kicked him sideways for good measure.

"Thanks," Holly said with feeling. The boathook was already back in her hand.

"Count to ten, then follow."

Running outside, Kat found the girls waiting in the van. The driver had already been trussed by Holly with rope from the boat. Kat had the ignition on and the van turned round by the time Holly hurtled from the house and jumped in beside her. The wheels spun briefly, then bit into the dirt as they roared off.

"They'll come after us," one of the girls said nervously, looking behind them.

"If we're right, they'll have more important things to think about," Holly said.

"Like what?"

"Like the CAC card I unwrapped earlier."

"What's a CAC card?"

Suddenly the farmhouse behind them exploded in a fireball of masonry and glass.

"In the present circumstances," Holly said with satisfaction, "it makes a fairly good IED."

Sixty-seven

DANIELE SAT ACROSS from Ian Gilroy and looked around the room. The table was a circular gilt monolith inlaid with Murano glass, made in the eighteenth century. From the walls, his disfigured image reflected back at him from a set of seventeenth-century mirrors with ornate gold frames. A fresco by Lorenzo Lotto covered the ceiling.

"My family used to own this villa," he said conversationally. "I remember playing here, as a child."

"Your family's foundation still does own it."

"And yet now *you* have the use of it."

Gilroy shrugged. "A villa by Palladio is a work of art in its own right, and as such the terms of your father's trust require the Foundation to be the custodian of Villa Barbo. I had no idea you cared about such things, frankly. Is that why you wanted to see me? To discuss your accommodation?"

"I want to negotiate. For my freedom, and that of my website."

"What makes you think I have any say in such matters?"

"Oh, I know you do," Daniele assured him. "I may not fully understand the game, but I recognise the player. Who else could be the link between Camp Ederle and Carnivia?"

Gilroy's expression didn't change. "I have no idea what you're talking about."

"The CIA was involved in the William Baker conference. According to Father Uriel – to Dr Doherty, that is – you were one of the organisers."

The other man sat back. "Well, you have been busy. And that's your bargaining chip? The knowledge – the *supposition*, I should say – that I was there?"

Daniele shook his head. "My bargaining chip is the whereabouts of your agent. Second Lieutenant Boland."

Gilroy looked genuinely surprised. "She's alive?"

"Both women are. And they have with them the evidence that links a former US Special Forces soldier, employed by a private military contractor, to atrocities in Bosnia."

The American was silent for a moment. "It's hardly much of a hand. I'll just stay here and wait for her to turn up."

"It'll be much easier for you to have her killed now, rather than when she reaches Venice."

"Killed!" Gilroy regarded him steadily. "You know, you've misunderstood this situation, Daniele."

"I don't think so. It's a classic CIA manoeuvre. You've long suspected there might be evidence out there somewhere that could turn up one day and incriminate you. So you're using Holly to flush it out. Then you'll get rid of the evidence, and her with it."

"Your reasoning is logical. But you've failed – and if I may say so, Daniele, this is perhaps a consequence of your condition – to understand the true motives of those involved. I want Holly alive, not dead. As my agent, she's my responsibility. Just as you are, in a different way. Which is why, incidentally, I've been protecting you for months."

"Me!"

Gilroy nodded. "You're quite right when you say that I could, if I wished, speak to those who want to destroy your website. You're also right when you assume that they'll happily destroy you, if it helps achieve their objective. *My* objective is, and always has been, to prevent that from happening."

"You were behind William Baker. You're just as much responsible for those atrocities as anyone."

"No. I was *at* William Baker. There's a difference. Here." Getting to his feet, Gilroy went and pulled a thick hardback from a shelf. He showed Daniele the cover. The memoirs of a former US Secretary of Defense. "You want to know how high William Baker went?" he demanded. Turning towards the middle, he located the section he was looking for and read aloud:

> The President and I discussed the situation in Bosnia. Clearly, Bosnia's very survival was at stake. We agreed to authorise a private company to use retired US Military personnel to improve and train the Croatian Army, and not to enforce the arms embargo too tightly.

He snapped the book shut. "The private company was MCI. Of course, 'retired' makes them sound like old warhorses put out to grass, instead of the well-organised army of ex-Special Forces mercenaries they actually were. The point is, once MCI had the administration's blessing to run the Bosnian conflict as their own private war, there was no reining them back. With the arms companies giving them anything they wanted, and NATO's warmongers egging them on, they became uncontrollable."

"You're claiming you tried to stop them?"

"I did what I could, which was admittedly very little. The CIA had been authorised to assist them – and MCI interpreted that as *ordered* to assist them. What could we do? Short of going public – that is, telling the world the US had not only circumvented a UN arms embargo, but used a private army to start a dirty war in the process – our options were limited. But I vowed that one day, after that administration had left office, I'd find the evidence and get it to the International War Crimes Tribunal."

"You're going after the former Defense Secretary?" Daniele said, flabbergasted.

"Not just him. The Secretary of State. The President himself. And all the other senior policy makers of that administration, the ones who spend their retirements running humanitarian foundations and giving advice to the Middle East about conflict resolution. They all knew what was being done in their name. I want to see them on trial for crimes against humanity, every last one of them. And now, at last, I have the opportunity."

"Because of Findlater?"

"Because of *Korovik*. General Korovik's arrest changes everything. He's the one man who can testify that the US knew what was going on. And Korovik will be happy to pass the buck, if it means saving his own skin. All we have to do is to find the proof that backs up his testimony."

"Wait a minute," Daniele said, confused. "You're saying the evidence Holly and Kat provide will somehow *help* Korovik. Surely it's there to assist the prosecution, as evidence of his crimes?"

Gilroy shook his head. "Think it through. Instead of denying the crimes took place, he'll admit to them but lay the blame at the door of the hawks in Washington."

"And that means," Daniele said slowly, "there won't be any need for me to negotiate for Carnivia. Once the truth comes out, the people who have been trying to destroy it will be in the dock themselves."

"Exactly. Daniele, I've spent years working towards this moment." Gilroy fixed him with his steady blue eyes. "But I must know where Holly is. I need to find her before MCI does. They've already seen the sense in trying to kill Captain Tapo and her, despite my explicit instructions not to."

"How much does Holly know about all this?"

The American shrugged. "Very little. Partly, that was to protect her. But she's also motivated by a very straightforward sense of loyalty. I was advised that she would work most effectively for me if I seemed to embody the simple, black and white values of her father."

"Would that advice have come from Father Uriel, by any chance?" Daniele said drily.

"We meet up from time to time to discuss matters of mutual interest."

"And I suppose it was Uriel who suggested that you get her to appear to take an interest in me?" Daniele said, avoiding the other man's eye.

"To do what?" Gilroy sat back, a look of amusement passing across his face. "Indeed not. In fact, it never even occurred to me to do so, although now that you mention it, I probably should have done. I had no idea you might be susceptible to that kind of thing."

"Since I came here today prepared to barter her life for my website," Daniele said coldly, "I can hardly be accused of sentiment."

"Ah," Gilroy said. "But you thought at the time that perhaps she was my *agent provocateur.* Where is she?"

"They landed south of Ravenna early this morning. Her CAC card was activated briefly, then went silent again. I took a look via a hacked weather satellite, and it appears there was an explosion – almost certainly, your friends at MCI having another go. Holly knew what would happen if the CAC card went live, so I'm hoping she must have planned it that way. Assuming they've got transport, they should be in Venice this afternoon."

Sixty-eight

JUST SOUTH OF Rimini Kat pulled off the road into the pine woods that blanketed the beach. In summer, these woods contained camping sites and nudist beaches. Now, in the depths of winter, they were utterly deserted.

Turning off the engine, she said, "Let's get this over with."

Holly nodded. They went to the back of the van and pulled out the trussed driver. Blood still seeped from his head where Holly had knocked him out.

They slid him none too gently onto the ground and loosened the boat rope from his mouth.

"This is how it's going to be," Kat said, squatting down beside him. "You're going to answer some questions. And if you don't, we're going to hurt you until you do."

"Go fuck yourself, whore," the man spat.

Kat sighed. "You think we won't do it? Because we're women, perhaps?" She brought her bag out and started showing him what was in it. "This paint scraper, for example, is the perfect size for scraping your pathetic cock and balls right off your body. This nail here, that'll go through your hand. The boathook, well, maybe we'll get that into your armpit and pull you about a bit. Oh, and if you think we're too weak and feeble to keep this up for very long, bear in mind we've also got the van. When we get tired, we'll just reverse back and forth over what's left of your legs. You know what? We might even turn the radio on, so we can listen to some nice girlie music instead of you screaming. And then, whether you've told us what we want to know or not, we'll leave an envelope on you with three hundred euros and a note of thanks, so that the scumbags you report to can spare us the hard work of finishing you off." She brandished the paint scraper in his face. "Now, I'm going to ask this once and once only. We're looking for a Croatian girl called Melina Kovačević. She was smuggled over on the same supply route *we* came on, about a year ago. Where is she now?"

"Piss off, bitch," the man said.

"Not good enough. Holly?"

Holly opened the man's trousers and, with a flicker of distaste crossing her face, pulled out his genitals. Kat placed the sharp edge of the paint scraper underneath his testicles.

"Pull it good and tight..." she said to Holly. "That's it. Ready? On three. One—"

"I heard they were going to move her," the driver said quickly. "I don't know where to, I swear. But they never found her."

"Why not?"

"She got away from her pimp, somewhere in Venice. They put a watch on the train station and the ferry but she never showed up. Word went out she was to be killed when she was found, to set an example to the other girls. But she just vanished."

"I think I believe him, Kat," Holly said carefully.

Kat put away the paint scraper. "Sadly, I think I do too."

As they drove off, leaving the hapless driver still trussed in the woods, Holly glanced at her. "That was pretty convincing."

"You think I'd actually have done it?"

"Back there, I wasn't sure."

"Neither was I," Kat admitted. "So, where does it leave us?"

"Three options. Either Melina's dead, or she somehow evaded the Mafia and got out of Venice undetected, or—"

"Or she's still there, and has been all along."

"Wherever she is, she must be well hidden. Venice is a small place, but neither Findlater nor the Mafia could find her, and they must have been looking pretty hard."

Sixty-nine

DANIELE TYPED IN a URL address ending in .ru, the suffix denoting an internet site based in Russia. In fact, he knew very well that this particular site was owned and run by two MIT dropouts currently residing in London who had made a fortune from applying permutation theorems to online gambling. One of them, known by his internet handle of Snap, was like Daniele a member of the Knights of the Lambda Calculus, a loose-knit association of programmers and mathematicians who delighted in solving abstruse coding problems.

This fraternity, despite defining themselves as hackers, considered it bad manners to steal or make alterations to another person's code: such activities were for *crackers*, and thus by definition *lusers*, *lamers*, *script kiddies* and *leets*. Daniele was careful, therefore, to observe the appropriate courtesies when he visited Snap's bulletin board.

hello world, he typed.

After a moment another board user replied. *hi2u2. long time, defi@nt.*

Snap about? he wrote.

Last time I heard he was in deep hack.

IRQ? Daniele typed, meaning: *is he interruptible?*

Snap here, the board owner typed, joining the thread. *Just parsing some joe code. My box is crunching, so I'm in laser chicken state. Whassup?*

Meaning: *while my computer processes a rewrite of some over-complicated code, I'm eating a Chinese takeaway and catching up on the news.*

I'm after some deep wizardry, Daniele wrote.

Last time I looked you had pretty good privileges yourself, Def.

Thnx, but I need a specific kluge and I don't have time to lift the bonnet.

What's the frob?

A Pr3D47OR Dron3, Daniele wrote, using leet substitutions to avoid alerting any roving search engines.

Hmm. I for one welcome our new insect overlords. Meaning: *messing with government shit is not to be undertaken lightly.*

Daniele waited. There was every possibility that his friend would refuse to help – not because he was afraid to hack into a Predator, or because it was illegal, or too difficult, but because of the ethical complexities involved. Tampering with matters of national defence was Bad Manners. He was hoping that Snap trusted him enough to help anyway.

Do you need knobs? Snap asked at last.

Nil. Just visuals.

Sec.

There was a pause of about three minutes before Snap returned.

My friend, your quest is almost done. Have satellite/p?

Certainly.

There's a kluge called Skygrabber. I'll hop over to foovax and FTP it. There shouldn't be any ice. HTH.

Indeed, it helps a lot. Thnx.

According to Newsweek, *the Taliban have been hacking drones for years. Some of them even claim they can spoof the GPS. YMMV.*

W00t. Thnx again.

Daniele logged off from the board and downloaded the software Snap had directed him to. If the hacker was right, all he had to do was install it, point his satellite dish at the sky and scan the airwaves for the Predator's video feed, just as if it were any other signal bouncing around the ether. According to Snap there wouldn't even be any Intrusion Countermeasure Electronics.

While he was waiting for the program to install he did a quick search. His friend was right: astounding though it seemed, *Newsweek* had indeed reported that feeds from Predator drones had no encryption whatsoever. Apparently, captured Taliban laptops had been found to contain, in some cases, hundreds of hours of intercepted surveillance footage. The Pentagon claimed that the problem was devising an encryption system that could be shared with allies on the battlefield. Daniele suspected the real reason was much simpler: whoever had designed the drones' software systems had made the mistake of assuming that their enemies were unintelligent, and that just because they didn't have running water they were incapable of writing computer code.

Twenty minutes later he had a menu on his screen that offered him a choice between twenty Italian satellite porn channels and the feeds from three Predator drones.

He opened a voice link and spoke to Gilroy. "I'm in."

"Can you see them yet?"

Daniele was flicking between the Predator's video feeds as

the other man spoke. From the look of it, two of the drones were locking onto a small van heading northeast from Padua. "I think so."

"Good. Let me know if anything changes."

Seventy

AS THEY CAME over the Ponte della Libertà, Holly looked across at Kat. "Now what?"

"We'd better drop off our passengers, I guess."

"If we leave them wandering the streets, the Mafia will scoop them up."

"I know. And if we hand them over to the police, they'll be deported back to Croatia, and the gangs will get them at that end."

"Any thoughts?"

"It's not ideal. But there's someone I can trust to do the right thing." Turning on her phone for the first time since she'd reached Italy, she dialled a familiar number.

"Aldo Piola," came the answer.

"Colonel, it's Kat Tapo."

There was a moment's stunned silence. "Where are you?"

"In Venice."

"I was told two days ago that you'd been killed in an explosion in Croatia."

"As you may have gathered, those reports were exaggerated. But it might be a good idea not to correct them just yet," Kat said. "I'll explain later. In the meantime, I have an immediate problem I need your help with."

This time the silence was more nuanced. "Kat, I've given my word..."

"I'm with a group of young women who have been trafficked into Italy from Croatia. The Mafia wants them as prostitutes. If they're sent back home, they're probably dead. They need a knight in shining armour, Colonel."

Another pause. "Where are you?"

"We'll be at the Tronchetto car park in about fifteen minutes. I'll pull up as close as possible to your car." She rang off before he could ask any more questions, then called another number. It was answered immediately.

"Daniele?" she said. "We're back in Venice."

"So I gathered. In fact, I'm watching you on my screen right now, courtesy of our friends at MCI."

"There are Predators on us?"

"Three of them."

"We need to lose them."

"Indeed. I suspect the only reason they haven't killed you already is that they're waiting for you to lead them to Melina."

"But we don't know where she is either. Only that she's somewhere in Venice."

"Yes, but maybe they aren't aware of that. Either way, I'd suggest you've only got one shot at finding her. Once they realise you're as much in the dark as they are, they'll have no reason not to strike."

"Then we definitely need to get rid of the drones."

"Kat..." Daniele paused.

"What?"

"How much do you trust Holly Boland?"

Kat resisted the instinct to glance sideways at the American. "As much as I trust anyone," she said, keeping her voice neutral. "Which is to say, quite a lot but not completely. Why?"

"It's just that I've been speaking to Ian Gilroy. He's clearly been running her. And although he's got an explanation for everything, it's all a bit *too* neat. I'm still not sure I trust him. And that means I don't trust his agent, either."

"I'll bear that in mind. Now, can you help us deal with the Predators?"

"I can certainly try. Where are you headed now?"

"Into the Tronchetto car park. We're meeting Colonel Piola there. He's taking the girls."

"That's perfect. A little risky for Piola, but perfect."

Fifteen minutes later, when Piola reached the Tronchetto, he found the van waiting by his Fiat.

"Here," Kat said, giving him the keys. "You're taking the van to Vicenza. We'll take your car."

"Why?"

"I'll explain later. But if Daniele Barbo calls with instructions, follow them to the letter, OK?"

Taking Piola's Fiat keys, she and Holly jumped into his car and waved him ahead of them to the exit.

The Predators, circling over the multi-storey car park, had lost visual on the van. In an air-conditioned room in Virginia, half a dozen pairs of eyes scanned the exits, looking for their quarry.

"There," one of the analysts said suddenly. "Leaving the car park again. They must have been trying to shake us."

"Keep two UAVs on the vehicle," the commander ordered. "One stays on the car park. Which way's the van headed?"

"Back over the bridge, towards the mainland."

*

Kat waited two minutes, then drove Piola's car to the exit. Pushing Piola's ticket into the machine, she paid the five-euro fee, then filtered out.

"Anything?" she said into the phone clamped to her ear.

Two miles away at Ca' Barbo, Daniele was watching the monitors. "Two drones have gone after the van. The other's still circling over the car park. I think you've got away with it."

"Excellent."

"How will you double back to Venice after you've crossed the bridge?"

"I'm going to drive round the lagoon to Chioggia."

"The ferry to Venice from Chioggia takes quite a while."

"We're not going to Venice."

"You know where Melina is?"

"It's just an idea at the moment."

"Don't say any more over the phone," he warned. "There's no reason they should have this number, but you can't be too careful."

In the car park, inside the overheated control booth, the attendant sat reading *La Repubblica*. It wasn't much of a job, to be honest, but he got paid handsomely for it, particularly if he smashed a few car windows occasionally to justify the high prices his bosses charged for the safe-deposit room.

Glancing at his screen, he saw that a ticket corresponding to one of the number plates on the watch list he'd been given had just exited the barrier.

Picking up his phone, he made a call.

"The third drone's just peeled off. I think it's following you," Daniele reported.

"Damn." Kat swung round at the end of the Ponte della Libertà and headed back to Venice. "In that case, change of plan."

"To what?"

"I'm not sure yet." She thought a minute. "Daniele, Carnivia's an exact replica of Venice, right?"

"Right down to the last stone."

"Is there any way you can use it to—"

"Yes!" he interrupted. "Kat, that's brilliant. Get to Piazzale Roma, dump the car in the parking lot there, and call me back. I'll do the rest."

Across Venice, cell phones were beeping. Discreet calls were being answered with monosyllabic grunts. On the Grand Canal, two gondoliers pushed away from a jetty without their passengers and turned abruptly north, up the Rio Novo. In the municipal casino, a man playing a slot machine ignored a sudden shuddering ejaculation of coins over his shoes and walked away without a backwards glance, his eyes glued to the screen of his phone. A hotel porter in Santa Croce handed a laden luggage trolley to the hotel manager with the terse instruction: "Take this. I'll be back later." A dwarf standing outside Santa Lucia station, a placard festooned with tourist maps around his neck, peremptorily snapped his fingers at a nearby tout.

It's sometimes said that organised crime in Italy is the only thing that is. Within five minutes of Kat turning back towards Venice, a small army of watchers was also converging on the Piazzale Roma.

Daniele logged into Carnivia. On an adjacent monitor he had the video feeds from the Predators. On that monitor, therefore, he could see exactly what those controlling the drones could see.

On the new screen, however, he could see what they couldn't – a pedestrian's-eye simulation of the tiny streets and alleyways of Venice, some no more than a metre wide, into which no sunlight ever penetrated.

And no overhead cameras, either. The passageways and canal pavements formed a labyrinth that even locals sometimes got lost in.

"There's a narrow *calle* to your right," he reported. "It leads to a fork where you turn into a *ramo*—"

"Daniele, slow down," Kat said, sounding breathless as she walked briskly down the little alleyway. "If we move too quickly we'll stand out."

"OK." Daniele glanced at the Predator feed. The drones were still circling, looking for the two women amongst all the people on the Strada Nuova. "OK, they don't know where you are but they're waiting for you to reappear. I'm going to take you on a walkabout."

He directed them down several more alleyways, then into a *sotoportego*, a walkway that ran underneath several houses.

"That should fool them for a while," he said with satisfaction.

Kat's voice said in his ear, "Daniele, I think we were just spotted by a gondolier. He's making a phone call." There was a pause, then her voice came back. "He definitely spotted us. He's turning round to follow."

"OK, so now we have to avoid the canals. Do a left up ahead, where the bridge is."

He took them through a number of other paved passages. "There," he said at last. "You should know where you are now."

"Thanks."

"And I think I know where you're trying to get to. But don't say anything on this line. Good luck."

Daniele had guided them back towards Cannaregio, the northernmost of Venice's *sestieri*. This was the last remaining part of Venice not to be overrun by tourists. Humble hardware stores, grocers and other working-class businesses were more in evidence here than ritzy fashion stores.

"Here," Kat said, turning off yet another *sotoportego* into a tiny boatyard that gave onto the canal. "I remembered the address from Barbara Holton's receipts."

There was a hand-painted sign high up on the wall. *Barche a noleggio.*

Boats for hire.

They asked to rent a small speedboat. The owner wanted ID and a credit card before he'd so much as untie it.

"Look," Kat said, losing patience. "We'll give you cash *and* have the boat back by nightfall."

The boatyard owner shook his head. "ID and a card. That's the law."

Quietly, Holly slipped away from the discussion.

Kat said, "Remember that boat you rented to the tourist who got killed? I'm the *capitano di carabinieri* you spoke to. This is a police emergency, and if you don't rent me a boat right now, I'm going to come back with a search warrant and turn this place over. OK?"

"Well, if you're a *carabiniere*, you can show me some ID, can't you?" the owner said reasonably.

Kat caught the sound of an outboard from around the corner. "I'll be back," she said, turning towards it.

The yard owner shrugged. Then he heard it too. "Hey! What's—"

The boat came into view, passing the two of them at speed. Without hesitating, Kat jumped, landing neatly in the prow.

"Nice," Holly said, opening up the throttle.

"I'm a Venetian. We don't fall over in boats."

Behind them, the boatyard owner reached for his cell phone. Then he hesitated. If she *was* a *carabiniere*, reporting it stolen might be the wrong thing to do. He'd check up the line before he did anything else.

Seventy-one

IN THE MCI surveillance room, an orderly turned to the suited man at the observation desk and said quietly, "Sir, Mr Gilroy's requesting videocon."

"Put him on."

"Good day to you, General," Gilroy said courteously as his face appeared on the screen.

"Mr Gilroy." There was just the faintest inflection on that "Mister". None of the men in the observation room were still in the military, but they carried their former ranks with them like invisible limbs. To be plain "Mister" meant you were either a civilian or a spook, neither of which categories of person the general had much time for. "How's the weather in Venice?"

"Oh, it's a beautiful day," Gilroy assured him. "Good flying weather, in fact. Although I believe I can spot a few clouds on the horizon."

The general glanced at the sensor screens. "So can I, Mr Gilroy. So can I."

"In fact, you're probably wondering why you can't see very much at all right now," Gilroy said bluntly.

"We do seem to have lost sight of our objectives," the general admitted.

"I can tell you where your quarry is going."

The general's eyes narrowed. "I thought you wanted them safe and sound."

"I did. Because I wanted them to lead us to the girl. But once we've established where she is..." Gilroy let the words tail off. "But please, no more loud bangs. Do you have someone nearby who can clean this up for us?"

"Our man never left the city. How solid is your intelligence?"

"It comes from someone close to the women. He's cooperating with me."

"You must be very persuasive, Mr Gilroy."

"It's what I do," Gilroy said flatly. "I find that if you give people a good enough reason to help you, they generally oblige. Does your man have a boat?"

"He can get one."

"Tell him to go out to the lagoon. I'll relay further instructions when he's on the water." Gilroy disconnected without waiting for the general to say any more.

Seventy-two

NEITHER KAT NOR Holly spoke much as they headed across the lagoon. The tiny outboard protested with a high-pitched whine at the speed it was being asked to do. Icy water exploded in their faces every time they crashed down onto a wave.

Eventually they came within sight of their goal, and Holly slowed.

“The jetty’s pretty rotten,” Kat said, remembering. “We can tie up by the shore.”

They cut the engine, and suddenly everything was very quiet. Waves sucked at the boat’s keel. They tied up and jumped onto the concrete.

“The old hospital’s over there,” Kat said, pointing. “Through the trees.”

“It looks like it’s derelict.”

“We’ll try the tower. That’s where the fisherman said he saw lights.”

They pushed their way through the hospital’s broken front door. The authorities still hadn’t bothered to come and board up the windows. There was the same debris lying on the floor, the same graffiti on the walls.

“Melina!” Kat hollered. “Melina!” After a moment Holly joined in, the two of them calling at the top of their voices.

Holly held up her hand for silence. "I think I heard something."

They listened. A bat see-sawed past their heads, tumbling over itself in a frantic effort to get past them to the door.

"Melina!" Holly shouted again.

And then they heard footsteps coming down the stairs, and in front of them stood a dark-haired young woman.

Seventy-three

"MELINA KOVAČEVIĆ?" Kat said gently.

The young woman nodded.

"I'm an officer of the Carabinieri, and this is a friend of mine. We've come to take you somewhere safe." Fear flashed in the girl's eyes, and Kat added hastily, "Don't worry. From now on, one of us will stay with you all the time. We know you've been in danger. Have you been here all along?"

"Jelena brought me here," the girl said in broken Italian. "She said it was a safe place. I didn't know it would be so cold."

So Melina had been here for over three weeks, living off the Pop-Tarts and tinned chickpeas the older women had bought for her. Mentally, Kat kicked herself for not having realised at the time what those supermarket receipts in the women's hotel room, and the smell of fires here on Poveglia, had meant.

"When the police came – me and my boss, and the forensic team – why didn't you give yourself up?" she asked.

"Barbara said not to trust the police." Melina was silent a moment. "I thought Barbara would come to get me. She said she would. Then my phone battery ran out."

"I'm afraid Barbara's dead," Kat said, as gently as she could. "And presumably you know about Jelena."

"I was here," she whispered. "I saw the man kill her, right in the middle of Mass. He didn't see me, but I saw him drag her to the sea."

"Did you get a good look at him? Would you know him again?"

"I think so. It was dark, but there was a moon."

"Do you know who he was, Melina?"

She shook her head. It was not the moment, Kat decided, for explaining exactly what relation Bob Findlater was to her. "Let's get you back to Venice. Do you have any things here? Clothes? A bag?"

"Just my sleeping bag. It's upstairs." She glanced sideways at Kat. "I had to burn things to keep warm."

"Don't worry. No one will care. They should have knocked this place down years ago."

They went with her to get her sleeping bag. It was marginally less derelict up there, but without heating the nights must have been bitterly cold. It occurred to Kat that without more supplies of food, a phone battery, or a way of getting off the island, Melina would probably have ended up dying on Poveglia.

It was as they were coming down again and making for the front door that a dark figure stepped out from a doorway behind them and said, "Stop."

They turned. Findlater was holding his pistol two-handed, his body aligned precisely behind it, knees slightly bent. He looked both alert and relaxed, like someone who had stood that way many times before.

"I'm surprised at you, Second Lieutenant Boland," he added.

"What do you mean?" Holly said warily.

"First rule of hostile territory. Secure a perimeter and your exfiltration point. You're a disgrace to the US Military."

Holly didn't reply.

"I want all three of you outside. Assume the captive position on the terrace. That means kneeling, hands behind your head. Don't look round, don't look at each other, don't talk, or I'll shoot you immediately. Go."

They did as they were told. As she knelt on the cold stone, Kat felt her arms lifted from behind, something soft and rubbery looping itself over and around her wrists.

"We call these Guantanamo restraints," Findlater's voice said conversationally in her ear. "Gitmos for short. No matter how much you struggle, they won't leave a mark."

He moved along to Holly and did the same to her. Melina he left until last: Kat heard her gasp in pain.

"You don't get the gitmos, daughter dearest," Findlater observed. "'Cause you don't need them. Plain old ratchet ties for you."

He came back over to Kat and Holly. "You two, stand up and come with me."

He made them walk at gunpoint through the bushes to the shore. Kat risked one glance back. Melina was lying on her side, her arms and legs immobilised. *Why separate us?* Kat thought.

Then, with a sudden chill of understanding, she realised why. It didn't matter whether Melina had bruises on her wrists or not because her body, with its incriminating DNA, was never going to be found. He'd kill her, take her out to the lagoon and dump her, properly weighted this time.

Why he wasn't planning the same for Holly and her, she had no idea.

She soon found out.

"Onto the jetty, you two," he ordered. "Careful now. If you go through it you'll drown for sure. That's it. Now lie down on your sides."

Kat felt him step onto the jetty, gingerly picking his way across the rotten boards. Then he yanked her bound wrists and fastened them with another tie to one of the sturdier posts that supported the structure.

"High water tonight," he said conversationally. "Which, as we know, washes bodies from this location right into Venice. Including yours." Standing over her, he put a boot on Kat's head and rolled it to and fro, thoughtfully, like a football. "The tide will reach about a foot higher than this, I reckon. I'll stick around, watch you both drown, then I'll just take off the gitmos and let you float back to town. Seawater in your lungs, and not a mark on you. Boating accident." With his boot he rolled Kat's head some more, pressing down on her cheek until she was forced to look up at him. "Question is, how shall I amuse myself in the meantime? Shame I can't mark that pretty face. But perhaps there's another way of having some fun."

The boot left her head and roughly sought out her crotch, pushing her thighs apart, making her hiss with pain as he leant his weight on her groin. "Indeed, I think there might be," he said. "Good thing I bought a condom. We wouldn't want any pesky DNA to be found at your autopsy, would we?"

He reached into his shirt pocket. "So, which one's it to be? The brunette or the blonde? Or even my pretty little Bosnian daughter? Hmm, it's a tough one. Oh, what's this?"

Crouching down, he flashed something in front of her eyes. A small blue packet.

"Would you believe it?" he breathed. "Looks like I've

bought a pack of three. Everyone gets lucky. But I think, just for novelty, my daughter gets it first."

Kat felt him lean in close, scrutinising her face, looking for the fear and revulsion in her eyes. She shut them so that he wouldn't have the satisfaction. Felt his breath on her cheek. He chuckled.

"Now you know what it was like in Bosnia," he whispered. "The strong or the weak. Life or death. Pleasure or pain. No rules. It's beautifully simple, really. There's no sweeter feeling than having the power to do whatever you want to another human being." He tucked a lock of her hair, almost tenderly, back behind one ear. "Unless it's doing what you want to an entire country, like we're doing to yours. Once you've tasted that, it's kind of hard to go back."

He stood up and sprang lightly onto the shore. "Maybe I'll bring my little girl over here so you can listen to us. How'd you like that, Captain? Like to listen to me screwing her as she dies?"

He turned, added "What the fuck?" in a belligerent voice. There was a single sharp crack, followed by another. It seemed like an eternity before there was any other sound: the splash of his body hitting the water.

Seventy-four

BECAUSE OF THE way she was lying, Kat couldn't see what was going on. Had Findlater stumbled on the jetty? Had that been the crack of a breaking board? Or had Melina somehow worked herself loose and come after him? Competing explanations tumbled through her mind, but none made any sense.

"What's happening, Kat?" Holly called.

But the voice that replied was American, male, and steady. "Findlater's dead. Are you girls all right? Don't try to move, that jetty's barely safe. I'm going to bring the boat round and cut you free."

"Mr Gilroy?" Holly said.

"Indeed. Captain Tapo, it's good to meet you at last, although I'm sorry about the circumstances. It took me a little longer to get here than I'd have liked. Was Findlater alone?"

"We think so. Melina's over at the old hospital—"

"I know. I already checked on her, she's fine. We need to get you back there too, and quickly."

"Why?"

There was an explosion out in the lagoon, half a mile away. Water pulsed into the air as if from a giant spout.

"Predator drones," Gilroy said bluntly. "Still watching, though they've been fed the wrong coordinates by Daniele –

GPS spoofing, I believe it's called. Let's get under cover, then I'll make some calls."

Kat felt a knife slide inside each of her restraints in turn. Painfully, she got to her feet. Gilroy was already cutting Holly free.

"And we'd better tow *that* back to Venice." He nodded contemptuously at Findlater's corpse. "Get a line round his feet, will you? We'll work out what to do with him later."

"Did you just use us as *bait*?" Kat said incredulously.

Gilroy turned his friendly blue eyes on her. "In a manner of speaking. But I assure you I had no choice. Let's get back to the hospital, and I'll explain."

Once they reached the relative safety of the old hospital, Gilroy went off to another room to make a series of phone calls, each one in a different language.

She overheard him saying, "We have the whole thing on film. One of my people has been recording the feed from your UAVs." There was a pause. "That's why I hold all the cards, and you none whatsoever. But listen, we're done now. It's quite straightforward—" Through the open door he saw Kat listening and moved away, lowering his voice as he did so.

A few minutes later he returned. "It's all taken care of," he said bluntly. "Game over. We beat them, people. Let's go home."

Seventy-five

TEN DAYS LATER, Daniele Barbo stood up in court to receive his sentence. To the surprise of many in the crowded courtroom, the judge gave a lengthy list of all the reasons why the convicted man should go to jail, but followed it by noting that he had received a report from the distinguished chief doctor of a respected psychiatric institution. This stated that the accused had now placed himself under the doctor's care, and that in view of the excellent possibilities for progress enumerated in his report, it would be entirely wrong to impose a custodial sentence. The sentence was therefore suspended for as long as the accused continued to receive medical treatment.

Daniele Barbo walked from court a free man.

But not an untroubled one.

Once he'd shaken off the pursuing journalists, he made the taxi take him not to Venice, but to Villa Barbo, the family's former summer residence near Treviso, now occupied by Ian Gilroy.

"I suppose you've heard the news from court," he said when he was shown into the older man's presence.

Gilroy nodded. "Indeed. Many congratulations. Though it was not, of course, entirely unexpected."

"Not the Italian court. I meant from The Hague."

"What news is that? General Korovik's trial doesn't start for another three days."

"There won't be any trial, now. He was found dead this morning." Daniele lifted his phone and read from the screen. "'General Korovik had recently claimed he was suffering from a heart condition, the severity of which made him unfit to stand trial. Preliminary reports suggest that he may have been trying to exacerbate his own symptoms with smuggled medication, but fatally misjudged the dose.'"

"How fast news travels nowadays," Gilroy mused. "I'm constantly amazed how everyone seems to know almost everything, right as soon as it happens."

"Except that in this case, no one really knows anything, do they?" Daniele said. "I suppose this makes your plan to impeach a former US president and his Secretary of Defense for war crimes a little impractical?"

Gilroy nodded thoughtfully. "Well, it's certainly a setback. I won't deny that."

"You know, I almost believed you for a moment," Daniele said. "I really thought you meant it."

"Oh, you mustn't think..."

"You played me, Gilroy. Just like you play everyone. Working out what we most want to hear, then constructing a story that we want to believe in."

"Daniele," Gilroy said patiently, "I thought we'd finally put the suspicious-teenager phase of our relationship behind us."

"You never intended to impeach anyone. Just like Carnivia was never going to be hacked, was it? You just made me think it might be. It was one of the first buttons you pressed, to make me do exactly what you wanted."

"What *did* I want, Daniele?" Gilroy asked, his pale eyes narrowing.

"The assassination of two men who knew too much. One – Bob Findlater – you killed yourself. The other – Dragan Korovik – was apparently out of your reach, in a prison cell in The Hague. And to make matters worse, he was about to talk, as a way of saving his own neck. But you knew that, given enough of an incentive, there were others who'd do your dirty work for you. Did Korovik know what was in those pills he was taking? His death has your signature all over it, Gilroy – persuading a man to willingly swallow poison, by making him think it's in his own best interests."

"Daniele, this all sounds very ingenious. Worthy, almost, of one of your internet boards. Father Uriel did warn me that you might experience increased paranoia during the early stages of your treatment. I take it there isn't a scrap of evidence to back up these fantasies?"

"Not yet."

"Not yet," the older man echoed. Just for a moment, Daniele glimpsed relief in Gilroy's clear blue eyes.

"In mathematics, when we think something is true but don't know how to prove it, we call it a 'conjecture'," Daniele said. "It doesn't mean it's wrong, just that the best way to examine it is to imagine it's true, and see where that takes you. And where this takes me is the conclusion that someone had to take the lead in planning William Baker. I don't believe MCI could have done it alone – they're mercenaries, not strategists. The Church, the Mafia, the ex-Gladio staff officers from NATO – none of them were big enough on their own to organise that coalition of vipers. It would have taken someone who really understood where all the levers of power in Italy were located, and how to pull them. Someone like you, in fact."

"Fascinating, Daniele. Fascinating and, as you said yourself, quite without foundation."

"Perhaps. But there might be one thing. Bob Findlater said it to Kat Tapo, before you shot him. He said, 'There's nothing sweeter than the power to do whatever you want to an entire country, like we're doing to yours.' Those were his exact words – 'like we're doing to yours'. Kat was very struck by that."

"A slip of the tongue. He meant 'like we were doing to Bosnia'."

Daniele shook his head. "He can only have meant Italy. And that 'we' – I don't see how it can have referred only to MCI."

Gilroy threw up his hands. "And that's it?" he demanded. "One ambiguous pronoun – and suddenly I'm not to be trusted?"

"I keep thinking about who we were up against here," Daniele said. "All those vested interests, working together at William Baker, still working together today to cover it up. Who's pulling the strings here, Gilroy? Why did googling 'Companions of the Order of Melchizedek' cause my computer to become infected with a tiny piece of spyware, one so quiet and well designed that even I almost didn't notice it was there? What's really going on in Italy?"

"I have absolutely no idea what you're talking about," Ian Gilroy said with a sigh, shaking his head. "Or what it can possibly have to do with me."

"As I said, I don't know yet either. But believe me, I *will* find out."

When Daniele had gone, Gilroy said, "I suppose you heard all that?"

Holly Boland stepped out from behind a painted screen. “Enough.”

Gilroy sighed. “He doesn’t trust me. I don’t blame him. He’s been dispossessed by his father’s Foundation, and I’m its representative. But what am I meant to do? The legal structures are quite unalterable.”

Holly touched his arm. “Just keep protecting him.”

“I can protect him from many things. But not, I fear, from the demons inside his own head.”

“Can I help?”

“Would you?” Gilroy said. “I’m getting too old for this, and he’s a responsibility I suspect I’ll never succeed in discharging.”

“What can I do?”

“Get close to him. Get inside Carnivia – that’s the key. If you can make sense of that website, I think you’ll begin to make sense of Daniele Barbo.”

“It’ll be a pleasure.”

“Thank you, Second Lieutenant.” He was silent a moment. “While we’re in confession mode, there’s something I should explain to you. Before you came to Italy, your predecessor, Carol Nathans, came to me with some correspondence relating to a Freedom of Information request she’d been asked to handle. I realised immediately what it meant, that the enquirer was somehow on the trail of Operation William Baker. Nathans said she wanted my advice, but it was clear she really just wanted to know how best to answer the letter so that she could get it off her desk before her transfer. The same day, a contact of mine at the Pentagon called to say you’d applied for an Italian posting. I encouraged him to grant the application. I guessed that, like me, you might feel a loyalty to this country as well as to our own, and be motivated to get involved with the investigation as a result."

"Why didn't you mention it when we first met?"

"I didn't want you to feel under any obligation to help me. But I promise, next time something like this comes up, I'll level with you."

"Next time?"

"There's always a next time in intelligence, Holly. You never beat the enemy, but if you're lucky, you might hold him in check for a while." He eyed her thoughtfully. "What about the Carabinieri captain? Will you keep in touch with her?"

"We're going to live together. For a while, at any rate."

Gilroy raised an eyebrow.

"I've been ticking off the days, waiting for my mandatory period on base to end," Holly explained. "I mentioned to Kat I was going to be looking for accommodation, and she suggested I stay with her until I'm sorted. She mentioned three times that she was very broadminded, before I twigged she was telling me that she didn't mind if I was gay. Something to do with my lack of lacy lingerie and kitten heels, apparently."

Gilroy laughed. "That's the very definition of a broadminded Italian. Happy to accept you as lesbian, but unable to believe that you're not one unless you put on a *bella figura*."

"I guess we'll figure it out. And she's told me I can borrow some heels, to practise in."

"So you'll all three stay close." He nodded. "Good. And what about Kat's unfortunate boyfriend, the Colonel? Where does he fit into the picture?"

Holly hesitated. "I believe she's seeing him this evening to discuss that very question, sir."

Seventy-six

AS NIGHT FELL, the tide rose. They said it could be the last *acqua alta* of the season. Venice's canals and squares slowly filled with silt-brown water, like a blocked drain spilling over a bathroom floor.

Kat waded across the flooded Campo San Zaccaria to the *osteria* near the Carabinieri headquarters, where she found Aldo Piola sitting alone, eating a bowl of *bigoli con le sarde*. A low wall of sandbags across the door protected the restaurant from the worst of the water's ingress, although the floor was damp from a trickle that had somehow managed to penetrate its defences.

She pulled up a chair; saw the complex mixture of emotions that flashed across his eyes. Surprise, delight, wariness, guilt.

"Will you join me?" He indicated the pasta. "It's good. Freshwater sardines from Lake Garda, with zibibbo raisins and a little ricotta cheese."

She shook her head. "But I'll have some wine."

He gestured to the owner, who came over with another glass. "The girls are safe," Piola said, filling it for her. "I found them all places at a rehabilitation project in the countryside, twenty miles away."

"Thank you. And Findlater?"

"His body, curiously enough, was found washed up at

almost exactly the same spot Jelena Babić's was, right by Santa Maria della Salute. That's the sea for you, I guess. Prosecutor Marcello is inclined to treat it as a case of suicide."

She raised her eyebrows. "Weren't there two bullets?"

"Apparently there's some doubt as to whether the first was sufficient to kill him. And if that isn't enough, his employers in America have provided medical evidence showing that he was on long-term leave of absence because of depression. It was a form of post-traumatic stress disorder, the company doctor said, probably related to his time serving in the US Special Forces."

"And you? What do you believe?"

"I believe that Prosecutor Marcello has shown his customary brilliance in finding a theory that fits all the known facts, before ordering us not to look for any more." Piola looked at her. "And since by some miracle you're still alive, I have absolutely no intention of trying to find out anything else."

"Thank you."

"Forget it. Tomorrow morning..." He waved a *bigoli*-laden fork at the water lapping at the door, "all this will have gone, and Venice will be clean again. Let the sea wash away its secrets."

"Clean? Venice?"

"Well, back to its usual filth, at any rate."

"Aldo..." she said.

"I can't stay long, by the way." His eyes were on his bowl as he chased the last strands of pasta around the sauce. "I promised I'd read to the kids."

"There's something I need to ask you."

"Go ahead."

"I want to go on working with you. Like we would have

done if we'd never slept together. Not pretending that it never happened: accepting that it did, and that it was wrong, and putting it behind us so that we can do our jobs."

Piola placed his fork in his empty bowl, then pushed the bowl aside. "I'd like that too, Kat," he said slowly. "I'd like nothing better. But I'd like it for the wrong reasons."

"You're saying no?"

"I'm sorry. I just can't do it."

"That's what I thought you'd say, but I wanted to be absolutely sure. You see, I've got a decision to make."

"Oh?"

"There's a vacancy that's come up in the Milan division. It's been suggested to me that I apply. *Strongly* suggested, in fact."

"Ah," he said. He looked at her. "And you're going to take it?"

"Did you know?" she asked, not answering him directly. "About the suggesting, I mean?"

He shook his head. "What have you decided?"

"That's why I've come to see you." She took a deep breath. "I wanted to tell you to your face that I'm going to enter an official complaint of sexual misconduct against you. I want you to understand why. It isn't because you slept with a junior officer. It's because you wouldn't work with her afterwards."

He stared at her, aghast. "You'd do that?"

"The letter's already written."

"But this is crazy, Kat. I'm not going to cause you any problems."

"You already have, by depriving me of the chance of working with the Carabinieri's best investigator."

"But... why? I know you're ambitious, but do you really

think trampling over—" He stopped. "Sorry. That was unforgiveable of me. I just don't understand what's making you do this."

She said slowly, "It's not you, Aldo. It's the system – the way it assumes that it's me, rather than you, who's got to be shunted off sideways. And it's Jelena Babić, and Barbara Holton. And Martina Duvnjak, and Soraya, and Melina Kovačević, and my own grandmother, who fought alongside male partisans in the war but was made to go back afterwards to baking cakes and having babies. It's the women who aren't allowed to be priests, because the Church looks at a two-thousand-year-old tradition of misogyny and calls it Holy Law. It's the women raped in the Birds' Nest camp during the Bosnian conflict, and the girls who are still being trafficked to Italy today. Not one of them wanted to be a victim. But they were." She stood up. "You asked me once, 'Why Italy?' Well, maybe this is part of the answer. Maybe it's only after we've changed things like this that we'll be able to start dealing with the things that really matter."

He didn't try to negotiate with her, or say he'd changed his mind, and for that she was grateful. She'd have hated to despise him now.

"I'm sorry," she added.

He didn't reply. There was nothing more to say.

She put a five-euro note on the table. "For my share of the wine," she said, and was pleased to see that he almost smiled. Then, going to the door, she stepped carefully over the sandbags into the icy waters.

Daniele and Holly were waiting in the Barbo launch at the edge of the Riva degli Schiavoni, where the spilling waters concealed the course of the canal. Kat stepped in. The engine spluttered into life. None of them spoke as Daniele opened up the throttle, turning a wide circle through the darkness before setting the prow back towards Ca' Barbo.

Historical note

Although *The Abomination* is fiction, much of the background is based on fact – even if, as you might expect, many of those facts are still disputed. For example, there now seems to be a reasonable weight of evidence that elements within the US intelligence services were covertly helping the Croatian side in the war in the former Yugoslavia, despite a UN arms embargo. In turn, this led to the NATO airstrikes on Kosovo, widely heralded as NATO's first "humanitarian" war, and to a subsequent expansion of NATO's sphere of operations. The expansion of US Military bases in northern Italy, such as the doubling in size of Camp Ederle near Venice, remains on-going. In all, there are over one hundred US Military installations in the country, established under terms that remain classified to this day.

References in *The Abomination* to events such as NATO's Gladio conspiracy are, in general, as accurate as I could make them. Additional background material can be accessed via the series website, www.carnivia.com, along with information about further books in the trilogy.

Acknowledgements

A number of people helped *The Abomination* to be born. In particular, I want to thank Laura Palmer, fiction publisher at Head of Zeus in the UK, not just for her spot-on editorial advice but also – along with CEO Anthony Cheetham – for their immediate enthusiasm on first receiving the manuscript, and for communicating that excitement to other publishers around the world.

My thanks, too, to Lucy Ridout for her thorough and unobtrusive copyediting, and to Anna Coscia for correcting my often-terrible Italian. I am especially indebted to Sara Cossiga in Venice, and to Colonello Giovanni Occhioni of the Venice Carabinieri for showing me round their headquarters at Campo San Zaccaria. But my greatest debt is to my agent, Caradoc King, who along with his associate Louise Lamont saw something in the idea when it was nothing more than a few scribbles on a page and a conversation in a restaurant. Grateful as I am for his generous counsel and unflagging support, I'll always particularly treasure the email he sent me from Goa, after he read the finished manuscript whilst on holiday. Here's hoping the prediction he made then comes true.

About the Author

Jonathan Holt studied English literature at Oxford, and is now the creative director of an advertising agency. He lives in London.